FOUR BOMBS EXPLODED AND BROKE THE WHEELBOAT IN TWO. A TORRENT OF WATER WAS RUSHING UP THE PASSAGEWAY AND FLOODING INTO THE ROOM...

The Jap wasn't finished. Before either Steve or Cadillac had time to react, Wantanabe threw himself towards the open door, seized hold of the precious keys that still hung in the lock, jerked the door clear of Cadillac's outstretched fingers and pulled it shut behind him.

'Steve!' screamed Cadillac. 'Stop him!'

Reversing the blade to put the curved cutting edge on top, Steve raised the blade as high as he could and plunged it downwards with all the force he could muster. The blade sliced through the lattice and sank deep into Wantanabe's chest before he could turn the key but as Steve withdrew it and his body slid into the rising water, his dead hand pulled the keys from the lock...

Oh, Sweet Mother! They were going to drown!

The Amtrak Wars
Book 4: Blood River

PATRICK TILLEY

SPHERE BOOKS LIMITED

SPHERE BOOKS LTD

Published by the Penguin Group
27 Wrights Lane, London w8 5tz, England
Viking Penguin Inc., 40 West 23rd Street, New York, New York 10010, USA
Penguin Books Australia Ltd, Ringwood, Victoria, Australia
Penguin Books Canada Ltd, 2801 John Street, Markham, Ontario, Canada l3r 1b4
Penguin Books (NZ) Ltd, 182 – 190 Wairau Road, Auckland 10, New Zealand

Penguin Books Ltd, Registered Offices: Harmondsworth, Middlesex, England

First published in Great Britain by Sphere Books Ltd 1988

Printed and bound in Great Britain by
Richard Clay Ltd, Bungay, Suffolk

In loving memory of my mother
born Agnes Rose Lewer
July 22nd, 1904–December 1st, 1987
who gave me the priceless gift of education
but whose formidable personality
caused me to censor everything I wrote.
God bless you, Ma. Hang on to your halo.
This is where it starts to get interesting.

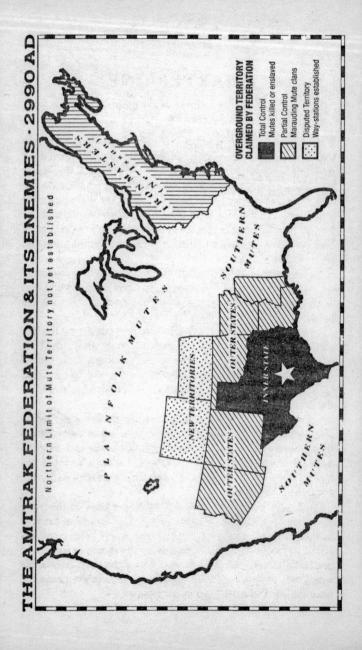

THE AMTRAK FEDERATION & ITS ENEMIES · 2990 AD

Northern Limit of Mute Territory not yet established

IRON MASTERS

PLAINFOLK MUTES

SOUTHERN MUTES

NEW TERRITORIES

OUTER STATES

OUTER STATES

INNER STATE

SOUTHERN MUTES

OVERGROUND TERRITORY CLAIMED BY FEDERATION

- ■ Total Control — Mutes killed or enslaved
- ⬚ Partial Control — Marauding Mute clans
- ⬚ Disputed Territory — Way-stations established

CHAPTER ONE

If it had not been for the fact that his youngest son suddenly took it into his head to totter through the partially-open door while his mother's back was turned, Izo Wantanabe would not have leapt up from his writing table and stepped out onto the deck of the house-boat. Had he not done so, the winter months would have passed with their usual tranquil monotony and the lives of several hundred of his comrades in arms would have been spared or, at the very least, expended on a more profitable enterprise.

But it was not to be. Fate, in the guise of fatherly concern, compelled him to follow and, as he scooped up the infant and lifted him shoulder high, he saw something which took his breath away.

Two dark stiff-winged objects were moving across the sky on a line that would take them almost directly above the boat on which he stood. The objects were heading in a south-westerly direction, along the ragged forward edge of a massive blanket of grey cloud now advancing over Lake Mi-shiga from the north-west.

Oblivious of the wind-driven snow-flakes that were beginning to swirl round him, Izo Wantanabe stood there open-mouthed with his small son clutched to his breast and watched as the objects passed over the jetty to which the wheelboat was moored then grew smaller and were finally swallowed by the advancing snow-cloud.

And there he stayed, his dark button eyes fixed on the point where the two winged dots had vanished, oblivious of the tiny fingers that pulled playfully at his bottom lip. The questions raised by what he had just witnessed caused him to forget the original reason for being there and it took the shrill cries of his wife, Yumiko, to alert him to the fact that his son's unprotected head was now liberally coated with snow.

Wantanabe meekly allowed Tomo to be snatched from him and followed his wife inside.

By the traditional laws of domestic etiquette, a wife was not permitted to upbraid her husband but, in practice, that convention was normally only observed when friends, relatives, servants or superiors were present. A wife was duty bound to respect and obey her husband but that did not stop the more spirited (or malicious) members of the female sex from giving their menfolk an earful in private – or showing their displeasure in other, more subtle ways.

Wantanabe seated himself on the mat behind his writing desk and endured the inevitable blast for endangering the health of his youngest child in dignified silence. He knew Yumiko's concern was well-founded but his mind was engaged on other, far more important matters which she, being a woman, could not be expected to understand.

He slowly twirled the point of his writing brush on the ink block and let her voice flow unheeded through his brain. Stripped of their meaning, the stream of words resembled the clucking of an irate hen driven from a newly-laid egg before she has had time to admire her handiwork.

Eventually, as the ten-month-old child was vigorously rubbed dry and his happy gurgles indicated that he was not about to expire, the reproachful clucking was replaced by the soft mothering sounds that humans and animals use when nurturing their young. And shortly afterwards, when he had been dressed in dry clean clothes, the glowing-cheeked child was presented to his father as a peace offering.

Musing upon the fact that his wife's moods were as predictable as night and day, Wantanabe gathered Tomo briefly in his arms, bestowed a kiss on his soft, downy skull then handed him back carefully. For Yumiko, the crisis was over, harmony was restored. Her husband's problems were only just beginning.

Izo Wantanabe and his wife Yumiko came from a race of people known to their neighbours as Iron Masters; a stratified collection of asiatic bloodlines in which the Japanese formed the top layer, followed by Chinese, Korean then the other ethnic groups in descending order. Each group's position related directly to the distance – in the World Before – of their ancestral lands from a sacred site known as Mount Fuji.

Successive waves of the Iron Masters' ancestors had landed on the north-eastern coast of North America between 2300 and 2400 A.D. Now, six centuries later, the seventeen domains that made up their nation state – known as Ne-Issan – stretched from the Atlantic to Lake Erie, and from the St Lawrence Seaway to Cape Fear, in North Carolina.

Wantanabe's family owed its allegiance to the noble house of Yama-Shita, holder of the exclusive licence to trade with the grass-monkeys who roamed the endless Western Plains. Izo's family formed part of the Japanese ruling class but he himself was a love-child produced by one of his father's Chinese concubines.

The resulting social stigma, while not catastrophic, meant he was permanently barred from the high appointments open to his peer group and that his future wife – should he choose to marry – would have to be Chinese. This had led to his decision to enter commerce, for it was here that many Chinese families had flourished, and his father's connections had secured him a junior position in one of the rich trading houses with a string of depots from Bu-faro on Lake Iri to the Eastern Sea.

His alert intelligence, plus a head for figures and a flair for organisation, won him quick promotion and a fortunate introduction to Yumiko, the fourth daughter of a Chinese merchant who, with a shrewd eye to the main chance, provided her with a handsome dowry.

The father's gamble on Izo's family connections did not bring the hoped-for rewards. After Yumiko had given birth to a son and a daughter, and was carrying Tomo within her, the senior partner's latent disapproval of Izo's mixed parentage was finally revealed when he was twice passed over in the annual round of promotions, putting an end to his hopes of reaching the top echelons.

His despair, however, had been short-lived. Summoned to the palace at Sara-kusa, Izo Wantanabe had been met by an official of Lord Yama-Shita's court who offered him the post of Resident Agent to the Outlands.

He would, explained the trade-captain, be one of a trial batch of five appointees – the first to be stationed beyond the borders of Ne-Issan. Aware that this was a heaven-sent opportunity to get in on the ground floor of a pioneering enterprise and escape from the veiled but vengeful discrimination that continued to shadow his marriage and career, Izo accepted the offer without hesitation.

The wheelboats of the Yama-Shita had visited the two established trading posts at Bei-sita and Du-aruta once a year for several decades, but in the summer of 2990 Domain-Lord Hiro Yama-Shita had decided to set up a chain of resident commercial agents to develop regular contacts with the Mute clans in the hinterland.

Izo and the other four appointees were to be the first links in this chain which – if positive results were obtained – would eventually extend right around the southern shores of the four, interconnected lakes which formed the Western Sea; the vast body of water the Mutes called 'The Great River'.

Each resident would live with his family aboard a houseboat, smaller cousins of the three-storied steam-powered monsters that made the annual journey to Du-aruta. It was envisaged that the houseboats would be permanently moored to purpose-built jetties but, if the need arose, they could always cast off and put to sea. Domestic servants would be provided and the boats would be maintained and, if need be, protected, by a small detachment of sea-soldiers.

For Izo, it meant assuming the leadership of an enclosed community of thirty-five souls. Food and other stores would be delivered by sea until adequate supplies could be obtained locally.

Yumiko had not been overjoyed at the prospect of an isolated existence in the back of beyond, but the chance to make a fresh start plus the generous lump sum payable on completion of a nine-year term and the promise of three months' paid home leave for every thirty-six served in the outlands had softened her protests.

The possibility that she and her family might not even

survive three years, let alone nine, did not appear to have occurred to her and Izo had wisely kept silent about the possible dangers of living amongst a horde of unwashed, unfettered savages.

The first four residents were posted to Detroit, Saginaw Bay, Cheboygan, and Ludington. Izo Wantanabe, the last far-flung link in the chain, was anchored at a place once known as Benton Harbour, twenty miles north of the point where, on pre-Holocaust maps, the Indiana state line met the eastern shore of Lake Michigan.

Their primary task was to forge closer trade links, including the recruitment of more 'guest-workers'. They were to achieve this by commercial and cultural 'counselling', the purpose of which was to change the Mutes' perception of the Iron Masters as cold and forbidding into something more ... paternal. Firm (the grass-monkeys despised weakness) yet benign.

That, in itself, was a job and a half but the residents had also been entrusted with an equally important, parallel assignment: the gathering of intelligence.

Following the first incursions by the Federation wagon-trains into Plainfolk territory in 2989, the conflict between Tracker and Mute had been drawing ever closer to the borders of Ne-Issan. Lord Yama-Shita had hit upon the idea of using the residents – Wantanabe in particular – as forward listening-posts. Their genuine effort to improve trade relations would provide both the cover and the opportunity to gather information about the Federation's war machine and its northward and eastward advance towards the Running Red Buffalo Hills – the Plainfolk's name for the Northern Appalachians.

As point man, Izo Wantanabe was nearest the action. Up to now, the probing advances of the warriors from the Deserts of the South appeared to have stopped at the west bank of the wide, meandering river the outlanders called the Miz-Hippy. The river had its source in a cluster of lakes to the north-west of Du-ruta. Wantanabe had only been on the ground for less than four months so much remained to be discovered, but according to his initial contacts, the iron snakes had never attempted to cross this waterway. Whether they could not, or did not wish to do so, remained to be seen.

The Plainfolk had said the iron snakes preferred to follow the lines of the ancient hardways – most of which, outside Ne-Issan, had long since crumbled into dust. From a captured Federation map acquired in exchange for six knives it was clear the iron snakes (which their owners called wagon-trains) would have to cross a number of smaller rivers to reach the Miz-Hippy.

Izo Wantanabe had not yet seen one of these much-feared killing machines for himself but perhaps because of their huge size or the manner of their construction they could not float across a river like a loaded cart drawn by oxen and supported on air-filled bags made from animal skins. So much the better. It meant that, until a bridge was built or suitable ferry craft were put in place, the iron snakes would be held at bay – perhaps indefinitely. Gangs of construction workers were a soft target and even if bridges and ferries were completed, they could still be attacked and burned by determined bands of men.

The Miz-Hippy was like the wide moats that surrounded the palace-castles of the domain-lords of Ne-Issan. It formed an almost endless defensive line which – as far as he knew – could only be turned by journeying northwards around the Western Sea. Densely-forested hills pitted with lakes formed the first line of defence. If this was penetrated the iron snakes would be halted by the San-Oransa, the wide river that protected Ne-Issan's border domains. But not the skies above them. These marauding serpents carried winged chariots that could travel through the cloud world of the *kami*. Rivers and mountains were no barrier to them. The grass-monkeys called these charriots 'arrowheads', and the soldiers who rode in them were known as 'cloud-warriors'.

Up to this moment, all the stories about 'arrowheads' dropping fire-blossoms from the sky and killing people with long sharp iron were nothing more than hearsay. Exaggerated rumours. None of his informants had ever seen an 'arrowhead'.

6

Neither had Izo Wantanabe until today – when he had seen two! Only these sky-chariots were not like the crafts his informants had described. Their wings were not triangular. They were stretched out on either side of their bodies like those of a gliding seabird. And they had a tail – not fan-shaped like that of a bird, but a tail nevertheless – attached by two beams to the plump body.

Their shape, in one sense, was immaterial. Izo Wantanabe was in no doubt that the sky-chariots were a product of the Federation. Merely to look upon them sent a chill down the spine. They were dark alien things whose form could not have been conceived in the soul of a noble samurai. But what were they doing in a sky filled with snow?

Lord Yama-Shita's trade captain had told him that the iron snakes retreated south to their underground lairs during the winter months and his own tame grass-monkeys had confirmed this was so. But . . . if there were sky-chariots aloft, it meant that somewhere away to the south-west, an iron snake was lurking. Hiding perhaps in a forest, awaiting their return.

Yes . . . News of its presence and its exact whereabouts would soon – if it was not already – become common knowledge among the locally-based Mute clans. And someone would bring the news to him in the hope of a reward. Izo had several trunkfuls of small gifts, some useful, some decorative, for such occasions.

Wantanabe gazed at the blank sheet of paper before him and continued to twirl his brush on the ink-block even though it was now fully charged. It helped concentrate his mind on the circumstances surrounding the appearance of the sky-chariots. The air had been getting progressively colder over the past two weeks but they sky had been clear, or dotted with broken cloud. And that very morning, the rising sun had warmed an empty sky. It was only later that a line of grey cloud had appeared on the northern horizon.

The two sky-chariots had approached from the north-east and had flown over the mooring in a south-westerly direction – back towards the Miz-Hippy. Which meant they must have either circled round from the north or round from the south –

driven back towards the ironsnake by the advancing snow-cloud. But before that, they would have been flying across a clear sky – so their course would have been observed by the sharp-eyed Mutes who occupied the lands around Lake Mi-shiga.

Perhaps his nearest neighbour, Saito Aichi, the resident agent at Ludington whose house-boat lay one hundred and twenty miles north of his own, had seen them crossing Lake Mi-shiga while the windswept blanket of snow was still beyond the far shore. *Hhhaaawww!* Cloud-warrior was an apt name for men bold enough to drive their winged chariots over such a huge expanse of water! But if they were ever rash enough to invade the sacred sky-world above Ne-Issan, the *kami* who guarded the heavens would send them crashing to earth like birds struck by a hunter's arrows.

Izo decided to pen a message slip that would be delivered to his neighbour by carrier pigeon. He would have to wait for the snow storm to pass, but if the bird could be released by noon, he might have a reply the following day that could help him pinpoint the location of the wagon-train. On the other hand, if the sky-chariots had circled round from the south, word of their sighting would take longer to reach him. But it would come – of that he had no doubt.

The high-born half-caste had made full use of his organizing skills since arriving in the outlands, putting his greatest effort into the area south and west of Benton Harbour. As a result, there were few grass-monkeys within a hundred miles of where he now sat who did not know of the rewards to be gained by being the first to report the sighting of an ironsnake or an arrowhead.

Selecting a smaller, much finer brush, Izo Wantanabe took a narrow slip of thin paper from a leather folder and began to compose his message to Saito. A string of tiny ideograms – the symbols the Iron Masters used instead of the roman alphabet – flowed effortlessly from the tip of his brush.

For 'Buffalo Bill' Hartmann, commander of The Lady from Louisiana, the word came in the form of a coded radio signal at 0625 hours Mountain Standard Time, some ten minutes before sunrise on the 12th November 2990. Hartmann was just easing himself out of his bunk when the VidCommTech on the redeye shift triggered the soft alarm bleeper in the headboard by his pillow. He looked across at the VDU above the small desk built into a corner of his private quarters and saw the screen fill rapidly with line after line of five letter code-blocks.

Hartmann's wagon-train, which had halted overnight seventy-six miles south of the Pueblo way-station, had been following a trail – once known as Highway 25 – that led down through navref point Trinidad and Raton, New Mexico and across the Canadian River before turning west to Roosevelt Field, the underground divisional base situated close to the long-vanished city of Santa Fe. Because the Federation maps of the overground were based on pre-Holocaust editions, urban areas, state lines and major highways had been retained as navigational reference points. So although the main part of the base was several hundred feet below ground, it was known by its composite title – Roosevelt/Santa Fe.

There were ten such bases buried deep within the earth shield under or near major cities of the southern mid-west, the majority named after past Presidents of the United States: the headquarters of the Federation, Washington/Houston – known informally as 'Grand Central' or Houston/GC, Johnson-Phoenix, Reagan/Lubbock, Nixon/Ft. Worth, Eisenhower/San Antone, Truman/Lafayette, Le May/Jackson, Lincoln/Little Rock and Grant/Tulsa. The latest, still under construction, was Monroe/Wichita.

These cities had vanished too, leaving only their names on the maps stored in the Federation's computer archives. Names which helped to soften the grey anonymity of the massive slab-sided constructions that had taken their place. The bunkers, which hugged the earth like a cubist sculptor's vision of a beached jellyfish, were the interface between the underground world of the Federation and the Blue-Sky World above.

Like the network of smaller way-stations and work-camps, they were artefacts of the third millennium. Some dated back to the early part of the twenty-fourth century; beyond that very few traces of human habitation remained. All outward signs of the twentieth century had disappeared – vaporised by nuclear

9

explosions or razed to the ground in the internecine struggles between crazed groups of survivors for control of uncontaminated resources in the immediate post-Holocaust period.

The shattered ruins, the ransacked shells and anything left standing by the gangs of looters had been slowly destroyed by wind and rain, storms and hurricanes and the relentless passage of time. But despite being dealt an almost mortal blow, the planet had endured; had begun to heal itself.

Unchecked for over nine hundred years, nature had reasserted its eternal supremacy over the transient, insubstantial works of humankind, grinding concrete into dust, and covering the piles of fallen bricks and forlorn debris with a shifting layer of sand or a carpet of red grass.

Like the Santa Fe interface towards which Commander Hartmann was travelling, the wagon-train under his command was also an artefact of the third millennium. Built in 2961, The Lady from Louisiana – known to its crew as The Lady – was an armoured land-train that stood over thirty feet high and measured a staggering nine hundred feet from end to end when fitted with its full complement of sixteen wagons.

This was the mobile home for a thousand Trail-Blazers – men and women who ate, showered, slept, fought and died alongside each other during the nine months of each year that the wagon-train spent on overground operations. They also used the same toilets, and it had been that way since the Holocaust. To date, the President-General had always been a man, and generations of women had served as guard-mothers to his children, but apart from these two immutable functions there was no discrimination on the basis of gender. In the Federation, men and women enjoyed total equality of status and opportunity from pipe-cleaning in the A-Level sewage farms to the top executive suite in the Black Tower and in front-line combat against the Mutes.

Each wagon, which was linked to its neighbour by a flexible passway, was fifty-five feet long by thirty feet wide, with room inside for three decks, and it was supported at each end by two pairs of giant drum-shaped low-pressure tyres, twelve feet high and twelve feet wide.

Hartmann sat in 'the saddle', the top deck of the forward

command car. This was like the bridge of a pre-H naval frigate and below it was the wagon-train's version of the ship's fire/command control center. Hartmann's deputy, Lt. Commander Cooper had charge of a second duplicate command car at the tail of the wagon-train which meant that, in tactical terms, there was no front or rear. The Lady could go back and forwards with equal facility or split up into two independently manouverable segments – a ploy that had often thrown attacking Mute clans into confusion.

The wagon mix could be modified depending on whether The Lady was on a supply run to way-stations or on a fire-sweep. In combat configuration, the train would haul ten 'battle-wagons' equipped with multi-barrelled gun turrets along the top and sides, a 'blood-wagon' crewed by a team of combat medics headed by Surgeon-Captain Keever and a flight-car which housed the wagon-train's own airforce – ten Skyhawk Mark 1's, the single-seat delta-winged microlite whose production centenary had been celebrated in 2983.

The flight car had an extra-wide flat roof which acted as a mini-runway. With throttles wide open, the Skyhawks were launched into the air from angled steam catapults and 'landed on' with the aid of an arrester hook just like the carrier planes of the twentieth century. Due to their interior layout, the flight-car and power-cars carried fewer guns than the others. It was the command cars and 'battle-wagons' that, quite literally, bristled with weaponry – body heat sensors, night-scopes and infra-red laser ranging devices.

Like the submarine and long-range bomber crews in the last big war of the pre-Holocaust era, Trail-Blazers lived surrounded by their equipment and weapons. Stores and ammunition were stowed in underfloor and overhead compartments, bunks folded down and were shared by day and night-duty personnel and, like the submarines of the Old Time, there were no portholes. Narrow vision-slits could be uncovered in an emergency but under normal conditions, batteries of video screens displayed what lay outside.

The wagon-train was a sealed environment, shielded against the radiation that still fouled the Blue-Sky World, and the air that circulated inside them was carefully and constantly filtered. In the nine centuries since the Holocaust conditions had improved but Trail-Blazers were still pulling 'tricks' – a slang term based on the acronym TRIC – Terminal Radiation-Induced Cancer.

According to the First Family, it was the sub-human Mutes who were responsible for the sickness in the air. And everyone knew that to be true because they weren't affected by it. Mutes had poisonous skins which, if touched with bare hands, caused the flesh of ordinary human beings to rot, and they exuded noxious chemicals which contaminated the atmosphere.

Any Tracker breathing unfiltered air was at risk. Even if they were not killed in combat, Trail-Blazers knew that a nine-month tour on overground operations could shorten their already brief lives by several years but that was a sacrifice they made without hesitation. 'They died so that others might live' was a phrase imprinted daily on every Tracker's consciousness from the age of two onwards, and the words were carved into the Memorial Walls to be seen in the central plazas of each divisional base. They could also be found painted in giant letters along corridors, galleries, the tunnel walls facing the platforms of subway stations, and the radials and ringways linking the network of accommodation deeps.

You had to be blind and deaf not to get the message for it was regularly screened during programme breaks on the nine tv channels piped through the Federation and was often included in voice-over station identification announcements, along with a clutch of other homilies issued by the First Family.

'They died so that others might live'. *Yay, brother. Amen to that . . .*

Although prolonged exposure to overground radiation was still regarded as life-threatening, the level had been falling at a steadily increasing rate over the last few decades. This was entirely due to the dramatic reduction in the numbers of Southern Mutes whose presence had infected the mid-western states now cleansed and reclaimed by the Federation – Texas, Arizona, New Mexico, Oklahoma, Arkansas, Louisiana and Mississippi, plus the New Territories of Colorado and Kansas.

That was a big chunk of territory and required constant policing.

Most of the Southern Mutes who had not been killed or enslaved had been driven towards the east and west coasts and down into the desert wastes of Mexico. A few marauding bands roamed the Outer States looking for easy pickings like scavenging crows but they did their best to avoid contact with patrolling wagon-trains and had become adept at concealing themselves from the circling Skyhawks whose presence announced the imminent arrival of one of the feared iron snakes.

The present threat to the Federation's plan to reconquer the Blue-Sky World was to be found in the New Territories and the vast rolling plains beyond. The Northern Mutes, who called themselves the Plainfolk, were proving a tougher proposition than their southern relatives. Raised to fight and die with the same dedication as the Trackers, they possessed animal cunning, incredible physical endurance and suicidal courage. Fortunately, they were illiterate savages locked into a nomadic, hand-to-mouth existence, and armed with primitive weapons – knives, clubbing axes and crossbows.

Welded into a cohesive force under a shrewd, informed leader, they might have found ways to neutralise the superior technology and fire-power of the wagon-trains but time and destiny were ranged against them. Despite their collective name, the Plainfolk clans had no sense of nationhood and were as keen to fight each other as they were to fight the Federation.

After rolling out of Nixon/Fort Worth in early March for a run of stateside patrols, The Lady had spent the summer roaming the central plains – Kansas, Nebraska and South Dakota where her crew had helped reduce the level of air pollution even further by racking up a body-count of seven hundred and twenty-nine lump-heads. Some were children but, as old Trail-Blazers were often heard to say: '. . . the little 'uns grow up to be as big, mean and bug-ugly as the bucks an' beavers who reared 'em . . .' Harsh but plain commonsense. By taking out the young and the child-rearing females, you effectively neutered the clan. And more often than not, their

13

deaths often goaded the surviving male and female warriors into launching suicidal attacks against Trail-Blazer combat squads sent out from the wagon-train.

Hartmann's crew had taken some casualties but, all in all, it had been a successful tour, in marked contrast to The Lady's first, catastrophic encounter with a strong force of Mutes in Wyoming, the previous year. On his return to the depot, Hartmann and his executive officers had been brought before a Board of Assessors to face a charge of recklessly endangering their train.

It was accepted that lump-heads might kill Trail-Blazers, but they were not supposed to damage wagon-trains or outwit their commanders. With only twenty-one currently in service and a present production rate of one a year the wagon-trains were the most precious item in the Federation's inventory. The Lady's execs experienced a few bad moments, but in the end, everyone had gotten away with a severe reprimand and the loss of a year's seniority.

It could have been a lot worse. Hartmann had a shrewd idea why things had gone so wrong, but like all experienced hands, had not attempted to defend himself by telling the truth. To have suggested that the wagon-train and its crew had run up against the malevolent powers of a Mute summoner would have gotten him into *real* trouble. Mute magic – something which many overground veterans accepted as a proven fact – was a taboo subject within the Federation.

The Manual, the video-archive containing the received wisdom of the First Family and the Behavioural Codes which governed the lives of Trackers from cradle to grave contained a cryptic reference to past allegations of 'Mute magic' and the Family's final word on the subject. Officially, it did not exist. The mere mention of it was a Code One offence. If you were caught, or reported to the Provos and subsequently charged, no plea of mitigation could be allowed. Anyone found guilty of a Code One infraction was guaranteed a one-way ticket to the wall.

This time, the homecoming would be different. The Lady had fallen short of the 1000-kill target that would have earned it a unit citation but after subtracting the time wasted on supply runs, 729 was still a respectable total. And there was always the chance they might nail down the odd clutch of Mute escapees or raiders on the way back to Nixon/Fort Worth.

Despite their poisonous presence, a number of Mutes from the decimated southern clans were used in the overground work-camps. They were supposed to be chained down at night but sometimes, through sloppy security or outside help, they went over the wire. Escapees were usually unarmed but it always made the home run interesting and Hartmann sometimes sent his men out after 'phantom' targets to keep them on their toes. Experience had taught him that it was when you were rolling with the hatches battened down and your feet up that the unexpected happened.

And it was a bit like that today. When decoded and screened, the TAC-OPS signal from CINC-TRAIN in Grand Central put an end to Hartmann's thoughts of celebrating New Year with his kinfolk in Eisenhower/San Antonio. The Lady was ordered to change course immediately and head east, towards navref Kansas City.

After crossing the Missouri, he was to take the wagon-train north through Des Moines, Iowa then east along the old US Highway 80 to Cedar Rapids. The Lady was to make the 1200-mile journey without the customary night halts and he was to ignore any targets of opportunity en route. On arrival at Cedar Rapids, he was to launch his Skyhawks on a search and rescue mission across the Mississippi.

The order to head north so late in the year with snow already falling on the lower slopes of the Rockies came as an unwelcome surprise. Winter was the period set aside for rest and refit. Hartmann would not normally have expected to be called topside until March for supply runs and security sweeps inside the Federation. And when he got to the part of the signal which told him who he was supposed to be looking for, he got an even bigger surprise.

Hartmann keyed the signal into the Command Log – the hard disk whose memory could only be accessed by a combination of his own ID-card and voiceprint – then screened himself through to the Duty RadCommTech and told him to send the standard IMMEDIATE ACTION response to Fort Worth. Having received the signal, the radio operator knew its time and reference coordinates, but at this point, no one, apart from Hartmann, was aware of its contents.

Leaving his quarters, he roused his Navigation Exec and told him about the course change they were to make at Trinidad instead of rolling down to Santa Fe. Hartmann also told him he planned to wait until they had covered the ten miles to the turnoff point before breaking the news to the rest of the crew.

Leaving the NavExec to draw up a new route and schedule based on a three-shift roll, Hartmann returned to his own quarters. CINC-TRAIN'S message had contained a third surprise that would be greeted with equal dismay by The Lady's passengers – Colonel Marie Anderssen, commander of the Pueblo way-station, and sixty-four officers and men from her 1000-strong assault pioneer battalion who, prior to CINC-TRAIN'S signal, had been expecting to be off-loaded at the Santa Fe interface.

The steely-grey lady colonel, referred to by her subordinates as Mary-Ann, had been summoned to Grand Central to attend a Forward Planning Review Board. And travelling with her were a mixed bag of officers and other ranks; soldiers, technicians and construction workers heading south for their first stateside leave after two years up the line.

For some of her party, the journey home would have ended with the fifteen-hundred-foot ride down in the elevator to Level One-1 of Roosevelt Field and its centrepiece, New Deal Plaza; the remainder, whose kinfolk were quartered in other divisional bases, were due to catch the shuttle at the subway station immediately below New Deal Plaza. After trading a few credits for a hot meal or a session on one of the range of video battle or proficiency quiz games in the Plaza's recreation arcade they would have trooped aboard the Trans-Am Express for a 120 mile an hour journey through the earth shield. A few hours later they too would have been home.

But now all that had changed. The digital wall clock was marking up the last seconds towards 0705 when Hartmann re-entered his private quarters. As commander of the wagon-train he was allocated more personal space than anybody else but it was still severely limited. Service protocol and simple courtesy required him to share his quarters with Colonel Anderssen and the designers had thoughtfully provided an extra fold-down bunk for such occasions.

Since there was only just enough room for one, it meant even less room for two. This called for a certain amount of coordination between host and guest, but on this trip it was not a problem. Hartmann and Anderssen were already well acquainted.

They had been classmates at the MacArthur Military Academy and had both graduated *summa cum laude*. Anderssen's posting to the Pioneer Corps who built and manned the way-stations caused them to lose touch for several years but both had moved with equal speed up the promotion ladder and with Hartmann's appointment as commander of a wagon-train it was only a matter of time before their paths crossed again.

In the intervening period, Hartmann had filed bond papers with Lauren, a young woman from a third generation Trail-Blazer family. A few months later, they were notified that she had been selected as a 'guard-mother'. They had gotten along fine from the moment they had been formally introduced and were looking forward to rearing the child but someone at the Life Institute had fouled up and Lauren had died two months after implantation of the microscopic embryo – the fruit of the President-General's seed.

Trackers were conditioned from birth to accept the loss of their kinfolk with a fatalistic shrug. Grief was permissible and in extreme cases counselling was available but you were expected to purge it in private. Death was to be viewed as a victory, not a disaster, which meant Hartmann had received notification of the event but no explanation. His partner's death through negligence – for which no one was ever called to account – left a sour taste and discouraged him from entering into another officially approved relationship.

Since he was not predisposed to jack up everything within sight Hartmann had opted for celibacy, contenting himself in off-duty hours with advanced video study-programs and the fraternal company of his fellow-officers. But whenever The

Lady had been detailed to make a supply run to Pueblo that entailed a night stop-over, he had quartered with his former class- and bunk-mate Mary-Ann.

And now and then, despite the tight-lipped disapproval of Mary-Ann's dark-haired sidekick, Major Jerri Hiller, they would cast aside the burden of command and put the horse between the shafts. They told each other it was just for old time's sake but they both knew there was more to it than that.

Anderssen poked her glistening head around the edge of the shower curtain as he came in. 'Hi . . .' She watched him lock the door and switch on the 'DO NOT ENTER' sign. 'You look as if you've got something to tell me.'

'I have.' Hartmann screened himself through to his deputy.

Lt. Commander Cooper's face appeared on the VDU. 'Morning, skipper.'

'Morning, Coop. I've got some items that are going to keep me busy for the next twenty minutes, so I'd be obliged if you'd get The Lady underway. CINC-TRAIN had ordered a course change and a three-shift roll. Tell Mr McDonnell to bring the section chiefs to the saddle at 0730. I want you and the rest of my staff there too.'

'Very good, skipper.' Cooper paused. 'Sounds serious.'

'Well, I don't think anyone's gonna feel like dancin' "Turkey in the Middle",' said Hartmann. 'But keep this under your hat till I go on the air – okay?'

'Will do . . .'

Hartmann blanked the screen and put the VDU into text and sound mode. He then stripped off the olive-drab tee-shirt he wore when sleeping and approached the shower with his thumbs inside the waistband of his matching boxer shorts. 'Mind if I join you?'

Anderssen opened up the curtain, revealing the now familiar lines of her firm, thirty-six-year-old body. 'Be my guest . . .'

Hartmann stepped into the shower cubicle. There was no way two people could stand under the spray head without their bodies touching in several interesting places – but that was something they'd long been accustomed to. At the Academy, male and female recruits shared the same sleeping quarters and bathroom facilities which included communal shower blocks with units that could house four at a time – or six good friends.

Hartmann pumped some soap out of the dispenser and worked up a lather. He hadn't joined Mary-Ann in the shower because he was feeling horny. When the water was running, it was the only place in the wagon-train you could talk without anyone being able to listen in. Hartmann had no firm proof that the train was bugged but he had not reached the rank of commander without discovering that careless talk could, on occasion, cost lives.

'Want me to scrub your back?'

'Yeah, why not . . .,' Hartmann faced the wall. Anderssen went to work with both hands. 'It's my *back* you're supposed to be doing.'

'Don't worry, I'll get there. We usually manage this twice a year. Twice in one week arouses all kinds of unhealthy appetites.'

'It's the wrong time and the wrong place, honeybun. Listen. CINC-TRAIN just came through. The Lady's not going home. Not yet, anyway.'

Anderssen's hands kept moving. 'So how do I get to Santa Fe?'

'We're going to fly you there.'

'Bill, be serious. I've never flown in one of those stick and string contraptions and I don't intend to start now.'

'Yeah, well, I'm under orders from CINC-TRAIN and while you're on The Lady, you do as I say. Which means you've got about forty-three minutes to get used to the idea.'

'Bastard . . .'

Anderssen tweaked his buttocks with iron hard fingers but Hartmann, anticipating a revenge attack, had already firmed them up so it didn't hurt too much.

'C'mon, Mary-Ann. Ease up. A few puffs of the stuff you keep hidden away and you won't feel a thing.'

'Great idea but I never carry it around – especially to Grand Central. But never mind that, just where the hell am I gonna sit? If you think I'm going to let myself be zipped into one of those buddy-frames you can forget it!' Anderssen's voice softened as Hartmann eased himself around. She smiled up at him as their loins came into contact.

Hartmann made himself comfortable. 'Don't worry. CINC-TRAIN already thought of that. One of those two-seat Skyriders is coming out from Santa Fe.'

'Oh, dandy . . .'

'Hey – snap to it! You got a reputation to keep up. Don't they call you the Iron Lady?'

'Yeah. But that's when I've got my feet on the ground.'

'Look, it's a hundred and seventy-two miles by road. By air, it won't take more than an hour and a half. All you've gotta do is hang tough for ninety minutes. You telling me you can't handle that?'

'How was it with you the first time?'

Hartmann responded, tongue-in-cheek. 'I'm still waiting for someone to offer me a ride.' He silenced her protest with a quick kiss. 'Listen, if it starts getting to you, just close your eyes, lay back and think of –'

Anderssen's firm thighs put the squeeze on his brace and bit. 'Don't say anything you might regret, Billy-boy . . .'

Hartmann pinned her arms inside his and locked his wrists against the base of her spine. 'You're right,' he said. 'This is no time to be kidding around. Do you realize we've only six good years left – maybe eight, if we're lucky?' He sighed. 'Wish I was going with you . . .'

Anderssen didn't resist as he pulled her even closer. She laid her head under his chin as they rocked gently from side to side under the raying jets of warm water. 'Do you still miss Lauren?'

'Not as much as I'm going to miss you.'

Anderssen slid her arms around his waist. 'Where are you headed?'

'Cedar Rapids, Iowa . . .'

'Never heard of it.'

'It's about twelve hundred miles north-west of here. On the same latitude as Chicago.'

'Christo! Doesn't it snow up there at this time of year?'

'So they tell me.'

'Must be pretty important for them to risk sending you that far north. Do you have any back-up?'

'Not that I know of.'

'So what's the bottom line – or haven't they told you yet?'

'It's a search and rescue mission. At least, that's what CINC-TRAIN calls it. Five of our people have gone missing up there.' He shrugged. 'Houston want me to find them and . . . bring 'em in.'

'Feds . . .?'

'If they are, they're not going to tell *me*.'

'Feds' was the nickname applied to special undercover agents thought to be employed by the First Family. No one had ever come up with any hard evidence that such people existed but that had not dispelled the widespread belief that they did.

'The only other kind of people roamin' around out there are breakers. Apart from FINTEL, of course. But it's the first time I ever heard of anyone operating east of the Mississippi.'

'Yeah. The other odd thing is, two of them are wingmen from The Lady – Jodi Kazan, the flight section leader did five tours with me before disappearing over the side in a ball of flame. In that battle I told you about when we –'

'Ran into some unexpected trouble . . .'

'Yeah, that one. The second was a new boy called Brickman. One of three we lost before we turned and ran south to lick our wounds. I've got nothing on the other three – apart from the fact one's a wingman – but everyone thought Kazan and Brickman were both posted KIA over Wyoming last June.' Hartmann shrugged. 'It seems we were mistaken.'

Anderssen leaned away from her shower-mate. 'This guy Brickman . . . would he happen to be 2102–8902 Steven *Roosevelt* Brickman?'

'Yeah, that's him. How d'you know his name and number?'

'Because he's the kind of guy you remember – for all kinds of reasons.'

'But why in particular – and how come?'

'He flew into Pueblo on a wing and a prayer almost a year ago today. Said he'd escaped after being shot down then captured and held prisoner by a clan of Mutes –'

Hartmann looked surprised. 'Held *prisoner*?'

'That's what he said. We radioed The Lady to check that you had a crewman by that name. Your Signals Officer obviously didn't tell you about our query. Anyway, he confirmed that Brickman was one of three wingmen listed PD/ET north-east of Cheyenne on June 12th – as the defaulter claimed.'

'Defaulter?'

'It's SOP. Anyone who comes wandering in from the overground adrift from his unit and without an ID is automatically regarded as a potential code-breaker until proved otherwise. You know that.'

'Sure,' grunted Hartmann. 'But up to now, the only breakers I've seen have been dead ones. So what was his story?'

'I never got to hear it.' Anderssen dropped her voice right down. 'When we called up Brickman's dope-sheet from Grand Central, it came prefixed with a Level Nine entry.'

'Which only you could read.'

'Lucky I did. Otherwise I might have got my buns roasted. Your Mr Brickman is on the Special Treatment List.'

The news caused Hartmann's eyebrows to rise. 'Is he? Well, well, well . . . Thanks for telling me – although, to be honest, I can't say it comes as a total surprise. I always have a one-to-one word with new crewmen when they come aboard then compare notes with McDonnell my Trail Boss. We both had him down as someone who might go far.'

'I know what you mean,' said Anderssen. 'He has that . . . look about him.'

Hartmann drew her to him. 'Yeah. It's the eyes.' He looked deep into hers.

'So, be careful, huh?'

'You too.' He planted a brotherly kiss on the tip of her nose. 'Okay, fun's over. Git outta here.'

'Sure . . .' Anderssen pushed the curtain aside. 'Just out of interest – do you always wear socks in the shower?'

Hartmann looked down at his olive-drab feet. 'Awww, shee-utt! Y'see what happens when you're around?' he peeled off the socks and started to wring them out.

'It might help if you turned the water off.' Marie Anderssen stepped out of the cubicle and picked up a couple of towels. She threw one at Hartmann then started to give herself a vigorous rub-down. 'So what's the word on the rest of my party? Are they being flown to Santa Fe too? Or do they have to walk it?'

'Neither,' replied Hartmann. 'They're staying aboard.'

Mary-Ann stopped drying her hair with one end of the towel as the other end stalled between her thighs. 'But these guys are –'

'Due three months leave, yeah. It's been postponed. Tough, but that's the way it is. They'll get home when we do.'

'That is outrageous . . .' Anderssen cast around for a solution. 'Can't you drop them off at Monroe/Wichita on your way through? I know the interface isn't operational yet but they could ride down the air shaft that was drilled through the floor of the old way-station.'

'We're not going through Wichita. We've been routed through Great Bend and Salina. The terrain is easier to navigate – which means we can maintain speed during our nighttime run.'

Anderssen swore violently then vented her frustration on her own body with an extra-punishing rub–down. 'There must be *something* we can do!'

'Uh-uh, not so much of the "we". This is your beef, hon.'

Her voice turned sour. 'Thanks, I'll remember that.'

'Listen, Marie, I've got my orders. If you don't like what's happening, take it up with CINC-TRAIN – when you get to Santa Fe.'

'Yeah, sure. It means going through channels. Any complaint I make has got to go all the way up to Pioneer Corps HQ before being sent over to CINC-TRAIN. By which time –'

'– assuming it ever gets that far –'

'– you'll be out of sight across the Missouri.'

'Exactly. You know the score – just like CINC-TRAIN knew your guys were hitching a ride home on The Lady. There was no order to off-load them because no one at Grand Central gives a shit whether they get home for New Year or not. All GC cares about is getting this wagon-train to Cedar Rapids. Pronto. So don't take it out on me.'

Anderssen turned away from him, sawed the towel rapidly across her buttocks and down the back of her legs.

Hartmann didn't need to see her face to know that she would have preferred to throttle him with it. Hanging his own towel round his neck, he fished a clean pair of socks and a set of underwear from one of the drawers in his clothes cupboard. He wasn't completely dry but he now only had four minutes in which to get dressed before he was due to break the bad news to his execs and section-chiefs – and he did not relish the prospect.

As a commander who had a genuine interest in the morale and general well-being of the men serving under him, he could understand Marie Anderssen being reluctant to abandon her soldiers but he was irritated to discover that she appeared to be more concerned about them than she was about him. In less than thirty minutes she would be flying out, leaving him with a glum-faced crew and the unwanted problem of coping for upwards of two months with an extra sixty-four disgruntled dog-faces.

He zipped up his khaki fatigues and set a yellow baseball cap at the regulation angle on his head. Anderssen, now in briefs and T-shirt, was stuffing her belongings into a trail-bag. She still had her back to him.

'C'mon, Anderssen – spare me the fire and ice. This new assignment CINC-TRAIN has thrown at us is going to be tough on everybody.'

As she turned around, the tight line of her mouth twisted into a wry smile. 'Everybody except me. You're right. You're the last person I should be dumping on. I'm sorry.'

'Don't say sorry. Just say goodbye.'

They hugged each other warmly. Anderssen raised her face to his. 'Till whenever, huh?'

'Sure. And don't worry about your guys. It's not going to be a joy-ride but I'll do my best to look after 'em.' Their lips met briefly then, as they disengaged reluctantly, Hartmann picked up his wristwatch. 'Christo! I'm late!' He buckled it on and gripped her shoulder, his voice now a whisper. 'Listen, this guy Brickman. Where did he go after he left you?'

'He was hooded and chained then flown to Santa Fe aboard a Skyrider from Big Red One and handed over to the Provost-Marshal of New Mexico for onward transmission to

Grand Central. And GC also ordered us to erase his name from our station-log.'

Hartmann nodded. 'That explains why we were never sent an up-date. We still have him listed K I A.'

'I don't get it,' breathed Anderssen. 'If he was sent to GC as a defaulter last November, what the hell is he doing up to his ass in snow in Iowa?'

'Good question,' said Hartmann. 'But even if I find him, you and I are never going to know the answer. Young Mr Brickman is on the Special Treatment List – remember?'

CHAPTER TWO

For Steve Brickman, any advantages bestowed upon those selected for special treatment were, at that precise moment in time, fated to remain unspecified and dubious. He certainly had no reason to feel privileged, except in the negative sense that he and his four travelling companions had been chosen to be on the receiving end of a sudden run of bad luck. Once again, hasty, ill-considered action had placed him in a situation fraught with difficulty and danger.

Their arrival, before dawn that same day, on the wind-carved dunes of Long Point, on the western shore of Lake Erie, had marked the end of the first phase of a perilous escape from Ne-Issan, the eastern lands over which the Iron Masters held sway. The second phase, a fifteen-hundred-mile journey by air to Wyoming lay ahead. It was this journey which, after a tense but triumphant start, had gone disastrously wrong. Two and a half hours into the flight, Steve had discovered they were rapidly running out of fuel – and there was worse to come.

With the help of two Tracker renegades – Jodi Kazan and Dave Kelso – Steve had made good a promise to rescue Cadillac and Clearwater, two gifted Plainfolk Mutes from the clan M'Call who had fallen into the hands of the Iron Masters. The promise had been made to Mr Snow, the clan's quirky, ageing wordsmith whose brain acted as the repository for nine hundred years of oral history. Mr Snow might be the guardian of the past and the clan's guiding intelligence but that did not stop him making mistakes. It was he who was responsible for sending Cadillac and Clearwater to Ne-Issan in the first place; a decision he had later come to regret and which Steve, in a rash moment, had offered to repair.

But as with most situations Steve found himself in, it was

not as simple as that. Before making his promise to Mr Snow, Steve had been recruited into the ranks of AMEXICO – the AMtrak EXecutive Intelligence COmmando – a top-secret organisation working directly for the President-General of the Amtrak Federation. So secret that only a select handful of the First Family knew of its existence.

Trained as a wingman – the airborne elite of the Federation's overground strike-force, Steve was now a *mexican* – a generic term proudly adopted by AMEXICO operatives along with the use of words and phrases from the pre-Holocaust language known as spanish; the language of the long-vanished nation which had once bordered the southern edge of the Federation and was now the refuge for some of the displaced clans of Southern Mutes.

Steve's new boss, Commander-General Ben Karlstrom had given him the same assignment as Mr Snow. But since he didn't regard Mutes as people, he had referred to Cadillac and Clearwater as 'targets', and the word 'rescue' had been replaced by 'capture'.

Mr Snow had also been targeted – to paraphrase Karlstrom – 'for removal from the equation'. Steve's mission was to bring all three back to the Federation alive, or leave their bodies for the death birds. Or else.

There had been a veiled threat of punitive sanctions that might be levied on Steve's kin-sister Roz and his guard-parents, Annie and Poppa Jack. The death or ill-treatment of his guard-parents would have caused him great distress but it was something he could have borne. It was the threats against Roz that could not be countenanced.

Steve had accepted the assignment because it offered a chance to get back into the Blue-Sky World where he had time to think and room to manoeuvre. Time to think how to rig the board so that everybody got what they wanted – or were fooled into thinking they had. He had the impression that Karlstrom didn't trust him completely. The feeling was mutual. In several action-packed months on the overground, Steve had discovered that the First Family had been lying to their loyal troops for centuries – perhaps from the very beginning when the ash-clouds from the firestorms that had swept across America turned the sun into a chilling, crimson eye for more than three decades.

But it was not all threats and double-dealing. When the chips were down it was Karlstrom who had provided the vital back-up Steve had needed to blast his way to freedom. Part of that back-up had been a fellow-agent code-named Side-Winder disguised as a lump-head with the aid of plastic surgery.

Side-Winder, who claimed to have been working inside Ne-Issan for years, had been just part of a baffling set-up that had included some hard cases from one of the Iron Masters' own intelligence networks. Steve, unaware of this linkage, had done a separate deal with a highly-placed samurai from another network, and there were probably more. Layer upon layer of deceit and intrigue, like the bland protective coating that concealed the ultimate truths about the First Family, the Amtrak Federation and their hereditary enemies, the Mutes.

The task he had been given by Karlstrom – and had voluntarily undertaken for Mr Snow – was difficult enough in itself since the popular belief among Mutes was that no one ever returned from 'the Eastern Lands'. But it was made doubly difficult by his feelings for the people he had been ordered to betray. Cadillac and Clearwater had revealed themselves to be 'straight' Mutes, with perfectly formed bodies and clear, unblemished skins – just like real human beings – which had been skilfully camouflaged by vegetable dyes to blend with the multi-coloured hides of their clanfolk.

Mr Snow was afflicted with the characteristic skin and bone deformities that had caused all Mutes to be labelled 'lump-heads' but he had also been blessed with an encyclopaedic memory, a piercing intelligence and a fund of ageless wisdom spiced with his own engaging blend of mischievous good humour.

Steve's dilemma arose from the fact that he had – to use the time-worn pre-Holocaust phrase – fallen deeply in love with Clearwater and she had responded with equal passion.

Raised in the Federation where the word 'love' was not even part of the vocabulary, Steve had never experienced this depth of emotional involvement before. But he had been extremely close to his kin-sister – closer than two normal human beings can get. He and Roz shared a secret telepathic link of extraordinary intensity that had set them apart from other Trackers since early childhood and on reaching puberty, she had coaxed Steve into a covert sexual relationship.

With his posting to the Flight Academy at the age of fourteen this had gradually broken down due to the long periods of enforced separation. Roz still felt the same but Steve, the reluctant partner, had moved on. With his kin-sister, it was the mental bond that was paramount; his feelings for Clearwater – which had caused Roz such anguish – were of an entirely different order.

Those feelings had caused Steve a great deal of soul-searching too. From the very first days at school he had been taught to regard the malformed Mutes as repugnant, disease-ridden animals; an insult to Nature that had to be ruthlessly exterminated. It therefore followed that an intimate physical liaison between a Tracker and a Mute was an unthinkable aberration; the product of a sick mind. But the attraction he and Clearwater felt for each other had been instantaneous and irresistible and, for Steve, the desire to possess her body and soul had developed into a dangerous obsession.

His bond with Mr Snow and Cadillac was based on a debt of gratitude. Even though he had taken part in a murderous air raid against their clan, they had nursed him back to health after a near-fatal crash and later had saved him from certain death. Had they been captured by Trackers, they would have been killed out of hand but these two so-called savages had shown a degree of forbearance and forgiveness which he did not deserve. His feelings for Clearwater had led him to betray their trust but, once again, there had been no recriminations and he could not bring himself to betray them a second time.

The Manual made it clear that normal moral considerations did not enter into the relationship between Trackers and the Mutes. Despite the superficial resemblances they were not people, they were mentally-defective anthropoids whose place on the evolutionary tree was approximately halfway between human beings and the vanished apes. Karlstrom, the head of AMEXICO, had told him that 'promises to Mutes don't count'. One half of Steve knew that to be true but the other, newly-awakened half told him it wasn't so.

From the moment he had emerged to make his first solo flight above the overground a profound change had taken place within him. He had felt himself being torn in two. The solidarity he felt towards his fellow Trackers, the solemn oath of unswerving loyalty to the First Family conflicted with the growing feeling that he was not and had never truly been part of their underground empire. Entering the Blue-Sky World was like . . . coming home. It defied all reason but every fibre of his being knew it to be true.

For the moment, however, the crushing burden of these emotional and mental pressures had been supplanted by the more urgent and fundamental problem of survival . . .

Steve, Jodi and Dave Kelso were all skilled pilots but they had never flown anything as sophisticated as the Skyrider. The instrument panel was overloaded with switches, dials and radio navigation aids, plus a video screen which showed the aircraft's position as a dot on a moving map which had to be programmed before take-off. They had been in too much of a hurry to discover how to do this, and they were also unfamiliar with the engine which was more powerful and operated on an entirely different principle to the battery-powered Skyhawks they were used to.

Steve had twice been a passenger aboard a Skyrider but the first time he had been too busy talking to the pilot – his late classmate Donna Monroe Lundkwist; on the second occasion, a night flight with a taciturn MX pilot who ignored most of his questions, he had spent the greater part of the trip gazing through the canopy at the star-filled sky.

Until that morning, Jodi and Kelso had never seen a Skyrider but, like Steve, they had enough basic savvy to get one off the ground and manoeuvre it through the air, flying it not with the aid of the overloaded instrument panel but by the seat of their pants. The chance of making a fatal error had been greatly reduced by the provision of an 'idiot board' – an abbreviated list covering the essential control checks and settings a pilot was required to implement on take-off and landing.

But the list did not tell them everything they needed to know before embarking on their journey. And since they had temporarily immobilized their guide, Side-Winder, and the two MX pilots sent to fly them back to the Federation, there was no one to tell them the planes were due to be refuelled for the return flight from a large storage tank buried in the sandy soil alongside the grass landing strip.

With Jodi's help, Kelso had filled two zipper-bags with food and other useful items from the beach store before leaving but if Side-Winder had not revealed its hiding place they would not have known such treasures lay buried beneath their feet. Similarly, it did not occur to them that there might also be a fuel dump. Even if it had, they would have been unlikely to discover its location. Like the beach store with its cunningly-arranged pebble lid, the access points to the fuel tank were hidden from unwelcome visitors beneath the weathered stump of a dead tree whose centre-section could not be unlocked without the aid of a special tool.

The truth was, they were so pleased at having outwitted the trio sent to bring them in, the idea that the planes might be short of gas never entered their heads. They had only one thought – to get the hell out of Long Point as fast as possible.

Steve was flying with Clearwater in the passenger seat and Jodi's haul from the beach store in the cargo bay; Jodi herself was riding with Kelso and they had Cadillac in the cargo hold plus the second bag of looted goodies.

Like Jodi and Kelso, Steve had checked the fuel state immediately after activating the batteries that powered the instrument panel and on-board systems. The visual display, which was graduated to show the fuel state as a percentage gave a reading of 75%. In the lower half of the dial there were four small rectangular windows set side by side. The first three were red and so was the bottom quarter of the fourth window; the upper part was white.

Since his mind's eye equated white as neutral and therefore representing nothingness, Steve assumed, not unreasonably that the three red markers matched the 75% reading, indicating three full tanks and one almost empty. There was a slight problem with the thin red strip in the bottom quarter of the fourth window but the fact that 3.25 did not divide neatly into 75% did not ring any alarm bells. He merely concluded that a zero per cent reading on the dial left the pilot with a quarter of a tank to cover those last few miles home before the engine went dead.

He was wrong all the way down the line. And Jodi and Kelso, by the same perverse logic, made the same mistake. It was almost as if their brains, not wishing to disappoint their owners, had obligingly interpreted the observable facts to fit their expectations.

The reverse was true. The red bar in each rectangle indicated an *empty* tank, and the percentage reading applied to the tank currently switched into the fuel supply system. The pilots of both Skyriders had flown in using the fourth, reserve tank and had already used up a quarter of its contents.

It was only when they were in the air and had been heading west for an hour and a half that his euphoric mood started to evaporate. The red segment in the fourth window was creeping *upwards*, not downwards and the needle indicating the percentage of fuel remaining was dropping too fast. He said nothing to Clearwater or to Jodi and Kelso – now flying off his starboard side with their wing tip lined up with his tail – but thirty minutes later, after checking every knob, switch and dial, his worse fears were confirmed. The other three fuel tanks were empty.

Shit, shit, and triple shit . . .!

Steve selected the plane-to-plane channel. They had maintained radio silence since leaving Long Point to prevent any electronic eavesdroppers getting a fix on their position. With no word from Side-Winder or the two MX pilots for over two hours, alarm bells would be ringing all over Grand Central and once Karlstrom found out what had happened – if he didn't know already – the long knives would be out. Now was not the time to start broadcasting their predicament but Steve had no choice; this was a life-threatening emergency.

'Breaker One to Breaker Two. What's your fuel state, over?'

Kelso's voice came back through his headset. 'Funny you should ask. Kaz and I have been trying to work out why we were burning up so much fuel at the optimum cruising speed and altitude. We started off with 75% and now we're down to 30.'

'I got 37 on the dial,' said Steve. 'That's the good news. The bad news is that reading only applies to one tank. We've been flying on the reserve since take-off. The other three are empty.'

'Jeeezuss!' Kelso cursed volubly. 'So how much does the tank hold? Hang on a minute – Jodi's tryin' to see if there's a vidifax version of the handling notes stashed somewhere. You got one?'

'Stay tuned . . .' Steve told Clearwater what to look for. They searched the cockpit and drew a blank. 'No joy, Dave. Best thing we can do is throttle back. Be careful though. These things fall out of the sky below 65. But if we can burn off less fuel we can maybe extend the mileage.'

'By how much? We're burning it up faster than you are because we got a bigger load! Or have you forgotten we're carrying a ratfaced 'coon skin in the back?'

'Go easy, Dave. He's wearing a paint-job just like you guys.'

'Maybe. But he aint the same underneath . . .'

'Now listen! Don't start peddling that shit! We're all in this together!'

'Yeah, except we aint all in the same airplane! I'm not happy about this, Stevie. Jodi's just shown me the map. There's a big stretch of water lyin' right cross our line of flight.'

'I know. Lake Michigan. The far side is the birthplace of the She-Kargo Mutes. The ancestral home of our two friends here.'

Kelso came back louder than ever. 'What good is that going to do us if we drown before we get there?!'

'We're not going to!' cried Steve. 'We can make it!'

'This side or that side – what's the difference?!' bellowed Kelso. 'We're gonna get our heads sliced off wherever we come down! I *knew* it was too good to be true!'

Turning to Jodi, Kelso said: 'Didn't I tell you that sonofabitch would foul things up for us sooner or later?!'

Jodi, who was studying the video position-plotter and checking distances on a plasfilm map answered him with her eyes but kept her mouth shut.

Steve also let it pass. 'Y'know what? There must have been a fuel dump at Long Point.'

'Brilliant,' sneered Kelso. 'You got any more useless information?!'

Jodi lost her patience. 'Cut it out, Dave!'

They maintained the same course for several minutes in stony silence. Steve looked across at the other Skyrider and saw Jodi's head bobbing around as she made another search of the cockpit. Eventually she held up a flat rectangular object and waved it triumphantly.

'Breaker Two to Breaker One. Got it, Steve!'

What Jodi had found was a vidifax, a slim pocket-sized databank measuring four by eight inches. The top surface was divided into an LCD screen and a set of special function keys including a Scroll command which allowed the viewer to scan blocks of copy by moving them line by line upwards or downwards across the screen at varying speed.

Jodi selected the main menu, moved into the Fuel menu and found the information they required. 'Okay . . . you there Steve?'

'Breaker One, listening out . . .'

'The reserve tank holds 30 gallons of fuel. The optimum burn-off rate is 1 gallon every 25 miles giving a maximum range of 750 miles –'

Kelso chimed in, 'But we only started with 75% of that.'

'I know,' said Jodi.

Steve fed the figures into the small calculator on the low console that ran out from the instrument panel to a point midway between the two seats. 'That still gives us a range of 525 miles.'

'Hang on. Don't get excited.' said Jodi. 'That burn-off rate only applies to an unloaded Skyrider with pilot only and no fuel in the other tanks. We got some more figuring to –'

Kelso exploded. 'Well get to it, Kaz! The needle on this dial is heading down towards the 20% mark.'

Jodi let him have it. 'Dave, for chrissakes gimme a break! You sound like a jackal whining after a bitch on heat.'

'We're close to 29,' said Steve. 'But that doesn't mean anything if we don't know how far we've travelled.'

'I think I can answer that. I managed to get this mapping screen working a while back. We're coming up to navref point Grand Rapids. That means, lessee ... we've travelled 312 miles so far.'

'Thanks. I'll get back to you.' Steve began to button in the numbers.

Jodi passed the map over to Kelso. 'Check how far it is from Grand Rapids to navref Milwaukee ...' Her fingers darted over the calculator.

After a short while, Steve came back on the air. 'Got it. The burn-off rate is one gallon every 22 miles. If this 29% reading is accurate, we can cover another 195 miles. How about you?'

'Not too good, Steve. With our extra loading we're only doing 18.9 miles to the gallon. There's only six left in the tank. According to the calculator, that's 113.5 miles. But that doesn't take into account this headwind we got blowing up our nose.'

Steve glanced at his folded map. 'We still got a chance. Lake Michigan is only 80 miles across.'

Kelso's voice ricochetted round the inside of his skull. 'We aint *got* to Lake Michigan, you dickhead! Look at your frigging map! We're just comin' up on Grand Rapids. That's a *hundred an' twelve miles* from Milwaukee! Look out the windshield! That's a fuggin ocean out there! You seriously expect me and Kaz to try and cross that with *maybe* just enough gas for one hundred and *thirteen*?!

'What d'you want me to do?!' shouted Steve. 'Jettison fuel so I've got the same chance as you? Get your brain into gear, Dave! We're eight thousand feet up. If the motor cuts, you can glide another ten, maybe fifteen miles.'

'Oh, really? The man who didn't know he was flying with empty tanks is now the expert on Skyriders! If you think I'm flying out over that stretch of water just to find out if this thing glides like a fuggin brick you got another think comin'! I want grass under my wheels when the juice runs out. Me and Kaz are headin' south!'

Steve dropped back and closed in until they were flying with wingtips almost touching. He looked across at Jodi Kazan who sat blocking his view of Kelso. 'Jodi, for crissakes! Can't you do something?!'

She drew her right hand swiftly across her throat – the signal used to tell pilots to cut the motor and which was also employed to indicate the abandonment of a fruitless situation or discussion. 'I think he's right, Steve. Have you seen what's up ahead?'

'Yeah,' said Kelso. 'Check the weather at two o'clock!'

Steve switched his eyes from Jodi to the north-west quarter of the sky. The long grey bank of cloud that had been poised ominously on the horizon had begun to move while his attention had been diverted by his lengthy investigation of the crowded instrument panel, the search for the vidifax and the calculations of the plane's fuel consumption. The cloud mass was now angling in rapidly across their front.

Clearwater levelled a finger at the ragged ash-grey wall of cumulus. 'Look! It carries the White Death in its belly!'

She was right. It was a snow cloud whose front edge stretched out of sight in both directions and whose lumpy top layer rose, in places, to almost double their present altitude.

Jodi spoke into the mike fitted to her borrowed crash helmet. 'We're gonna have to run ahead of this, Stevie. It must stretch from here to South Dakota. On the fuel we got left we're not gonna be able to climb over it and flyin' through it aint gonna do us no good either. If we end up being' forced to land in what the good ole boys call a 'white-out' we could be in all kinds of trouble.'

'We're in trouble whatever we do,' grunted Kelso. 'This is as far as we go, Kaz.' Easing back the throttle, he pushed the control column forwards and over to the left and dived under Steve's tail.

Steve caught an over the shoulder glimpse of the Skyrider as it slid beneath him. He banked to the left and saw it reappear in front of him. He cursed quietly and stabbed the transmit button. 'Breaker One to Breaker Two. What's your new heading?'

'Just follow my ass, Brickman!' shouted Kelso. 'I'm aimin' for the southeast corner of the lake. We can head west from there!' His eyes met Jodi's. 'Providin' this goddamn weather doesn't beat us to it!' He held the nose down and pushed the throttle wide open. 'What a pisser!'

Jodi didn't say anything. She'd been here before.

Swallowing his anger, Steve piled on the speed in an effort to catch up with Kelso. He knew they were obliged to change course but he was annoyed at having lost control of the situation. Kelso had played his part in the breakout from the Heron Pool but he had been nothing but trouble from Day One.

When you were in the kind of jam they were in, the one thing you didn't need were guys who were constantly back-biting instead of coming up with positive answers. Jodi's long-suffering attitude had no doubt grown out of comradeship born in adversity but Steve's patience was wearing thin. He mentally gave Kelso one more chance to shape up. If not, the red-headed loud-mouth would find himself surplus to requirements – and Jodi would have to decide whether to stick with a loser or join the winning team.

He looked across at Clearwater and saw she had become tense and withdrawn. She sat hunched up in her seat, one hand braced against the side of the cockpit, the other on the centre console.

Steve laid his left hand over it and gave a reassuring squeeze. 'Hey, hey, relax! A little while back you were enjoying this. What's the matter? You not feeling too good?'

Her lips tightened, then she said: 'I do not understand these things you talk about. Only that something is wrong and that there is much anger between you. Cadillac should have come with us. The two sand-burrowers would then have been free to go where they wished.'

'You're right. Would have made things a lot simpler. The idea was to split the risk so that – if this plane, or Kelso's, powered down, one of you might still have a chance of getting home.'

Her gaze steadied and her mouth relaxed a little. 'We will all get home. Were we not born in the shadow of Talisman?'

'You and Cadillac maybe. I don't think he's too bothered about the rest of us. Don't worry about Kelso. Jodi and I will straighten him out. He's one of these people who only feels happy when he's complaining. But his heart's in the right place.'

And if I find it isn't, I'll put a hole in it . . .

Clearwater turned her right hand upwards and took a firm grip on his. 'I fear the White Death.'

'You?' The idea made Steve laugh. 'C'mon! You're not frightened of anything! You and Cadillac have seen more of this stuff than any of us! Kelso's lived through three winters, Jodi's survived one. It's *me* who should be worried!'

'And are you?'

'Naahh . . . I've got you, haven't I? Trust me. It'll all come out right in the end.'

'Yes, I know,' said Clearwater. 'Even if you and I don't live to see it.'

With the need to keep his eyes fixed on the plane ahead, Steve was not able to examine her face and gauge just what she meant by that cryptic remark. But it was not the first.

Sensing she had unsettled him, she added, 'I do trust you. My life has been placed in your hands. It is the will of Talisman.'

Steve checked the weather to his right then brought his eyes back onto Kelso's plane. 'Why do we always have to keep coming back to that goddamn prophecy? Just for once it'd be nice to think *I* had something to do with the way you feel.'

'But you *do*, golden one. You do . . .'

'Yeah . . .' Steve stared straight ahead. It must be great, he thought to have someone you could rely on. Someone who genuinely cared, who did all the worrying, all the figuring out, and made sure nothing bad happened to you. Why was it he who always seemed to end up carrying everybody else?

Perhaps that was the way it was for people who liked running the show. But Jefferson the 31st, the current President-General – who he'd met – ran the greatest show on earth. You could bet your last meal credit *he* didn't give a damn about anybody lower down the wire. Including Steven Roosevelt Brickman. You could see it in the eyes. Jefferson was the kind of guy who could walk you all the way to the revolving door to his office, a smile on his lips, a fatherly hand on your shoulder – knowing that the hit-squad he'd ordered was waiting for you to step out of the turnstile.

Pure naked power ... At the level the P-G was operating on, it must give you a real buzz ...

As the two planes lost height, the grey wall of cloud began to tower over them like a giant tidal wave that threatened to swallow them without trace. The strong north-westerly wind that provided its motive power was driving the snowflakes forward from its leading edge as they fell in their countless millions.

Steve glanced at the gyro compass. He was currently tailing Kelso on a heading of two zero zero. They had lost altitude steadily and were now down to nine hundred feet. It was clear that Kelso wanted to maintain visual contact with the ground; a wise decision in the circumstances but if they were to avoid being engulfed they would soon have to swing onto a more southerly heading.

He consulted his map and tried to find a matching feature on the lake shore beneath. And then it happened. As his left index finger edged over the folded sheet of plasfilm towards navref Benton Harbour, map and ground coincided and he glimpsed the squat, rectangular outlines of a boat moored to a wooden jetty. It was not one of the massive wheelboats that visited the trading post, but it was still of appreciable size, with a paddle wheel running across the full width of the stern.

Colour and detail faded rapidly beneath the first wash of snow. In perfect visibility, Steve might have seen the upturned face of the figure standing on the bow deck as a pale dot set against the dark wooden planks but not today. Izo Wantanabe saw the two Skyriders pass overhead but those aboard did not see him.

Steve didn't need to. There was only one place the boat could have come from – Ne-Issan. The Iron Masters had put it there, and had built the square jetty to which it was moored. Its positioning far beyond the present borders of Ne-Issan must have taken place several weeks, if not months, ago. The boat and its invisible crew could only belong to domain-lord Yama-Shita; it was his family who held the exclusive licence to trade with the Mutes. But Yama-Shita had been dead for a week – killed by Clearwater during the break-out. Did the dead-faces down there know that? Or know that his assassins had escaped?

Steve thought it unlikely, even though the Iron Masters used carrier pigeons for urgent long-distance communication. The Yama-Shita family were probably still reeling from the shock and were more likely to be concerned with fighting off bids from envious rivals anxious to grab a slice of their trading empire than alerting their front men in the outlands. For the moment, anyway.

No. The real question was more basic: Why would a boat-load of Japs be moored near the southern end of Lake Michigan in the second week of November? Had Hiro Yama-Shita got some kind of extended operation going with the Plainfolk Mutes in this area?

The need to press onwards, ahead of the advancing snow made detailed observation impossible but Steve had not seen any on-shore installations out of his side of the cockpit, and neither had Clearwater. The boat's occupants might be armed but they were sitting ducks. Steve toyed momentarily with the agreeable notion of capturing it and making a slow but stately progress to the trading post at Du-aruta. They would be assured of absolute safety at sea, coming ashore only for timber to feed the boiler – the source of power and warmth. The problem of what to eat could be solved by catching fish like the Iron Masters did.

Winter would give way to the time of the New Earth. Freed from the grip of its icy fingers the soil would burst open as the buried seeds awoke. New pink grass would put a warm blush on the face of the world and as the air softened with the approach of spring they would linger off Du-aruta until the M'Call delegation joined the other Plainfolk emissaries near the end of May for the annual round of trading with the Iron Masters. Then, before the massive three-storeyed wheelboats steamed into view, they would beach their stolen vessel in full view of the waiting Mutes.

Steve pictured the faces of the Plainfolk as he lead his party ashore. Yes . . . a lot better than walking to Wyoming. And if Kelso got lippy he'd end up tied to the paddle wheel . . .

'Steve!!'

Clearwater's cry snapped him out of his reverie. Kelso's

Skyrider had disappeared. Visibility was now zero. The cockpit was surrounded by driving snow.

Steve rolled the Skyrider to the left, held the nose down and slammed the throttle wide open. The snow started to thin, then fell behind as they outraced the bank of cloud. He knew they had gained only a temporary respite. The only way to avoid it was by flying south-east – back towards Ne-Issan – the one place he didn't want to go.

Applying a touch of right rudder, he brought the Skyrider back onto a heading of 180 degrees – due south – and peered through the canopy. It was now streaked with melting snow. 'Can you see them?' His own eyesight was extra sharp but he had discovered that some Mutes were able to get a visual fix on moving objects at amazing distances – like birds of prey.

Clearwater searched the sky ahead of them.

'Hang on . . .' Steve made the plane weave from side to side, dipping the left wing then the right to provide her with a better all-round view. The southern end of Lake Michigan which lay just beyond his right shoulder fell under the shadow of the advancing snow cloud.

Looking down, Steve saw the sand dunes and swamps that had repossessed the area once drained and flattened under the concrete bases of steel-making plants and petro-chemical complexes. Poisonous effluents and sulphurous smoke-stack emissions in the pre-Holocaust era had turned the area into a wasteland but nine centuries later, the waters of Lake Michigan were as clean and blue as when the first 17th century French fur trappers had canoed down the Wabash.

Clearwater flung her arm across the cockpit in front of Steve's face. 'There!'

He followed her pointing finger. Several hundred feet below them, a winged speck was heading south-west. Kelso and Jodi. Any minute now they would be running out of gas and they would both be searching for a reasonably safe place to put down.

'Don't lose sight of them,' said Steve. He switched on the plane-to-plane channel. 'Breaker One to Breaker Two. What's your fuel state? Over.'

It was Jodi who replied. 'Breaker Two. We've had zero on

the dial for the last six minutes but the motor's still – uh-oh, correction. It just cut out on us. Over.'

'Okay, hang in there. I know you'll be fighting gravity from here on in but try to find a spot that's big enough for both of us. We'll be coming in right behind you.'

'Roger Wilco. Dave says he can't wait. According to the map there's a hardway running east to west. We're aiming for that. Breaker Two over and out.'

As Jodi went off the air, the plane ran into another blinding flurry of snow. A knot formed in her stomach. 'Are we gonna be able to get down?'

Kelso wrestled with the controls. 'Kaz – that's the one thing you can be sure of. Whether we walk away is another matter entirely.'

They broke out into a relatively clear patch of sky. Two hundred feet below them they saw the vague outline of the hardway – the remains of US Highway 30. With the coating of snow thickening by the minute, it was impossible to gauge what condition it was in and without power they could not make an exploratory low-level pass. Once again they were wrapped in a swirling white cloud, the flakes turning to translucent sludge as they hit the canopy. The slipstream blew the sludge into ragged waves that crept slowly up the windshield. Jodi and Kelso leaned forward and peered through the gaps, trying to get a clearer view.

'This is hopeless,' shouted Kelso. 'I'm gonna make a down-wind landing!' He selected full flap. 'Pull your straps tight!'

Without power, any turn has to be made nose down to avoid a stall which, at low altitude, is usually fatal. Putting the snow behind their tail increased the forward visibility a little but decreased the speed of the air flowing over the wings, robbing them of valuable lift and increasing their rate of descent.

The snow-covered hardway came up to meet them at an alarming rate before Kelso could line up the nose properly.

'Dave! For crissakes –!'

BLUMMFFF! Jodi's skull and spine collided with a sickening jolt as the three plump tyres flattened onto the axles then bounced the plane back into the air on the north side of the hardway. Trees loomed up ahead. Kelso kicked on some right rudder to bring the nose round. With the Skyrider now close to stalling speed its response to control movements was mushy but with the help of a stream of invective from Kelso, it wallowed back towards the centreline of the makeshift runway.

'Okay! This is it!' Kelso tried to correct the drift to the right but the controls no longer responded. Jodi braced herself as they dropped through the last fifteen feet like a stone.

The main wheel on her side of the plane hit the ground first. The undercarriage strut had survived the first punishing blow but this second impact tore it loose. The Skyrider crashed forward onto its nosewheel, buckling the supporting strut and driving it upwards through the fuselage. The right wheel landed on the sloping, overgrown grass verge, tilting the Skyrider further over to the left. The tip of the wing on Jodi's side was ripped to pieces as it came into contact with the ground. She tried to steady herself as the plane slewed round, jolting and bouncing over the uneven surface of the hardway. There were sharp cracks and rending noises as other parts of the plane to the rear of the cockpit broke loose. The Skyrider spun around once on its belly then slid sideways along the axis of the undamaged starboard wing into the snow-covered undergrowth on the northern side of the hardway.

Jodi could now only see where they'd been and not where they were going but during the ground-loop, she had caught a whip-pan glimpse of several more clumps of trees. Her internal radar sensed they were now probably on a collision course. She dropped her chin onto her chest and hugged her arms. If there was an afterwards, she knew they would discover there was more than enough room for half a Skyrider to pass between the trees but by Sod's Law they were bound to hit one. She was not disappointed.

With the fine tuning only Destiny can provide, the leading edge of the starboard wing lost its top coat of paint as it scraped past the rim of the trunk of the last tree of the last clump at a neat tangent, leaving Kelso's side of the cockpit to take the full impact.

KERR-RUNCH!! Jodi was held in her seat by the safety harness but her head was thrown back against the bulkhead with a force that not even her crash helmet could absorb. In the split second before she lost consciousness, the last thing her mind registered was an overwhelming sense of relief: she might die, but she would not burn . . .

The weather was even worse when Steve and Clearwater arrived on the scene but with their lighter all-up weight, they still had some gas in the tank. Skimming perilously close to the tops of the trees, Steve flew up and down the highway, searching for Kelso's Skyrider.

Now flying into the teeth of a full-scale blizzard, Steve had to give his full attention to keeping the plane on course. He had to rely on Clearwater but even her sharp eyes missed it on the first two attempts. She spotted it as Steve made a third, westward, pass.

'There they are!'

'Good! Keep your eye on it!'

'But, ohh – its wings are broken!' She turned around in her seat, pressing her face against the canopy. 'And nothing moves!'

'In this weather, they're better off staying inside,' said Steve, trying to sound optimistic. He hadn't seen the wreckage for himself but it didn't sound too promising. On the other hand, there was no point in worrying about what might or might not have happened to Jodi, Kelso and Cadillac. The first thing they had to do was make a safe landing themselves.

Banking to the left, he flew eastwards roughly parallel with the hardway, passing the Skyhawk on the downwind leg. Its charcoal-grey outline was fast disappearing under the snow. Another thirty seconds on the cockpit's digital clock took him three quarters of a mile down the road and clear of the trees.

As he circled round and prepared to land, he spoke to Clearwater over the radio channel that linked their headsets. 'Okay! I'm gonna be busy trying to keep this thing lined up on the hardway so give me a shout when you see 'em. Should be any second now!'

Clearwater unbuckled her safety harness and sat on the edge of her seat, bracing herself against the instrument panel.

Forward visibility was atrocious. The ground on all sides

was now completely blanketed with snow and the sky was full of it. The instruments told Steve he was flying more or less straight and level at just under fifty feet but his stomach told him they were being buffeted up, down and sideways by the gale-force gusts of wind. The only reliable guide to where the ground ended and the sky began were the dark sheltered recesses of the trees where the inner branches met the trunks.

'Now! Now!!'

Steve waited till the wheels touched before cutting the motor. He caught a fleeting glimpse of the front half of Kelso's Skyrider wrapped around a tree as they flashed past, rocking and juddering along a six-lane highway that had not been resurfaced for over nine hundred years. It was like rollerskating over corrugated iron. He pulled the brake lever back as far as it would go, locking the two main wheels. And just as he was wondering what had happened to the other half of the Skyrider, they ploughed into it.

Steve, who had received a split-second advance warning from his resident guardian angel, threw his arm across Clearwater's chest and yanked her backwards. He succeeded in stopping her going head first through the canopy but the sudden deceleration caused everything from the waist down to slide forwards off the seat. Her knees crashed against the instrument panel with a sharp, bone-cracking noise that made him wince.

Clearwater didn't utter a sound. A secret combination of true grit and mental discipline rendered Mutes – with a few exceptions – almost totally impervious to pain.

'Christo! That sounded terrible. You okay?'

She eased herself slowly into an upright sitting position and rubbed both kneecaps. 'I'll tell you after I've tried to walk.' She searched for the lever that opened her side of the canopy. 'We must find Cadillac –'

Steve grabbed her shoulder and held her down. 'You stay right there. I'll go check what's happened.' He slid out quickly, landing with his weight on his right foot. The wound in his thigh gave him a sickening reminder that she wasn't the only one who might not be in the best shape for an overland expedition.

He shut the canopy and checked to see what they'd run into. The mangled tail-boom section of Kelso's plane was caught against the rear wheel struts. They had also passed over an unseen but unyielding projection – probably a rock – which had mangled the tips of the propeller blades.

Well done, Brickman ... Opening the hatch of the cargo bay, he rummaged through the bag of odds and ends they had brought with them and pulled out a straw poncho – one of the items of clothing issued to Mute slaves by the Iron Masters. Lowering the visor of his crash helmet, Steve leaned against the howling wind and hobbled down the hardway towards the wrecked Skyrider.

The buckled fuselage pod with its rear-mounted engine and one and a half wings lay hard up against a huge tree – now a dark silhouette against the white landscape. The impact had shaken the snow off the branches, dumping it on the wreck below. There was no sign of movement and no sound.

The canopy release handle on the port side was jammed. Steve broke open the emergency rescue panel behind the cockpit and used the spiked axe to prise the canopy open. The hinges were warped and stiff. Steve forced it upwards and saw that the other half had shattered. Snow was blowing in, covering Kelso's body. Jodi's had twisted towards the point of impact. Her left arm was bent over her chest, the other lay across Kelso.

Steve leant in and laid a hand on her shoulder. 'Jodi . . .?'

Her head rocked slowly against the bulkhead as she started to come round.

'Hi. How're you doing?'

Jodi's eyes fluttered open. It took a few seconds to get her eyes into focus. Her brain took a little longer. 'I, uh . . . uhh . . .' Her painted hands fumbled ineffectually with the release clip of her harness.

Steve undid it for her then loosened the chin strap of her crash helmet and eased it off. 'Does it feel as if anything's broken?'

Jodi moved her arms and legs. 'Nuhh . . . think I'm okay. It's just my neck.' She raised her head gingerly. 'Oww –!'

'Here – lemme have a go at it.' Steve massaged the muscles

and bones at the top of her spine, causing her to gasp with pain.

'Hey! Go easy!'

You'll survive. It's gonna hurt for a while but everything seems to be in place.'

Jodi carried on where Steve had left off. 'Can always give myself a shot, I suppose. Dave and I picked up some morphine jabs and a few packs of Cloud Nines when we raided the beach store.'

Steve nodded towards Kelso. 'We may need all of that for him – assuming he's still with us. 'C'mon, shift your butt.' he gave Jodi a helping hand as she climbed stiffly out of the cockpit. They saw Clearwater limping unsteadily towards them.

'Looks like another candidate for the sick parade.' Jodi's teeth were chattering with cold but she could not help laughing at their predicament. 'What a mess! Still, I s'pose things can only get better.'

Steve was already inside the cockpit checking Kelso's heartbeat. 'He's alive . . . Dave! Dave! Can you hear me?'

The big man gave an answering groan. Steve lifted the visor of Kelso's helmet and saw his eyelids pressed tightly together as he mastered a wave of pain. The alloy ribs and plating on his side of the cockpit was ripped and mangled and Kelso was pinned underneath from the hips down. Steve realized it would take a while to free him.

'Is he hurt bad?' asked Jodi.

'Can't tell yet but it don't look too good.'

Clearwater reached them and leaned against the cockpit sill, breathing in and out through clenched teeth.

'Welcome to the A-Team . . .' said Jodi.

The joke was lost on Clearwater. She turned towards Steve and waited for him to acknowledge her presence.

The acknowledgement, when it came, lacked the easy charm that many of his admirers found so irresistible. 'What the hell are you doing here? I told you to stay in the plane!'

'Where's Cadillac?!'

'One thing at a time!' snapped Steve. 'We got a badly injured man here!'

47

'But Cadillac may be hurt too!'

'Make up your mind! A little while back you told me every-thing was gonna be okay 'cause you were both protected by Talisman!'

'Ohh, Sweet Mother! You're as pig-headed as he is!' Momentarily forgetting she had two badly bruised knees, Clear-water stamped her right foot to vent her frustration and almost fainted from the searing pain that filled her leg from hip to ankle.

Jodi caught her as she swayed and sat her down on the sill. 'Easy now, just . . . hang in there, okay? We're on his case.'

Steve clambered out of the cockpit. He shared Clearwater's concern but temper tantrums he could do without. 'Jodi – that hole in the canopy is proving a real pain in the butt. We need some kind of cover to keep the snow off him while we get him out.'

'How about using the hatch off the cargo bay?'

'Brilliant. . .' Steve fished the axe out of the cockpit then, adding a dash of acid, he said: 'And if it turns out Cadillac's still in one piece, we can ask him if he'd care to give us a hand.'

Clearwater met his narrowed eyes but refused to take the bait.

Steve got to work with the axe. The cargo door was designed to lift upwards, but with the plane lying on its belly and tilted towards them, the release catches were pinned against the ground. After chopping through the hinges, Steve used the axe handle to lever the curved panel open far enough to get one foot on the top edge then he and Jodi trampled it to the ground.

Clearwater helped Jodi to pull out the bulging, overweight bag of swag Kelso had slung in on top of their passenger. As they lifted it clear, Cadillac's limp body slid into view, head first, face down.

Fearing the worst, Steve turned him over. There wasn't a mark on him. His eyes were shut, but he wasn't unconscious. He was fast asleep – snoring contentedly.

With a cry of exasperation, Clearwater scooped up a handful of snow and rubbed it over his face then, when he didn't respond quickly enough, she stuffed a second helping down the front of his tunic.

'Yyyu-ughhh! Wha – wha's happening?!' Cadillac hoisted himself up on his elbows, bonked his skull on the low roof of the cargo bay and fell back clutching his forehead. 'Shee-ehh!'

While Steve worked to free the bottom edge of the hatch, Clearwater and Jodi hauled Cadillac out and stood him upright. His legs were still rubbery. The Mute had drunk so much *sake* at Long Point they'd practically had to pour him into the cargo hold. But with hindsight it had proved to be the safest way to travel. It was amazing. The sole injury he'd sustained was the bump he'd collected on waking up.

Pulling the sodden front of his tunic away from his chest, Cadillac draped an arm across Clearwater's shoulders and gave her, then Jodi, a lop-sided grin of recognition.

Jodi watched as he took stock of his surroundings, ending with a puzzled stare at the dark grey sky from which white flakes were dropping silently onto his upturned face. His sodden brain finally worked out what was happening. 'Snow,' he said. 'It's snowing!'

Incomprehension gave way to understanding followed by a wave of cautious elation. Cadillac seized both girls by the arm. 'Where are we – Wyoming?'

'Not quite,' said Steve. He wrenched the battered cargo hatch clear of the fuselage. 'But you're getting warm . . .'

The wind picked up again and the snowflakes – now as big as communion wafers – began falling thicker and faster than ever.

CHAPTER THREE

When Kelso had been heavily sedated and prised loose, it was immediately obvious that his right arm and leg were broken but without x-rays and an examination by a paramedic, it was impossible to tell if he had additional internal injuries. Once again, Clearwater came to their rescue. Using a previously unrevealed gift allied to her powers as a summoner, she was able to 'read' what she called 'the fire devils'. Laying her hands gently on Kelso's body, she located the fractures in his upper arm and thigh and found he also had four cracked ribs. Worst of all, he had a broken hip-joint – or perhaps a fractured pelvis.

Not good. Not good at all . . .

Steve was tempted to put an end to him there and then. The alternative was to carry him all the way to Wyoming, but by the time they got there – assuming they ever did – he would be beyond even the amazing skills of Mr Snow.

It was a stark choice that might yet have to be faced if their situation deteriorated and it was bound to cause dissension. Steve knew that Jodi would fight to keep him alive until the last moment. But then maybe, if he was in Kelso's place, he would be glad to have someone close at hand with the same protective feelings.

In the meantime, the only thing they could do was to apply splints and bandages to his broken limbs, secure his hip-joint from further dislocation by strapping his body to the door of the cargo hatch, keep him warm and dry, and heavily sedated.

Thanks to Kelso's decision to plunder the beach store at Long Point they had a supply of bandages, medicine, food and fire and – best of all – several mirror-foil emergency blankets. But their long-term survival was threatened by totally inadequate footwear and clothing and the lack of shelter.

Steve had already taken steps to deal with the latter problem.

In order to free Kelso they first had to ease the fuselage away from the tree using branches as levers. The broken port wing was now propped up by those same branches, tilting the plane over so that the starboard wingtip touched the ground. Kelso had been moved underneath as soon as he had been disentangled and now lay wrapped in two of the foil blankets on a floor made of smaller branches cut from neighbouring pine trees. The soft ever-red foliage gave off a sweet reassuring smell when crushed underfoot.

Under the direction of Cadillac and Clearwater, more branches were laid at an angle against the front and rear edge of the wing. When several more layers had been applied and interwoven to keep out the snow, the result was a snug, wind-proof little hideaway into which they crawled to silently nurse their various aches and pains.

Compared to the scale of Kelso's injuries, the week-old arrow wound in Steve's right thigh was a minor inconvenience but he would not regain full use of his leg unless he gave it proper care and attention. Clearwater was temporarily crippled by two bruised and swollen knees and the whiplash injuries to Jodi's neck had left her extremely sensitive to any jarring of her spine. Without a pain-killer, even walking was now a disagreeable exercise, forcing her to tiptoe around like Doctor Caligari. That left Cadillac as front runner – a situation Steve was not at all happy about but one he was going to have to live with.

Despite the injury to her neck, there was nothing wrong with Jodi's legs but it would be two or three weeks before his own and Clearwater's would be strong enough to face a thousand mile hike – carrying Kelso all the way. Steve knew that putting their feet up for so long was a luxury they would have to forego; the most they could allow themselves was two or three days – not to rest, but to prepare for the journey ahead.

They had to keep moving. If Karlstrom's electronic ears hadn't picked up their panic-stricken air-to-air exchanges, he would soon learn they had taken off with almost empty tanks. All he had to do then was draw a circle on the map. And it wouldn't take long for someone of his intelligence to figure out which part of the circle they were most likely to be in.

There was the added, and quite unexpected, threat posed by the presence of Iron Masters at Benton Harbour – only sixty or so miles from where they had landed. Since he had been able to see the wheelboat it was reasonable to assume that someone on board *might* have seen the two Skyriders passing overhead. Even if they didn't know what they were looking at, their curiosity would be aroused and if they were linked by carrier-pigeon to the Yama-Shita household the news would travel fast. Iron Masters were compulsive scribblers; a constant stream of paperwork flowed back and forth through the government-run postal system and the parallel private networks of couriers – some of them winged – employed by each of the seventeen domain-lords.

Steve and his companions had given the Yama-Shita family ample cause to regret their involvement with flying machines. The domain-lord's relatives might confuse a report about the two Skyriders with the rocket-powered gliders he and the others had used to escape from the Heron Pool.

Given the time of the year, the present weather and the distance now separating them from the family's headquarters at Sara-Kusa the possibility of intervention from that quarter was remote but there was no point in taking chances – especially with an unknown number of Japs moored just up the coast. From here on in, pursuit by the agents of AMEXICO *and* the Iron Masters were factors that had to be considered when evolving what political and military strategists called 'the worst case scenario': it would be foolish to base their future moves on anything else.

Steve, who now sat huddled together with Jodi, Clearwater and Cadillac in front of the fire can, warmed his hands alongside theirs and shook his head as he reflected on their predicament. Why did it get more difficult and more complicated instead of easier and simpler? When would it ever end? And why had he ignored all the warning signals and walked into this mess in the first place?

The answer was locked away somewhere inside him – maybe held by the stranger whose whispered voice he heard from time to time. With Uncle Bart's connections, a safe, comfortable desk job in the Black Tower could have been his for the asking but that would have been too easy. The example set by Poppa Jack and his own need to measure himself against the brightest of the best had led him to become a wingman. And that, in turn, had led him to discover his affinity with the overground, a mind-blowing experience which released feelings that had shaken his previously unswerving allegiance to the Amtrak Federation and left him wondering where he really belonged.

Steve had always believed himself to be smarter than his classmates, had enjoyed pitting his wits against the system but *why* did he have this insatiable desire to know everything, to be Number One? Why him and not the next guy? What had given *him* the idea that he was some kind of super-hero who could solve any problem and triumph over impossible odds? Where had this arrogant certitude come from? It was insane. And how had he – who from an early age had cultivated a steely detachment – become *involved*? Why had he begun to care about what other people felt and what happened to them? What the hell difference did it make? The Plainfolk believed it was all going to happen anyway: 'The Wheel turns, The Path is drawn . . .' Mr Snow, Cadillac and Clearwater had all trotted out that line at one time or another. But it didn't *explain* anything – like who had drawn The Path. Talisman? Mo-Town? The Sky Voices? And *who* had given whichever one of them it was the right to interfere?

The same question could be asked of the First Family. Perhaps that was the reason why he couldn't let go: run for cover, take the soft option – and why he also felt so torn and confused. He would like to have been comforted by the thought that he had a friend out there, watching over him, ready to extend a helping hand, shoulder some of the burden but he still couldn't bring himself to really trust in anybody or anything. There were times when he even began to have doubts about Clearwater. If you dug deep enough, everyone had an angle. And what *really* went against the grain was the idea that someone else – be it a person like the President-General, or some imagined power like Talisman – had already planned each move he would make in life and that he, Steven Roosevelt Brickman, could do nothing to change the future course of events.

Like many young men, Steve was confusing the material world – external reality – with the world of the spirit. And as there were no books in the Federation and the only moral philosophy – spiced with a large measure of self-interest – was dispensed through the Federation's televideo network by the First Family, he was unaware of the nature of his dilemma and a key pre-Holocaust quotation that might have helped to set his mind at rest: 'We may not be master of our own destiny but each of us is the captain of our soul'.

Regardless of our physical or material circumstances, whether we are fated to be showered with good fortune or dealt the cruellest blows (or a mixture of both) we have the power within us to make the conscious decision to retain our humanity, the ability to love, and our sense of what is right and just, and true.

When Jodi had gone back down the hardway to pick up the trail bags from Steve's Skyrider, she had used her newly acquired knowledge of the nav-systems to get a fix on their present position. The undamaged cockpit contained an inertial plotting device which automatically monitored speed and direction throughout the flight. Since it had logged the coordinates of Long Point, it was able to work out where it was now. When the latitude and longitude readout was applied to the map, she was able to tell Steve they had landed a few miles to the east of navref point Merriville, Indiana.

Their flight had taken them into the next time zone. The on-board digital display had adjusted itself automatically, leaving their wristwatches running an hour fast – something she failed to notice. Not that it mattered; they had other more pressing concerns. But for the record, it was now 1416 hours Central Standard Time and it snowed steadily for the rest of the day.

Nine hundred miles to the southwest, the clocks aboard The Lady from Louisiana were still set to Mountain Standard Time. Colonel Marie Anderssen had signalled her safe arrival at Santa Fe and would soon board the inbound afternoon shuttle for Houston/GC. So far, The Lady had made good headway, maintaining an average speed of 18 miles per hour.

54

She had succeeded in crossing the Arkansas River west of an old reservoir without having to decouple the wagons, and was now heading towards Lamar, the last navref point before the Colorado/Kansas state line.

The next morning, when Izo Wantanabe emerged from his quarters on the wheelboat, the skies had cleared. Climbing up the newly-swept steps to the bridge, Izo scanned the surrounding landscape. A deep covering of snow – heaped in places into mountainous drifts – stretched away to the north, east and south as far as he could see.

Because of the weather, Izo had been unable to send the message he had prepared the previous day and it was now probably a waste of time to do so. If the bird-men had managed to outrun the snow cloud and return to their roost the answer to his query would be largely academic. On the other hand, the receipt of his message and its contents would be duly noted in the log. If examined by his superiors it would provide proof of his alertness. But even if the agent at Ludington had nothing to report it did not significantly alter the overall situation. The iron snake, which carried the cloud-warriors in her belly and killed all those who came too close with its white-hot breath, might still be lurking on the west bank of the Miz-Hippy River.

Offensive actions during the winter months were unprecedented but they could not be ruled out. The cloud-warriors could have seen the wheelboat. If their masters concluded that its presence signified a strengthening of the links between the Iron Masters and the Plainfolk they might return to attack it with the much-feared fire-blossoms. From now on, he and his staff must remain vigilant. Summoning them on deck, he told them what he had seen the previous day and explained its importance. Starting immediately, the entire crew, working in pairs on two-hour shifts, were to maintain a sky-watch from dawn to dusk until further notice.

After adding a hasty postscript to his original message, Izo ordered the pigeon-keeper to prepare the fastest bird they held from the Ludington coop. While the message, in its tiny capsule, was being attached to the bird's leg, a carrier-pigeon arrived from Di-taroya, the first outland station, on the straights of Hui-niso. Reports passed on by 'friendly' Mute clans, whose turf lay to the northwest, spoke of two 'arrowheads' that had flown 'out of the east.'

From Ne-Issan . . .

An inner voice told Izo that these were the same pair he had seen running ahead of the snow-cloud. The agent at Di-taroya, who was preparing a report to send to Lord Yama-Shita, wanted to know if these craft had been sighted by the staff of the other stations. If the answer was 'yes' they were to contact Lord Yama-Shita directly.

Seized by a premonition that he had accidentally become a player in an intriguing and mysterious drama, Izo tore up his first message and swiftly prepared another. The thought that the account of what he had seen, signed and sealed with *his* name, would soon be on its way to the palace at Sara-kusa excited him. The original query to Ludington might lay unnoticed for months, even years; this report would reach people of importance in a matter of days, drawing their attention to the diligence with which he performed his appointed task. Izo closed his eyes and called upon the Goddess of Good Fortune to bless his actions. He felt her calm hand on his brow; his brush hand ceased quivering. This was not the end of the affair. There would be more questions. When they came, he intended to have some of the answers.

The pigeon circled several times as it got its bearings then flew off eastwards on rapidly beating wings.

Calling the master-sergeant to his quarters, Izo informed him that he had decided to make a four-day journey on horseback into the interior, accompanied by two sea-soldiers, packmules, and one of the male domestics to act as forager. By making contact with the scattered clans whose turfs lay to the south of his station Izo hoped to establish with some precision where the 'arrowheads' had gone after passing over Benton Harbour. He asked the sergeant to select three dependable men and appointed him to command the house-boat in his absence.

Each agent had been supplied with four horses and six pack mules for overland sorties. The weather was far from ideal for a horseback ride but the primary reason for the animals' presence was to impress the natives. The enormous size of the Great River wheelboats and the formidable appearance of the masked nobles and samurai created an atmosphere of authority and power that could not be matched by the agent's modest house-boat and relatively puny entourage. Nor could the sense of occasion that accompanied their brief annual visits to the trading post be sustained for months on end.

The boats anchored at the outland stations could have been easily overrun but the agents had been assured they were unlikely to be attacked. The Plainfolk clans – who were not as dumb as they looked – had long realized that any unprovoked aggression would be counter-productive. But that realization did not automatically engender respect – especially when you were inferior both in numbers *and* physical stature.

That was the real problem: the average grass-monkey stood head and shoulders above the average Iron Master. Since they did not have the awesome bulk of three giant wheelboats to act as a backdrop to their negotiations, Izo and the other agents needed something to enhance their status as Sons of Ne-Issan. Horses – which the Plainfolk had never seen before – had been the answer. Once seated in the saddle, Izo was immediately elevated to an impressive height and wherever they went, horse and rider were greeted with universal awe.

After the necessary preparations for the journey had been completed, Izo took leave of his tearful wife and children and set off in a southwesterly direction. The Iron Masters were used to harsh winters but the deep snow hampered the movement of both men and horses.

Since this was the first winter spent in the outlands, they did not know that with the onset of the 'White Death', the Plainfolk went to ground, living in a state of semi-hibernation like wild animals. Their brains tended to fall asleep too, and the inhabitants of the few settlements Izo managed to find were even more doltish than usual and could offer no assistance even when their spirits had been warmed with a cup of *sake*.

On the fourth day, numb with the cold, hungry and ill-tempered, Izo turned back towards Benton Harbour. His patient escort, hardly able to believe their luck, followed in grateful silence, buoyed up by visions of steaming tubs, hot food, warm beds and glowing charcoal braziers. Their expectations of an early return to 'civilization' were shattered when Izo, acting on a sudden impulse, turned left and cantered off along an ancient hardway which the cutting wind had partially cleared of snow.

The three-man escort exchanged weary glances then followed with sinking hearts, tugging the reluctant pack-mules behind them. Head down, face averted, man and beast leant their right shoulders into the wind as it tore thin white streamers from the razor-edged crests of the drifts and sent them snaking across their path. On they went for the rest of the day, covering some twenty-five miles – much of it on foot – urging their exhausted animals through the more densely-covered sections where the snow was often thigh-deep.

As darkness fell, Izo's party sought the shelter of a clump of pine trees that stood huddled together in the freezing wastes like beleaguered sentinels. Cutting branches to provide the tethered horses and mules with a warm footing, they tied blankets to their backs, fed them the last of the hay then set up the communal tent at the foot of the innermost tree.

Supper consisted of balls of cold rice and meat washed down with hot green tea cooked over a small charcoal firepot. Izo sent one of the soldiers out to make a last check on the animals then, on his return, poured a small cup of *sake* for each man as a nightcap and announced his firm decision to start out for Benton Harbour at first light. Since their rations were almost exhausted and their search had so far failed to turn up one single piece of useful information his companions were ready to believe that this time he meant it.

Warming their feet and hands over the embers, they slid into their fur-lined sleeping bags, pulled the hood tops tight around their faces and dreamt of home: of boughs heavy with pink cherry blossom, sun-dappled meadows, the quicksilver flash of fish rising from the mirrored surface of a lake, the laughter of children as they lay sprawled on top of a wagonload of sweet-smelling hay, the autumn sun, a vast red disc, sinking through a golden haze, the scent of pollen and wild flowers lying heavy on the still evening air.

*

On the morning of the fifth day, they awoke to discover they had passed the night less than a hundred paces from another encampment: a curious structure which betrayed its alien origin even under a thick coating of snow. Arming their bows, the two soldiers approached cautiously. Izo, brandishing a sword that had never drawn blood while in his hands, called upon the occupants to show themselves. His imperious command in Japanese was unlikely to be understood, but the sound of his voice breaking the stillness ought to have produced some response.

Nothing moved, no one stirred.

Covered by the drawn bows of the two sea-soldiers, Izo and his servant made a circular tour of inspection and found themselves confronted by the snow-covered remains of a straight-winged vehicle which lay tilted on one side. The body of the vehicle, whose width was less than the span of his outstretched hands contained a windowed compartment, one side of which had been crushed against the nearby tree.

Izo made a cursory examination of the snow-covered interior of the compartment from a safe distance, noted the coverless, empty storage space that lay behind it then walked round to the other side.

The downward-pointing wing had been turned into a make-shift shelter using branches cut from the surrounding pine trees. Izo ordered his servant to check that it was empty then followed him in. Smaller branches had been laid inside to make a floor. A few charred pieces of wood lay around a small soot-covered metal container. There were several similar open-topped containers which, from their smell, may have contained outlandish food. There were also some irregular-shaped pieces of a mysterious flexible material with a surface like polished steel and – most significant of all – some torn strips of blood-stained blue-grey cloth.

One of them bore part of a house-symbol which Izo recognized instantly. The dark-brown eight-petalled flower of the Min-Orota. Pale blue-grey was the colour of the clothes worn exclusively by the slave workers of Ne-Issan. This was part of a tunic and the blood seemed to indicate the owner had been injured when the sky-chariot had come to earth.

The reason for him being on board was obvious – this was an attempt to escape. But how had an ignorant slave gained access to such a craft and where were the long-dogs who had guided it and its twin companion through the air?

A shout from one of the soldiers put an end to further speculation. Emerging from the shelter, Izo hurried round to the other side of the wrecked sky-chariot and saw one of the sea-soldiers floundering towards him through the knee-deep snow. The soldier pointed to his companion who had moved some considerable distance along the hardway and was waving his arms excitedly.

Izo broke into a high stepping run, trying to place his feet in the holes already dug by the two soldiers.

'Another sky-chariot!' gasped the first soldier. 'Empty – but this one –' He paused to gulp down more air, '– unbroken!'

Izo ordered him to rejoin the servant by the wreck and pressed on. Halfway there, when his thigh muscle began to burn, he abandoned the high step and began to kick his way through the snow like a blunt plough, leaving a ragged furrow behind him.

As he drew closer to the second soldier, Izo caught sight of the second, snow-covered craft and began to share his excitement. Viewed from a distance, it was almost invisible against the white landscape. The wind-driven flakes had stuck to the freezing cold surface, covering all but the extreme underside of the dark grey body.

Bursting with pride, the sea-soldier led Izo towards his find, stamping the snow down ahead of him. The sky-chariot stood on three legs with its feet buried in snow that rose to within inches of its belly. With its straight wings spread out on each side at shoulder height it looked like a plump-bodied duck gliding down to alight on a pond.

Its tail – which Izo could just touch by reaching up with his fingertips – was attached to two parallel hollow beams that grew out of the rear edge of the wings. A raised hatch, held open by a stay, revealed another empty storage space. Moving onto the passenger compartment, he ordered the soldier to scrub away the frozen coating from one of the side windows then peered inside.

The snow lying on the rest of the canopy cast an eerie light over the dark-coloured interior. Despite their outlandish design, the two seats with sets of straps to secure the occupants were easy to identify. As to the function of the strange devices that lined the four sides of the compartment, that was a mystery Izo did not intend to pry into. He had seen enough to convince himself that it was an exceedingly dangerous place which he and his men should not attempt to enter. The craft, and everything within it, was the work of the sand-burrowers, slaves of The Dark Light; the evil force that had totally destroyed The World Before.

Izo was left in no doubt that these were the two sky-chariots that had been seen flying out of the east and had later passed over Benton Harbour. He and the soldier scoured the surrounding area but the intermittent blizzards that had hampered their progress during the first three days had obliterated the tracks made by the departing cloud-warriors.

It would make finding them more difficult but Izo was not unduly worried. Since his party had not encountered tracks of any small groups during their southward journey, it meant the cloud-warriors must have headed in the direction he expected – towards the west. If they were travelling on foot through deep snow with at least one wounded companion, their progress would be painfully slow.

The condition of his quarry and the direction they had taken were guesses based on the most tenuous evidence but, in the past, Izo had always been lucky when he had backed his own judgement. If he was right again (and he was convinced he was) then there was a reasonable chance of picking up their trail before they reached the Miz-Hippy.

But without food for themselves and their exhausted horses, Izo knew that immediate pursuit was impossible. Given the present weather they would need fresh mounts and more pack-animals before undertaking another overland journey. The first move was to return to the house-boat and send word to his masters. Signalling the sea-soldier to follow him, he turned back towards the campsite and broke into a stumbling run . . .

*

Steve's unknown adversary was right. Since abandoning their first makeshift shelter beneath the wing of the wrecked Skyrider, progress across the snow-covered landscape had been painfully slow but the problem of keeping warm had been partially solved prior to their departure. Leaving Clearwater to look after Kelso, Steve and Jodi had gone out hunting with Cadillac. The hand-guns lacked the range of the Mute crossbows but after two days of plugging away at anything and everything dressed in a fur coat they amassed enough skins to keep the worst of the cold out.

The problem of stitching them together had been foreseen by whoever had designed the survival packs that came with each Skyrider; each pack contained a variety of needles and reels of stout waxed thread. Squatting around the fire like immigrant tailors fresh from a *shetl* in Czarist Russia, they set to work. By dawn, the sewing circle had produced some rough shapeless over-garments which they then tied in place around each other's bodies using electric wiring and strips of fabric culled from the wrecked Skyrider. It was fortunate they were concerned more with keeping warm than keeping up appearances for when the last knots were tied and they emerged to test their yeti-boots in the snow, they looked like a ragamuffin quartet of stone-age primitives in search of a mammoth beefburger.

The collective but somewhat reluctant decision to head west along the hardway was taken round about the time that Izo Wantanabe decided to head in the same direction. A bitterly chill wind was driving the snow horizontally across the landscape but Steve would not allow them to wait until it stopped. They set out in a somewhat acrimonious mood but despite the appalling weather they chose the right moment for the snow and wind quickly obliterated their tracks.

Dave Kelso, trussed up like a Bacofoil mummy in his reflective blankets, and covered with a bear skin – still raw and bloody on the inside – lay on an improvised stretcher with Jodi's half of the canopy lashed over the top part of his body as extra protection.

With Steve paired with Clearwater at the front, and Cadillac with Jodi at the back, the load was evenly and easily distributed but after they'd covered the first few miles, Steve realized there was no way they could carry him through the snow to Wyoming.

Besides being not physically possible, there was no point in doing so – as Steve had already concluded. Kelso's fractures would be incurable by the time he got there. But even if they dumped him, it was highly doubtful whether they themselves could survive such a journey, ill-prepared, and in the depths of winter.

They had to find somewhere to hole up until spring. Steve only knew of one place – the dugout he'd used in Nebraska. It was warm, dry, well-concealed and just about big enough for the five of them. Nice idea, but there were two big snags. The dugout had been set up by AMEXICO, which meant there might be another undercover agent in residence – in radio contact with Karlstrom. And – the real killer – it was more than seven hundred miles from their present position.

With a pang of regret, Steve recalled Baz, the playful wolf-cub whose brief life had been blown away by Malone. He wiped the scene from his inner eye and turned his thoughts back to the problem of finding suitable winter quarters.

There had to be another solution . . .

There was – but the elements did not drop into place until several days later.

Warmed by an hour-long soak in a steaming bath-tub and the loving embrace of his wife, Yumiko, Izo Wantanabe's spirits rose even further when his trusty sergeant presented another dispatch which had arrived by carrier-pigeon the day before his return.

Izo broke the tiny container with trembling fingers and unrolled the ribbon of paper. It was longer than usual and double-sided. The dispatch – sent directly from the Sara-kusa Palace, home of Yama-Shita – was signed by Aishi Sakimoto, one of the domain-lord's uncles and key member of the family's Inner Council. But Sakimoto had also written the dispatch with his own hand, using the intimate form of address normally reserved for correspondence between noblemen of equivalent rank. The gesture was not lost on Izo.

The contents of the dispatch were startling. The house of Yama-Shita sought five slaves who had murdered scores of high-ranking Iron Masters with a deadly combination of black powder and The Dark Light, then had escaped by means of 'flying-horses'.

Izo was requested to do his utmost to discover the subsequent fate of the two straight-winged craft. If it was found that their aerial journey had continued, Sakimoto wished to be informed of their last known heading. If, on the other hand, the weather had forced them to come to earth in the area mandated to him, Izo was urged to do his utmost to discover the present whereabouts of the riders – alive or dead.

Sakimoto acknowledged that the search might prove fruitless but the honour of the Yama-Shita family was at stake. If the riders were found alive, Izo was to use the subtlest means at his disposal to detain them in the area without giving then cause for alarm. A punitive expedition would be mounted to bring them and their accomplices to justice but this could not leave Ne-Issan until spring of the following year.

A delaying action was therefore essential but Izo was ordered not to intervene directly with his own small force. The riders had powerful friends and secret means to summon them in the twinkling of an eye. Izo was empowered to offer inducements to the Plainfolk to secure their cooperation. He was, of course, expected to use his discretion but the Yama-Shita family undertook to honour any such promises he made on their behalf – *if* they led to positive results.

The message ended with a warm greeting and the promise that, if Izo was successful, he and his family would be richly rewarded with lands and titles. Izo needed no further prompting. With the discovery of the two abandoned 'flying-horses', his dream of attaining social status and material rewards commensurate with his abilities was already within his grasp. If the cloud-warriors were to be apprehended, there was not a moment to lose.

While the engine room crew laboured to raise a head of steam, Izo watched from the bridge as a second pigeon bearing the latest report – humbly addressed to Aishi Sakimoto – was launched towards Sara-kusa. A small guard-detail was put ashore to look after the stables and log store then, when his sergeant reported the boat was ready to put to sea, Izo gave the order to raise the anchor and directed the helmsman to steer due west across Lake Mi-shiga towards the legendary birthplace of the She-Kargo Mutes.

The preliminary schedule drawn up by Captain Ryder, the navigation officer, showed The Lady's E T A at Cedar Rapids as 1615 hours on the 15th November. Given the time of year, it proved imprudently optimistic but although Ryder bore the brunt of CINC-TRAIN's subsequent displeasure, he could hardly be blamed for getting it wrong. No wagon-train had ever ventured beyond the snow-line before.

From Trinidad, Colorado, to the banks of the Missouri, everything went according to plan. Travelling round the clock on what Trail-Blazer crews termed a three-shift roll The Lady logged an average of 18 mph over the first 620 miles of her journey, arriving at Kansas City in the late afternoon of the 13th.

Although the night air and ground temperatures were plunging with the onset of winter they had not encountered a drop of rain or a flake of snow, despite the cloudy, threatening skies. That left The Lady rolling over a dry-bed – the optimum conditions for a long haul over the crumbling, grass and weed-infested foundations of the pre-Holocaust highway system.

The bridges spanning rivers and gorges had vanished long ago. Shallow, slow-running rivers could be negotiated by simply driving across at the marked fording points; the deeper, wider ones – like the Missouri – could only be crossed with the aid of special ferrying equipment. Rivers with precipitous banks or rock-strewn rapids formed impassable barriers that had to be circumnavigated.

Where possible, the Federation's wagon-trains also followed the gentle curves and gradients fashioned by the predecessors of Amtrak, the company that had inherited the shrunken remains of the American railway network – the giant, epoch-making enterprise which had tamed and transformed a savage continent.

The width of the wagon-trains meant they could only travel along lines where, in the distant past, two or more sets of tracks had been laid and because of their height, the tunnels – many of which, in any case, had fallen in on themselves – were as impassable as river gorges.

One of the tasks the First Family intended to dedicate itself to after the conquest of the Blue-Sky World, was the restoration of the American railroad system. The Founding Father, George Washington Jefferson the First had been one of the dedicated visionaries who had helped to create the MX missile trains that had ridden the rails before the Holocaust and it was to honour his memory that the historic lines were to be rebuilt. Not only rebuilt. History was to be recreated. The new rolling stock would not be overground versions of the Trans-Am shuttle with its high-speed linear induction motor, they would be lovingly-constructed replicas of the giant 4-6-4 Union Pacific locos from the glorious era of steam when brains and brawn formed an enduring and unequalled partnership that could – and quite literally did – move mountains.

Disguised as ordinary freight trains, the MX launch vehicles and command modules circulated around the Amtrak system from coast to coast. The concrete ICBM silos buried beneath the prairies had been targeted by the enemy for decades, but the MX trains – the Pentagon's best-kept secret of the last years of the 20th century – remained safely hidden from the prying camera lenses of hostile reconnaissance satellites: impossible to find, fix and strike.

Some perished through random targeting – being in the wrong place at the wrong time during the first strike – but many more survived, their crews protected in their sealed, radiation-proof environments. It was from these trains, as America was turned into a giant funeral pyre, that the second devastating strike had been launched – the strike that utterly destroyed the enemies of freedom but which also triggered the detonation of their orbiting Doomsday weapons, bringing about the end of what the Mutes called The Old Time.

The knowledge of that particular piece of history was confined to the very top echelons of the First Family. As far as the rest of the Federation was concerned, the history archives that could be accessed by courtesy of COLUMBUS left the viewer in no doubt as to who was responsible for the Holocaust: the Mutes.

Since leaving Pueblo, two of The Lady's complement of twelve new Mark Two Skyhawks had been constantly aloft during the hours of daylight on what were known as Forward Air Patrols. The single-seat rear-engined microlites were the airborne equivalent of the sharp-eyed horsemen who once rode ahead of the ox-drawn pioneer wagons and US Cavalry columns that blazed their way across the continent and into history.

Now, twelve centuries later, the Skyhawks – like the birds of prey who were their namesakes – drifted back and forth across the cloud-filled blue with the same effortless grace, scanning the flanks and the route ahead for any obstacles or hidden dangers.

In the gathering dusk, Gus White, a classmate of Steve Brickman and leader of the last patrol of the day, switched on the two landing lights mounted behind perspex fairings at the front of the slim fuselage pod and turned westwards over the wide placid waters of the Missouri. His wingman, curving in from a last search of The Lady's northern flank, followed suit, throttling back to put half a mile between them as he lined up on Gus's tail.

The Lady, who had already turned into wind, switched on the required illumination. A green laser beam, designed to act as a long-range beacon was fired vertically from the roof of the command car. As it punched through the cloud base and went on up, a row of lights set into the top of the train rippled on to form a centre line and the four edges of the flight deck were outlined in blue.

On the wide deck, atop the extra-long flight car, three sets of arrester wires had been raised to snag the hook which had now been lowered between the two fat rear wheels of Gus's Skyhawk, and the ground crew, stationed in the 'duck-holes' on either side of the deck, stood poised ready to leap into action.

Apart from the total absence of deck officers waving bats, or the succeeding generations of electronic aids, the procedure

67

– as noted earlier – was essentially the same as that used for landing US Navy jets on pre-Holocaust carriers. But instead of several astronomically-expensive metric tons of airframe thudding down at speeds in excess of 120 miles per hour, the Skyhawks breezed in over the stern at a modest thirty-five.

BB-BMMMFFF! As Gus White snagged the second wire and touched down, the ground crew leaped into action. His wingman, now a mile downwind on the same glide path would be landing on in just under two and half minutes. More than enough time to unhook the Skyhawk from the arrester wire, fold each wing in two places, unlock the twin tail booms, swing the rear section downwards and underneath the wings, and run the resulting package onto the starboard bow lift.

With Gus still in the cockpit, it dropped swiftly out of sight looking like the crumpled creature that emerges from a chrysalis then unfolds in the drying rays of the sun to become an elegantly-proportioned dragonfly. The plane was quickly wheeled into the hangar deck, the lift came back up and – BB-BMMMFFF! The second Skyhawk landed on, bonking down hard on its nose wheel as the arrester wire brought it rapidly to a halt.

Ordinarily, apart from the watch, the crew of the wagon-train would have stood down until dawn, but the evening's activities were just begining. CINC-TRAIN had decided to refuel The Lady on its outward journey rather than get locked into sending a tank-train further north to an uncertain rendezvous on the return journey from Iowa. 'Let's face it,' said the tanker captain to Hartmann with disarming honesty, 'There's no point in both of us ending up with our asses stuck in the snow.'

Since The Lady had already replenished its stock of hydrogen granules during the stop-over at the Pueblo way-station, Hartmann was directed to hitch up two of the tank-train's hopper wagons – one at each end, next to the power-cars. Two more would be left at the Monroe/Wichita interface in case The Lady needed to top up on its southward run to the wagon-train depot at Fort Worth. It was reassuring to hear that their return was envisaged.

Hartmann and the men and women of his Trail-Blaze battalion set to work, assisted by the tank-train crew and the sixty-four Pioneers from the Pueblo way-station. Most of them had gotten over their initial grouchiness at having their leave abruptly postponed but whatever their feelings they were now rostered for trail-duty just like their hosts.

A handful, led by a pugnacious lieutenant called Matt Harmer and a VidCommTech-4 by the name of Deke Haywood, had volunteered their services. Buck McDonnell, better known as Big D, the Lady's Trail Boss, gathered the remainder together before The Lady began its crossing of the Missouri and announced in his gruff but fatherly fashion that he sympathized with their undeserved plight. They had, as he put it, 'drawn the shitty end of the straw'.

However (and here the tone and tempo of his delivery changed) they had now had two whole days in which to adjust to the situation and/or cry their eyes out. From here on in, he did not intend to have a disaffected bunch of moon-faced sack-happy lump-sucking shit-assed piss-brained Pioneers lying around feeding their faces and doing sweet fuck-all.

Regardless of their rank or special qualifications they were, as of now, under his orders and assigned to general duties until they disembarked. No slacking or malingering would be tolerated and anyone reporting sick who was not actually dead would very soon wish he were. So they had better buckle to. Over and out . . .

Ferrying the wagon-train across the Missouri kept both crews busy for the next twenty-four hours. Each of The Lady's sixteen wagons plus the two hoppers had to be carefully loaded one at a time onto a steerable bridging raft. The raft, which had been assembled in advance by the tank-train crew was mounted on two dozen large inflatable pontoons and was powered by heavy-duty water-jet motors. In Texas, the Inner State, several rivers had permanent pontoon bridges made from these assemblies and more were being installed at key points in the safer areas of the Outer States.

The designers of the wagon-trains had solved the transmission problem by giving each wheel its own electric motor. Emergency batteries, fitted in each wagon, enabled it to move backwards or forwards at low speed under its own power.

Both sets of wheels were steerable and the movement of the wagon could be controlled by an on-board operator, or from the outside by means of an umbilical unit.

This facility made it relatively easy to marshal a train in the depot, or re-sequence the wagons to meet altered operational requirements. It also meant that the individual wagons could be driven on and off the bridging rafts without having to be coupled to one of the power-cars.

Once safely across and re-assembled, The Lady headed north, retracing the line of the old US Highway 35 that linked navref Kansas City with navref Des Moines. It was on this leg that Ryder's timings started going out the window. The first flakes blew across their path as they neared the Missouri/Iowa state line and it was not long before their average speed dropped to around 8 mph. The dramatic slowdown was due, in almost equal parts, to the deepening layer of snow that cloaked the natural hazards of the terrain and the fact that the chosen route was criss-crossed with minor tributaries draining southwest into the Missouri River or southeast into the Mississippi.

Approaching Des Moines with The Lady at times over axle-deep in snow, Commander Hartmann had the genial notion of using the battery of superheated steam jets mounted under the nose of his command car to clear a path down to ground level. That way, at least, they would be able to see what they were running into. The jets, which had been fitted to repel close-quarter attacks by Mutes, were angled to cover the underneath and flanks of the train without melting the armoured rubber wheels. If they could blast flesh clean off the bone in seconds, snow would present no problem at all.

And so it proved. Like all brilliant ideas, it was incredibly simple. The reason no one had thought of it before was because the problem hadn't arisen. There was only one drawback. The superheated steam jet system was not designed for continuous operation. This meant frequent stops to replenish the water tanks which, on this part of the journey, meant filling up with melted snow.

Onwards they pressed, through pitch dark nights and days of eerie twilight that seeped through an endless grey blanket of cloud so heavy with snow it seemed about to collapse under its own weight. With its batteries of bug-eyed headlights blazing and its nose and flanks wreathed in clouds of hissing steam and whirling snow, The Lady looked liked a latter-day Loch Ness monster, surrounded by a foaming wake as it ploughed its way across the surface of a bleak Arctic sea.

By late afternoon on the 21st November, they reached Iowa City twenty miles south of Cedar Rapids, five days behind schedule and nearly nine days after Hartmann's dawn tryst in the shower with Colonel Marie Anderssen. Once again, as on their arrival at navref Kansas City, the light was fading. It was also snowing. Heavily . . .

The next day, more snow fell – for an unbroken fourteen hours, burying the lens housings on the tv cameras which acted as their windows on the world. Working under the eagle eye of Big D, groups of Trail-Blazers and press-ganged Pioneers from Pueblo struggled to keep the roof of the train clear of snow, using ordinary steam hoses and deck swabs. It proved a thankless task – like picking up leaves in an autumn gale – and by the morning of the 23rd another eight-inch thick crisp white carpet lay waiting to be cleared.

This time, however, the roof details found themselves working under a still blue sky. Most Trail-Blazers weren't too enthralled by the sights and sounds of the overground but it was such a gorgeous sight, several people – including Deke Haywood from Pueblo, who was a covert cloud-freak – went up just to take a look and fill their lungs with crisp, cold air.

On days like this, reflected Deke, it was hard to believe the overground was still cloaked in an atmosphere that had to be filtered before it was fit for Trackers to breathe. According to the First Family, those few deep breaths had shortened his already all-too-brief life by a few more months.

What the hell. Everybody had to die of something. And if you were a Tracker, it sure as hell wouldn't be of old age . . .

Hartmann huddled over a map of the area with Ryder, The Lady's navigator. A meandering cluster of lakes and old reservoirs lay across the shortest route linking his present position and navref Cedar Rapids. To get there would mean going the long way round. In Ryder's opinion, given the present weather conditions, it just wasn't worth the hassle.

If CINC-TRAIN wanted them to get closer to where they thought Brickman and his friends might be, it made more sense to push along the line of the Interstate towards Davenport on the west bank of the Mississippi. But as Ryder was quick to point out, that meant finding a place to cross the Cedar River. On the other hand, it would put them seventy miles closer to the primary search area, south-west of navref Gary, Indiana.

To fly there and back from their present position plus the standard square search-pattern when they got there meant a round trip of over five hundred miles. That was uncomfortably close to the limit of the Skyhawk's range but, more importantly, it meant that any planes they dispatched would be airborne for over four hours. If the weather suddenly deteriorated – and on the journey north it had proved it could, with frightening rapidity – they might not make it back to the train.

Hartmann took the point but decided it was a risk his wingmen would have to live – or die – with. In an exchange of messages with CINC-TRAIN – already chafing at the time he'd taken to get as far as he had – he obtained permission to re-route The Lady in whichever direction he thought best, having taken into account the suitability of the terrain and the prevailing weather. The First Family only required two things of him: he was to do his utmost to bring in Brickman and his fellow-travellers, but in attempting to do so, he was not to pursue any course of action that might jeopardize the security of the wagon-train. Crewmen were expendable. The Lady from Louisiana wasn't.

It was the typical double-bind he had come to expect – and one which every wagon-train commander had to live with.

After discussing the weather situation with Captain Baxter, the Flight Operations exec, Hartmann told him they'd been sent to recover five 'bodies' but did not identify them. CINC-TRAIN's first transmission had stated that the details of the mission were only to be disclosed on a 'need-to-know' basis. When Baxter had grasped what was required of his ten wingmen, Hartmann called McDonnell up to the saddle and asked him to put some men up to clear the roof.

'Start 'em on the flight-deck then work outwards, towards

both ends. A fast clean job, Mr McDonnell. We need to get our birds in the air by eleven hundred hours.'

'Yess-SURR!' The Trail Boss slammed his brass-topped drill stick under his left arm, gave Hartmann an impeccable salute then left to galvanize his underlings. He was a big man, above average height for a Tracker, but he was capable of moving with surprising speed and agility.

At 0927 hours, the first two Skyhawks were catapulted off the angled ramps at the front of the flight deck within seconds of each other. The clouds of steam drifted round the ground crew as they quickly dragged the launching shackles back to the start position. Two more Skyhawks waited their turn on the rear lifts, wings and tails still folded, their helmeted pilots already strapped in the slim-nosed cockpit-pods. Behind the rear bulkhead lay the tanks of liquid methane that powered the hyper-efficient engine mounted at the rear, its two-bladed propellor in the vertical position, ready to turn over at the touch of a button.

Gus White, was the first pilot away. The only wingman to have survived The Lady's first encounter with the Plainfolk Mutes the previous year, Gus had been posted to The Lady along with Steve and several other classmates. Gus had seen them all die or disappear over two days of nightmare action. He'd been with Steve when Jodi had been lost overboard, and he had seen Steve's Skyhawk plunge into a burning cropfield they had both set alight with canisters of napalm.

A new section-leader with three years line experience had been drafted in to head up the replacements – most of whom were as raw as Gus, but after a shaky start when he'd fallen foul of Big D, he had applied himself diligently to his allotted tasks. Since he was also bucking for promotion he had worked hard to make himself Captain Baxter's blue-eyed boy.

The reward for his brown-nosing had been his appointment as deputy section-leader. It was a post which brought no extra credits or any real executive clout. The only thing the holder earned was the chance to go boldly where no wingman had gone before. To lead, in other words, the more hazardous missions. Since the post was an essential stepping-stone to further promotion, they were risks a young ambitious schemer had to take.

73

Gus White knew he was searching for five survivors from two Skyriders that had been forced down through lack of fuel but he had not the slightest inkling they were being lead by his ex-classmate and rival, Steve Brickman. And while, on occasions, he experienced a vague nagging regret about leaving the trapped and injured Steve to burn in that Mute cropfield he had, to all intents and purposes, wiped the incident from his mind. There was really nothing he could have done with a jammed gun against so many screaming hostiles. Right or wrong, what did it matter? Gus didn't believe in weighing himself down with moral burdens. Steve Brickman was dead. KIA, Wyoming, June 12th, 2989. End of story.

Except, of course, it wasn't. And there was something else that Gus didn't know. Steve had silently sworn to get even. Had Gus been aware of what was waiting for him down the pike, he might have searched the landscape with something less than his customary zeal.

Lieutenant Matt Harmer, who also figured on Steve's hit list since he'd headed the welcoming committee at Pueblo, stood beside Buck McDonnell on the empty flight and watched the four Skyhawks spread out then disappear as they rose higher and higher into the eastern sky.

Normally, once the given task had been accomplished, Trail-Blazers rarely lingered for any length of time on top of the train – especially in Plainfolk territory where anyone standing in an exposed position ran the risk of being skewered by a ten-inch bolt from a Mute crossbow. But today wasn't like any one of the countless days spent on previous overground fire-sweeps. Despite having spent six years up the line, McDonnell had never seen so much snow before – a smooth dazzling white carpet under a vast, unblemished blue sky. He wanted to take in the scene for real, in its true awe-inspiring dimensions rather than in miniature through a tv screen.

Even so, he was not a man to take needless risks just to ogle the landscape. As a seasoned campaigner he knew they were reasonably safe – for the moment, anyway. The wagon-trains were fitted with body scanners mounted in the lead and rear command car which could detect the presence of warm-blooded animals and differentiate between the two-legged and four-legged variety.

The scanners were always switched on prior to any activity on the flight deck and had been used to cover the work parties clearing the snow off the roof. Their invisible beams, which could calibrate and pinpoint heat sources at a range of eight hundred yards, were linked to the wagon-train's fire-control system. Once a target had been located, its position was passed directly to the gunners manning the turrets covering the relevant sector.

That was the theory; in practice – like most electronic gizmos in the Federation – the set-up aboard The Lady had never been 100% operational but it had greatly reduced the number of surprise attacks. And it meant Big D and the lieutenant from Pueblo could relax for a few minutes and take in the view instead of standing back to back with their eyes peeled, pumping out adrenalin, guns cocked and trained, ready to blow away the first thing that moved.

Harmer pivoted slowly on his heel, scanning the vast white emptiness that surrounded them like a hungry wolf, then returned and caught McDonnell's eye. 'The only thing that's been keeping me going up to now is the thought I might get a chance to flatten a few lumps and thread some beaver. But up to now, we've rolled right past everything the scanners picked up. Okay, the heat is on. But now we're here and you promised we'd see some action. So tell me – where are all the fuggin' Mutes?'

'Don't worry,' said McDonnell. 'They're out there.'

'So when do we get started?'

'Probably sooner than you think. I reckon they aint gonna take too kindly to us barging in just when they're getting ready to celebrate the New Year.'

Harmer's narrow eyes gleamed. 'Great. There's nothing I like better than spoiling some lumpshit's day. Especially when they're having a party. That's the best time to hit 'em – when they've got nothing but smoke between their ears.'

CHAPTER FOUR

Buck McDonnell was right. There *were* Mutes out there and they weren't all – as Izo Wantanabe believed – in a state of suspended animation.

While it was certainly true that, compared to the rest of the year, the winter months were marked by long periods of sleep and inactivity, the Plainfolk were still able, when awake, to get their brains in gear.

Like the other Iron Masters who had preceded him to the outlands, Izo Wantanabe was, by his very nature, unable to make a dispassionate study of Mute behaviour. Like the Trackers, he had come imbued with an unshakeable belief in his own superiority and full of second-hand information and preconceived ideas about the people he would be dealing with. None of the Resident Agents had been in place long enough to form a detailed picture of the daily life of Mutes during a bleak winter and, what was more, it was not something they had been asked to record.

As a Johnny-come-lately, Izo was forced to rely on the information gleaned by previous visitors and they – for the reasons stated above – had learned surprisingly little about the way Mutes *really* lived, how they thought – or what they thought about. As a result, Izo did not know that one of the defensive tactics employed by Mutes was to pretend to be even more stupid than they looked.

Many Mutes were hampered by a genetic fault that affected the link between the part of their brain which stored acquired knowledge and their mouth. In computer language, you could input data but due to a software fault, you couldn't get a print-out. The severity of the problem varied widely between individuals but, in a social context, it made it difficult, and sometimes impossible, to put what they *knew* – as opposed to what they had seen, thought or felt – into words. And since

Mutes did not know how to read or write, the knowledge they possessed often remained locked away.

In captivity, shackled and beaten, treated and worked like beasts of burden, they became morose and silent. 'Mute', an abbreviation of mutant, took on an added meaning. But they were far from dumb. In the history archives of the Federation they were referred to as 'the wily Mute', but the attributes they were considered to possess were low animal cunning and primal ferocity. Courage and a lively intelligence were not qualities that could be ascribed to sub-humans.

Trackers – who believed themselves to be the only true human beings to have survived the Holocaust – knew how 'real people' were supposed to look. Since the Mutes did not conform to this model they were regarded as misshapen and ugly, and this lack of symmetry, this ugliness was proof of their sub-human status and irredeemable stupidity.

Their enemies from the dark cities beneath the deserts of the south, convinced they were opposed by witless savages, had been lulled into a false sense of security. Believing themselves to be superior in both firepower *and* brainpower, commanders of overground units had, on numerous occasions, made tactical errors they would probably not have committed against a more respected opponent.

The irony was, when the inevitable post mortem took place, the sand-burrowers were so convinced they were the master-race they preferred to find scapegoats among their own ranks rather than face up to the proposition that they might have been outsmarted.

The same tactics had been employed to cope with the threat from the east. The Plainfolk, whose warrior ethos was based on the courage of the individual in one-to-one combat, were quick to realize they could not fight a war on two fronts against foes who both possessed what Mutes regarded as weapons of mass destruction; long sharp iron that could kill or maim whole groups of people with a single blow delivered from a great distance.

Apart from a few bloody skirmishes when the wheelboats had made their first forays along the shores of the Great River, relations had been reasonably smooth and mutually beneficial despite the fact that the Iron Masters appeared to be calling the shots. The leaders of the delegations from the Mute clans who gathered annually at the trading post were painfully aware that the barter deals negotiated by the masked yellow dwarfs were loaded against them but it had been agreed (amongst hereditary blood-enemies who could agree on precious little) that a bad bargain was better than no bargain at all.

There was much to be learned, by adopting the role of the awed and not very bright savage and much to be gained in the way of quiet satisfaction – as was the case with the Mutes whose winter slumbers Izo had so rudely interrupted.

As it happened, none of the inhabitants who emerged from the three settlements he had approached on his initial sortie had seen any arrowheads flying through the sky or coming to earth. Given a warm spring or summer's day, the prospect of looking for such an object and being rewarded for finding it would have aroused their enthusiasm. Only an idiot – or an Iron Master – could sustain the necessary level of excitement with intermittent blizzards sweeping in from the north over a thigh-deep layer of snow.

So the reception committees of warriors and elders had stared at him with sleepy eyes and slack mouths, pretending not to understand. When all the fire-water that was on offer had been drunk by a fortunate few, and the pompous little fart finally abandoned his attempts to persuade every available adult to join in the search for the elusive arrowheads, they watched him wobble off astride his strange, four-legged beast then returned to their huts to warm their chilled bodies over blazing hearthstones.

And while Izo and his weary escort struggled on through the snow, they squatted on their talking mats, passed around a pipe of rainbow grass and laughed at the Iron Master's absurd behaviour. Only clever people, they agreed, who used silent speech to record everything they saw and did but understood nothing were capable of such foolishness. Winter – the period known to the Mutes as The White Death – was the moment when Mo-Town, the Great Sky-Mother who breathed life into the land each spring mourned its passing. As the last leaves were stripped from the trees by the icy winds that came howling out of the northern wastes, her heart grew chill and the world was covered with her frozen tears. Everyone knew that the cloud-warriors – unlike the dead faces – had the good sense to stay in their burrows from the end of Yellowing to the time of the New Earth.

But not this year – as some of their blood-brothers were soon to discover . . .

The same hostile weather system that had almost doubled The Lady's journey-time to navref Iowa City had also wrecked Steve's hopes of making a speedy getaway. Driven by the fear that Karlstrom might send in an MX snatch squad but without having any clear plan of action, Steve's prime objective had been to put as much distance as possible between themselves and the point at which they had come to earth. But since leaving their first campsite beneath the wing of the wrecked Skyhawk they had been moving with painful slowness, taking several days to cover just over sixty miles. On two of those days, bitterly cold winds and driving snow had prevented them from moving at all and it was only the expert trail-craft of Cadillac and Clearwater that saved them from dying from exposure.

Although Kelso was kept liberally dosed with pain-killer, he had recovered from the initial shock of the accident. The morphine substitutes Jodi and Steve injected him with produced a state of drowsiness interspersed with periods of lucidity. And during these latter moments it soon became evident that, despite his injuries, he was as combative and caustic as ever and there were occasions when Steve found himself wishing Kelso had broken his jaw instead of his pelvis.

Day eight dawned bright and clear. Stepping out from the shelter of the pine trees, they scanned the cloudless blue sky and the dazzling white landscape. An overnight frost had brushed a thin layer of ice crystals over the undulating carpet of snow, making it gleam and sparkle with countless points of rainbow-tinted light.

It was a scene which, on any other occasion, would have inspired feelings of pure joy at just being alive but, despite its breathtaking beauty, the four stretcher bearers took in the view then eyed each other with something less than total enthusiasm. The fact that there was no razor-sharp wind and no threatening cloud-wall of snow lurking on the horizon meant there was no excuse for not moving forward. But the same good weather could also entice the warriors of hostile Mute clans out into the open in search of fresh meat.

Each of them knew that the atrocious conditions they had encountered since landing were the main reasons why the Plainfolk clans who inhabited the area had not put in an appearance. So far. Without having it spelled out, everyone knew there was no way they could reach Wyoming without stepping on the turf of a hostile clan. Snow or no snow, it was only a matter of time before they would have to face their first challenge. And again, without having someone spell it out they also knew the first would probably be their last. If attacked by a determined and numerically superior group the handguns they carried would only afford them a brief respite and would probably be more effective if turned against themselves. Suicide was infinitely preferable to an excruciating death through ritual mutilation.

The subject of how to defend themselves when this inevitable – and terminal – encounter took place had been broached on several occasions as they sat huddled over a fire inside their overnight shelters but no one had put forward a coherent plan. Jodi was left with the impression it had been tacitly agreed that if the problem *did* arise, Clearwater would somehow use the inexplicable power she possessed to get them out of trouble.

Since the first day, when the four of them had staggered like drunken sailors through a blizzard carrying Dave Kelso's stretcher shoulder-high, they had got themselves better organized. The hatch cover to which he was strapped had been turned into a sled which they pulled along with a lot less effort two at a time. It gave Kelso a much smoother ride and meant that the two who weren't pulling could hump the home-made backpacks into which their supplies had been loaded.

Towards noon, the trouble they'd been expecting appeared in the shape of solitary fur-clad Mute warrior who ambled up out of a dip in the ground and stopped as he caught sight of

Cadillac and Clearwater who were walking about a hundred yards ahead of Steve, Jodi and Kelso.

Everyone froze – including the Mute, who was carrying a crossbow. Steve weighed up the distance between them and decided there wasn't a lot he could do. The warrior was a couple of hundred yards away from where he stood – too far even for Cadillac to pick off with a handgun. And it was just as well none of them tried because more fur-clad Mutes rose into view on either side of the first.

'Shee-iitt . . .' breathed Jodi. 'What the eff-eff are we gonna do?'

'Stay calm and start counting,' said Steve. There were thirty of them – five hands – spread out in a long line that started behind Steve's right shoulder then angled in past Cadillac and Clearwater barring the way ahead. Roughly a third of them carried crossbows; the rest were armed with a mixture of spiked head-crushers and knife-sticks. Without the rapid intervention of Talisman, the presence of so many bowmen beyond the reach of their handguns made the outcome of any fight a foregone conclusion.

Steve and Jodi watched with bated breath as Clearwater raised her right hand and made the traditional sign of greeting. As she did so, Cadillac produced the fat-barrelled pistol he'd taken from the Skyrider's rescue kit and fired a white signal flare vertically into the air.

'Sheee-ehhh!' The sibilant Mute cry that signified amazement, awe and admiration burst from the throats of the warriors as they watched the dazzling fireball rise some two hundred feet before curving over their heads and falling to earth behind them, leaving a drifting trail of smoke to mark its passage through the air.

It was the equivalent of the 'white arrow', the crossbow bolt that carried a smouldering sheaf of dried grass aloft as a signal that the hunter or the hunted wished to parley.

After a suspense-filled moment when nobody in the Mute line reacted, the four warriors in the centre went into a huddle then raised their right arms and returned Clearwater's greeting. There was then a second, longer confab between the leader of the Mute posse and Cadillac. From the amount of head-nodding, some sort of agreement seemed to have been reached. Steve eyed Jodi and let out a husky sigh of relief.

A rapid tap-tap-tap drew their attention down to Kelso whose hatch-sledge lay between them. He was knocking on the inside of the perspex canopy that covered him from head to hip with the knuckles of his good left hand. Jodi hunkered down beside him.

'What is it, Dave?'

'Get this cover offa me and give me a gun!' The words came out as a hoarse, muffled whisper.

'Are you crazy? What for?'

'What a dumb question! If we're goin' down under this heap of shit-balls, I wanna take one with me!'

Jodi reacted with an angry gasp then slapped the canopy alongside his face. 'Dave! Do everyone a favour will you!? Just go back to sleep!'

Jodi stood up in time to see Cadillac trudging towards them through the snow carrying both back-packs. Clearwater was still engrossed in conversation with the four leaders of the Mute posse.

Cadillac handed Clearwater's pack to Jodi and gave his own to Steve. 'I don't want to sound too optimistic but we may have struck lucky. I was worried we'd run into one of the D'Troit clans but these guys are M'Waukee Mutes – braves from the Clan Kojak.'

'Aren't the M'Waukee supposed to be friends of the She-Kargo?'

Cadillac responded to Steve's question with a faintly patronizing smile. 'That's an over-simplification. Even clans from the same blood-line will kill each other to protect their turf. Let's just say they dislike the She-Kargo slightly less than they dislike the D'Troit.'

'Terrific . . .' Steve eyed Jodi. 'So where does that leave us?'

'Alive – for the moment.'

Jodi surveyed the impassive line of Mutes. The fact that they weren't psyching themselves up with warlike noises somehow made the situation seem more threatening. She nudged Steve. 'I don't get it. By rights these guys should be leaping all over us. Are they frightened by signal flares?'

'No. Must have been something he said.' Steve turned to Cadillac. 'What did you do – hit 'em with some fancy fire-speech?'

'On the contrary. It was what *they* had to say that floored *me*.' Cadillac glanced over his shoulder at Clearwater then ran his eyes slowly along the line of Mutes before coming back to Steve and Jodi. 'The reason we're not dead is because they regard us as something special.'

'Special . . .?'

'Yes. They've been expecting us.' Cadillac saw them exchange puzzled looks and explained. 'The Kojak's have got a wordsmith like Mr Snow. He is the guardian of the Talisman Prophecy but he has also kept alive another centuries-old prediction which – on the face of it – appears to concern us. It's very strange . . .'

Steve blew his top. 'Caddy, for chrissakes spare us the suspense! We appreciate the build-up but this isn't the time or place! Just give us the bottom line!'

'Okay. Hang on to this. Besides teaching them about Talisman, their wordsmith has been telling them for years that one day ". . . a small group of Plainfolk – The Chosen – would fly out of the east in the bellies of iron birds" –'

'I don't believe it –'

'Hold on, I haven't finished! ". . . and that their arrival would herald the birth of Talisman and the return of The Lost Ones" – the Mutes held in Ne-Issan.'

'I see . . .' mused Steve. 'And this is why they haven't killed us.' He looked across at Jodi. 'What d'you think?'

Cadillac cut in before she got her mouth open. 'Christo! What a dumb question! It's what *they* think that matters! If they believe we're "The Chosen", why disillusion them? Let's go along with it. I mean, who knows? It might actually be true.'

'It might,' admitted Steve. 'If you believe that stuff.' He eyed the motionless warriors. 'Did you tell them we flew here from Ne-Issan?'

'No.'

'So how did they know about the "iron birds"?'

'The same way as the Plainfolk knew about cloud-warriors and iron snakes centuries before wagon-trains emerged from beneath the deserts of the south. That's the magic of prophecy.'

'Yeah . . .'

Jodi, who had been following their conversation with growing puzzlement said: 'Would you mind telling me what all this iron bird shit is about? And who or what is Talisman?'

Steve flagged her down. 'Some other time, Jodi. So – where do we go from here?'

Cadillac smiled. 'Well, for the moment, you three aren't going anywhere. We can't risk Kelso shooting his mouth off.'

'Ayy-men to that,' said Jodi.

'They wanted to take us all back to their settlement so their wordsmith could question us but I told them our "blood-brother" had contracted a malady that lurks in the land of the dead-faces. And until he got better, he should not be brought into the settlement. I explained that we were not infectious. It was only young children in the general vicinity of the invalid who were in danger.'

'Neat. So we stay and you go . . .'

Steve looked at Jodi. His eyebrows formed the silent question.

'That's okay by me, Steve. Clearwater gave us all great paintjobs but even if Dave kept his mouth shut neither of us know the ropes. You may be able to wing it but it's not gonna take 'em long to cotton on to the fact *we* aren't the real thing.'

'Yeah, you're right.' Steve slapped his fur-clad hands together. 'Okay – how does it play from here?'

'They're taking me and Clearwater back with them to meet their wordsmith. That's why I'm leaving you the back-packs.'

'And what do we do,' asked Jodi. 'Camp here?'

'Yes. There shouldn't be any trouble. We're on their turf.' Cadillac made a quick appraisal of their surroundings and pointed to a nearby stand of tall pines whose lower branches dropped under the weight of the accumulated layers of snow. 'That looks like a pretty good spot. Why don't you check it out?'

'We will,' said Steve, feeling distinctly upstaged. 'Where're they taking you?'

'They didn't say exactly. Just somewhere north of here.'

'So you can't tell us when you'll be back . . .'

'No. But these guys are travelling light – which means their settlement can't be all that far away. My guess is we'll be back in the next couple of days.'

'Or never,' said Jodi.

Cadillac replied with a philosophical shrug. 'Depends on how we make out with their wordsmith. If we can convince him we're the real thing we may be offered a warm bed and free meals for the rest of the winter.'

Steve absorbed the scenario with a thoughtful nod. 'That takes care of you two, and maybe Jodi and me at a pinch. But that leaves Kelso out in the cold – or is his "malady" going to be suddenly and magically cured?'

'Be realistic, Brickman. We both know there's only one cure for Kelso and –'

'Now wait a minute –!'

Cadillac rounded on Jodi. 'No! *You* listen! Because without me and Clearwater your life's not worth shit! Even if Mr Snow was here right now he couldn't put Kelso back together. He needs major surgery – and only your people can handle that –'

'But –'

'Look! I'm not going to argue about this. Kelso's *your* problem – and you've got two days to make up your mind what to do about it.'

'You miserable piece of lumpshit!' Jodi lunged at Cadillac's throat.

Steve saw Clearwater start running towards them as he stepped in between the warring pair, deflecting Jodi's hands before they could do any damage. 'Cool it! Christopher Columbus! What d'you wanna do – blow the whole deal?!'

She rounded on Steve, eyes blazing. 'I'm not going to let you kill him!'

'Shut your face!' hissed Cadillac. 'I'll give you this one last time.' He lowered his voice further. 'The one chance we have of getting out of here alive is by pretending to be who these guys think we are. Which means passing you two off as Plainfolk Mutes. And *that* means,' – he jabbed a finger at Jodi – '*you* gotta act like one! For the Plainfolk, death is just part

85

of a continuing cycle of existence. When a warrior is badly injured –'

'Yeah? Well, you're gonna have to get rid of me too!'

Cadillac waved dismissively. 'That's it. I've had enough. You handle it, Brickman.' He turned away as Clearwater arrived anxious to discover what all the shouting was about. Cadillac put her in the picture.

Clearwater came over in an attempt to calm things down. 'Jodi, please, I know how you feel about Kelso but you're only prolonging his agony. If you'll just let me explain –'

'I don't wanna *hear* any explanations!' yelled Jodi. 'You can both go fuck yourself!'

Steve wrestled with her as she tried to break free. 'Jodi! For chrissakes! Keep your voice down!'

Cadillac strode off purposefully to rejoin the leaders of the Mute posse. Halfway there, he looked back and summoned Clearwater with an imperious wave. Clearwater signalled him to be patient. She didn't want to leave until Steve and Jodi had finished arguing.

'I'm serious, Brickman. I'm not gonna let you do it.'

'Look! No one's gonna kill Dave. I promise! I'm on your side in this. We'll sort something out! Okay?'

'If you say so.' She stopped struggling but her body was still shaking with anger.

'Good. Now back off and simmer down. Hell – I mean – after all we've been through . . . it'd be stupid to blow it now.'

Jodi eyed them both resentfully. 'Yeah, it would be, wouldn't it?' She knelt down to check on Kelso. He had drifted off to sleep.

Clearwater took Steve aside. 'Will she be all right?'

'Yeah. No problem. It's you I'm concerned about. At times you've been barely able to put one foot in front of another. Are you gonna be able to handle this run?'

She laid a hand on his arm. 'Don't worry about me. "Mutes feel no pain" – isn't that what they say?' Her eyes became clouded. 'I don't want to leave you but I have to go with Cadillac. You understand why, don't you?'

'Sure. Take care. Of him *and* yourself.'

'We'll be back soon. I promise.'

'I'll hold you to that.' Steve stepped back and shooed her away. 'Better hurry. Your lord and master is getting impatient.'

Preceded by six Kojak braves and flanked by the remaining twenty-four, Cadillac and Clearwater jogged away through the snow without a backwards glance. Steve watched them until they disappeared behind a fold in the ground then looked down at Jodi.

'Cadillac's right,' she said, shouldering one of the backpacks. 'There's no point in arguing. One more, one less ... what does it matter? That's the way lump-heads think.' Her eyes met Steve's as she straightened up. 'I guess that's the difference between them and us. That's supposed to make us the good guys and them the bad.'

'It's not that simple, Jodi.'

She gave a derisive laugh. 'No. With you it never is. But then, you're not really one of *us* any longer are you?'

They picked up the rope leads of Kelso's sledge and headed towards the trees. Neither of them spoke for a long time.

Led by Gus White, the four Skyhawks climbed to five thousand feet and flew due east in parallel lanes, each pilot keeping visual contact with his neighbour. Forty odd minutes after take-off, the patrol crossed the Mississippi, a smudgy grey line that meandered across the snow-covered landscape like the first, haphazard scrawl made by a young child on a pristine white page.

An hour later, the northernmost wingman caught sight of the lower end of Lake Michigan. It was his first sight of one of the Great Lakes. Neither he nor his companions had ever seen so much water before. In the centre of the curving shoreline, between Izo Wantanabe's base at Benton Harbour and the legendary rainbow-ice city from which the She-Kargo Mutes had sprung, lay navref Gary, Indiana.

On the map-table around which all ten wingmen had gathered to be briefed by Baxter, the Flight Ops Exec, navref Gary was positioned halfway along the top edge of a shaded rectangle which, on the ground, was fifty miles square. This was the primary search area. Somewhere within it were two

Skyriders – either whole or in pieces. The first task of the air patrols launched by The Lady was to discover where the planes had come down. Having done that, they were then required to establish the fate of the five people known to have been aboard. If they were not lying dead in the wreckage, they must be presumed to be alive and proceeding westwards on foot. If so, the flight-section was required to make a major effort to discover their present whereabouts and assist in their recovery.

This was the reason, continued Baxter, why four sets of ski attachments – which would allow the Skyhawks to land and take-off from snow – had been fabricated by the engineers during the journey north from designs supplied over the video–link by Houston/GC.

Gus White asked the question that was on everyone's mind. 'Are we working to a time limit on this, sir?'

'Nope. We're here for as long as it takes,' replied Baxter.

It sounded ominous. Since nobody wanted to be out here in the first place, it meant the rest of the crew would be constantly on their backs, pressurizing them to get the job done so that everyone could get home in time for New Year.

But there was more. Baxter had concluded the briefing by applying another turn of the screw. Whilst in the search area, and on the outward and return legs they were also to record the position and size of any Mute settlements and take note of the level of over-ground activity. But they were not, repeat not, under any circumstances to attack any ground targets – even if they came under fire from the ground – without first obtaining specific authorization to do so from Hartmann himself. The only situation in which the use of weapons *might* be sanctioned would be to cover a landing to investigate clearly identified wreckage or to evacuate survivors.

Gee whizz . . . thanks a bunch, sir . . .

Picking the mutinous undercurrent from his ten pilots, Baxter privately questioned the wisdom of 'non-aggressive' patrols but got no joy from Hartmann. The wagon-train commander shared his reservations but he had been given clear and precise instructions by CINC-TRAIN who, in turn, were acting on orders emanating from the Oval Office. Karlstrom, the Operational Director of AMEXICO was the prime mover behind the search for Steve and his companions but the signals were prefixed with 'Eagle One'; the President-General's code-name. The acronym AMEXICO never appeared on any video-screen or hard copy and this 'invisibility' was one reason why, over the centuries, the organization's existence had been successfully concealed from all but a chosen few.

From the moment that Kelso had broadcast his covert May-Day signal and alerted the organization to what had taken place at Long Point, AMEXICO's sophisticated intercept system had been monitoring the range of radio frequencies utilized by the stolen Skyriders.

During the brief exchange with Kelso via the airborne signals unit there had not been time to query the fuel state of the two aircraft. Kelso had been instructed to fake engine trouble, providing him with a valid excuse to change course, flying around Lake Michigan instead of across it. With Cadillac locked in the cargo hold, Brickman would be obliged to follow. A lot depended on how well Kelso stage-managed events but he was to try and land in Iowa, as close to the Mississippi as possible.

It was only after contact with Long Point had been restored that Karlstrom learned the aircraft had taken off without being refuelled. By then it was impossible to contact Kelso and modify the arrangements without risking blowing his cover.

The rapidly-emptying fuel tanks had provided him with an even better excuse for changing course but the Skyriders had been forced down, in the middle of a snowstorm, some two hundred miles short of the point Karlstrom had selected. The heated conversations between Steve, Jodi and Kelso about their predicament had been recorded but because they had gone off the air prematurely, AMEXICO's signals unit had been unable to obtain an exact fix on the point where they had landed. And they had stayed off the air ever since.

Now, almost two weeks later, Karlstrom was unaware that Kelso – the man he was counting on to keep him posted – was lying with his broken body strapped to a make-shift sledge and that the compact but powerful walkie-talkie he had used to such good effect at Long Point had been crushed when he'd wrapped his Skyrider around the unyielding trunk of a big pine.

Given Brickman's action against his fellow operatives at Long Point, Karlstrom had decided against sending in more mexicans. The first three had only been temporarily disabled, but had Brickman's attempt to steal the aircraft misfired, the consequences might have been a great deal more serious – perhaps fatal.

In seeking Side-Winder's help to escape from Ne-Issan with Cadillac and Clearwater, Brickman had spoken of the need to reach Wyoming to capture his 'third target': Mr Snow – the most powerful summoner known to the First Family. If this was true, if Brickman was only *pretending* to have changed sides, Karlstrom could foresee a situation where – in order to reinforce his credibility as a dependable ally of the Clan M'Call – he might be obliged to take more drastic measures against any new attempt by AMEXICO to bring in Cadillac and Clearwater before he was ready to deliver them. His original assignment had been to capture all three. Perhaps the plan he'd worked out needed the presence of Cadillac and Clearwater to bait the trap for Mr Snow . . .

So be it. If Brickman believed he could pull off a hat-trick there was no point in throwing away highly-trained men who could be used more effectively elsewhere. Far better to give him as much rope as he needed. As long as he delivered the goods what did it matter if he ended up hanging himself? That was why Karlstrom – who flattered himself that his own devious mind was more than a match for Steve's – had selected The Lady from Louisiana to conduct a search of the area.

Since Brickman and his friends lacked the necessary clothes and equipment to make an overland trek in the depths of winter, he might have second thoughts about going it alone. If the correct signals were received, assistance – in whatever measure required – would be quickly and discreetly provided.

On the other hand, if sacrificial goats were needed, they too would be provided – from amongst the crew of The Lady.

The whole exercise rested on the assumption that the principal players had survived the forced landing and its attendant dangers. Through his daily contacts with Roz Brickman, Steve's psychic kin-sister, Karlstrom was confident they had. So, barring some unforeseen disaster, it would only be a matter of time before Steve and Jodi Kazan came up against their old bunkmates. Yes ... It would be an interesting test of *her* loyalty and the extent of *his* duplicity.

Cadillac saw two of the patrolling Skyhawks pass overhead as he and Clearwater jogged northwards with their escort of warriors. For a brief instant, the posse halted and stared open-mouthed at the 'arrowheads'. Several braves armed their cross-bows but Cadillac advised them, through their leader, not to waste their precious bolts. The craft were too high for their skins to be pierced even by a well-aimed shot.

Through their contacts at the trading-post, the Clan Kojak knew of these craft and were aware that their appearance usually signalled the presence of one of the dreaded iron snakes, but up to that moment, no arrowheads had ever appeared east of the Mississippi. That in itself was amazing but what were they doing here during the White Death? The paramount clans of the She-Kargo had claimed that the iron snakes always returned to their burrows by the end of the Yellowing! – crawled back to their lairs beneath the Deserts of the South?

Death Leopard, the leader of the posse, waved the column forward. Clearwater, tight-lipped but uncomplaining, kept pace using the mental powers that Mutes possessed to block off the pain from her badly bruised knees. Beside her, Cadillac was quietly pleased to discover that he was not short of breath despite the lack of practice.

Glancing up from time to time he saw the two aircraft hold the same steady eastward course, becoming tiny specks that were soon swallowed up by the unbroken blue. He believed he knew why they were here but this was not the moment to speak of such things.

On the journey to the search area, Gus White's patrol spotted a handful of settlements and a number of ground movements.

All four pilots would dearly have loved to indulge in some low-level strafing but the plastic muzzle caps of their nose-mounted machine guns had been taped on to catch anyone tempted to violate the order not to fire.

Failing to find any sign of the crashed Sky-Riders within the allotted time, Gus ordered the others to head back to The Lady and continued the search until he had just barely enough fuel to make it home. He had been secretly hoping he might locate one or both of the aircraft and thus take the entire credit himself instead of getting into an argument with the others about who saw what first. In this he was destined to be disappointed but he turned for home content in the knowledge that the extra effort would not go unnoticed by the top brass.

He locked on to The Lady's radio beam and gradually lost altitude, levelling out at two thousand feet in order to get a closer look at what lay below.

As soon as Kelso had been installed under the close-packed groups of pines, Steve left Jodi in charge and went out with a brace of hand-guns in the hope of felling some fresh meat. In the time they'd been overground, both Jodi and Kelso had overcome the revulsions all Trackers had towards eating the real thing — no easy task for someone raised on a diet of synthesized soya been papo.

Steve had promised to be back in an hour but it was close on two before Jodi sighted him through the 'scope she'd been using to scan the surrounding landscape. Her relief at his return was tinged with disappointment when she saw he was empty-handed.

She went out to meet him. 'One of those days, huh?'

'Yeah.' He rubbed his wounded thigh. 'Saw all kinds of stuff out there but it was either too fast on its feet or too far away.'

'Never mind, we can always open —' Jodi broke off as Steve's attention fastened on something in the sky.

Following his gaze, she saw the blue-grey speck and hurriedly focused the 'scope on it. The blurred image resolved itself into a straight-winged aircraft painted in the standard Federation blue and flying directly towards them.

Jodi gasped as she caught sight of its white wingtip markings. 'I don't believe this – Steve! Look! It's from The Lady!'

Before her involuntary separation from the wagon-train during the battle of the Now and Then River, Jodi had been a member of The Lady's crew for five years, rising from wingman to section leader. 'Christo! Talk about luck! D'you realize what this means?'

Steve, who had only served aboard for some three months before being shot down, didn't share her sudden gush of nostalgia. He took a brief look through the 'scope. 'Yeah. I'll tell you exactly what this means. That plane up there is one of the new model Skyhawks I told you about. We're looking at the wrong end of a six-barrelled machine gun!'

The information didn't appear to register. 'So what? Don't you understand? This changes everything!'

'You're right. We're in even bigger trouble than we were before.' Steve pulled her back under cover of the pine trees where they had set up camp.

Kelso's improvised stretcher lay on the far side of the bivouac area. His face was turned away from them and he appeared to be sleeping. Steve turned back to Jodi and sank to his knees, pulling her down with him. He held up a warning finger as he let go of her wrist. 'Calm down, okay? I can tell from your face your brain's working overtime. I don't know what you're cooking up but if it's what I think it is, you can forget it!'

It was Jodi who now grabbed hold of him. She seized his left forearm with both hands and shook it excitedly. 'Listen! If Hartmann and Big D are still aboard, there won't *be* any trouble! If I can make contact with them and get back on board I can explain what happened to me!'

'And . . .?'

'Brickman! I did five operational tours with those two guys! If they testify on my behalf I'd have a better chance of getting a fair shake from a board of Assessors! I could be reinstated!'

'That's what they *want* you to think,' said Steve. 'For chrissakes, Jodi! The Federation's got at least twenty wagon-trains on the overground. Do you think it's just a coincidence that plane just *happens* to be from The Lady?'

Jodi's excitement faltered momentarily. 'It's the first time

93

to my knowledge that a wagon-train has ever made an offensive sweep at this time of year. But apart from that, the fact that it's The Lady who's prowling around out there doesn't strike me as being particularly sinister.'

'Really? What d'you think she's doing here?'

'Hunting Mutes, what else? You've seen for yourself there's plenty of 'em around.'

'C'mon, Jodi. You can do better than that. That guy up there was looking for *us*!'

'How d'you figure that out?'

'What's the matter with you? You got frostbite on the brain? When that ape Side-Winder woke up and found us gone, he knew where we were heading –'

'How?'

'Because, like a fool, I told him! And those two pilots knew just how far we could get on the fuel that was left in the tanks!' Steve shook his head and cursed under his breath. 'We should have shot the bastards . . .' Steve's eyes hardened. 'Kelso was going to and –'

'I know. I stopped him.'

'Big mistake. But I still take the booby prize. We should have burned those Skyriders instead of just leaving 'em standing there like a couple of signposts.'

'Without bodies inside that wouldn't have fooled anybody for long. And although I've never flown anything that wasn't battery powered I would guess that planes with empty fuel tanks don't catch fire unless someone puts a torch to 'em.'

'No . . . you're right,' muttered Steve. 'But with this snow covering what was left of them they'd have been a lot harder to find. Once they pin-point those planes – if they haven't spotted them already – they'll know we're out here. We only saw one today but they must have the whole flight-section patrolling this area.'

'D'you think he spotted us?'

'Hard to say. There's plenty of tracks out there, ours *and* the ones made by the Kojaks. But it doesn't matter because unless someone plants a big arrow besides ours there ain't no way they're gonna be able to spot the difference.'

'Do you think they'll come back? The planes I mean.'

'Yeah. Bound to. I'm only guessing here, but given the time of day and the fact that he was flying due west, I'd say he was probably heading for home. So where would you say that puts The Lady – on the far side of the Mississippi?'

'Sounds reasonable . . .'

They consulted the map together. The Mississippi River wasn't depicted. The left hand edge ran down through Joliet, Illinois.

'Terrific . . .' Steve shoved his half of the map towards Jodi. 'I still don't think Hartmann's gonna put any line-men across the water. My geography's a little hazy but I reckon we must be about a hundred, maybe a hundred and fifty miles from the river.'

Jodi smoothed out the crumpled map. 'At least . . .'

'Well, you know him better than I do but I can't see Hartmann sending a combat team that far out on the limb without the proper backup – can you?'

'No.' Jodi chewed on her lip. 'So . . . what happens now?'

'For the moment, nothing. We sit tight and stay under cover until we find out what kind of a deal Cadillac and Clearwater have managed to put together.'

'But suppose there isn't a deal? What do we do if they don't come back in a couple of days like they said? How long do we wait here – for ever?'

Steve sighed impatiently. 'Jodi, if there isn't a deal, we'll know soon enough. Those Kojak braves'll be swarming all over us!'

Jodi considered this unappealing prospect with a thoughtful nod then said: 'Lemme make you a proposition. You were sent out to bring in those two smart Mutes. Okay. With some help from Dave and me, you got 'em out of Ne-Issan. But now they've gone – and they might not be back. So before we find ourselves up shit creek without a paddle, I suggest we cut our losses and try to rejoin The Lady.'

Steve gave her a disbelieving stare. 'Are you crazy?'

'Brickman, be realistic. What chance do we have out here?'

'The same chance as everyone else! You made it through one winter. You can do it again.'

'Last year I was one of ninety renegades in a highly organized group. Run by Malone, remember?'

'I'm not likely to forget.' Steve's laugh had a bitter edge to it. 'I also haven't forgotten he managed to lose over thirty breakers, including you and Dave, to the M'Calls. Some organizer!'

'Okay, so he makes mistakes too. But he was onto *your* number in nought seconds flat.'

'Yeah, that's right. He was . . .'

Jodi lowered her voice. 'The point I'm trying to make is, I was with my own kind. I don't trust that bunch of Mutes your two smoothies are trying to do business with. Like I said, those lumps are soon gonna find out I'm not regulation issue, but even if there was some way to swing it I'm not prepared to come with you if it means dumping Dave.'

'Jodi! For chrissakes, be reasonable! We've done our best for the guy. Most people would have put a bullet through him and left him in the wreckage!'

'Yeah? Well, I'm not most people. You promised me no one would kill him – that we'd work something out. Now it sounds like you're ready to hit the Delete button. Whose side are you on, Brickman?'

'Yours. At least I'm trying to be – but it's not easy when you keep changing your fucking mind!'

The accusation riled her. 'Jeez! You got a nerve! You chew me out for switching tracks but you been rewriting the programme ever since we ran into each other back in Nebraska. First you tell me you're dressed up like a lump-sucker just to save your hide. It then turns out you're an undercover Fed out to kidnap some smart Mutes – and you lay that True Blue stuff on me and how helpin' you will save the day and your kin-sister's ass.

'Finally, at first hiccup – when Kelso and I start having second thoughts – you're ready to dump little sister and kiss goodbye to the Federation! It just doesn't figure. You're up to something, Brickman. This ain't exactly the time and place to fall out but the fact is, I don't trust you.'

'Yeah . . .' Steve let out a long, weary sigh. 'You're right to be suspicious, Jodi, but you're reading things the wrong way. I *was* pressured into this operation by threats against Roz. And yes, I *did* ask for help from the Federation. If it hadn't been for them we would never have gotten out alive. I promised I'd help you escape from Ne-Issan and I did. But I never intended to go back in.'

'So why all the talk about me being True Blue and how we were all going to be heroes?'

'That's simple. I couldn't do it without you. But for us to escape *I* had to work with the Federation and *you* had to agree. Sooner or later you'd have asked where all the hardware was coming from – so I had to appeal to your loyalty. One Lindbergh Baby to another.

'When we talked after we'd been captured by the M'Calls you were pretty negative about the Federation so when you agreed to help I couldn't be sure whether you'd had a permanent change of heart, or whether you were just hitching a ride on the wagon.'

Steve paused and watched the colour flood into Jodi's cheeks. 'I didn't find out you'd been stringing *me* along until we were in that inflatable on our way to Long Point.'

'I didn't lie to you, Brickman. I was ready and willing to go back in. It was just, well . . . that whole set-up at Bu-faro. And that guy Side-Winder, not just painted up but with *lumps* stuffed in his face! The discovery that the Family had people working hand-in-glove with those dinks spooked me. It suddenly made me realize we were just a small part of a much bigger deal and I felt . . .'

'Expendable . . .? We've never been anything else, Jodi.'

'Yeah, strange . . . I don't know why it came as such a shock.'

'That's because until we broke loose and were able to give our brains some elbow room it never occurred to us that there might be an alternative to what was on offer. From the moment we were old enough to understand it's been drummed into us that the only reason for a Tracker's existence is to die so that the dream of the First Family can be fulfilled. The conquest of the Blue-Sky World . . .

'But no one has ever questioned their right to it – or whether it's worth the lives that have been lost, the sacrifices that have been made, and the untold numbers that still have to die before they repossess the overground.'

'It's not just *their* dream,' said Jodi. 'It's something we all share. Well, most of us . . .'

Steve picked up the 'scope and moved to where he could see the western half of the sky through the branches. The Skyhawk was now a long way away, a tiny dot on the vast, cloudless yellow canvas that hung above the western horizon.

He returned and crouched down facing Jodi. 'The question is – if that dream becomes reality, what will happen to the Plainfolk?'

Jodi shrugged. 'If the Federation gets its way, I guess there won't be any.'

Steve found Roz's words on his lips. 'Don't they have a right to exist?'

Jodi responded with a blank stare. 'I don't know what you're getting at.'

'They're *people* Jodi! Human *beings*, like us! Our ancestors were their ancestors too!'

Jodi was unmoved. 'So what? If it's true, which I doubt, that was a long long time ago. And even if you could prove it, who'd wanna believe you? D'you think everyone's gonna kiss and make up after all the sacrifices that generations of Trackers have made? Stop trying to kid yourself, Brickman. Lumpheads and breakers don't mix. Whether you're inside or outside the Federation, they're the enemy and always will be. If we don't kill them, they'll kill us.'

'The M'Calls didn't kill you and the other guys.'

'No. They sold us down the river so the Iron Masters could stick it to us instead!'

'Haven't you learned *anything* since you've been out here?!' hissed Steve. 'Cadillac and Clearwater helped us *escape*! If it wasn't for her we wouldn't *be* here!'

'And *we* helped them. But it's different now. In Ne-Issan, we had a common enemy – the Iron Masters. That deal fell apart the moment we reached Plainfolk territory. We're back in *their* country. They're amongst their own kind. Just look at the way Cadillac's behaving.'

Steve nodded. 'He has been coming on a little strong . . .'

'You can say that again. A couple of weeks ago he was falling apart and you had to glue him back together one day at a time. Now he's behaving like an arrogant sonofabitch!' snapped Jodi. 'That may be okay by you but he's not walking over me!'

Steve appraised her thoughtfully. 'You know what? I think all this guff you've been laying on me about Us and Them, who did what to who, and whether you can trust me or not is pure buffalo shit. This is really about Kelso, isn't it? You've got it into your head that if we can get him aboard The Lady –'

'What other chance does he have?' cried Jodi. 'C'mon! There's a complete combat surgical team riding around in that blood-wagon! If we could arrange for a pick-up, they could get to work within minutes of him getting there!'

Steve glanced over at Kelso. He hadn't moved.

Maybe he was dead. Some chance. Good ol' Dave wasn't the kind of guy who'd do everyone a favour by going quietly ...

He turned back to Jodi. 'They could, but now you're kidding *yourself*. You know as well as I do they're not gonna put Kelso on the operating table. They're gonna put three rounds into his brain. He's a renegade, remember?'

'You're wrong. He isn't ...'

Steve frowned. 'What d'you mean?'

'He's an undercover Fed. Just like you.' She watched Steve trying to grapple with this revelation. 'You don't believe me, do you?'

'How long have you known about this?'

'Since we left Long Point. D'you remember me coming back from the beach store ahead of Dave and how we sat there with the motors running wondering where the hell he'd got to?'

'Yeah ...'

'Well, while I was cursing him with every name I could think of, I fiddled around with a few of the knobs and switches and ... I accidentally turned on the tail end of a radio transmission.'

'Go on ...'

'It was Dave.'

'You sure about this?'

'Absolutely. He was talking to Sky Bucket Three, the same bunch your friend with the lumps in his face got in touch with just after we landed at Long Point.'

'Did you manage to get a handle on what Kelso and this Sky Bucket were talking about?'

'Not really. Skybucket was relaying instructions from someone called Mother. That make any sense to you?'

Steve's face gave nothing away. 'A little . . .'

'Mother' was the soubriquet coined by AMEXICO operatives for Karlstrom. It had entered their private language over a generation ago and had proved so popular, the then Operations Director had allowed it to supersede his official code-name MX-ONE. Karlstrom, who appreciated its shades of meaning, had continued the tradition.

'Did Kelso use a code-name?'

'Yes, Rat-Catcher . . .'

Steve absorbed Jodi's revelations calmly. There was little to be gained by being angry. 'Why'd'you wait till now to tell me about this?'

Jodi hesitated then said: 'It seemed like the right time. Let's face it, we've had more important things to think about over the last few days. Cadillac was always around and, well, I was . . .'

'Confused . . .?'

'Yeah. Truth is, I didn't know what to think. I was surprised, naturally. I'd spent nearly a year on the run with Dave. Okay, at times he could be a pain in the ass but I'd gotten pretty close to him. I thought he was genuine. But then . . . I thought you were too. A little mixed-up, perhaps, decking yourself out as a Mute. But when we met up again in Ne-Issan and you finally came clean and told me *you* were an undercover Fed, plus all that other shit – like your thing with the Herald –'

She waved it all away. 'I'm just a simple, straight down the line type person, Brickman. With all the deals you had going there were times when I lost track of who was shafting who. My first reaction – after I'd recovered from the surprise – was to think that maybe you and Dave were in cahoots, but working both sides of the track.'

Steve nodded. 'Yes, I can see how you might think that . . .'

'Then we ran out of fuel and the way Dave acted made me think that maybe you *didn't* know what he was up to. By which time he'd picked a tree to run into and broken half the bones in his body.'

'So you started feeling sorry for him . . .'

'What was the point of telling you? You might have tried to shoot him there and then!'

Steve's anger rose. 'What makes you think I won't do it now?!'

Jodi grabbed hold of him. 'Because you don't *have* to, and I won't let you! What harm can he do now? The poor bastard can barely move!'

'So what do you care? I just don't get it, Jodi. He helped get us into this mess. Why are you trying to protect him?'

'For the same reason when you were tied to a post face to face with a corpse, I persuaded Malone to let me come back and cut you loose! Because I *cared*! And Dave cared enough to come with me! The same way *you* cared enough to get me out of Ne-Issan – or was that because Dave and I were needed to make up the numbers?'

'No! I meant it! I promised to get you out and I did. We're all from Big Blue, right?'

'Exactly. We're the best. That's why I want to do what's right for both of you.'

'Go ahead. I'm listening . . .'

'If those planes come over again I'm gonna let 'em know that Dave and I are down here. And if they ask where you are, I'm gonna say that you, Cadillac and Clearwater never came back from a hunting trip. That you were probably captured by a bunch of Mutes and the only reason I escaped was because I stayed behind to look after Dave.' Jodi paused. 'How does it sound so far?'

'Keep talking . . .'

'I'll probably have to tell them you'd talked about trying to get to Wyoming – but that everyone could forget about that now because if you weren't already dead, you probably soon would be.' She shrugged. 'Mutes kill anyone who invades their turf, right?'

'Right . . .'

'Of course, I won't say anything about all that stuff Clearwater did at the Heron Pool. They probably wouldn't believe it anyway. And besides, talking about Mute magic's a Code One offence.'

Steve waited a while. 'Is that it . . .?'

'Yeah.'

'Aren't you forgetting one thing? Kelso might be an undercover Fed but you ran with a bunch of breakers for over a year. What do you think they're gonna do, Jodi – pin a lifesaving medal on your chest? You've seen too much and you know too much. If they take you back to Fort Worth you'll probably end up against the wall.'

'I know. But that's the only way I can save both your asses. Two lives for one.' She grimaced ruefully. That's not such a bad percentage.'

'This is crazy. There must be some other way to get Kelso on board and keep you off the –'

'No!' Jodi grasped Steve's wrist firmly. 'I want to go in.' She searched his eyes for some sign of encouragement and drew a blank. 'I know it looks as if I'm running out on you but . . ,' she paused awkwardly, '. . . this is the best chance I'm ever going to get to straighten things out.'

'Then take it. With the top deck of The Lady on your case you should come out cleaner than the P-G's underwear.'

'It'd be nice to think so but if I draw a ticket to the wall I'll go quietly and say my piece. I've had enough, Brickman.' Her mouth twisted into a tired smile. 'Once upon a time I believed in the Federation – that the First Family could do no wrong. Then Dave and Malone and Medicine Hat showed me another whole new way of living, feeling and thinking and I believed that too.

'I realized we'd been fed a whole pack of lies only to discover that Dave – one of the guys who saved my life – wasn't for real either. I don't hate him for it. But it made me realize there ain't no truth to be found anywhere, Brickman. So you might as well pick the most comfortable lie and live with it.'

'I think you're wrong but I know what you mean.' Steve sighed with genuine regret. 'It's your decision, Jodi. So where do we go from here?'

'Well . . . before I do anything rash, maybe I should talk things over with Dave.'

'Leave that to me,' said Steve. He saw the flicker of alarm in her eyes. 'Don't worry, I'm not going to give him a hard time. I'm pretty sure he went along with you because he wanted to see which way I'd jump. He probably had orders not to make contact. The high wires who run this scummy business back in Grand Central have some strange ideas. They don't like us guys at the sharp end getting too friendly with one another.'

Jodi nodded. 'Tell me something . . .'

'What's that?'

'When we were crossing Lake Erie. If Dave and I hadn't told you we didn't want to go back in, what were you planning to do?'

'I'd have taken you out with the gas just like the others,' said Steve.

Jodi checked the sky for herself then stood up and moved out into the open. She looked back at Steve. 'When the new intake came aboard The Lady in '89, Big D told me you were the one to watch. I'm not surprised they made you an under-cover Fed.'

Steve shrugged modestly. There hadn't *been* a plan. From the moment they'd boarded the wheelboat for Bu-faro he'd been playing it by ear. Plagued by divided loyalties, his mental confusion had steadily increased until Roz had come through on their own private line with the reassurance he needed. But given their present perilous situation this was not the moment to reveal any hint of weakness or indecision. If Jodi was convinced he was ten moves ahead of everyone else in the game, why spoil the illusion?

CHAPTER FIVE

For the wingmen aboard The Lady from Louisiana, the second day produced more encouraging results. The primary search area had been assailed by new snow flurries overnight but the accompanying wind, which sculpted the landscape into a new pattern of knife-edged dunes and hollows, blew most of the accumulated snow from the abandoned Skyriders.

They were spotted by the afternoon patrol led by Nate Stinson. He had been Deputy Section-Leader aboard Sands of Iwojima before being transferred and moving up a notch into the post that Jodi had held aboard The Lady. Stinson radioed news of the find to Hartmann then, after all four pilots had made a low-level check on the area, he detailed Vickers to land and examine the crash site.

The wingman, one of two on the present patrol whose aircraft had been fitted with ski attachments wasn't too thrilled at having drawn the short straw but there was nothing he could do except say 'Roger, Wilco'. He put down alongside the remains of the highway and taxied back to where one of the Skyriders still stood more or less upright with its wheels buried in the snow.

Leaving his motor running, in case he needed to make a quick getaway, Vickers made his way towards it. The wind had cleared patches of the crumbling highway but the vegetation on the overgrown slopes had trapped the snow beneath an icy crust.

This was Vickers' second operational tour but, up to this moment, he had only ever set down on the flight-deck of the wagon-train. Well, that was not *quite* true. He *had* made four touch and go landings to try out the skis but this was the first time he had actually walked more than ten yards on Plainfolk territory and prior to crossing the Missouri he had never, in his whole life, seen so much snow before. Pressing ahead on the blithe assumption it was all ankle deep he crashed through the brittle surface and sank in over his knees. Recovering from his initial surprise, he attempted to resume the purposeful stride with which he'd left the Skyhawk but was quickly reduced to an ungainly waddle by the buried tangle of roots and stalks that kept trapping his feet.

Goddamn fuggin' overground ... First Family wanted their brains examining ... who'd wanna live in an asshole place like this?

It was not all that far to the highway, but by the time he reached it, Vickers had run out of obscene swear words to heap upon the heads of the shit-brained high-wires who had dreamt up this operation.

From the air, the plane had appeared to be undamaged, but as he drew closer, Vickers saw that the Skyrider had been reduced to a mere shell. A horde of scavenging Mutes, working with the same expertise that desert vultures bring to the job of removing the edible parts of a dead camel, had picked the metal carcass clean: seats, cables, control rods and wires, instruments, hatches, parts of the canopy, every square inch of fabric and anything that could be unscrewed, unpicked or torn loose had vanished.

An examination of the snow-covered debris wrapped around the nosewheel revealed that this Skyrider had ploughed into the severed tail section of its companion during its landing run. Vickers used his walkie-talkie to report his findings to his airborne companions then climbed back into his 'hawk and taxied eastwards till he came opposite the last of the trees where the forward half of the other aircraft had come to rest.

This too had been stripped but a close inspection provided some useful clues. Smears of dried blood on the jagged ends of metal stringers and formers in the crumpled cockpit section testified to the force of the impact and the likelihood that one of the five people they were looking for had been either killed or seriously injured on landing.

Beneath the broken starboard wing, Vickers found – like Izo before him – the remains of a fire. The pine branches that Steve's party had woven together to form the walls of the shelter had been thrown aside and scattered but several remained intertwined giving a clue to their use. The fire-cans and food tins — which might have told him a great deal more than they told Izo — had been carried away as trophies but the scattered circle of ashes and a solitary ring pull-tab from a standard-issue ration can suggested that the surviving crewmen had spent some time under shelter before vanishing into the snow-covered wastes.

Whether they had vanished of their own accord or had been overwhelmed by the same force of Mutes who had descended on the two aircraft in search of booty could not be established. Backing clear of the tree under which the wreckage lay, Vickers gave his section-leader a status report and his views on what had happened.

'Roger, Blue Two. Well done. Put some sky under your wheels.'

They were the words Vickers had been waiting for. He hurried back across the highway and waded up the other side to where he'd parked his Skyhawk facing into wind. He didn't waste time brushing off the snow or strapping himself in. He just rammed the throttle wide open and held his breath until he had regained the comparative safety of the air. The audible sigh of relief came as the altimeter showed the Skyhawk at five hundred feet and climbing.

Made it . . . Yeeee-HAAAHH!

Fresh snowfalls and cloudy skies limited the air search during The Lady's third day on station. The flight-section were stood down but the remaining two hundred and sixty crew plus the Pueblo contingent found themselves with plenty to do. Following the discovery of the two Skyriders, Hartmann had decided to press forward to Davenport. The move, when completed, would extend the Skyhawks' range by another one hundred and forty miles, allowing them more time in the air east of the Mississippi.

Several squads of heavily armed line-men, dressed in the white coveralls that had been airlifted to the Kansas City rendezvous with the tanker-train, were sent out to reconnoitre a twenty-mile stretch of the Cedar River. When a suitable crossing point had been found, The Lady moved forward and unloaded the two bull-dozers she carried. Under the direction of Buck McDonnell, they began the task of cutting an access ramp down to the water. Lt. Commander Moore, the senior Field Officer had already put two combat squads onto the east bank to form a bridgehead and the usual perimeter defence that was always deployed when the crew were 'shifting dirt' was set up around the wagon-train.

The river at this point was only six to eight feet deep over a firm gravel bed which meant The Lady could roll across without even getting her belly wet. The crossing was delayed when the engineers decided they would have to use explosives to blast loose the rocks buried in the escarpment on the far side but just after dawn on the fourth day, the 'dozers had cut the required exit ramp and The Lady was on her way to Davenport.

The increasing numbers of arrowheads criss-crossing the sky did not go unnoticed by Cadillac's hosts. The settlement had not come under attack, but having watched several blue and white Skyhawks pass almost directly overhead, Carnegie-Hall, the Kojak wordsmith, became sufficiently concerned to ask his honoured guests if the appearance of the cloud-warriors and the attendant iron snake was linked to their own descent from the skies.

Cadillac who, from the outset, had been anxious to leave Carnegie and the Kojak elders in no doubt that he and Clearwater were the stars of the select group the clan had been eagerly expecting, ignored her warning glance and answered in the affirmative.

Having already held the clan spellbound with his faultless command of the Iron Masters' language and his graphic descriptions of life at all levels in Ne-Issan, he now revealed that Clearwater was a summoner who held the key to several Rings of Power.

Hey-yahhh . . .

Like all wordsmiths, Cadillac could not resist the lure of a receptive audience – especially when the story he was telling enhanced his own importance. Let the elders of the Clan Kojak mark this! He, Cadillac, son of Sky-Walker out of Black-Wing and she, daughter of Thunder-Bird out of Sun-Dance, had been born in the shadow of The Thrice-Gifted One. And Mr Snow – who was known and respected by his peers through the annual gatherings at the trading post – had declared them to be the Sword and Shield of Talisman!

And had not the M'Calls, the paramount clan of the She-Kargo, caused nine cloud-warriors to fall from the sky before forcing the first iron snake to venture into Plainfolk territory to turn tail and flee? Cadillac described the parts he and Clearwater had played in that great victory, allying their powers to those possessed by Mr Snow – The Storm-Bringer.

Carnegie-Hall and the elders roared their approval. In truth these were mighty deeds!

But there was more, declared Cadillac. And with his audience hanging on every word he went on to describe how, before leaving the eastern lands, they and their three companions had dealt the Iron Masters a mortal blow, killing mighty warlords and decimating their armies with sky-fire and earth thunder.

Hey-yahhh . . .

This, concluded Cadillac, was why they and their companions were feared and pursued by the sand-burrowers just as, in time, the dead-faces would seek to avenge their wounded pride.

This last remark of Cadillac's was totally off-the-cuff; mere verbal embroidery. Had he been drawing images of the future from a seeing-stone with their meaning spelled out in letters of fire, he could not have made a more accurate prediction. But he was not destined to discover the chilling truth that lay behind his boastful words until the danger burst upon him like a sudden rockslide sweeping down upon travellers in a narrow mountain pass.

Carnegie-Hall, a dark, sinister-looking lump-head with a bushy black beard – who Cadillac judged to be half the age of Mr Snow – was quick to pick up on the unexpected news that Clearwater was a summoner. If she had aided Mr Snow to defeat the attack on the M'Calls could she not – as a simple gesture of thanks for the protection and hospitality which the Clan Kojak was honoured to offer them – drive these cloud-warriors from the skies and force the unseen iron snake to return to its burrow?

The question left Cadillac open-mouthed but he had gone so far over the top there was only one thing he could say: 'If it is the will of Talisman, this thing shall be done.' Then, feeling that his reply needed more of a flourish, he added: 'And in its doing the Plainfolk shall witness the power of The Chosen, and the Clan Kojak shall be justly rewarded for being the first to receive them.'

How true, my young friend, thought Carnegie-Hall. How true. But the rewards he had in mind were of an entirely different order.

As soon as they had a moment to themselves, Clearwater treated Cadillac to a withering look. 'Well done. This time you've excelled yourself.' Her eyes blazed as her anger mounted. 'How dare you speak of the secret gifts that are mine alone to reveal!?'

'I got carried away,' said Cadillac. He spread his hands apologetically.

'You idiot!' Clearwater vented her fury by drumming her fists on his chest. 'I sat there wishing your tongue would drop out! How can we do what you have promised!?'

Cadillac fended her off gently. 'Calm down! *I* didn't promise we'd *do* anything. I said it would be done *if* it was the will of Talisman!' He stepped back, drew himself up and said loftily: 'It's time you understood that I don't just *say* things. These words are given to me. You or I may not understand their meaning when they spring from my lips but in time, Talisman's purpose will be made plain to us. Learn to be patient, for all will be well.'

'Bravo,' replied Clearwater. 'I hope you're right.' He was beginning to sound more and more like the gifted young man she had grown up with and whose life had been entrusted to her care. Stubborn, complicated, tormented, petulant but also brave, loyal, imaginative and likeable. A true friend. The Cadillac to whom she had given her body and soul until the fateful day that the Sky Voices had spoken of when the golden-haired cloud-warrior had fallen from the skies.

Changing the course of all their lives . . .

Cadillac abandoned his contemplation of the cosmic mysteries and patted her shoulders reassuringly. 'Don't worry. I've got a good feeling about this.'

As darkness shrouded the snow-covered wastes to the east of navref Joliet, Illinois, Steve sat with his knees drawn up to his chin, contemplating the glowing embers of the fire they had lit within the small circle of trees. On the other side of the pool of orange light, Jodi was feeding Kelso some soup she had made from a foil sachet of beef-flavoured concentrate and melted snow.

During the day, Steve had built a waist-high circular wall of snow around the campsite with four exits that could be blocked by branches. A layer of more slender branches covered the floor. Besides concealing the brightest part of the fire at night, the wall gave shelter against the icy wind, and once inside, they were able to keep themselves reasonably warm and snug.

When Kelso could not be coaxed into eating any more Jodi came over and offered Steve what was left.

'No thanks, you have it.' Steve watched her gulp it down then scrape out the can. 'Is he still awake?'

'Mmmmm . . .' She sucked the spoon clean then licked her lips.

'Good.' Steve dropped his voice. 'It's time he and I cleared the air.'

'Can I sit in?'

'No. The less you know the better.' He saw her bristle. 'Look. I know you find it difficult to trust me but try – just this once. Have you said anything to Kelso about, uhh . . .?'

She shook her head. 'There didn't seem to be any point.'

'You're right. Well done. I'll tell him it was *me* who caught him in the act. That way you're in the clear. You've got enough problems without getting mixed up in whatever *Kelso*'s mixed up in.'

Jodi shrugged. 'I know about you.'

'Yeah. And even that's too much.'

'So what if someone starts asking questions?'

'Just tell 'em what you did, and that you did it because *I* told you I was acting on behalf of the Federation and . . . *you believe I still am.*'

'Got it.' Jodi smiled. 'You really know how to put over the old sincerity routine. I remember you tryin' to buffalo me when we first met at Fort Worth. Your eyes actually glow. D'you know that?'

'For chrissakes, Jodi! I'm not trying to put one over on you! This is for your own good!'

'Just kidding. That's the trouble with guys like you.'

'What d'you mean – "guys like me"?'

'Over-achievers. They got no sense of humour. But seriously – these people who may question me . . . do I tell 'em I know about Side-Winder and the tie-up with the nips?'

'Only if they ask you first. Stick to the golden rule. Don't hide anything but don't volunteer any information. Above all, don't attempt to justify your actions. Let *me* take the heat. You did what you did because *I* asked you to. Okay?'

'Okay . . .' Jodi got to her feet.

Steve followed her up. 'Do my eyes really glow?'

Jodi laughed. 'You tryin' to tell me you never practised in front of a mirror?' She stepped outside the snow circle and looked up through the outer branches. 'Christo! Take a look at this . . .'

Steve joined her. A hard white moon rode high in a blue-black satin sky, edging a majestic procession of dense black clouds with a fleeting glow of silver. The light, which was strong enough to cast shadows on the snow, turned the night frost at their feet into a carpet of pearls. The landscape beyond, harsh and blinding in the winter sun, had been coloured in with mysterious, washed-out shades of blue. At moments like this, it was easy to understand why Mutes thought such beauty was the inspired handiwork of some all-powerful being. Like Mo-Town, the Great Sky-Mother . . .

Jodi surveyed the scene then said: 'This is one of the things I'm gonna miss.'

'Yeah. Not bad, is it?' Compared to this, the vistas offered by the John Wayne Plaza paled into insignificance.

She fisted his shoulder. 'Think I'll stroll around for a bit while you guys swap secrets. Have fun . . .'

Steve laid a few more branches on the fire then settled down beside Kelso. 'You and I need to talk.'

'S'posing I don't feel like it?'

'S'posing it means living instead of dying?'

'You mean I got a choice?'

'Wanna know something? Adversity really brings out the best side of your nature.'

'Move it along, Brickman. Otherwise I may fall asleep on you.'

Steve outlined Jodi's plan to get them both aboard The Lady, and the reason why she thought she'd get a friendly reception.

'Because of her connections . . .'

'Yes. I think it's a runner, don't you?'

Kelso greeted this with a husky sneer. You could see by his face it hurt even to breathe. 'She might get away with it but what about me? When they feed my serial to that bug-eyed monster back in Houston, they'll know I've been on the run for over three years. Those guys on that wagon-train'll dump me over the side without even bothering to change the bandages!'

'It's true they rarely take renegades back alive, but in your case I think they'll make an exception.'

'Oh, yeah? You must know somethin' I don't.' Kelso tried to keep his voice and expression neutral but the way his lips froze up around the words gave him away.

'Wrong. I heard something I wasn't meant to.' Steve's eyes fastened on the left side of Kelso's head. 'Hold still. You got a bug crawling up your neck.' He reached over and flicked away the imaginary insect then slid his forefinger upwards under Kelso's ear and located the pea-sized transceiver lying beneath the skin just below the edge of the skull.

Kelso tried to move his head away but Steve's own transceiver had already picked up the signal and fed it into his eardrum as a mosquito-like whine. Jodi was right. David Kelso *was* a mexican – as Steve had once suspected back at the Heron Pool when he'd encountered the irascible red-headed breaker humming 'Down Mexico Way'.

'Just testing. Let me guess your call-sign – R T – C R . . .?'

With only one free hand and the rest of him tied to the hatch, Kelso knew he was at Steve's mercy. 'How long have you known?'

'It was just before we took off from Long Point. I heard this character called Rat-Catcher asking Sky-Bucket Three to pass a message to Mother.' Steve fed him an edited version of Jodi's story.

'What can I say?'

'Plenty. That evening back at the Heron Pool – when I met you in the alleyway and –'

'I was humming our signature tune –'

'Yeah. When I responded with my call-sign – why didn't you answer back?'

Kelso shrugged his good shoulder. 'I was checking you out. Jodi'd told me what you had in mind. I just wanted to make sure you really *were* one of us.'

'Are you telling me that, on top of everything else, there are guys who *pretend* to be mexicans?'

'There are some strange people out here, Brickman – grinding some very peculiar axes.'

'And you thought I might be one of them . . .'

'The question did crop up. Jodi wasn't one hundred per cent sure of you either. You're a hard man to pin down.'

'Look who's talking. What about *your* change of heart on the way to Long Point?'

'Simple. It was Jodi who suddenly got cold feet. I pretended to go along with her to see which way you would jump.' He saw the doubt creep into Steve's eyes. 'C'mon, Brickman, you know the way Mother likes to run things. If we're not sent in as a team, individual agents do not link up without prior instructions. It's SOP.'

'Except in an emergency.'

'Right. But response to a May-Day is not mandatory if it risks jeopardizing your own operation. The same applies to the situation where you came on to me. If it's not in the script, then it's up to each individual agent to react as he thinks fit. Depends on the circumstances. He may not want to blow a deep cover that's taken years to acquire. Okay, that may mean there are times when the right hand may not know what the left hand is doin', but it's the only way AMEXICO and its operations can remain watertight.'

'Yeah, I suppose so . . .' A sudden thought struck Steve. 'Did we run into each other by accident in Nebraska, or did –'

'By accident, of course! Jeez! What a question! If I'd known I was gonna get captured by those fuggin lump-heads you wouldn't have seen me for dust!' Kelso was lying, but now that Brickman thought he knew all the answers, it was easier to slip one past him.

Besides, it was half-true. They had been alerted to Brickman's arrival. As a brand new member of AMEXICO, he had been 'posted' to test the limits of his physical and mental endurance – and had passed with flying colours. Kelso and Medicine-Hat had been detailed to go back to cut him loose before he suffered serious injury and, by a happy coincidence, Jodi's genuine concern had provided a convenient cover. The bit which hadn't been planned was their unexpected encounter with the clan M'Call.

'So what were you doing out there?' Steve knew it was a waste of time asking but his curiosity got the better of him.

Kelso replied with a croaking laugh. 'You never cease to amaze me, Brickman.'

'How about Malone? He seemed to know a great deal about under-cover Feds.'

'That's a question you'll have to ask him.' Kelso yawned. 'Is there much more of this? I'm findin' it hard to keep my eyes open.'

'I want you to give a message to Mother.'

Kelso yawned again. 'Hope it's not a long one . . .'

'No. But listen carefully. I was sent out to capture three smart Mutes. Cadillac, Clearwater and their teacher – an old guy called Mr Snow.'

'Well, two out of three ain't bad. Especially on your first assignment.'

'Will you listen to me!?' demanded Steve angrily. 'This is important! Those two are piddle-shit compared with Mr Snow. You saw what Clearwater did at the Heron Pool? Yeah? Well, Mr Snow can unleash ten times more power than that!'

'So just how d'you propose to bring him in?'

'The only way I can get to him is through his pupils. They have been raised to take his place when he dies and they're his *only* weak spot.'

'Go on . . .'

'Knocking out Side-Winder and the two MX pilots was necessary to give *me* the deep cover I need. Cadillac and Clearwater have to believe I'm totally committed to the Plainfolk. That's why I promised Mr Snow I'd do my best to rescue them from Ne-Issan. If I can get them back safely to their clan in Wyoming, I'll be the local hero and –'

'That's when we snatch all three.'

'Exactly.' Steve grinned. 'Y'see, the thing is, I don't really give a damn about saving your ugly hide. I just need someone I can trust to explain what's happening. Someone with the right connections. The first thing you must do when you get aboard The Lady is contact Mother, relay what I've just told you, and ask him to arrange for Hartmann to get his marching orders. I want that wagon-train out of here A S A P and I don't want to see another one north of the Kansas state line until I send word.'

'Some chance. They may pull out The Lady but I can't see 'em holding up the whole fuggin' war while you get your act together.'

'Just pass on the message, okay?'

'Okay. But I think I ought to warn you. If someone offers me a quick rebuild under a general anaesthetic, your message may have to wait until I come round.'

'Bad, huh?'

'I've known better days.' Kelso fought down a wave of pain and clutched at Steve's arm. 'Listen. I appreciate you sticking by me. Thanks for fixing me up with a ride home.'

'You're not there yet, *amigo*.'

'All bar the shouting. I owe you one – okay?'

'If you get that message through, we're even. But if you feel like doing me a favour, just make sure Jodi comes out of this in one piece. She's putting her neck on the line to save yours. Remember that.'

'I will . . .'

'Good. Here's the bottom line. Apart from Mother, if

anyone wants to know, you two are the only survivors. You didn't see anything. It's Jodi who's got the full story. Got that?'

'Yeah . . .'

Jodi came over to give Kelso his nightly jab of pain-killer then stroked his forehead. 'Okay, get some sleep, champ. We want you in good shape for the big event.'

'When's, uhh . . . tomorrow . . .?' Kelso's eyes started to close.

'Soon,' said Steve. It would have to be. There were only two more shots of morphine left in the locker.

For the return journey to the campsite, the Kojak elders provided Cadillac and Clearwater with an escort of two hands instead of the original five. Although this appeared to devalue their worth it was, in fact, intended as a compliment. Having listened to Cadillac's extravagant claims, the elders had come to the conclusion that even if only half of it were true the 'Chosen Ones' would be more than capable of protecting themselves and their escort.

The decision was not unanimous, but taking their lead from Carnegie-Hall, the dissenters did not declare themselves. Having netted this prize catch, the wordsmith was reluctant to jeopardize their safety but questions of etiquette were involved. To have provided their honoured guests with the same, or an even larger escort would have implied that Cadillac's testimony regarding their status and Clearwater's powers had not been taken seriously.

Time-honoured tradition required wordsmiths to speak openly to one another. They might not declare all they knew but everything they declared *had* to be true. For one member of this select band to imply by word or deed that a brother-in-spirit had used his gifts to weave a tissue of lies would have been a serious affront with unpredictable consequences.

The elders had another more practical reason for reducing the size of the escort; the warriors were needed elsewhere. The appearance of the iron snake had disturbed the winter slumbers of the Mute clans whose turf lay close to the Mississippi. Had they been capable of submerging their individual interests they might have put up a concerted and vigorous defence but the day when the Plainfolk clans exchanged their implacable hostility towards one another for a sense of nationhood was still a long way off.

Instead of standing their ground, they had begun to withdraw in a northeasterly direction. That very morning, a posse of Kojak braves had encountered an advance party of C'Natti Mutes from an unidentified clan who were in the process of planting marker poles on land already claimed by the M'Waukee.

The C'Natti – the fawning jackals to the wolf-packs of the D'Troit – had been driven off without a fight but they threatened to return in greater numbers and this had given the Kojak elders cause for concern. With some nine hundred braves of both sexes, the Kojak did not fear an attack by a rival clan but they could not withstand simultaneous invasions of their turf by several adversaries – as was bound to happen if the iron snake continued its advance.

A damaging conflict could only be avoided if the threat from this fearsome beast was eliminated. Since Cadillac M'Call had claimed its arrival on the scene was directly linked to the appearance of the Chosen Ones, it was only reasonable to expect these gifted individuals to use their combined powers to remove it. Carnegie was given the task of explaining to Cadillac before he left that defeat of the iron-snake was no longer regarded as an optional, goodwill gesture: it was now essential to prevent the clan being overwhelmed by the pressure from its displaced neighbours.

Clearwater's heart sank as she listened but Cadillac accepted the assignment with the confident air of a man for whom nothing is impossible. He chose to ignore her reproachful glances as they ran southwards but behind his purposeful 'can-do' demeanour he was silently castigating himself for his uncontrolled eloquence. And the phantom personality that dwelt within his brain was running around in mounting panic repeatedly asking the same unanswerable question: '*What am I gonna DO!!?*'

Steve intercepted the column a mile north of the campsite and took Cadillac and Clearwater aside. 'You had me worried. We were expecting you the day before yesterday.'

'The journey took longer than we thought,' said Cadillac.

Steve's eyes met Clearwater's. Her face looked drawn. 'You okay?'

Cadillac cut in ahead of her. 'She's fine. What have you done about Kelso?'

'He's still with us but hold onto your hat. Jodi has come up with an interesting solution and I think it's something you and I should talk over.' He searched the sky. 'Let's get under cover . . .'

Cadillac told their escort what was happening. The fur-clad braves followed them into the nearby stand of pines and settled down out of earshot.

Steve cast his eyes over the Kojak Mutes then asked: 'How d'you make out with their wordsmith?'

Cadillac responded with a self-satisfied smile. 'We're here, aren't we? I did a real number on him.'

Clearwater's expression didn't change but her eyes conveyed a different story.

'I bet . . . But something struck me while you were gone. How come you and Mr Snow didn't know of this prophecy about the Chosen Ones? I thought you wordsmiths passed this kind of stuff around during your annual get-together at the trading post.'

Cadillac did not attempt to hide his exasperation at what he perceived to be an attempt to undermine his new-found authority. 'Brickman! Just leave the business of prophecy to those whose minds are trained to dwell on such things!'

Clearwater, in an effort to keep the peace, said: 'The Old One may have kept it secret to protect us. Ignorance of the terror and humiliation we were fated to endure in the Eastern Lands gave us the blind courage we needed. Foreknowledge of these things might have weakened our resolve.'

'Nice try,' said Steve, with an admiring nod. 'But it doesn't answer the question.' He inclined his head in the direction of their seated escort. 'If those guys were expecting us to drop in – as their wordsmith said we would – it means you were destined to survive the trip to Ne-Issan. So it doesn't make 'any difference whether you knew what you were letting yourself in for or not.'

'Can we get back to the *real* purpose of this conversation?' snapped Cadillac. 'We are not here to justify *our* actions but to hear *his* excuse for failing to deal with the problem of Kelso!'

'I was coming to that. Those guys over there . . . are they in charge, or are you?'

Cadillac glanced at the twelve Mutes then frowned. 'How do you mean . . .?'

'Jack me! It's a simple enough question! Will *they* do what *you* tell 'em!'

Cadillac looked at the Mutes again then studied Steve warily. 'Just tell me what the plan is, Brickman. I can see you can't wait to tell me.'

'It's brilliant. Those Skyhawks that have been flying overhead are –'

'– from The Lady. I know. They have white wing tips. Only these are Mark Two's – as opposed to the delta-winged models you and Jodi were flying last year in Wyoming. Before the M'Calls cut short your promising career.'

'Correct . . .' Steve didn't let the interruption needle him. Cadillac was just trying to level the score. Some chance. But he would have to be watched. If he wasn't slapped down soon he'd start believing he was running things. Meanwhile it was time for some soft soap. An easy smile. 'When you break into a guy's brain, you really clear out the shelves . . .'

'Just thought I'd remind you – in case you were trying to put one over on me.'

'On the contrary. This is a chance for you to look good in front of your new friends.'

'Don't tell me. Let me guess. Jodi wants to try to get back on board The Lady – and she's going to take Kelso with her.'

'Very good. Flushing that *sake* out of your system has really sharpened you up.'

'Okay. That gets rid of Kelso but how does it benefit us?'

'Jodi is going to swear, hand on heart, that she saw the three of us caught by a big posse of Mutes while we were on our way back from a hunting trip. She wasn't spotted because she'd stayed under cover with Kelso but she had the 'scope on us. We were cut down and stabbed repeatedly then our naked bodies were carried away slung on poles.'

Cadillac and Clearwater exchanged loaded glances.

Sensing there was something going on that he wasn't part of, Steve tried to feel them out. 'You're probably wondering if Kelso can be relied upon to corroborate her story. It's not a problem. Since you left we've been keeping him heavily sedated. He doesn't know what day it is.' He studied their faces but neither was giving anything away. 'So it's down to her. And since she was a trusted member of the crew for five years . . .'

'They'll believe her . . .'

'Sure,' continued Steve. 'When the news gets back to Grand Central, they'll tell Hartmann to pull out. You can take the credit and everyone'll be able to go back to sleep again.'

Cadillac mulled it over. Brickman had handed him the opportunity he'd been looking for. The plan began to crystallize in his mind. 'Neat . . . I like it.'

'Good. 'Cos you're going to have to sell it to those twelve guys over there. We don't want 'em going apeshit when those planes come in for the pick-up.'

'I'm not a total idiot, Brickman.'

Steve rolled his tongue around a tart reply then decided to swallow it. There would be time enough to nail this grassmonkey to the wall.

When Hartmann came on screen to announce that an eight-figure serial number had been sighted stamped in the snow one hundred and forty miles east of their present position, the news was greeted with a spontaneous cheer. Since the crew had been told they were searching for five Trackers, everyone was genuinely pleased they'd been found but the real excitement was generated by the prospect that their successful recovery would mean an early return home.

Summoned to the saddle, Trail-Boss McDonnell recognized the serial tapped onto the screen by the RadCommTech who had received the message. Hartmann, who knew there were more to serials than met the eye, had it run through the computer.

Sure enough, up it came: 2096-5341 KAZAN, JODI, R. MUSTERED ABOARD THE LADY FROM LOUISIANA, 5 APRIL 2984. PROMOTED FLT.SEC/LDR 1 MAY 2986. MIA/BELIEVED KILLED WHILE ATTEMPTING TO LAND ON DURING STORM NEAR NAVREF CASPAR, WYOMING, 12 JUNE 2989. FILEXTRANS ENDS

Nobody who was on board at the time was likely to forget the 12th of June.

Hartmann had known Jodi was out there since being ordered to change course at Trinidad but he was genuinely surprised to have been handed a positive ID *and* a precise location on a plate just when the search, after a promising start, had entered a needle-in-the-haystack phase. He turned to McDonnell. 'That's incredible . . .'

'Doesn't surprise me at all, sir. That is one tough *hombre*.' Coming from the lips of Big D, the term – applied regardless of the recipient's gender – was the ultimate accolade. And one that was rarely bestowed.

Hartmann turned to the execs and technicians on duty in the saddle. 'Well, there it is, gentleman. Our first contact – and she belongs to The Lady.'

Everybody within earshot gave an exultant yell and punched air. 'YO!'

Hartmann gave his Flight Exec the nod. 'Initiate recovery procedures, Mr Baxter. I want Kazan back on board as soon as possible. And that includes anyone who's with her. Keep me posted throughout. I want the full story as it develops.'

'Yessir!' Baxter saluted happily and went to work.

Hartmann took McDonnell aside. 'I don't want to be a killjoy, Buck, but as and when she's brought in I'm relying on you to keep the reception strictly low key.' He watched the broad grin fade from McDonnell's face. 'A lot can happen in seventeen months.'

The Trail-Boss got the message. 'I just can't figure her as a cee-bee, sir. Kazan was a straight arrow. It's partly my fault she went missing. As soon as the flood waters went down, one of her section – a guy called Brickman – came onto me. He wanted to take a search party down river. I turned him down flat. Told him we didn't waste wingmen on bag-jobs!' He grimaced ruefully. 'I know that a short while later we were hit by a screaming mass of lumpshit but I felt bad about it then – and I feel even worse now.'

'You did what was right, Buck. Regret is a wasted emotion – especially now she's been found and is apparently well enough to trample her serial number in the snow. I share your high regard for her but – much as I'd like to – we're not going to be able to keep her to ourselves. In fact, it's likely to be some considerable time before she's re-instated. If at all. When those Assessors get to work . . .'

'She'll come through, sir. I'll bet my badge on it. The crew-chief told me how she went over the side. If you ask me, she'd need more than just luck to get out of a jam like that. Wyoming to Illinois is a long way to travel without a wagon-train wrapped around you. Yessirr. I can't wait to hear what she's been up to.' He threw Hartmann a knowing look. 'Would I be right in thinking she's linked with those two Skyriders we've been lookin' for?'

'I'm afraid we won't know that until she comes aboard,' said Hartmann. Apart from his deputy, Lt. Commander Cooper and Ryder, the Nav-Exec, no one else on board knew Kazan and Brickman were two of the five people The Lady had been sent out to recover. Kazan's name was now out of the bag but Hartmann judged it prudent to avoid linking her with the downed aircraft for as long as possible.

''Cos there are people who say those Skyriders are often used by Feds.'

Hartmann stiffened. Since his instructive shower with Colonel Marie Anderssen, he'd become convinced The Lady had been sent out to pick up the pieces of a covert operation that had gone wrong. But he wasn't prepared to share his thoughts with anyone else. 'No comment, Mr McDonnell. And a word of advice. I would suggest you avoid further speculation on that particular subject in public *and* in private.'

McDonnell leapt to attention and gave Hartmann an impeccable salute. 'Yesss-SURR!'

Moore, the senior Field Commander approached with his

deputy, Captain Virgil Clay as the Trail-Boss left the saddle.

'What is it, Bob?'

'Virgil has an idea he wants to run by you.'

Clay explained. 'I've got this gung-ho lieutenant from the Pueblo way-station who's offered to take a detachment across the Mississippi – so we've got backup out there on the ground.'

'Harmer . . .? Is he the guy with the broken nose and no . . .?'

'That's him. He claims to have nineteen men prepared to go with him. They've all had winter combat experience.'

'Does he know how far he's got to travel? Kazan is a hundred and forty miles due east of here.'

'He's already solved that. We've got four Skyhawks fitted with skis. His plan is to fit two buddy frames – one each side of the fuselage.'

Hartmann turned to Lt. Commander Moore. 'Can they lift two passengers in full combat gear?'

'They can if they strip out the multi-gun.'

'Harmer's checked all this with Baxter. If all four aircraft fly three sorties we can have twenty men on the ground in seven and a half hours. The round trip will take approximately three hours.'

'That also means the first eight men will be on their own for three hours.'

'He's thought of that. The other 'hawks will have to fly top cover during the build up. In fact, they'll need air cover during daylight hours the whole time they're out there.'

Hartmann didn't look impressed. 'Which means our entire air component is going to be tied up while this goon tries to grab himself some glory and another citation, and it'll take seven and a half hours to fly 'em all back in.' He shook his head. 'It seems a very extravagant waste of airpower . . .'

'On the other hand –' began Moore.

Hartmann cut in. 'I know exactly what you're going to say, Bob. I just think we should wait until we've got Kazan aboard. Let's see how she fits into this assignment and just who else is out there.'

'Okay. I can live with that . . .'

Captain Clay looked disappointed. He'd been hoping to

hitch a ride and grab a citation of his own. 'So what shall I tell Lieutenant Harmer, sir?'

'Give him a map to play with and tell him to prepare a list of the equipment he and his men will need. Have they got their own weapons?'

'Only side-arms, sir.'

'Arrange for them to be issued with the full ordinance load, Mr Clay. And tell Harmer he's responsible for inspecting his team's weapons and making sure everything is in perfect working order. I want them at combat-alert status twelve hours from now!'

'Yess-S I R R!' Clay's right hand flew up to the long peak of his yellow baseball cap. He spun on his heel and left the saddle at the double.

Moore glanced shrewdly at his commander. 'That should keep the lieutenant busy for a while.'

'Yes,' sighed Hartmann. 'Those goddam Pioneers. Just because they didn't make it onto a wagon-train they can't resist trying to prove what eager-beavers they are.' He dragged his fingers over the ends of his bushy white moustache – a sign he was mulling something over. 'Do you think he could be a plant?'

'Hard to tell,' said Moore. 'Why don't you ask Mary-Ann?'

'I might just do that. Meanwhile, keep the pressure on him, Bob. With a bit of luck, he might get overexcited and shoot himself in the foot.'

Moore smiled. 'I'd say that was unlikely. But it can always be arranged.'

Hartmann's question about the gung-ho lieutenant from Pueblo referred to the covert deployment of military personnel attached to the Department of Assessors. They performed the same duties as regular soldiers of varying rank and grade but their real task was to monitor the operational 'zeal' and competence of wagon-train commanders and their crews.

Their presence aboard a wagon-train, or inside a way-station, usually only came to light when they appeared as witnesses for the prosecution at disciplinary tribunals. No one knew how widespread this unpleasant practice was but the knowledge that the testimony of these scum-bags had sent good men to the wall helped keep everybody on their toes.

In certain aspects of their work, notably their assessment of a crew's 'attitude' to the leadership and directives of the First Family, the active service evaluators – for that was their official title – resembled the political commissars attached to units of the Soviet Army – notably during the pre-Holocaust conflict known as World War Two.

The commissars, however, were highly visible and could take issue with military commanders over the 'correctness' of tactical decisions. An ASE had the same power to wreck a man's career; the trouble was, you couldn't even see the tip of the iceberg. By the time you discovered it was there, you were usually already badly holed and sinking because, for serious code violations, no pleas of mitigation were allowed.

To the Department, an evaluator serving with an operational unit was referred to as 'an ace in the hole'. The time they stayed with a particular outfit could be a month or a year. An ASE could be a senior or junior officer, a technician, or a lowly dog-soldier manning a weapons barbette – or there might not be anyone from the Department on board at all. That was the strength and the beauty of the system; there was no need for a vast army of snoopers. Like so many of the controls exercised by the First Family, it operated on the classic principle known as 'FUD' – Fear, Uncertainty and Doubt.

Lieutenant Harmer might have proved to be a pain in the butt but one of his fellow-travellers from Pueblo, Deke Heywood turned out to be a real find. The VidCommTech-4 had an unsettling enthusiasm for cloud-filled skies, but as far as anyone knew it was not an arrestable offence – although it might be a certifiable disorder. Whatever the official verdict, the crew of The Lady regarded Deke's addiction as a minor and forgiveable abberration when set alongside the fact that the guy was an electronic genius. Since coming aboard he had already debugged several systems and was now working his way through a list of equipment whose intermittent malfunctions had resisted the diagnostic skills of The Lady's own repairmen.

In anticipation of this first air-to-ground contact, Deke had also assembled two identical black boxes – one for each of the alternating four-plane patrols. When fitted to a Skyhawk it would enable someone on the ground below to be patched through to The Lady. All the wingmen had to do was drop a suitably-packed walkie-talkie and Hartmann would be able to talk directly to whoever was out there.

As it happened, Steve's party had *two* radios – one from each of the emergency survival packs fitted to the Skyhawks. As a result of which, Jodi came on the air and was put through to the man himself while some guys in the flight car were busily fitting a drag chute to the canister containing the walkie-talkie that Gus White was waiting impatiently to deliver.

Gus, who had pictured himself coming over the rise like the legendary 5th Cavalry, was not well pleased.

'Never mind,' said Baxter. 'You can go out and pick her up.'

It was the patrol led by Stinson who had spotted her serial number and reported it to The Lady. Vickers, having made a landing, had swapped planes with a guy called Owens and it was he and the No. 4 – Marklin – who were now flying what had quickly been dubbed the 'Skihawks'. Both men offered to go down and investigate but Stinson decided against it.

Up to the moment of sighting the serial number, the aim had been to maximize the time spent in the air. Since the ski attachments produced a significant amount of drag, the two planes had not yet been saddled with the additional burden of the 'buddy' frames – which meant they were unable to pick anybody up.

Stinson radioed for instructions. Baxter, the Flight Exec told him that the second pair of 'Skihawks' aboard The Lady were now being fitted with the emergency stretcher-type attachments. Owens and Marklin were to bring their planes in for the same treatment; he and Vickers were to circle the recovery point until relieved.

Hidden at a safe distance beneath a dense cluster of pines to the north of the campsite, Steve, Cadillac and Clearwater took turns to watch events unfold with the aid of the 'scope that had come from the same survival pack as the handset that lay beside them. The set was turned to the standard frequency used by the Skyhawks for air-to-air and air-to-ground transmissions.

Holding the 'scope steady on the clump of trees under which Kelso lay, Steve saw Jodi emerge holding the second handset in her left hand and a flare pistol in her right. She looked up at the Skyhawks circling high overhead then fired a green flare almost parallel with the ground. The dazzling ball of light landed near the middle of the huge block of numbers Steve and Cadillac had helped her trample in the snow during the night.

Steve watched the smoke drift from the burning magnesium and mentally reviewed their preparations to reassure himself they had covered all the angles.

To add weight to her claim that she had spent the last several days alone with the injured Kelso, they carefully concealed their last moves around the camp by treading the same path through the snow. And when they withdrew northwards to their present hiding place, they again walked in single file. Jodi followed for part of the way then doubled back to create a return track as they entered the trees.

Before leaving the campsite, Clearwater used some of the pink soap leaves and melted snow to scrub the dye off Kelso's face, neck and hands then helped Jodi do the same. The clean-up was designed to prevent a knee-jerk reaction by her rescuers. If they suddenly found themselves confronted by what looked like a Mute they might shoot first and feel foolish afterwards. It then occurred to Steve that when her painted body came to light it would inevitably lead to more awkward questions. Jodi agreed and was soon standing naked and shivering by the small fire. They all pitched in and with everybody scrubbing away like crazy, she didn't stay cold for long.

Kelso's injuries meant they couldn't do the same for him but that, decided Steve, was his problem. The mexican would be hospitalized as soon as he got on board and Karlstrom, alerted by the RX code attached to the mexican's serial number would ensure he was surrounded by a wall of silence.

While Steve went over the scenario with Jodi to make sure she was word perfect, Cadillac and Clearwater had given Kelso a last examination, making sure his splints and bandages were still firmly in place to avoid further dislocation of his limbs during his aerial journey. And when that had been done,

Cadillac helped Steve check the campsite to make sure all evidence pointed to it being occupied by the two people that would be found there. Clearwater having persuaded Jodi to kneel down, proceeded to massage her neck in an effort to soothe the pain from the whiplash injury she'd suffered in the crash and which had flared up again during the big scrub-down. At one point Jodi appeared to fall briefly asleep but when she opened her eyes she was able to move her head freely without the slightest twinge of discomfort.

'That is amazing!'

'Not to the Plainfolk,' said Cadillac.

'It's all in the mind,' explained Clearwater. And she took hold of Jodi's hands and looked deep into her eyes. 'When the time comes to act, heed the voice within you and you will be able to summon up the strength required to achieve that which is asked of you.'

At the time, this had struck Steve as a slightly odd thing to say but they had then gone out to stamp Jodi's number across the landscape and he had not given it a second thought.

CHAPTER SIX

Now, in the early afternoon of the following day, the plan was coming to fruition. Steve, who had been listening with the others to the chatter of The Lady's wingmen as they spoke to each other, knew the giant numbers sighted on the ground had been confirmed as being those issued to Jodi and that a recovery operation was now underway.

He watched Jodi ready the handset as one of the Skyhawks which had been circling high above her spiralled down and made a low pass over the dying flare. Nate Stinson, the pilot, dipped his wings as he sped past Jodi. She waved as it banked away in a climbing turn to her right. Levelling out at five hundred feet, Stinson kept the starboard wing down and let the Skyhawk's nose travel along the horizon in a gentle 360-degree turn.

Jodi switched on the handset as the blue and white machine flew over the snow-covered pines beneath which Steve lay hidden. '2-0-9-6-5-3-4-1 calling Skyhawk. How do you read, over?'

'Blue One to 5-3-4-1. We have you in the frame and read you five by five. Your call-sign is Snow Bird, repeat Snow Bird. Need your sit-rep to facilitate recovery. Stand by while we patch you through to Sun-Ray Lady, over.'

'Roger, Blue One. Snow Bird standing by . . .'

Switching channels, Stinson called up The Lady and received confirmation that his black box was relaying Jodi's transmission. The exchanges were being taped and a digital voice transducer was simultaneously translating it into text onto one of the many video screens. Sun-Ray Lady was Hartmann's call-sign.

'Blue One to Snow Bird. Sun-Ray Lady now on line. Proceed with sit-rep. Blue One listening out.'

Steve, Cadillac and Clearwater listened intently as Jodi gave

Hartmann a succinct run-down on the state of health of her travelling companion and told him that she and Kelso were all that was now left out of the original five-strong party.

Hartmann thanked her then asked for Kelso's serial number.

Jodi reeled it off, adding: 'I was told to mention there's an RX-suffix – whatever that means, over.'

'Roger, Snow Bird. Stand by.' Hartmann turned to Dexter, the Duty RadCommTech. 'Is our video-link with Houston up and running?'

'It is now, sir.'

'Key that latest name and number through to Central Records Control with a ten-ten rating. I want immediate verification and procedural guidance!'

'Yessir!' Dexter's fingers moved nimbly over his keyboard.

RX was shorthand for 'Refer to Executive'. It meant that no administrative action could be taken in regard to an individual without reference to AMEX, the Executive Branch of the Amtrak Federation housed in what was known as the Black Tower. Old hands like Hartmann knew that AMEX was an extension of the First Family. That meant Mr Kelso was working for the White House. Could Jodi Kazan – as Buck McDonnell had hinted – be working for them too?

Steve, Cadillac and Clearwater caught intermittent glimpses of Stinson's Skyhawk as it continued to circle over the camp-site. Jodi had gone back under cover and was now standing beneath the tips of the outermost branches with the handset close to her ear. Its twin lay between Steve and Cadillac, quietly dribbling static.

Hartmann came back on the air. 'Sun-Ray Lady to Snow Bird plus one. Recovery now underway. Two, repeat two pick-up vehicles air-borne at fourteen-fifty hours. ETA your position sixteen-twenty hours Central Standard Time. Do you have time-check, over?'

'Snow Bird to Sun-Ray Lady. Affirmative. I make it fifteen-fifty-five, over.'

'You're running an hour fast, Snow Bird. It is now fourteen-fifty-five. We have to withdraw your top cover but don't worry. The cavalry is on the way. Do you have any coloured flares?'

'Affirmative, Sun-Ray. Three red, two green.'

'Okay, Snow Bird. Put up a green if recovery can proceed. If there are hostiles on the ground fire a red in their direction. Escort will lay down covering fire on your range and bearing.'

Steve and Cadillac exchanged glances.

'So hang in there, Kazan,' continued Hartmann. Despite the distance you could hear the smile on his face. 'If everything goes according to plan we should have you back on board in plenty of time to muster for the red-eye shift.'

'Can't wait, sir. Snow Bird listening out.'

It was the turn of Clearwater and Cadillac to look at each other. Steve, who lay on the far side of Cadillac, was unable to see the glint of triumph in his eyes.

Jodi, three-quarters of a mile to the south, watched the low-flying Skyhawk dip its wings as it turned westwards and climbed to catch up with its high-flying companion. As the sky emptied she was seized by a sudden anxiety. So near and yet so far . . . Never mind. She looked at her watch. Their replacements would arrive soon. By eighteen hundred hours, all being well, she'd be back on board and whooping it up with some of the good ole boys.

She ducked in under the branches and went over to check if Kelso was still awake. Maybe the news that in three hours time he would be in the capable hands of the medics aboard The Lady would bring a smile to his face. Finding him asleep, she decided not to wake him.

For the next forty-five minutes, the sky above the campsite remained empty. Jodi had never thought of herself as a patient person but since meeting up with Kelso she had discovered a hidden reserve of that precious commodity. She needed to draw upon it now but with her expectations raised by the friendly exchange with Hartmann she became increasingly anxious as she began imagining all the things that could go wrong. Brickman might have offered her a reassuring word but they had agreed to maintain radio silence in case one of the incoming planes picked up the transmission.

The minutes ticked by with agonizing slowness, each one

underscored every ten seconds by Kelso's rhythmic snores. It sounded as if his nose was full of gravel. Finally, she sighted three Skyhawks flying towards her, strung out in line abreast. She checked her watch then focussed the 'scope on each of the planes. These early birds all had clean sets of wheels and, sure enough, they stayed high. As their leader began to circle overhead like a buzzard looking for breakfast, the outer pair turned away north and south and kept on going. These guys certainly weren't taking any chances.

The handset crackled as it came alive: 'Blue Four to Snow Bird plus one. Update your sit-rep, over.'

Jodi thumbed the Transmit button. 'Snow Bird to Blue Four. We are still up and running and have you in the frame, over.'

'Roger Snow Bird. Pick-up team report their ETA still stands at sixteen-twenty hours on your green. Blue Four listening out.'

At ten minutes past four, Jodi sighted three more dots heading towards her at a lower altitude. The 'scope revealed that the lead and starboard aircraft in the formation had short skis attached to the three-wheeled undercarriage. When they drew near enough to be seen clearly with the naked eye, the port 'wheeler' broke away to meet Blue Four who had begun to descend in a gentle spiral. His two companions whose return had been timed to coincide with the 'Skihawks' arrival converged to follow the same flight path. The 'wheeler' tacked himself onto the end of the line as the trio levelled out some eight hundred feet above Jodi's head, then all four began to orbit the pick-up zone, chasing the tail of the man in front.

As the two 'Skihawks' approached in a shallow dive, Jodi sent a green flare soaring high into the air. Passing under the arching trail of smoke from the flare, the two planes skimmed past the campsite in rapid succession, dipping their wingtips to within inches of the snow as she bounced up and down, waving her arms excitedly. Jodi watched them make a second, higher pass to select a suitable landing site then dodged back under cover and knelt beside Kelso.

'Dave! Dave! Wake up! They'll be with us any minute!' She patted his cheek then shook his good shoulder excitedly as his eyes fluttered open. 'We're on our way!'

Seizing the rope leads of the make-shift sledge, she dragged Kelso out into the open. Apart from the flare pistol, the 'scope and the handset there was nothing else to carry. Steve and the two Mutes had carried away the trail bags containing the rest of their plunder.

The first of the two pick-up planes turned off its crosswind leg and began its final approach from the northeast – to Jodi's right. The second, now flying downwind, was temporarily obscured by the trees behind her.

Brickman and his friends would be able to see them both. Jodi wondered if he was having second thoughts. She felt a sudden pang of regret at leaving him behind at the mercy of those lump-heads, but what the hell – he had made his choice and she had made hers. She had found herself again. And the inner certainty about the rightness of her decision had given her the courage to face whatever lay ahead.

Only one more hurdle remained to be cleared. Having convinced Kelso that Steve had been killed, she was now saddled with the task of selling the story to everyone else. All the way up the line. And unlike good ol' Dave, *their* brains weren't befuddled with pain-killing drugs. She'd just have to do her best. It was too late to back out now. But it would be the last lie. The very last . . .

The second 'Skihawk' was still on its final approach as the first slid to a stop about fifty yards from where Jodi stood. She pulled the shapeless fur hood clear of her face and waved to the pilot as he pushed open the canopy and climbed out, then she started to haul Kelso's sledge towards it. The pilot raised his tinted visor and jogged towards her. Behind him, the second aircraft touched down smoothly on the undulating carpet of snow.

Jodi greeted the first wingman with a broad smile. 'Nice of you to drop in.' She thrust out her hand. 'Good to see you, Gus.'

Gus's eyes rested on her briefly then flickered away as he checked their surroundings, easing his handgun in its holster as he did so. When he'd gone full circle, he looked at her again – as if he couldn't make up his mind as to whether she was worth rescuing or not.

Jodi thought that maybe he didn't recognize her. 'Kazan. Jodi Kazan. A year last April I was your –'

'Yeah, I know . . .' Gus gave the hand that was still on offer a perfunctory shake. 'What happened to your face?'

'If you're that interested, ask me again when we get back on board.'

Gus pointed to Kelso who lay strapped to the cargo hatch. Beneath the hatch, was a crude frame made of saplings which acted as runners. 'Can he be moved off that contraption?'

'We can cut away the saplings but he has to stay strapped to the hatch. That's what's holding him together.'

Gus swore under his breath and took one of the rope leads from Jodi. 'Okay, c'mon. Let's get him stowed away and get the hell out of here. You can ride with Ruddock.'

'Sure. No sweat . . .'

'He's one of the new boys. Graduated this year. I'm Deputy Section-Leader now. How about that?'

'Congratulations,' said Jodi. 'You've come a long way . . .'

And you've got a long way to go. Dickhead . . .

They dragged Kelso towards Gus's plane. Ruddock, the second pick-up man, throttled back and drew up on the far side. He left the motor on tickover and ran over to help. 'How're we doin'?'

'Fine,' grunted Gus. 'Just get that frame ready while I cut this shit off.' He drew his combat knife and started to saw through the raw animal sinews that Cadillac had used to lash the sapling underframe to the hatch.

Jodi did the same on the other side.

Ruddock folded down the buddy frame that was attached to the port side of the Skyhawk's fuselage pod, clipped the upper and lower support stays into position and deployed the clear plastic zip-up bodybag in which the passenger would ride – protected from the gagging rush of air and the freezing cold.

When the three of them offered up Kelso's aluminium stretcher, it was clear that it wouldn't fit inside the body-bag.

'Awwwhh, SHIT!' cried Gus. 'I don't fucking believe this!'

'It's okay!' cried Jodi. 'He's got two foil blankets wrapped around him plus these furs. Just cut the bag and use the front section to cover his head!'

'But the hatch is too fuckin' wide! The straps won't go round it.'

'Then DO somethin', you asshole!' boomed Kelso. 'Just get me the fuck outta here!'

'Shut your face, soldier!' snarled Gus. 'You're lucky we're here to pull you out of this mess!'

'Go piss up your nose!'

Jodi banged her fist down on the hatch. 'Dave! For crissakes! Stop making waves!' She turned to Gus. 'We can lengthen them by using the ones off Ruddock's plane! I got two good hands to hang on with – and believe me, after getting this far I ain't gonna let go!'

Ruddock was already on the move. 'I'll get 'em . . .'

Jodi watched Gus take another anxious look around. And she suddenly remembered what Steve had said. This was the guy who had left him trapped in the wreckage of his Skyhawk in the middle of a burning cropfield. Underneath the bombast, the guy was scared shitless at the prospect of coming face to face with a bunch of screaming Mutes.

'This is one helluva job you're doing here,' she said soothingly. 'And I know what's on your mind. Relax. I ain't seen nor smelt any lumpshit for days.'

'Yeah . . .?'

From their hidden vantage point to the north of the pick-up zone, Steve, Cadillac and Clearwater watched the proceedings. Steve had his eye glued to the 'scope. Clearwater lay alongside him.

Cadillac who was kneeling a couple of yards behind them asked: 'What's happening?'

'I'm not sure,' said Steve. He had been trying to interpret the gestures that accompanied the heated exchange between Jodi and the pilots. 'They seem to have run into some kind of problem.'

'Hope it's not serious.' Cadillac swung round and caught the eye of one of the Kojak braves who was positioned deeper in the woods, some fifty yards to his left. Cadillac raised his left hand and brought it down with a swift chopping motion.

The Kojak brave acknowledged his signal and placed his fingers together in front of his mouth. The shrill terror-stricken cry of a small animal caught in the jaws of a sharp-toothed predator pierced the silence for a brief instant. Not loud, but chilling.

Startled by the sound, Steve rolled over onto his side. 'Jeez! What the hell was that?'

Cadillac moved back alongside them. 'Some poor creature about to come to a sticky end, I imagine. Could I, uhh . . .?'

'Sure.' Steve placed the 'scope in the Mute's outstretched palm.

As Ruddock ran back with the two securing straps, the air around Gus's Skyhawk was pierced by a quite different, but equally chilling sound.

Zzzzzzwheeeeee!

Gus ducked instinctively. 'What the fu –?'

Zzzzzzwheeeeee! Something else flew past them then – *Zzzzzzzwhikkk! Zzzzzzzwhokkk!* Two crossbow bolts hit the Skyhawk. The first passed straight through the port tail fin and kept on going. The second entered the nose, just missing Ruddock on the way in, and came to rest with six inches of the sharp end sticking out the other side right where Gus White was standing.

Gus leapt away like he'd been electrocuted. 'Hoh-lee SHIT!' He pulled his gun out and dived for cover.

Ruddock joined him. 'Can you see 'em!? Can you see 'em!? Where the hell are they!?'

Jodi knelt down beside them. 'Don't panic, boys. They're a long way away.'

'How can you tell!?'

'Because those guys don't usually miss. If they were close, that bolt would have skewered all three of us.' Jodi sighted along the embedded crossbow bolt and pulled out her handset. 'Blue Four this is Snow Bird. May Day. We're under crossbow attack by unknown number of hostiles. Estimate range one thousand yards from our position. Watch my red for bearing. Over!'

Jodi tossed the handset to Gus and hurriedly loaded a red flare into the fat-barrelled pistol. Resting her hands on the top of the fuselage above the bolt, she fired the flare towards the distant line of trees. The range was not one thousand yards but one thousand three hundred and twenty-five. She had gone out there with Brickman and the others to lay the false trail during the night and she had mechanically counted the paces on the way back. And the red flare was aimed directly towards the point where she had last seen them. Jodi could not even begin to guess what had gone wrong but there was nothing she could do to protect Brickman now. If the lumpheads he'd opted to run with had decided to get into a shooting match it was a simple case of Them and Us.

Zzzzzzwhonkk! A crossbow bolt sped in from a different direction and bounced off the open canopy of Gus's Skyhawk. Ruddock, who was tying the extra straps to the pair on the buddy frame, ducked and swore, but kept his fingers busy.

'See that!' shouted Gus. 'Came from over there!' He thumbed the handset. 'Blue Four, this is Ground Hog One. We got incoming fire from hostiles at one o'clock as well as our eleven! What are you waiting for!? Go get the suckers!'

'We're on our way, Ground Hog. Blue Four out.'

Jodi fired a second red flare towards the right hand end of the treeline as the four circling planes split into two pairs and dived towards their invisible targets.

Ruddock grabbed her shoulder. 'Get over to my ship and pull down the buddy frame. Can you do that – and get into the bag?'

'Sure. No problem.'

'Okay, go for it! Gus and I'll get your friend stowed away and I'll be right with you.'

Jodi dodged round the back of Gus's plane, crouched by the propeller then darted towards the second Skyhawk. *Zzzzzzwheeeeee!* Another crossbow bolt flashed past her. Then a couple more, overhead this time, wider of the mark. *Zzzz-wheeee-zzzzzwheeeee!* The lumps behind the crossbows must have realized those four planes were now coming down to nail their asses.

A voice came into her mind. Insistent. Demanding. Reminding her of something she had to do. Yes, of course. It all made sense. *This wasn't an attack. Nobody was meant to be killed.*

This was a diversion, to draw away the attention of those who might not understand while she helped her friends . . .

It might have seemed like a lifetime to Gus and the others who were pinned down on the ground but the four orbiting Skyhawks were on the case in under thirty seconds. The delay was due to the fact that Blue Four, flown by Sheela Cray, had to give Hartmann a rapid sit-rep before she could obtain clearance to lay down covering fire. But now, at last, it was open season for Mutes. Cray, who was leading the attack on the left hand section of the wood, switched on the electric motor that would spin the six barrels of the Thor needle-gun and placed her right thumb on the firing button. When she pressed it, Thor would spit out a deadly hail of razor-sharp flechettes at the rate of twelve hundred rounds a minute.

In the target area below, the twelve Kojak Mutes were already on the move, racing back deeper into the wood and converging on the crude shelter of woven saplings they had built during the night to Cadillac's instructions whilst he and the other Sky Travellers had been busy elsewhere.

Steve and Cadillac were still in the danger zone, locked in violent argument and on the verge of coming to blows. Clearwater, temporarily forgotten by both men and oblivious to their presence, stood several yards away, eyes closed, feet apart, hands on thighs, face turned towards the sky, her mind turned to something beyond it.

'What the hell is going on?' raged Steve. 'I thought you were in control of these people!'

'Calm down! They know what the score is. Nobody's been killed. All they did was take a few pot shots!'

'A few pot shots!? Those apes nearly wrecked the whole fuggin' exercise!'

'Don't you understand!? These guys are warriors, Brickman! That's the enemy out there. There's a question of pride involved here. The honour of the clan! It took a lot of arguing to get them to hold back. I had to agree to let them make this gesture of defiance.'

'Yeah? I suppose it didn't occur to you that the guys up there might respond with a little gesture of their own!'

'In that case we'd better get going.' Cadillac reached out to take hold of Steve's arm.

Steve brushed his hand aside and turned towards Clearwater.

Cadillac grabbed him firmly. 'Don't interfere, Brickman! She *knows* what she's doing!'

Clearwater's body shook as the initial jolt of earth power entered through the soles of her feet and travelled upwards to meet a similar charge that came funnelling down from the sky like an invisible lightning bolt. The muscles in her body hardened, the sinews became taught, her face turned into an implacable mask and when her eyes snapped open, they glowed with an intensity as terrifying as the legendary Medusa of ancient Greece, part-bird, part-beast, part-woman whose gaze turned men to stone.

Her arms shot forwards and upwards, the index fingers pointing towards the two oncoming planes and the shrill ululating cry that was the mark of a summoner burst from her lips. An inhuman, unearthly sound, impossible to describe. Heartstopping, gut-shrivelling, brain-piercing. A sound that left an indelible scar in the minds of those who heard it, turning bones to jelly and blood to water.

As she had learned in Ne-Issan, Clearwater could only enter the minds of others if a door was open, but had no need to confront those whose blood lust was roused and whose killer instincts were directed against herself or those she had been chosen to protect. The energy that fuelled their hatred acted as a conduit for her power, sucking it into the very centre of their being.

The same madness that had seized Steve's classmate Fazetti over the forests of Wyoming and caused him to turn upon his wingman, Naylor, now gripped Mark Riddell, who was flying behind Sheela Cray. He turned on his laser ranging sight, brought the red dot onto the fuselage of Cray's Skyhawk and blew her out of the sky. The shattered plane flipped over to port and went in nose first.

Riddell didn't give it a second glance. Only one all-consuming thought filled his mind. He had to protect the lives of those below from his misguided companions. Banking steeply to the right, he made a successful beam attack on the leading Skyhawk then turned towards the fourth plane, piloted by his friend Essex, and flew straight into him with a feeling of unutterable rapture.

Ruddock who had run over to zip up Jodi's buddy bag froze momentarily, his mouth and eyes wide open. The scale of the disaster, its inexplicable nature and the rapidity with which it occurred had left him speechless.

Jodi, who sat up in time to see the last three planes go down shared his sense of shock and desolation but she had already been introduced to the destructive powers of a Mute summoner – and she recognized Clearwater's handiwork. But there was no point in trying to explain what had happened to Ruddock. No time either.

She wriggled back into the bag face down and hugged the frame. 'Don't bother zipping me in! Just get this thing out of here before the sky falls in!'

Ruddock didn't need any further encouragement. He leapt into the cockpit, pulled down the canopy and slammed the throttle wide open.

Gus White's Skyhawk was ahead of them, racing away over the snow. Jodi saw it lift off and climb steeply, with Kelso strapped to the port side. A second or two later, they were in the air too. A wonderful buoyant feeling.

We made it, Dave. We're going home . . .

Hartmann received the news of the successful pick-up and the sudden, spectacular loss of the four escorting Skyhawks soon after lift-off. He thanked the two pilots for their part in the recovery operation and wished them a safe return flight. Hartmann knew something about summoners. The wagontrain commanders contributed to an unofficial pool of knowledge, and the subject of summoners and Mute magic was one of the items that were discussed in hushed whispers when two or three of them got together.

There was no hard evidence of the existence of such people nor was there a logical, or even plausible explanation of where their alleged power came from but no one could deny that some appallingly destructive force unconnected with natural phenomena had, from time to time, been directed against the forces of the Federation. More specifically, it had been directed against The Lady. In Wyoming, and now here. A force that could warp minds and conjure up a storm out of a clear blue sky.

Cray had been the first victim, but White had been uncertain which of the other three pilots was responsible for the carnage. It had a depressingly familiar ring but Hartmann knew his thoughts on the matter would have to be kept to himself and the few close associates whom he could trust. To talk about it publicly was a Code One violation. Some face-saving formula would have to be found for the official log. But this time, with four brand new planes involved, it would have to be something more plausible than 'pilot error'.

Gus and Ruddock set down smoothly atop the snow on the port side of The Lady and taxied back towards the flight car in the gathering dusk. The ground crew and some of the medics from the blood-wagon were waiting alongside. Hartmann had used the steam jets to blast away the snow beneath the wagon-train and the ramp in the belly of the adjoining section had been lowered for people to come in and out.

Buck McDonnell was on hand as Jodi slipped out of the bag on the buddy frame. He had been planning to smile but with the loss of four wingmen, there was little to smile about. Even so he was relieved to see her. He cast a jaundiced eye over her ragamuffin fur outfit. 'Kazan . . . You look like somethin' people shoot for lunch.' He threw his arm across her shoulders. 'C'mon. The Old Man wants an urgent word with you. In private.'

'I'll be right with you – *sir*.' Jodi broke away as the medics started to free Kelso from the buddy frame. She listed his probable injuries and the treatment she'd been able to give him, then added: 'I'd forget the stretcher. Best thing is to leave him strapped to that hatch until you get him into surgical on a pre-op trolley.'

The medic who'd come out to supervise Kelso's transfer to The Lady agreed. 'Good idea. Okay, boys, let's do that.'

'Dave?' His eyes had glazed over. Jodi shook hands with Ruddock and waved to Gus White. 'Check you guys later, huh?'

As she walked up the ramp with McDonnell, the flight crew chief signalled the boom operator to start winching up Ruddock's Skyhawk. Four ground crewmen stood on the lowered port bow lift ready to unhook the plane and man-handle it into the twenty-foot-high hangar deck. Below them, other members of the ground crew hurriedly folded the wings and tail of Gus's plane and pushed it into position under the boom as the first few flakes of fresh snow drifted down.

On board The Lady, the medics laid the cargo hatch and its foul-smelling fur-wrapped load onto a trolley. One of them stuck his nose close to Kelso's body. 'Think we've got some gangrene here . . .' They ran the trolley down the centre aisle towards the blood-wagon, three cars aft of the ramp.

Moving forward, Jodi and McDonnell passed through the flight car before Ruddock's Skyhawk came down on the forward lift. With four planes gone, there'd be a lot more room in the hangar. And empty seats at the mess table. McDonnell ushered Jodi onto a battery powered wheelie parked in a side bay and sent it gliding along the aisle towards the command car.

The belly ramp of the wagon behind the flight car closed as the last man came aboard. Gus White's Skyhawk was brought down into the hangar then the lift rose, sealing the rectangular hole in the flight deck. The remaining wingmen and other crew members clustered round and listened intently as Gus and Ruddock described how the whole operation had almost gone down the tube. Harmer, the hardnosed lieutenant from Pueblo simmered with anger. If his request to put his men out there on the ground had been taken seriously it would have been lump-heads lying gutted and bleeding into the snow instead of boys in blue.

In the blood-wagon, Surgeon-Captain Keever's team checked to see that Kelso was still alive, and listened to the report of his suspected injuries. Keever decided to make a visual examination followed by a top-to-toe sonar scan. He told the medics to remove the straps holding Kelso to the cargo hatch then cut away the furs and reflective foil wrapped around his broken body.

Jodi and McDonnell stepped off the wheelie and entered

the command car. Baxter, the Flight Operations Exec came down the steps from the saddle.

'Is the Commander up there?' asked McDonnell.

'Yeah. He'll be down directly.' Baxter offered his hand to Jodi. 'Long time no see. How does it feel?'

'To be back on board? Kinda strange but – it gets better by the minute.'

'What happened to your face?'

Jodi fingered the disfiguring slab of pink scar tissue that ran down the left side of her face and neck and responded with a twisted smile. 'I got that when I kissed goodbye to The Lady. I'm hoping the "welcome home" is gonna prove less painful.'

Baxter gave a disinterested nod then turned to McDonnell. 'Go on through. Everything's in there. I'm just gonna catch up with my guys in the flight car.'

McDonnell shunted Jodi along the passageway into Hartmann's private quarters. A clean wingman's uniform lay in a neatly folded pile on the bunk alongside a couple of fresh towels. 'Okay, strip off.'

'Strip off . . .?'

'That's what I said, soldier. We can't have you up front of the Old Man looking like that. So c'mon. Peel that rancid junk off your back and get in the shower.'

Jodi looked confused. 'I – I – can't!' She clutched her forehead. It felt as if someone was stabbing her brain with a red-hot knife.

'Kazan, I said strip off!' He grabbed her by the shoulders and shook her roughly. 'What the hell're you tryin' to pull!?'

Jodi shrank away, snarling like a cornered mountain cat as the pain in her head reached a new crescendo. 'Get away from me, you sonofabitch!' Her right hand flew towards the combat knife tied to the outside of her thigh. 'Touch me again an' I'll kill you!'

McDonnell's mental radar registered a troubling echo. There was something badly wrong and it called for immediate action. His pile-driving punch knocked her senseless before the knife was clear of its scabbard. As he knelt over her crumpled body, he sensed someone behind him. Hartmann was in the doorway.

'How much did you get of that?'

'Enough.' Hartmann stepped inside and knelt down beside them 'What's going on, Buck?'

'Can't say, sir. But I've got a feeling we're in deep shit.' As he spoke, he started to rip the loosely sewn furs from Jodi's body. He came to the now grimy blue-grey cotton tunic she wore as a slave-worker in Ne-Issan, pulled it open and saw what looked like square stick of wood wedged under the sash around her waist. Except that *this* piece had a radio-controlled detonator embedded in it.

'Christo!' gasped Hartmann. 'That's not wood, that's –'

'A fucking BOMB!!' yelled McDonnell. He grabbed hold of the stick of P3X, tore the detonator out and flung it through the open door into the passageway beyond. 'Sound the general alarm!'

Hartmann straightened up and lunged towards the big red slam button on the wall by his video console.

The move which would have automatically sealed each wagon from its neighbour came too late.

As five medics lifted Kelso off the cargo hatch, the detonator in the passageway outside Hartmann's quarters shattered with a loud bang and two simultaneous explosions ripped through the wagon-train.

The most catastrophic blast was centred on Ruddock's Skyhawk. The charge placed beneath the pilot's seat, caused the fuel tanks of the adjacent tightly-packed aircraft to explode. This, in turn, triggered further detonations as the racks of napalm canisters and underfloor pressurized fuel tanks ignited, causing the flight-car to erupt with the convulsive fury of a mini-volcano.

Blazing fuel and glutinous fireballs of napalm combined into a hellish tidal wave that swept along the aisles of the adjoining cars, engulfing those standing in its path. Two car-lengths away in both directions, shocked crewmen had the presence of mind to close the emergency doors, containing the fire but sealing the fate of all those trapped on the other side.

Among those who disappeared, or whose bodies were among those found later, charred beyond recognition were Baxter, the Flight Ops Exec, Gus White, Ruddock, Lieutenant

Harmer, the remaining wingmen and the entire ground crew. And many other good men besides . . .

The second blast, in the blood-wagon, blew Kelso to pieces, killed the five medics holding him and Surgeon-Captain Keever, and wrecked the operating theatre. Like all P3X explosions in confined spaces, it was murderously efficient. Several more of the hospital staff who were in the compartment or working close by were either killed outright or fatally injured. Those lucky enough to survive emerged from the debris, concussed, lacerated and badly burned.

The explosions were triggered by the same radio transmitter Steve had used to such good effect during the escape from the Heron Pool, but it was Cadillac and Clearwater who had engineered them.

Three charges remained from the Heron Pool exercise and, on landing near the Hudson River, Steve had carefully removed them from the rocket-powered gliders they had used for the first part of their journey. During the boat trip to Bu-faro, the plastic explosive, detonators and the radio transmitter had been packed in the bag that Cadillac had kept safely in his cabin.

From Bu-faro, the bag had been ferried to Long Point, stowed aboard one of the stolen Skyriders then lugged through snow to the final camp-site. And when Cadillac had learned of Steve's plan to put Jodi and Kelso on board The Lady he had decided to strike a blow that would impress their hosts and remove, at a stroke, all further opportunity for Steve to continue his double-dealing.

Using a length of twisted animal gut and a piece of bent metal prised loose from the cargo hatch, Cadillac had rigged the handheld transmitter so that the buttons controlling the three explosive charges would be depressed when Kelso was lifted clear of the hatch.

The transmitter and one of the charges had been placed beneath Kelso's body when they had checked his splints and bandages. Clearwater had then used her powers to enter Jodi's mind while massaging her neck.

Acting on a planted mental imperative, Jodi had concealed the second charge against her own skin. Later, during the diversionary attack by the Kojak Mutes, she had taken advantage of the confusion to place the remaining charge in Ruddock's Skyhawk. She had no memory of having carried out these actions but the original programme remained embedded in her subconscious. So when Buck McDonnell proposed an action that would reveal the charge hidden under the tunic — and thus violate the plan — she resisted like a deranged zombie.

Kelso had been given the same treatment, making him insensible to the lethal package placed in the small of his back. Sudden, violent death overtook him before his brain could register the sickening realization that he had been betrayed. It was ironic — for had there been time, he would have cursed Steve with his dying breath.

Ironic and rather sad because, for once in his life, Steve was blameless. He had played it straight. Well . . . straight-*ish*. And he had ended up being outsmarted. But at that moment in time, Cadillac hadn't told him the good news. So as the three of them ran northwards with their jubilant Mute escort, Steve was unaware that The Lady from Louisiana lay gutted and burning and that, with Kelso's death, his carefully-laid plans had also gone up in smoke.

CHAPTER SEVEN

Even though there were no further falls of snow, it took Steve nearly three days to cover the forty or so miles separating their abandoned campsite and the Kojak settlement. Hampered by the arrow wound in his thigh he had been unable to match the pace set by the posse and Cadillac had taken the opportunity to further underline his new-found superiority by urging him on mercilessly.

Steve gritted his teeth and willed the pain to disappear but on the second morning his leg simply gave way. Stumbling forward like an exhausted horse, he ended up nose down in the snow.

Cadillac stood by, hands on hips while two Kojak braves hauled his rival upright. There was a brief discussion as to whether he should be carried the rest of the way on tracking poles but Steve, aware that he risked losing any 'standing' he might have acquired as one of The Chosen, insisted on arriving on his own two feet – in his own good time.

Clearwater announced she would stay with him and asked for two braves to accompany them as guides. Since she had already demonstrated the power to demolish any opposition they might meet on the way, there was no lack of volunteers. Cadillac pressed on with the remaining ten and by the time Steve limped into the ring of firelight, he was already installed in the principal place of honour.

Arriving ahead of the others enabled Cadillac to grab the lion's share of the acclaim as his escort recounted what had happened and boasted of the part they had played in the downfall of the four cloud-warriors. Among the Plainflolk, this macho display was known as 'strutting their stuff'.

But that was not all, declared Cadillac, when it was his turn to speak. He had kept his promise to drive the iron snake back to its lair. As his escort would confirm, two of The Chosen, acting on his orders, had used their power to enter the minds of the enemy, forcing the surviving pair of cloud-warriors to carry them back, like avenging angels, into the belly of the beast.

Even now, as he spoke, it lay broken and burning, consumed by the deadly fire it harboured within its belly. The clans to the west, whose turf lay closest to that of the valiant Kojak would eventually pass on word of its destruction by a series of invisible blows striking with the force of earth-thunder.

In unleashing their awesome power, The Chosen had perished – but not for long. Their spirits, borne aloft on the flame-tinted smoke would be gathered by Mo-Town, the Great Sky-Mother and returned to earth in the bodies of mighty warriors. What the fortunate braves had witnessed – and the testimony of their neighbours would soon confirm – was the power of Talisman acting through those born in his shadow.

Heyyy-YAHHHH! The cry came from close on a thousand throats. The subsequent celebrations, accompanied by ritual drumming, dancing and chanting, and enhanced by copious lungfuls of rainbow grass had been underway for most of the night when the tail-enders arrived. Clearwater still rated a triumphal entry and was borne shoulder-high into the crowded arena where a giant bonfire, ignited by the Kojak in honour of their guests fuelled a scorching hot column of flame some twenty feet high. One of the more parsimonious elders estimated that it had consumed, within hours, more than a month's supply of winter fuel for the whole settlement but his carping fell on deaf ears.

Steve, the lame duck – literally and metaphorically – was also warmly received, but as he had not as yet, figured in any spectacular action or displayed any mystical attributes, he found himself relegated to the sidelines.

Cadillac's new grandstanding style was beginning to get under his skin but Steve did not allow it to throw him off course. In their present situation, it was much better to have the Mute fired up with a good head of steam. His inherent personality problems would eventually cause him to come off at the bend and Steve intended to be there when it happened. And this time, he would not be in any hurry to pick up the pieces. Besides, it was not all bad news: with the Mute's star now in the ascendant he had accepted without demur Clearwater's expressed wish to bed down with the competition.

Cadillac who, from an early age, had always taken a tremendously earnest view of himself and his allotted role as Mr Snow's successor, was now very close to achieving the philosophical detachment he had sought for so long. Jealousy and other petty emotions could not be allowed to deflect a true warrior from The Path. Cadillac's mind was now directed towards greater and far nobler concerns – the forging of the Plainfolk into one nation in readiness for the long-awaited coming of Talisman.

His rivalry with Steve was no longer centred around the possession of Clearwater's body and soul: it was for the leadership of this great enterprise. Only he, Cadillac M'Call, descended from the bloodline of the She-Kargo, the bravery of whose warriors had no equal amongst the Plainfolk, possessed the qualities and the vision to assume the role of the First amongst The Chosen.

In any case, his earth-longings were now amply catered for. The council of elders of the Clan Kojak, recognizing him as the chief architect of the spirited attack on the cloud-warriors and the predicted death of the iron snake had offered him a multiple choice of the available female braves to grace the hut placed at his disposal. To while away the long hours of darkness, Cadillac chose three complaisant 'body-slaves' named Tight-Fit, Stone-Fox and Afternoon-Delight.

Yes. It was all beginning to come together. Through his own quick thinking, and Clearwater's power, he had reproduced his favoured existence in the service of Domain-Lord Min-Orota except now, he had 'standing', the respect and admiration of his hosts; something the Iron Masters had denied him. The recognition of his abilities made him feel whole again, gave him a feeling of boundless confidence. That, plus the generous pipefuls of rainbow grass and the attentions of his fragrantly-oiled, full-bodied bedmates *almost* made up for the gnawing desolation caused by the complete and utter lack of *sake*.

*

The clan's huts had been set up in a series of concentric circles in a forest clearing to the west of what had once been known as Arlington Heights; a sub-division of the pre-Holocaust city of Chicago. Fur-clad sentinels patrolled the perimeter and the paths through the otherwise impenetrable undergrowth. Other, unguarded paths were false trails sown with hidden death pits bristling with sharpened stakes and other, equally lethal, tree-mounted devices.

As a mark of honour, Steve and Clearwater were allotted a hut in the 'inner circle' normally reserved for the elders and other notables like Carnegie-Hall and Flying-Tiger, the clan's paramount warrior. Cadillac and his three foxy ladies had taken up residence next to the wordsmith whose hut lay on the opposite side.

The huts were shaped differently to those made by the M'Calls. Steve's previous hosts used a system of socketed frames and curved saplings to build skin-covered huts shaped like the tops of button mushrooms about five feet from floor to smoke ring whereas the Kojak used six straight rough-hewn poles tied together near the top to form a triangular structure over twice as high. This meant you could stand up inside and exit on your feet instead of having to crawl out through the doorflap – a marked improvement. But despite the extra space, or perhaps because of it, they were not as warm or as cosy as the womb-like constructions of the M'Calls.

Steve crawled into bed as the celebrations slowly tapered off sometime after dawn. Clearwater followed, lying quietly beside him with tantalizing submissivness. Steve was not immune to the warming presence of her naked body and the delicious way it matched the curves and hollows of his own when he turned his back to her. But even when he felt that electrifying zing as she pressed that soft spot between the top of her thighs against the base of his spine the best he could manage was a mumbled, vaguely grumpy 'G'nite.' After what he'd been through in the last ten days he could barely raise his little finger let alone a head of steam – and he stayed buried up to his nose under the thick layer of furs either asleep or dozing for the rest of the day.

It was the morning after, when he woke up with hunger

pains and a terrible thirst and was searching through the tote bags for a fresh wound dressing that he noticed the square sticks of explosive, the detonators and the transmitter were missing. The discovery made his stomach turn over. Two more increasingly frantic searches confirmed his worst fears and he knew, with mind-chilling certainty who had taken them – and why.

Throwing aside the doorflap, he strode across the central reservation towards Cadillac's hut.

Clearwater who happened to be walking back from that direction met him halfway. One look at his face said it all. 'You know . . .'

'Damn right. Where's Cadillac?'

'He's with Carnegie-Hall and the elders.' She blocked the way as he went to step past her. 'If you want to talk –'

'Talk?!!' Steve's fury exploded. He tried to brush her aside but she deflected his arm before his hand reached her shoulder and took a firm hold of his wrist, pulling it down to waist level in one swift movement. 'Vent your anger then. Let your wrath fall on me. For without my help this thing could not have been done.'

'I have no quarrel with you. The bone I've got to pick is with Cadillac.'

Her fingers didn't relax their vice-like grip. 'He and I acted together. I will answer for him.'

Steve knew she was strong but this time he had the impression that, if she tightened her fingers any further, she would crush the bones in his wrist. Her eyes were like sapphires set in ice, devoid of love or compassion. He relaxed the muscles in his body. Whatever the provocation, he did not intend using brute force to subdue her.

She relaxed her grip and led him towards the south side of the settlement. They passed through the last ring of huts towards the dense surround of trees and when they were no longer in earshot of the nearest clanfolk they came face to face again.

'The explosive I brought out of Ne-Issan. Where is it?'

'It was placed in the belly of the iron snake.'

Of course. Where else . . .? 'How?'

Clearwater told him. The tone of her voice was neither triumphant nor apologetic. It all seemed so absurdly easy. All Steve could do was cling on to the vain hope that something might have gone wrong. He glimpsed Cadillac coming towards them as she ended her account with a fatalistic shrug of the shoulders. 'This thing had to be done. For only by demonstrating our power could we obtain the necessary standing in the eyes of our hosts and gain a secure shelter during the time of the White Death.'

'You'd already killed four wingmen!' cried Steve. He waved angrily at Cadillac as the Mute reached them. 'Wasn't that enough for this conceited, lumpsucking sonofabitch?!'

'Grow up, Brickman. That wagon-train had to be stopped dead in its tracks. Did you think it could just be wished away?'

Steve rounded on him. 'It would have pulled out once Grand Central learned our carcasses had been carried off by Mutes! That was the whole point of putting Jodi and Kelso on board!'

Cadillac greeted this with a bitter laugh. 'Really? We're not idiots, Brickman – and neither are your masters who rule the Dark Cities. Or have you forgotten Rozalynn, your kin-sister? Even if Jodi kept her promise and steadfastly held to the story that the three of us were dead, whether under forced interrogation or worse, your masters would know *you* were alive!'

'Not necessarily.' Steve hadn't figured on the Mute getting that deep inside his skull. He'd have to tread carefully. 'Roz, uh . . . knows what the score is now.'

'Oh?' Another bitter laugh. 'And just what *is* the score, Brickman? Your tongue and your intentions are as sinuous as the iron snake that carried you to us in its belly!'

Steve fought down the urge to fatten Cadillac's mouth. 'Jack me! You got one helluva nerve coming out with shit like that! The only reason you're standing there with your head on your shoulders is because I promised Mr Snow I'd get you and Clearwater out of Ne-Issan. And damn nearly got my ass busted doing it!'

'Yeah? You wanna know the reason why your ass *wasn't* busted? Because *we* saved it for you! You're so busy trying to claim all the credit, you've overlooked the fact it was *Clear-*

water who saved the day for *all* of us. And it was the planes *I* designed and built that gave us a flying start on the road home!'

'*You* designed?! Ha! That's the best joke of all! If you hadn't hacked your way into my memory-bank, you wouldn't have known how to join two pieces of wood together!'

'Oh, yeah?'

'Yeah! You'd still be the same stupid lump-head I met in that cropfield who didn't know one end of a rifle from the other!' As the words came out, Steve wished he hadn't said them but it was too late.

'You're right,' admitted Cadillac. 'Saving you was an act of incredible stupidity born of conceit. I should have let you burn.'

'Stop this!' cried Clearwater. She lashed out with both fists, striking them in the solar plexus. The force of the blows made them step back, breaking their nose-to-nose confrontation. She moved in between them. 'Is this the way The Chosen are to be remembered by the Plainfolk? Squabbling like bad-tempered children?!'

'Keep out of this,' said Steve. 'Ever since we landed this balloon-head's been treading on my toes and I'm not taking any more of it.' He squared up to Cadillac again. 'Okay. I was out of line with that cropfield stuff. You saved my life then, so I reckon that makes us even. And yeah, you *did* put together a few spruce and silk flutterbugs. We won't bother to ask where the sudden burst of expertise came from but there's one thing you can't deny. That project would never have gotten off the ground without rocket-power.' He jabbed a thumb against his chest. 'And that was *my* idea!'

Cadillac did not lose his new-found cool. 'Was it? Was it *all* your own work? Or did you get a little help from your high-flying friends you talked to every night?! The same thoughtful people who dropped whatever you needed into that pond at the back of the Heron Pool? What were *they* expecting in return? These people who used their influence with certain Iron Masters to secure us safe passage through the domain of the Yama-Shita to the waters beyond? What promise did you give them? The same you gave to Mr Snow? To deliver us out of Ne-Issan? Into whose hands, Brickman? Answer me! Into whose hands?!'

Steve saw the same accusing look in Clearwater's eyes but he managed to conceal his confusion. 'Nice try, *amigo*. But you can't score off me with this one because I've got nothing to hide. The Federation dropped those supplies to me 'cos they thought I was working for them. Sure . . . they sent me out to capture both of you. I accepted the assignment because it was the only way I could get back up onto the overground. They had me over a barrel because of the threats to harm Roz. I figured once I got out here I might be able to find a way to get her off the hook –'

'By capturing us.'

'No!' cried Steve. 'I went along with the idea to buy some time – so as I could get things sorted out! But when I got into this mess I had no idea you were in Ne-Issan. I couldn't see much hope of rescuing you but . . . when you didn't turn up at the trading post Mr Snow was so, well – distressed, I agreed to give it a try.'

He glanced at Clearwater then said: 'If you want to know the whole truth, *she's* the reason I came riding to the rescue. I didn't really care what happened to you but since the Old One was due to die and the clan couldn't function properly without a wordsmith . . .' He threw up his hands. 'My only concern now is to make sure you're delivered safely to Wyoming.'

'And you're not planning any more betrayals on the way.'

Clearwater opened her mouth to protest but Cadillac silenced her. 'I have every right to ask such a question! If the cloud-warrior is ready to betray his blood-brothers how can we be sure he will not turn against us?!'

Steve's eyes met Clearwater's and held them. The blue of her pupils had softened. 'Ask this lady here. She knows what the truth is. I came back to the overground because – don't ask me why – this is where I feel I belong. With her.'

Her gaze did not waver. 'Your words bring warmth to my heart, cloud-warrior. But what will become of your kin-sister?'

'Can't say. But while we were crossing towards Long Point, her voice entered my mind. It was she who told me to stay with you. She no longer fears those who are trying to control our lives.'

'So you have chosen to throw in your lot with the Plainfolk.'

'Isn't that obvious?'

Cadillac laughed derisively. 'A typically devious reply from the man who can never answer with a straight "yes" or "no"! In a few days – with luck – we'll know if our coup against the wagon-train was successful. If it is, then last year's slaughter of our clan-brothers and sisters will have been partly avenged and we will have earned ourselves a safe haven for the winter.

'But do you know the *real* reason why I planted those explosive charges aboard The Lady? To put an end – once and for all – to your double-dealing! To force you to choose sides by leaving you only *one* side to be on! If those charges have gone off as planned, many will die and that murderous machine will be permanently crippled.

'There will be questions, investigations, accusations. And in the end, the finger will point at the one person with the means, the opportunity, and the necessary degree of ruthlessness and duplicity to commit such an outrage. Not some stupid lump-head who doesn't know one end of a rifle from the other, but *you*, Brickman.

'So you can kiss goodbye to the idea of keeping a line open to your powerful friends in case things don't work out the way you'd planned. You're with us from here on in, whether you like it or not.'

There was no doubt about it, thought Steve. He had seriously underestimated Cadillac. The young Mute was a lot sharper than he'd thought. But then – why wouldn't he be? How foolish not to have realized that he was now pitting his wits against a mental mirror image of himself!

He appraised each of them in turn, trying to guess how well he had defended his corner. Since that last climactic, blood-soaked day at the Heron Pool, his relationship with Clearwater had moved onto another level. Although less feverish, the physical relationship was still as strong as ever but other, more disturbing elements now lurked in the depths, like the cold lake-creatures that had brushed against his naked body during his moonlight swims, sending shivers down his spine.

At times, when the brilliant blue was veiled with grey, her eyes became those of a stranger, filled with a mysterious, brooding malevolence. Not directed at him personally, but at the world – or perhaps at the world he represented.

But not now.

Now they were the eyes he had seen in that perfectly-formed face half-hidden among the ranks of M'Call warriors on the night he had bitten the arrow. The eyes that had lain in wait for his, capturing his heart and mind, drawing him into a web of intrigue, deception and high adventure. A dangerous, mind-twisting game which, if the Talisman Prophecy was fulfilled, would end in the death of one nation and the birth of another.

He sent Clearwater a silent message and on receiving the reply he sought, he focused his attention on Cadillac. Any anger he felt was concealed beneath a note of grudging admiration. 'I've gotta hand it to you, Caddie. I didn't think you had it in you. Even if the idea of taking out The Lady had occurred to me I don't think I could have used Jodi and Kelso as bomb-carriers. Still . . . now that it's done and you've both explained why, there's no hard feelings.'

'I'm glad to hear it.'

'No, I mean that. When you think of it as an abstract problem you came up with the ideal solution. In fact – and I hate to say this – it was pretty damn brilliant.'

'I had a good teacher . . .'

Steve caught the irony but he could see that the new Cadillac lapped up compliments just like the old model. He laughed. 'I doubt if I can teach you anything now. But you're wrong about one thing. It's true about me trying to keep a line open to the Federation but it wasn't because I was planning some kind of double-cross. I was hoping to use the connection to our advantage and give Roz time to get her act together but . . . you've decided to do it the hard way.' He shrugged. 'I can live with that. So why don't we wipe the tape and start again from the top?'

Drawing his knife, he slit open one of the small veins on the inside of his right wrist and extended his hand towards Cadillac. The Mute made the same ritual cut then they gripped each other's forearms in a Roman-style greeting.

Clearwater cupped her hands round their wrists, pressing them together so that their blood mingled. 'Now you are truly brothers. Let there be peace and friendship between you. Offer love and loyalty to your clansmen, dedicate your life to the service of Talisman and save your anger and hatred for the enemies of the Plainfolk. Do you so swear?'

'On this, our blood, I swear,' said Cadillac.

Steve repeated the oath with appropriate solemnity. It meant as much as the Tracker Prayer he'd mouthed daily for fifteen of his eighteen years. But it was an arrangement he could live with until the time came to get even . . .

With his air component and medical team wiped out in two swift hammer blows, upwards of a hundred dead and with scores of injured crewmen who could only be given basic first aid, Hartmann had no alternative but to withdraw southwards.

Abandoning the two shattered wagons plus three which had been completely gutted by fire, Hartmann reformed The Lady and headed back across the Cedar River towards navref Des Moines. On learning the bad news, CINC-TRAIN wired back the necessary approval and ordered The Lady to head for the Monroe/Wichita interface.

The choice of Monroe instead of the wagon-train's home depot at Nixon/Fort Worth was significant. It made sense to disembark the casualties at the nearest divisional base where they could receive skilled medical attention but it was also to be the end of the line for Hartmann and his execs. Monroe/Wichita was the terminus for the northern spur of the Trans-Am Expressway and the last paragraph of CINC-TRAIN's signal listed everyone from Hartmann down to and including Trail-Boss McDonnell who were required to board the first available south-bound shuttle.

Those named had no illusions about the kind of reception awaiting them at Grand Central, and the atmosphere aboard The Lady on the homeward journey was as grim and bleak as the winter landscape that fought them remorselessly, every inch of the way.

Jodi Kazan, on recovering from McDonnell's knock-out

blow, was found to be in deep shock; a condition that was later diagnosed as catalepsy. She seemed incapable of speech, did not respond to questions, and did not react to her surroundings or any other external stimuli, such as when food was placed before her. Unable to stand unaided, she lay vacant-eyed on her bunk. When placed on a chair, she remained in the position chosen by whoever put her there, like one of those stiff-jointed mannikins used by artists.

CINC-TRAIN, who had been told of her role in the attack on the wagon-train, ordered her to be confined to a punishment cell until handed over to the Provost-Marshal's office at Monroe/Wichita.

When The Lady reached the interface, the Base P-M came aboard personally to place Hartmann and the other fall-guys under close arrest, and Jodi, now wearing a defaulter's black jumpsuit with a big yellow X front and back, was hooded and shackled and put aboard the same shuttle.

The injured crewmen, mostly burn cases, were off-loaded together with the bodies of those who had died en route and the victims of the two initial explosions who had been identified. Those blasted or charred beyond recognition had been buried in a mass grave cut by the remaining 'dozer on the banks of the Mississippi.

A new, stripped-down team of execs came aboard to run what was left of The Lady back to Fort Worth, closely followed by six grey-uniformed Assessors. The legal eagles took over the aft command-car and immediately notified their presence by screening a preliminary list of crewmen required for interrogation. By the time The Lady reached Fort Worth, everyone on board at the time of the disaster had been thoroughly questioned and some, judged to be implicated in the overall failure to apply the proper on-board security measures, finished up in the slammer.

With the aid of drugs, an AMEXICO medical team – who were no strangers to mind control – managed to neutralize the mental imperative Clearwater had planted in Jodi's brain, and restore her to some semblance of normality. The failure to carry out the order to destroy herself and The Lady had triggered complete mental and muscular paralysis; a self-inflicted punishment that without remedial treatment could have eventually killed her.

Once programmed, Jodi was like a computer which throws itself into a loop trying to obey an instruction it is unable to execute; a condition known as 'lock-out'. The only way to break the cycle is to pull the plug on the machine before it goes round the bend and burns out the mother-board.

Karlstrom, the head of AMEXICO met the President-General to discuss how the investigation should be handled. They decided that Hartmann and those arrested with him should appear before a Board of Assessors, but because of the sensitive nature of much of the evidence, those selected to conduct the proceedings would all be disguised members of the First Family who knew of the existence of AMEXICO and were also familiar with the Talisman Prophecy and the concept of 'Mute magic'.

Karlstrom agreed to take the role of President of the Board, and the P-G also nominated Fran Delano Jefferson – a young relative of his, who was Steve Brickman's controller. The nomination raised Mother's eyebrows but when the P-G explained what he had in mind, Karlstrom found himself wishing he'd thought of it first.

Jodi squared her shoulders and snapped to attention as the young, dark-haired woman entered the interrogation room. Her hood had been removed when her escort left the room but she still wore wrist and knee shackles and was chained to a floor loop. The woman who was dressed in a grey jumpsuit – the uniform worn by the Legal Division – sat down at the desk in front of Jodi, activated the video and adjusted the angle of the screen. She keyed in a call-up code and read the top line on the screen. '2086-5341 Kazan, J.R?'

'Yes, sir-ma'am.'

'Take the weight off your feet.' The dark-haired woman smiled sympathetically as Jodi sat down on the moulded cushionless swivel chair fixed to the floor behind her. 'I'm sorry about the chains but it's regulations – you understand?'

'Yes, sir-ma'am.'

'You can drop the "sir",' said the dark-haired woman. 'Maybe I'd better start by introducing myself. I'm Nancy Reagan Delaney.' She smiled. 'Could be coincidence but maybe they picked me because you and I both come from the same base. Anyway . . . because yours is a somewhat complex case, the Legal Division has appointed me as your defence counsel.'

She smiled again as she noted Jodi's surprise. 'I know. I had a similar reaction. Code One offenders are not normally allowed to enter pleas of mitigation. But as I said, you're considered to be a special case.' The woman glanced at the screen. 'Your record – up to the time you went over the side is exemplary and I want you to know that I intend to do my utmost to see that after due process, the Board moves for an acquittal.

'But before you say anything, I must warn you that I will not be allowed to be present during the hearing. My plea on your behalf – which I hope to construct from these interviews – will be presented for the consideration of the court *before* you come before the Board of Assessors. So tell me, Jodi – are you prepared to confide in me on that basis?'

'Yes, ma'am. I realize my situation doesn't look too good but I have nothing to hide.'

'I'm pleased to hear it.' Delaney scrolled through the data she'd called up on the screen. 'In my book, anyone who's earned five stars and the kind of commendations I see listed here is a True Blue who knows *exactly* what they're doing and why.'

For the first time since boarding The Lady, Jodi started to feel like a human being again. She felt immensely reassured by the woman facing her but at the same time it was a strange experience. Delaney could almost have been her kin-sister. She had an oval face and short lustrous dark hair – except Delaney's was parted on the right and swept neatly back over her ears whereas her own unkempt locks had been shorn off, leaving her with a boot-camp crew-cut.

She also had a wider fuller mouth and larger, violet-blue eyes whereas Jodi's lips had thinned out from years of playing hard-ball with the hairy-assed Trail-Blazers under her command, and her deep-set eyes were the colour of weathered granite. And of course, her own face was hideously scarred down the left hand side whereas . . .

Delaney placed her forearms on the desk and laid her hands one on top of the other. 'Let me tell you what my biggest problem is . . . Commander Hartmann and the Trail-Boss of The Lady have both made statements in your defence. They believe you did not knowingly, and with intent, carry explosives onto the wagon-train.'

'It's true, ma'am. I didn't.'

'I want to believe you. But apart from the two pilots, you and Kelso were the only people to get within an arm's length of the two Skyhawks you flew out on. Now we know it couldn't have been Steve Brickman or the two Mutes that were with you because we have a tape of you telling Commander Hartmann they'd been killed some days previously. So since it's obvious that Kelso wasn't in a position to do anything, it must have been you. Why don't you just admit to the charge and get this business over with?'

'Because I didn't *do* it, ma'am! I wouldn't do anything to harm my trail-mates. I joined The Lady when Commander Hartmann became wagon-master and I've served the –'

Delaney cut off the rest of the sentence with a slicing movement of her hand. 'I know all about your record. But strange things happen when people become renegades. Their attitudes change – sometimes quite profoundly. It's something in the air. They become . . . contaminated.'

'I didn't become a renegade, ma'am. I was *found* by renegades. The group never undertook any hostile action against units of the Federation and anyway, for most of the time I was with them, I was recovering from the injuries I sustained when my Skyhawk –'

'Yes, yes, I know all about that. You still haven't explained who, if it wasn't you, planted those explosives charges. On Kelso, in one or both of the Skyhawks that landed, and how you came to be carrying another charge concealed on your person.'

'I didn't know they were there, ma'am I swear it!'

'So you keep saying. I'm trying to help you, Jodi, but

you're not helping me! You resisted an order to remove your clothes – and even tried to draw a knife in an effort to delay the discovery of the explosives you were carrying. Two witnesses, senior officers – fellow Trail-Blazers you profess to care about, have testified that you were only a split second away from destroying the forward command car – killing them and probably everyone else in the saddle!'

The accusation brought tears to Jodi's eyes. 'I didn't do it, ma'am. At least I didn't *know* I was doing it. They must have made me –'

'They . . .?'

Jodi's mouth fluttered open. 'B-b-beg pardon, ma'am?'

'Don't play games with me!' Delaney slammed her palm against the desktop. 'You said "*They* made me do it". Who are we talking about, Jodi?'

The expression on Jodi's face reflected her mental anguish.

'Brickman's still alive, isn't he? And so are his Mute friends. You, the loyal Trail-Blazer, the True Blue – or so you would have us believe – lied to Commander Hartmann, didn't you? He trusted you – like McDonnell and the rest of the crew – and you betrayed them. Am I right?'

Jodi hung her head as her eyes flooded with tears. 'That's the way it looks ma'am, but . . .'

With a tired gesture, Delaney tapped out the command to clear the screen then sighed. 'I'm sorry, Jodi. I don't think there's anything I can do for you. It's obvious what happened. You and Brickman saw the patrols from The Lady and realized the game was up.'

'No ma'am, it wasn't like that,' murmured Jodi.

Delaney ignored her. 'It was only a matter of time before you were found and brought in. You knew the punishment meted out to renegades. There was nothing to lose. You lied because you were a willing party to Brickman's plan to destroy The Lady.'

'No! It's not true!' cried Jodi. 'He didn't have anything to do with it! Neither did I – at least, not knowingly. *She* must have made me do it – the same way she made those Skyhawks destroy each other!'

'Oh, really?' Delaney had cleared the screen, but their conversation was still being secretly videotaped. 'Tell me about that.'

Jodi recounted how she had watched with growing horror as the second Skyhawk in the first formation blasted the lead aircraft out of the sky then turned on his colleagues, shooting one down before crashing into the other – with fatal results for all concerned.

Delaney listened with a blank expression.

Jodi then described what had happened after Clearwater had entered the fray at the Heron Pool. When she reached the point where Domain-Lord Hiro Yama-Shita had thrust his sword through his body eight times before falling dead at Clearwater's feet, Jodi paused and grimaced ruefully.

'I know I'm committing a Code One offence in claiming to have witnessed Mute magic but every word of that I've told you is true. One more violation – what difference does it make? I'm finished anyway. But I figure if you or someone could get word to the First Family and let them know what some of those lump-heads are capable of, they might be able to do something about it. At least that way, my death would serve some purpose.'

Delaney responded with a sympathetic smile. 'The thought does you credit even if the events, as you describe them, are totally unbelievable.'

'Ma'am, if I hadn't been there I'd've reacted in exactly the same way. But it's the truth. I swear it. And there's something else I think you ought to know. Brickman wasn't a renegade. He was an undercover Fed.'

Delaney looked puzzled. 'An undercover *Fed* . . .? I don't think I understand you.'

'It's Trail-Blazer jargon for some kind of secret agent . . .'

'Did *he* tell you that?'

'Yes – 'cept he didn't use that word. And I accidentally found out Kelso was one too. As to what outfit they were working for, or who's in charge . . . all that side of thing's a mystery. They didn't say and I didn't ask. Officially such people don't exist – right? But this is not something I dreamt up. This is a big deal – and the guys running it are tied in with the nips who helped us get out of Ne-Issan.'

'I see . . .' Delaney mulled over this latest disclosure then sat back and placed her elbows on the arm rests of her padded chair. Steepling her fingers, she said: 'Go back to the beginning. I want to know everything that happened from when you went over the side during the storm.'

Jodi took a deep breath and launched into her story. It took quite a time. But then it was quite a story.

When she got to the point where she and the others had transferred to the powered inflatables just before dawn and were heading across Lake Erie towards Long Point, Delaney checked her wristwatch then leant forward and raised her hand. 'Okay, we're going to have to hold the rest over. Tell me – referring back to our earlier discussion – whose idea was it for you to try and get back on board The Lady?'

'Mine, ma'am. Soon as I saw those white wing-tips, I knew what I had to do.'

'Ye-esss, I can imagine . . .'

Jodi leapt to attention with a rattle of chains as Counsellor Delaney rose from behind the desk and eyed her reproachfully.

'A slow start but we may eventually get somewhere. However, I must say I'm very disappointed you had to be pressured into admitting you covered up for Brickman and his Mute friends. It seriously weakens the case I was hoping to make on your behalf. And in view of your latest claim about Brickman and Kelso I am now obliged to seek the guidance of my superiors. I leave in a less hopeful state than when we began. Perhaps you will reflect on that.'

'Yes, sir-ma'am!'

Delaney nodded curtly. 'Good. Till tomorrow then . . .' Pressing the delayed-action buzzer to call the Provo escort waiting in the next-door office to take Jodi back to the cells below, she left the room. At the end of the short corridor was an elevator that could only be operated by those carrying the very highest levels of ID-cards. The buzzer summoning the meat-loaves – by now totally bored out of their skulls – did not sound until the doors closed, concealing the identity of the exalted passenger.

As Delaney was carried melodiously upwards in deep-pile

carpeted luxury to the higher levels of the White House, she carefully removed the violet-blue contact lenses to reveal the less striking but more compelling grey-brown eyes belonging to Franklynn Delano Jefferson – one of the President-General's favourite nieces, and controller, for the last six years, of Steve and Roz Brickman.

The next day, when Jodi was brought up for interrogation, she found that Delaney was accompanied by a man of indeterminate age; slim build, medium height, lean angular face topped by a high forehead and dark eyes that missed nothing. He was dressed, like Delaney, in the grey uniform of AMEX's Legal Division.

The thin, hard mouth and jaw suggested this was a man used to getting what he wanted. But the reassuring lines that converged on the corners of the eyes and the quirky twist to his lips said this was a man who used intelligence and humour to elicit the truth instead of a blackjack and a bath-tub full of cold water.

'This is a colleague of mine,' said Delaney. 'He has special knowledge of the, uh . . . areas you mentioned yesterday. You may talk freely with him of matters I'm not qualified to discuss.' She turned towards the door.

'Uh . . . beg pardon, sir-ma'am –'

Delaney stopped and looked back expectantly.

'Does, uh – does this mean you're no longer going to act as my defence counsellor?'

'Not necessarily . . .'

Karlstrom took over as Delaney walked out. 'Because of the complex nature of this case the full facts may have to be withheld from the Board of Assessors. In order to make sure you get a fair shake, the Department will probably modify or annul the sentence when it comes up for confirmation or . . . we may find a way to avoid you coming up for trial.'

'I understand, sir. Thank you, sir.'

'Delaney and I are here to offer whatever help we can.' A hint of a smile. 'There are always ways of accommodating deserving cases such as yourself – providing, of course, you tell us everything – exactly the way it happened.'

'I will, sir. I don't have anything to hide.'

'Yes ... well, not now perhaps. However, I should warn you, I've been allowed access to certain files. The First Family know a great deal more about Brickman and his friends than you might think.'

'I came back in of my own free will and at the first opportunity, sir. I'm here to tell the truth.'

'Good. Tell me the whole story from the beginning.'

Jodi looked confused. 'From when I went over the side of The Lady?'

'No. From when you went over the side of that fishing smack on Lake Erie into the powered inflatable and decided to throw your lot in with Brickman and his Mute friends.' Karlstrom's lips tightened into a thin smile as he noted Jodi's discomfiture. 'Delaney told me you were having problems trying to recall certain recent events. Do you think you can remember that far back?'

'Yes, sir.' Jodi told him what happened: explaining why she changed her mind while still being held in the slave-dealer's compound at Bu-faro, how Kelso had agreed with her, telling Steve, and the collective decision to make the break at Long Point.

'You needn't tell me how,' said Karlstrom, 'I've read a copy of the report made out by the person you know as Side-Winder.'

Jodi picked up the story at the point where she had accidentally overheard Kelso passing a message through SkyBucket Three to someone called 'Mother'. She had no inkling that Mother, the head of AMEXICO was standing right there in front of her.

She went on to give details of the crash landing and the subsequent trek through driving snow, the encounter with the Mutes and the appearance of the Skyhawks from The Lady. The reassuring sight of their white-tipped wings had aroused an overwhelming desire to be reunited with her trail-mates. Brickman on the other hand, had greeted her decision to go back in with astonishment.

'Astonishment ...? Are you sure?'

'Yes, sir. He tried to talk me out of it. Said they'd probably send me to the wall and shoot Kelso out of hand – because of his injuries.'

'Did you believe him?'

'Yes, sir. I've seen summary executions of renegades in the field whilst serving aboard The Lady and I've watched 'em going to the wall on Channel Nine. I told him I didn't care what happened to me. It was Dave I was concerned about.'

Karlstrom gave an understanding nod. 'And that's when you told Brickman that Kelso was an undercover agent . . .'

'Yes, sir.'

'How did he react? Was he surprised? Angry? Or did you get the impression you were telling him something he already knew?'

'Well, sir – with Brickman it's sometimes kinda hard to tell. He looked both surprised and upset – but it was more to do with the fact that I hadn't told him earlier.'

'But Brickman showed no sign of changing *his* mind and coming in with you.'

'No, sir.' Jodi fed Karlstorm the edited version. 'He'd gotten himself tied in to some kind of deal with the two Mutes who came out of Ne-Issan with us. Don't ask me what it was. All I know is they and Brickman had to get to Wyoming. Maybe he explained things to the big guy with the red bandana. Side-Winder.' She spread her hands. 'You gotta understand, sir. When you've got Trackers walking around – not only painted up but with lumps stuck in their faces, and others pretending to be renegades it's kinda hard for a simple-minded dog-soldier like me to know which way is up!'

'Ye-essss, it must be . . .'

'The thing was, Brickman sorta came round to my way of thinking but I was worried that the Mutes wouldn't let me and Kelso get back on board. That's when I offered –'

'– to lie on his behalf and say that he and his two friends were dead . . .'

Jodi felt the undamaged side of her face go pink with embarrassment 'Yes, sir. After that he was one hundred per cent behind the idea.'

'I imagine he was . . .'

Jodi was acutely conscious that her testimony was proving as damaging to Steve as it was to herself. This was not how she'd wanted it to go. 'I'm sure he had a good reason, sir.'

'So am I. What happened then?'

Jodi told him about taking a midnight stroll while Steve and Kelso had their fireside chat.

'Any idea what they talked about?'

'No, sir. But I think it must have been something secret 'cos Brickman wouldn't let me listen. He said I already knew too much for my own good. They talked for about twenty minutes or so.'

'More than enough time for Brickman to plant the explosives.'

'No, sir! When I got back, Dave – I mean, Kelso was still conscious! And anyway, if I'm supposed to have planted the explosives in the Skyhawk and inside my shirt, how did he make me do that?'

Karlstrom shrugged lightly. 'Brickman's a very persuasive fellow. He talked you into helping him get those Mutes out of Ne-Issan – and you offered to lie to save his skin even though you knew you could be sent to the wall. Blowing yourself to pieces is messier than facing a firing squad but the end result is the same. And a lot faster, too.'

'No, sir!' cried Jodi. 'If I'd been sent to the wall only *I* would have died! The sole reason for coming back in was to try and save Kelso's life!'

'The sole reason . . .?'

'No, no, uhh – I mean the *main* reason,' stammered Jodi. 'The two Mutes wanted to kill Dave! I offered to cover up for Brickman because it was the only way I could get them to co-operate!'

'And once you were safely aboard, you were going to tell your commanding officer you'd been forced to lie and that Brickman was still alive . . .'

'I never got the chance, sir.'

'No. You were too busy trying to blow up The Lady.'

'That wasn't my doing, sir. I tried to explain that to the counsellor yesterday.'

'Yes, she told me. It's certainly an intriguing idea . . .'

'That's the way it happened, sir. Brickman didn't have anything to do with it. It was Cadillac and Clearwater. They're from the clan M'Call. Their turf's in Wyoming. It was The

Lady's wingmen who fired their crops last year and strafed their warriors with napalm then when they tried to hit back, The Lady took 'em apart.

'They had both motive – revenge – and opportunity.' Jodi told Karlstrom what happened during the night prior to the pick-up, and backed up her thesis with an account of the skills and knowledge Cadillac had displayed in Ne-Issan.

Karlstrom allowed Jodi to present her case without interruption then said: 'Thank you. If this is true, it seems that Brickman bears a great deal of responsibility for allowing – perhaps even encouraging – this transfer of knowledge to one of the enemy. You know the official view of Mute magic but we will bear in mind the possibility that you may have been subjected to some . . . how shall I put it – unorthodox mind-warping techniques?

'However, because of the prima facie case against you arising out of the attack on The Lady you will remain in detention for the time being –'

Jodi shot out of her chair and stood rigidly to attention. 'I understand, sir!'

'– charged with a Code One offence . . .' He gave her a narrow-eyed look. Karlstrom did not like being interrupted. 'I don't need to underline the seriousness of your present situation but bear in mind my opening remarks about the special nature of this case. You will undergo a thorough debriefing covering the period between your last take-off from The Lady and your return.

'You've already gone through much of this with Delaney but I'm sure I can count on your whole-hearted cooperation.'

'Yess-sirr!'

'On the other hand, don't go overboard. In your own interests and that of the Federation, I advise you to structure your replies to avoid any mention of "Mute magic". It's entirely up to you, of course. I'm not asking you to tell lies.'

'No, sir. How d'you mean, sir?'

'Just stick to the facts, don't embellish them. Take the incident at the Heron Pool. You could describe what you *thought* you saw then, and on any other similar occasion where you were an eye-witness. Just take care not to make it sound too far-fetched and, above all, don't attempt to explain it. The last thing we want is for your mental state to be called into question. D'you follow me?'

'Yess-sirr!'

'Good. I can't promise anything but I'll do my level best to see you get a fair shake.'

The following day, Karlstrom and Fran Jefferson were summoned to the Oval Office. The President-General had already scanned the edited video-tapes and text summaries of the two interviews.

'What d'you think, Ben? Have they turned him?'

'This is one of those times when I don't have a neat answer.' The set of Karlstrom's mouth plus a tired wave underlined his frustration. 'We always knew Brickman was a tricky customer. But then I've got a naturally suspicious mind.'

'We both have,' said the P-G. 'That's why I'm still in the hot seat and you're head of AMEXICO.'

'It certainly helps. But we both know there's more to it than that.'

'Absolutely. But this is no time to dwell on the mysteries of natural selection and the precarious path of preferment.' The P-G swivelled his chair a few degrees to his left and aimed a questioning glance at Fran.

'I'm sticking with the Commander-General's original reading of the runes – based on what happened at Long Point and events prior to that. I think Brickman's still on the case,' she said.

'It's possible. But then, as his controller, you're going to resist, for as long as you can, the idea that he's finally jumped the rails.'

Fran admitted the truth of this with a smile. 'I won't deny I have a vested interest in maintaining an aura of infallibility.'

'So do we,' replied the P-G. 'It was Ben and I who recruited him into AMEXICO and sent him back out there.' He treated Karlstrom to a genial smile, enjoying his predicament. 'Could young Brickman have outfoxed us? Me, the man who's supposed to know everything – and you, the man who likes to think he knows everything?'

'Don't rub it in . . .'

'Just kidding, Ben.' Karlstrom was one of the few people the President-General could relax with. 'Okay, if you don't yet have the facts, Fran, make an informed guess.'

'Kazan is confused but her background material shows her to be a dedicated Grade A soldier. I'm inclined to believe her testimony – even though much of it is not admissible.'

'Ben . . .?'

'I agree. If Brickman had been part of the plan to cripple The Lady he'd have killed our three operatives at Long Point. We deliberately kept the reception committee small to allow him some elbow room, some flexibility. But it didn't enter his plan of action. It was Kelso who went through the motions – and allowed Kazan to talk him out of it. The two incidents just don't square – and whatever else he might be, our golden boy is consistent.' Karlstrom outlined what he thought Steve's game-plan might be.

'And you think, when he discovered Kelso was a fellow Mexican, he put him in the picture . . .'

'Let's call him Rat-Catcher and her Jodi. That way, we'll know which "K" was working for us. And the answer to your question is "Yes", I think he did. Jodi says Brickman talked to him for about twenty minutes and both of them kept their voices down. Rat-Catcher was an old hand. He wouldn't have spent time swapping case-notes and –'

'– it was too early for them to be saying goodbye . . .'

'Exactly. What is more, the two Mutes weren't around. If their eventual fate was the subject of the conversation Brickman couldn't have picked a better time. As to his game-plan, well – there I'm only guessing.'

'But it does fit in with what we know of his character?' The President-General aimed the question at Fran.

'Oh, yes. Brickman is more than capable of that degree of deception.'

'The question is – was that all Rat-Catcher was supposed to tell us? Or was there something else?'

The P-G smiled. 'I'll leave you to wrestle with the imponderables, Ben.' He stood up to indicate the meeting was over. 'Brickman knows what will happen to his kin-sister if he steps too far out of line.' A thought struck him. 'Can't *she* tell you what he's up to?'

'Only in general terms. The psychic feed-back is much more precise when she's trying to establish his location. But for some reason, the heavy snow that's currently blanketing Illinois and Indiana makes it impossible to relate the images she is receiving to the map I gave her.'

The P-G accepted this with an understanding nod. 'While we're on the subject I took another look at that video tape you sent over.'

'Oh – you mean when Brickman was forced to bite the arrow?'

'Yes. Very disturbing . . .'

'I know how you feel. It never ceases to amaze me. But the one interesting point to emerge from our study of this pair is the fact that the link only appears to work one way. Brickman doesn't seem to be aware we *know* he's alive. If he did, he wouldn't have gotten Jodi to tell Hartmann that he and the Mutes had been killed.'

'Or given Rat-Catcher a message telling us – perhaps – that he was still up and running.'

'Exactly.'

Fran was slow to grasp the point Karlstrom was trying to make. 'You mean, uh . . . he could have telegraphed his true intentions through Roz . . .?'

'Yes . . .'

'Maybe he did,' mused the P-G. 'And maybe she decided not to tell you about it.'

'The thought *had* occurred to me,' admitted Karlstrom. 'I was hoping you wouldn't mention it.'

'Do we have any way of finding out *how* this mind-bridge works – or how effficient it is?'

Karlstrom shook his head. 'We know as much about telepathy as we do about Mute magic. All we have is empirical proof that it works. Roz can get specific messages through to him. We have a tape of them in Santanna Deep where he mentions this.'

'Yes, I remember. They connected on that incoming shuttle. So in theory, she could have told him that we're using her to monitor his movements and his state of health.'

'She could have but it would appear she hasn't. Brickman's loyalty may be in doubt but his sister's isn't. I've been playing up the jealousy factor. She regards Clearwater as a rival who has to be eliminated. That came over very clearly on the same tape and the video recordings of our subsequent meetings prove her feelings haven't changed.'

'Good . . .'

'She's also receptive to his mental state. The distance separating them is not a limiting factor. The link with Brickman is usually triggered by a specific incident involving a high degree of stress or emotion. The tapes of the psychosomatic woundings demonstrate the most striking aspect of the connection but Side-Winder's report confirms her ability to relate mental pictures of Brickman to specific activities and identifiable locations.

'Again the traffic appears to be one-way. Roz is trying to deepen their mental kinship. He, on the other hand is trying to shut her out. We only have her word for that but it's backed up by what she says on the Santanna tapes. To prove the *true* extent of their telepathic abilities would require a controlled experiment.'

'And the participation of both subjects . . .'

'Exactly. So until Brickman comes back in, we'll have to put that particular piece of research on hold.'

'And hope in the meantime she's playing ball with us.'

Karlstrom nodded. 'Thanks for spoiling my day.'

'My pleasure, Ben.' The P-G ushered Karlstrom and Fran towards the turnstile. 'We're running *They were Expendable* on the big screen. Why don't you join us for supper tonight?'

'I will. That's one of my all-time favourites.'

'Contains a message for all of us,' said the P-G. His hand slid across Karlstrom's back and gripped his right shoulder.

Karlstrom, who had grown up with the President-General and aided his accession to the high-backed chair in the Oval Office, knew the precise meaning of the P-G's affable gesture; the momentary but unmistakable steely pressure of fingers on bone. Behind the smiles and the jokes, Jefferson the 31st was saying: *Don't fumble the ball on this one, Ben-baby, because your ass is well and truly on the line . . .*

When Fran had been rotated through the turnstile into the circular reception hall beyond, Karlstrom said: 'There's one subject we haven't touched upon. What to do with Jodi Kazan . . .'

'Do we have any choice?'

'Not a lot. The pity of it is she's a good soldier. Or rather she was. Under normal circumstances, the active duty she put in helping get those Mutes out would have earned her a commendation and two full stripes. But because of what she now knows we can't put her back with the dog-faces and she's temperamentally unsuited for intelligence work. Then there's the wagon-train. We've used drugs to counter the destabilizing influence of that lump-head bitch but it's no more than a holding operation. What she helped do to The Lady has blown her mind.' He grimaced. 'Emotionally, she's a real mess . . .'

'Physically too,' said the P-G. 'That face . . .' He banished the image with a shake of his head. 'Pump her dry, then get rid of her. Oh, by the way, we'll be eating at seven-thirty sharp.'

Karlstrom nodded and stepped into the turnstile.

CHAPTER EIGHT

Poppa Jack, the guard-father of Steve and Roz Brickman, gave up the losing battle with radiation-induced cancer during the night of the 23rd/24th December 2990 – three days short of his thirty-sixth birthday. Since the quasi-religious pre-Holocaust celebration known as Christmas had been discarded soon after the birth of the Federation, there was ample time for the ex-wingman's body to be bagged, burned and re-membranced before the New Year Festivities began.

As a double-six – the rating given to those rare individuals completing twelve overground tours and winning twelve successive commendations for meritorious service, Poppa Jack qualified for an Honour Party composed of stiff-backed, young ensigns dressed in the tricolour uniforms of the White House Guards.

The ceremony, which included a brief televised homily by the President-General, took place on Level Six of the upward-spiralling Wall of Heroes, a vast marble-clad shaft at Grand Central. And it ended with the tear-inducing strains of an electronic Last Post as Poppa Jack's ashes – now sealed in a slim brass shell-case – was inserted into the wall alongside his engraved name. The firing pin had been replaced by a small circular keyplate, and when the base of the shell slid flush with the lustrous black marble, the plate was turned, locking Poppa Jack's ashes into the wall for all time.

The upward spiral was not without significance. When the grand design was realized and the time came to take possession of the Blue-Sky World, the final exodus from Grand Central would be made along this winding ramp past the recorded names of those who, down the centuries, had made the ultimate sacrifice to turn the cherished dream of the First Family into reality and ensure the long-term future of the Amtrak Federation.

'They died so that others might live.' This inspirational utterance attributed to the Founding Father was one of the two inescapable exhortations emblazoned on every available wall-space throughout the Federation. The second, more chilling, addressed those who might be tempted to question the wisdom and supremacy of the First Family: 'Only people fail, not the system'.

Wearing her green blue and white jumpsuit with its big arm chevrons that identified her as a student surgeon-physician and the tasselled parade lanyard that denoted her existing rank as a general medical practitioner, Roz stood at attention facing the Wall of Heroes, chin held high, right arm raised in a military salute. She was flanked by Annie, her guard-mother, in a standard orange and grey outfit and Uncle Bart, Annie's kin-brother, resplendent in the all-white uniform and stetson of a States Provost-Marshal. Annie's eyes, like Roz's, were misted with tears. Bart, as befitted his status as head of internal security for New Mexico, remained stony-faced throughout.

As she listened to the last, echoing notes of the invisible trumpet, Roz was conscious that Poppa Jack had not been accorded the final honours that were his due. His combat record should have earned him enrolment into the select company of Minutemen which, like the Foragers, was the ultimate achievement – short of becoming a member of the First Family – to which ordinary Trackers could aspire.

The exclusiveness of these two companies rested upon the fact that membership was restricted to a hundred living 'names' at any one time. The ranks of Minutemen were reserved for combat personnel – Trail-Blazers, Pioneer Battalions and the foot-soldiers who had preceded the wagon-trains; the Company of Foragers comprised those who had rendered equally meritorious service whilst assigned to one of the other overground units – the Survey and Exploration, Mills and Mines, and the General Quarter-Master Corps whose tanker-transports provided the fuel, food, munitions and the host of other items required to keep the aforementioned groups in business.

With so few places available only those with the most outstanding records of service could be considered as candidates and, as a result, enrolment was often a last-minute affair; the reward for a lifetime of endeavour bestowed around the age of 40.

Since this was the average life-span of an ordinary Tracker it was, for many deserving cases, a death-bed promotion. And, human nature being what it is, the initials DBP had entered the underground language of the Federation as a synonym for intangible or illusory rewards linked to the completion of a particularly shitty assignment.

But this was not strictly true. Although Poppa Jack had been allowed to die without the proud knowledge that he'd been chosen to join the select company of Minutemen, his posthumous election would have brought extra lifetime privileges for Annie, including uprated living quarters in one of the new deeps. But despite Uncle Bart's connections, this last honour had been denied him.

Roz suspected that Karlstrom and the faceless members of the First Family who were directly involved in Steve's case had decided to accord their guard-father only the minimum recognition he could not reasonably be denied. So be it . . . Come what may, his name was now chiselled deeply into the black marble wall on the south side of Level Six and there it would stay regardless of what she and Steve did from here on in. Poppa Jack was finally home free and the veiled threat by Karlstrom to strip him of his field decorations could no longer be used to browbeat them into blind obedience.

That left Annie. Despite the declaration of his desire to help them, Karlstrom had hinted that his freedom of manoeuvre was limited by less sympathetic superiors. Annie could also be in jeopardy if Roz and Steve did not do what was asked of them. But as of today, their guard-mother appeared to be out of danger. Prior to the funeral ceremony, Uncle Bart had announced that Annie would be joining his personal staff at Roosevelt/Santa Fe. Working that closely with one of the 'high-wires' – plus the fact they were related – made Annie a lot less vulnerable. After mulling over Uncle Bart's news, Roz decided that if the First Family were going to dump Annie in the A-Levels – or worse – they would not have allowed the transfer, and her promotion to JX-1, to go through.

With one guard-parent reduced to ashes and the other in a relatively safe haven, Roz felt able to breathe again. Her own future as a surgeon-physician still hung in the balance but it no longer mattered whether she was allowed to continue her studies or not. In the months that had passed since Steve returned to the overground she had discovered her life had a deeper purpose.

This knowledge had given her a greater awareness of the nature of the power within her. She no longer feared those who sought to control their lives. When the time came she would use that power to bend their minds to *her* will.

But despite this increased awareness, there remained a great many things about which she knew nothing. Take, for example, three aspects of Poppa Jack's funeral. Roz might have viewed the future with less confidence had she known that the fifteen-minute televised appearance of the President-General during the ceremony, which had left her heart bursting with pride and her eyes filled with tears of gratitude, was not the live broadcast or pre-recording she might have expected but an electro-mechanical creation.

As the biological begetter – in theory, at least – of the present generations of Trackers, George Washington Jefferson the 31st was the benign, *in vitro* father of them all. This progenitive feat – made necessary because the majority of both sexes were born sterile – was lauded in the prayer which Trackers were called upon to recite twice a day whilst facing one of the countless portraits of the President-General. Like the slogans which met the eye whichever way one turned, the holographic portraits had to be displayed in every public access area, workshop, mess-deck and accommodation unit containing over thirty square feet of floor space.

. . . *Saviour of the Blue-Sky World, Creator of the Light, the Work and the Way, Keeper of all Knowledge, Wisdom and Truth, in whom the Seven Great Qualities are enshrined, and from whose sacred life-blood our lives spring* . . .

Since, in biological terms – or so ran the popular belief – every Tracker was related to the present or previous holder of the office of President-General, he or she was expected to display the same seven qualities which characterized the unique nature of the First Family and their right to eternal leadership of the Amtrak Federation. Qualities without which the nation would have perished centuries ago: Honesty, Loyalty, Discipline, Dedication, Courage, Intelligence and Skill.

To contravene the Behavioural Codes was not only an act of disloyalty to the Federation, it was a betrayal of parental trust. Paternalism, however, is a two-way process, and in return for their unquestioning devotion and allegiance, it was only fitting that the President-General should say a few words when the more deserving of his 'children' were buried. It was part of the firm but caring image the First Family wished to project. But the sheer numbers involved made a personal appearance in front of the video cameras a logistical nightmare.

The problem, like nearly all those encountered by the First Family, had been solved with the usual mixture of ingenuity and cold-eyed efficiency. Like his predecessors, the 31st President-General had provided the programmers with a comprehensive holographic film portrait which had been used to produce computer-generated audio and video master-tapes. Using digital processors, these tracks and images could be manipulated to produce a totally authentic-sounding speech on any subject, tailored to the required length, and underscored by the appropriate gesture or expression.

In the case of Poppa Jack – 2003–4093 John Roosevelt Brickman – his file had been pulled from the archives by a keyboard operator in the Obit Section of the Disabled Veteran's Division and combined with an appropriate funeral oration from a regularly renewed selection of over two hundred. The only other information required was the transmission date and time and whether it was to be networked or 'vectored' which meant the President-General's speech praising Poppa Jack would only be screened in specific locations such as Roosevelt/Santa Fe – his home base – the Air Force Academy at Lindbergh Field beneath the deserts of New Mexico where he trained as a wingman, and on the sets dotted around the Wall of Heroes in Grand Central where the ceremony was taking place.

COLUMBUS, the central computer that was the guiding

intelligence of the Federation – or one of its many satellites – had done the rest, slotting Poppa Jack's name and glowing references to the salient points of his military career into the speech in the same way that pre-Holocaust form letters offering credit on easy terms, or car-winning 'lucky numbers' tied to trial magazine subscriptions were warmly and personally addressed to the recipient throughout.

The result was slick, seamless and, to Trackers raised from birth with the aid of video screens, indistinguishable from the real thing – right down to the carefully-engineered catch in the throat.

Secondly, Poppa Jack's listing on the Wall of Heroes was not as permanent as Roz imagined. In the Federation you could become a non-person just as you could under earlier totalitarian regimes. Her guard-father's name might have been carved with graceful precision by a computer-controlled mechanical engraver but it could be obliterated overnight by the application of a special silicon paste mixed with the black marble dust. When ground and polished, the virgin surface was restored – ready to receive the name of someone deemed more fitting for eternal remembrance.

This third and last point concerned the identity of the man that Steve called 'crazy Uncle Bart'. Bart Nixon Bradlee, Annie's kin-brother was one of the many members of the First Family who had been given permanent 'deep-cover' assignments in the community at large. These individuals, however, were not agents of AMEXICO. Like the majority of the Family, Bart did not even know such an organization existed. Indistinguishable from ordinary Trackers, their task was to act as role-models for their 'comrades-in-arms' and through their rapid promotion to high ranking positions, demonstrate what ordinary Trackers could achieve through hard work and selfless devotion to duty.

The truth was somewhat different. While people like Hartmann and Anderssen could rise from the ranks to command wagon-trains and way-stations, they were deployed overground. The scope of their operations – and by extension, the power they were able to exercise – was governed by the logistical back-up supplied by the Federation.

Control of the interfaces, and the divisional bases within the earth-shield was a quite different matter. No one outside the First Family was permitted to occupy senior positions or any key posts in sensitive areas such as communications, policing, food-processing, inter-state transportation and the all-embracing environmental services.

Had Roz known that Bart was Family, she might have been tempted to believe that Annie, as his kin-sister, was now immune to any threat of reprisal. It would have been a mistake to think so. The female egg and male sperm that formed Annie were brought together in a laboratory dish while Bart was the product of normal sexual intercourse. It was this reproductive act – identical to that employed by the primitive Mutes – which set the First Family apart from their subjects. But even if Annie had been conceived in this fashion it would not have made her invulnerable. In the past, when the future of the Federation had been threatened, the Family had never flinched from devouring its own – and it would not hesitate to do so now.

When the ceremony was over, Roz stayed with Annie while Bart Bradlee went to a meeting at the Black Tower – home of the Amtrak Executive. Annie had two hours to kill before she and Bart boarded the west-bound shuttle for Santa Fe. Stepping into one of the two elevators that ran up and down the central core of the spiralling ramp, they descended to Level One and used Annie's ID-card to pull a wheelie from the head of the line. There were over fifty of them parked obliquely along the roadway, plugged nose first into a long, low recharging unit.

Running on four small fat tyres, the battery-powered wheelies were like topless, pre-Holocaust golf-carts. The type Roz and Annie had selected functioned as a self-drive taxi; a larger version consisting of a prime mover hauling a string of open trailers ran at pre-set times over fixed routes.

When inserted into the dashboard, Annie's ID-card switched on the motor, and when it was withdrawn at the end of the journey, an appropriate number of credits was deducted. The micro-chip control unit also recorded the ID-number of the card owner and when the wheelie was parked on the next recharging plug, it transmitted this information to COLUMBUS along with the grid coordinates of the entire journey. These coordinates were stored as magnetic data on flat metal ribbons buried at regular intervals beneath the road surface, and should someone in authority wish to do so, they could be reproduced on a VDU to give a visual display of the route taken.

The turnstiles and elevators which gave access to specific areas and levels operated on the same principle. In this way, everyone's movements could be continuously logged and, if necessary, impeded. Access to certain areas, services and levels of information available over the public channels of the video network depended on your rank and function and this was controlled by having ID-cards with differential ratings. The micro-processors at the various control points also rejected any card if the credit balance was within five points of zero, and could be programmed by COLUMBUS to swallow the card carried by a wanted person and sound a piercing alarm to alert any Provos nearby.

The ID-cards, which had to be presented for 'topping-up' every eight weeks in the same way that pre-Holocaust workers lined up to collect their pay cheques, was one of the many ways in which the First Family kept their hold on their loyal subjects. Without an authenticated card, a Tracker could not obtain food directly from one of the mess-decks, could not send a videogram or use a videophone, could not use any of the available means of transportation, change levels, or move from one control area to another. He or she could not even play Shoot-A-Mute – the most popular arcade game in the Federation. Deprived of the means to stay alive or move around – unless sheltered by card-carrying friends – a code-breaker or a 'diss' was like a rat caught in a trap. There was only one way to avoid being caught and to those who knew how, it was known as 'eating your way through the brick-work'.

Roz sat silently beside Annie as they drove down the curving four-lane tunnel that linked the Wall of Heroes with John Wayne Plaza. As they passed the turn-off to the shrine of the

Founding Father, George Washington Jefferson the 1st, Roz saw Annie glance towards the brightly-lit arched colonnade.

'Do you want to visit?'

Annie slowed the wheelie. 'D'you mind? We don't have to wait in line. Just sit on one of the benches for a minute or two.'

'Whatever you want. We got plenty of time . . .'

Annie let a couple of oncoming wheelies pass then turned right and drove into the crowded parking area. Pressing the 'Hold' button on the dash, she pulled her card and returned it to its protective wallet. This action reserved the vehicle – which would now only start if the same card was inserted, and a slow wink-light on top of the dash came on to indicate the wheelie was still in use. But not for ever. The 'Hold' button had a count-down mechanism. If the card-holder didn't return within an hour, the micro-chip turned off the wink-light and put the wheelie back on offer.

The memorial shrine of the Founding Father attracted a steady stream of visitors like Lenin's Tomb in Moscow's Red Square. The red marble mausoleum, along with the nearby Kremlin had been vaporized in the global Holocaust that had obliterated virtually everything ever built from the time of the Pharaohs to the beginning of the 21st century. Lenin's tomb had lasted less than a hundred years but the Founding Father's last resting place, fifteen hundred feet below ground, had been kept safe and secure for nearly five hundred years and would remain so. Not just for another five hundred years but for five hundred *thousand*. That proud boast was an indication of how long the First Family planned to stay at the helm.

Skirting the slowly moving eight-deep line, Annie and Roz found an empty bench carved out of the same white marble as the fifteen foot-high sculpted portrait head of George Washington Jefferson the 1st. The base of the neck rested on a deliberately rough, jagged granite plinth, standing ten feet high so that no matter how many people crowded into the rotunda, his face could always be seen by those entering. His two immortal phrases were carved into the surrounding wall on either side so that those queuing up on the left to touch the spot worn smooth by pilgrims approached under the words,

'They died so that others might live' and walked out past the ominous reminder, 'Only people fail, not the system.'

The Founding Father had actually died in 2045 AD, some thirty years after the Holocaust but his vision of the Federation and the future had been stamped indelibly on his descendants. The shrine, formally opened in 2500 AD, had been built to commemorate the Break-Out in 2445: the long-dreamed-of moment when the first Pioneer Battalions broke through the earth-shield and began construction of the first permanent interface, above Houston/Grand Central.

This return to the overground, which the Founding Father had laid down as the overriding objective of the following generations, had been the first step in the present battle to repossess the Blue-Sky World. Five and a half centuries of unrelenting guerrilla warfare with the wily Mute, to which was added the equally violent struggle to tame the vast, hostile landscape. A landscape which was overlaid by an invisible, poisonous blanket of air. Those five and a half centuries of conflict had taken its toll, as the Wall of Heroes and the lesser Monuments to The Fallen in the divisional bases testified. And now Poppa Jack's name had been added to the list.

As they gazed up at the strong, serene face of the Founding Father, even Roz – who had become increasingly prey to doubts about the integrity of those who ran the system – felt a sense of security, solidity, continuity. And with good reason. Had not the First Family protected and nurtured them for nearly a thousand years? Had they not sheltered their flock from the fires of the Holocaust and the freezing darkness that followed? Had they not led them back towards the light that filled the Blue-Sky World?

The Founding Father had foreseen the dangers, had laid plans by which the Four Hundred and their families would survive. And when the world of the Old Time was put to the torch by the ravening hordes of Mutes that poured out of the cess-pits the once-proud cities of America had become, he had dared to dream: that one day, when the corrupt and evil elements had choked to death by feeding on their own poisonous flesh, the strong and the brave would emerge to cleanse the earth and take their rightful place in the sun.

The succeeding generations of the First Family had cherished that dream and, as a result, vast areas of the overground were now controlled by the Federation. But the poisonous presence of the Mutes still polluted the atmosphere. According to the Manual, their sweat, their excreta, their breath were charged with lethal toxins. Death radiated from their bodies like heat from a ceramic hob. And it was an accumulated dose of these poisons, absorbed over years of active duty, which had laid waste to Poppa Jack's body and finally killed him.

In Roz's own lifetime, the newscasts had carried figures showing that the level of poison in the atmosphere had been dropping. Years ago, when Steve had dared to ask if there might be another reason – apart from the presence of the Mutes – that made the air bad for Trackers to breathe, Poppa Jack had become angry, warning them both that a person could get into deep trouble for having bad ideas like that. And when pressed to explain why the danger was decreasing, he had slammed his fist on the table, shouting: 'That's because every year that goes by, we're killin' more 'n more of the foul-smelling sons of bitches! Ain't it obvious? The less there are, the better it gets! But it won't ever be fit and proper to breathe until the bones of the last lump-head have been bleached white and ground into the dirt!'

But Steve had spent six months as a prisoner of the Plainfolk Mutes, had eaten their food, breathed same air, had even – Roz shuddered at the thought – shacked up with one and was, apparently, none the worse for the experience . . .

'Always makes me feel good – comin' here,' murmured Annie. 'Makes you realize how long the Family's been lookin' after us. And how well they done it. That man up there, he held it all together. All those hundreds of years ago . . . he knew where we was headed, an' what had to be done for us to get there. An' every year that passes brings us a step closer.' She sighed. 'I won't live to see the Blue-Sky World but you might. A lot can happen in ten years.'

Annie was referring to the Family's promise to repossess the Blue-Sky World by the year 3000 A D.

'I have a feeling, from what –'

Roz broke off abruptly. She had been about to say 'from

what Steve told me' but, as far as Annie knew, Steve had never returned from his first overground tour aboard The Lady from Louisiana. Officially, he was dead; missing in action over Wyoming, last year. She made a new start.

'– uhh, from what, uh, y'know, one hears around the campus. From guys who have kinfolk on the wagon-trains . . .'

'Yeah . . .?'

'That it could take a whole lot longer.'

'Scuttlebut!' snapped Annie. 'Never heard Poppa Jack spreadin' spineless rumours like that. An' I don't want to hear any from you. Now or ever!'

'No, ma'am . . .'

They sat in silence for a while then Annie produced a tissue and wiped the tears from her eyes. 'Y'know what I wish? That Poppa Jack and Stevie could have been remembranced to-gether. I know they didn't always see eye-to-eye.' She smiled, remembering. 'Never knew a boy who wanted to know so much. Every time Poppa Jack answered a question, he came back with two more. Just couldn't seem to make him under-stand that things were just the way The Manual said they were. The rows they had . . .'

'And the beatings . . .'

'Yeah . . . still, they thought the world of each other. Would have made me real proud to see their names set side-by-side on that wall. I know the rules 'bout those who go missin' but it don't seem right for Stevie's body to be lyin' out there somewhere and not be remembered.' She dried her eyes again then wiped her nose.

Roz hesitated then reached out and took firm hold of her guard-mother's hand. Bracing herself, she said: 'Annie, I couldn't tell you this over the video-phone but . . . Stevie isn't dead. I can't tell you *how* I know. I just do. He's going to come one day, I'm sure of it. And he'll be a hero. Just like Poppa Jack.'

To her surprise, Annie did not reproach her for going against the official word concerning Steve's fate. She patted Roz's outstretched hand. 'Glad you told me. I've had that feelin' too.' She looked around to see who was in earshot then lowered her voice. 'But it doesn't do to talk about such things.

Even if it's true – an' I pray to the Foundin' Father to make it so – it won't bring him back any quicker.'

'Just don't lose hope.'

Annie shook her head. 'The bag-men'll have to show me his body first. Have you spoken to anyone else about this?'

'No . . .'

'Then don't.' Annie hugged her. 'I appreciate you tryin' to soften the blow.'

'I'm not making it up, Annie. It's true, as sure as I'm standing here.'

Because when he dies, so will I . . .

'I know, I know, sweetie.' Annie stood up. 'C'mon. Let's go before we lose that wheelie.'

They spent the next half-hour wandering around a small part of John Wayne Plaza, the biggest rock chamber in the entire Federation. The free-flight dome at Lindbergh Field was the only other excavation that approached it in size.

The Plaza's ground plan was in the form of a five-pointed star lying within a circular ringway with a diameter of one mile. The V-shaped areas grouped about the central pentagon were lined with galleries which came together in a smooth semi-circular sweep above the arches that gave access to the encircling ringway. The views across the Plaza were spectacular but they were nothing compared to the view upwards; the tapering vault above the pentagon measured a dizzying eight hundred feet from floor to apex.

Above the apex, Pioneers were already sinking a shaft through the last layer of rock and earth to link the plaza with the overground and when the final stage was completed, a steel and glass tower would continue the lines of the vault upwards, converging to form a glittering five-sided pyramid eleven hundred feet high, topped by a covered observation platform. The world above would become one with the world below, linked by express elevators that would carry you upwards towards the clouds and a breathtaking view of the Blue-Sky World.

Even now, there was a lot to see (some said too much) and a leisurely visit took the best part of two days. Parties shuttling in from outlying bases on three day passes were quartered in units running off the top galleries of the V-shaped vistas; the Trackers who staffed the Plaza were stationed immediately below.

'Working the Plaza' was viewed by many as the best underground posting a guy could pull, better even than promotion to executive rank. 'High-wiring' it up the Black Tower might prove ultimately more rewarding but it was also a great deal more precarious. Like the dog-soldiers said: 'The higher you go, the further you fall'.

As Commander Bill Hartmann and the disgraced executive officers of The Lady knew only too well.

But back to the Plaza. The second and first street-level galleries contained a variety of arcades, mess-decks, space parks – combinations of architectural and landscaping elements where you could just sit or stroll around and enjoy the view – and exhibition areas covering every aspect of the Federation, past, present and future.

Twenty credits brought you a 10-minute ride in a cockpit of a Skyhawk surrounded by a computer-generated bird's-eye view of the overground. Artfully placed jets of air created a slipstream to complete the illusion of movement and a series of targets were presented for the rookie-pilot to gun down by firing a soft laser. Another exhibit, a full-sized walk-through mock-up composed of three sections of a wagon-train: the command module, power car and a typical battle-station, attracted a steady flow of visitors.

After watching the accompanying video-display, many yippies – Young Pioneers, who spent their 13th year as unskilled labourers, digging subway tunnels, air shafts and other backbreaking engineering projects – left the mock-up and headed straight for the recruitment information bureau to add their names to the list of would-be Trail-Blazers. And for the even younger visitor, aged four to seven, there were seats to be had aboard a minature, open-topped wagon-train that made regular trips around the Plaza. They, too, stepped down, filled with a wide-eyed sense of adventure and a restless desire to grow up as soon as possible.

Few, from either group, would ever step on board a full-sized, battle-worthy wagon-train but the illusion of choice was carefully fostered to counter the impression of a suffocating regimentation being imposed from the top down.

You obeyed the orders of the First Family because you believed that it was right and proper to do so, not because you were forced to. The Family gave you life, fed you, reared you, gave you a valued role in society, a sense of purpose and a promise of a better future. The President-General, like those who had preceded him, regarded you as his own kin; sons and daughters of one great extended family. And like the father of any family he placed his trust in you and, not unreasonably, expected that trust to be returned. Plus undying gratitude and life-long obedience. Sanctions were only applied to those who betrayed that trust. Such irrational behaviour was the product of a diseased mind; a sickness that was judged to be highly contagious. Code-breakers were like plague-carriers; they had to be removed from society and if they could not be cured then they had to be destroyed.

Roz and Annie enjoyed a leisurely cup of Java by the cooling fountains and greenery in the spacious central pentagon beneath the soaring light-filled vault. It was not the only source of illumination but its warmth and brightness gave a hint of what it would be like to live in the rays of the sun that generations had died without ever seeing. The lush broad-leaved vegetation had been grown from seeds carefully preserved by the First Family. Back in the Old Time, before the hell-fires that spawned the Mutes, the overground had been green too. Now the trees and grass were blood-red, flesh pink and fireball orange but one day that would change. When the air had been purified and the earth was purged of all that was unclean, a new world would be created; a world that embraced the simplicity and goodness that had been lost along the way and – as in the words of the song – the good ole boys would return 'to the green, green hills of home'. . .

Roz gazed around the Plaza and down the tapering broad-walks filled with air, light, colour and movement and mentally compared it to the grey, cinder-block face of Roosevelt/Santa Fe, her divisional home. 'How the other half live . . .' She turned to Annie. 'Still, you should be okay, now that you're moving in with Uncle Bart. I seem to remember you took me there once. When I was . . . six?'

'Five . . .'

'It was pretty fancy.'

'It's certainly better than the quarters me an' Jack started out with. But things improved when you two came along. Bart lives better'n most but then . . . he had an important job to do. When those high-wires from the Black Tower come out to see him, you can't have 'em sittin' with their knees under their chins.' Annie gestured towards their surroundings. 'You mark my words. One day, everywhere's gonna look as good as this.'

They took the elevator to the top gallery of the south-west vista. Because of the funeral, Roz had been given a pass from Inner State U which allowed her to stay overnight with Annie. They picked up their zip bags from the janitor's office and, after keying in their onwards destinations, they inserted their ID-cards and logged themselves off the accommodation roster.

The information was relayed through the network to COLUMBUS enabling it to record where they'd been and where they were going, just as later, it would note their arrival. The current location and destination of any individual was temporaily recorded on the ID-card's memory. This enabled the Provost-Marshals to identify a valid card. Provos, the visible internal security force of the Federation a.k.a. 'meat-loaves', often carried out random ID checks at what were known as 'choke-points'. Using portable plug-in terminals they could run an immediate check on the card's status and, by pressing the Run Data key, obtain the full story on suspect card-holders from the files held by COLUMBUS in under two seconds.

During several of the Saturday night sessions hosted by Chisum at Santanna Deep, Roz had joined in conversations with her student friends about the rumoured existence of a hidden sub-culture inhabiting disused service tunnels and the long-abandoned subterranean installations of the pre-Holo-caust era.

Whenever one of these underground workings was dis-covered it was explored then demolished with explosive charges or sealed and filled with gas. Over the years, Roz had watched several newscasts in which the discovery of these installations and their subsequent destruction had been featured but there was never once any mention of people having lived in these dusty vaults and tunnels.

Apart from the televised trials and execution of Code-One defaulters – who were charged with specific, individual crimes – the First Family did not acknowledge the existence of any organized groups of dissidents. And if the official view was that such groups did not exist then any reference to them was, by definition, an unsubstantiated rumour and rumour-mongering was a Code Three offence which, if repeated, could make you a candidate for 're-education'.

Yes, thought Roz, as she slipped her ID-card back into its own special pocket inside her jump-suit, life in the Federation contrasted starkly with the unfettered existence of the Plainfolk that Steve had described and which, on occasions, she had shared through the telepathic link that enabled her mind to unite with his. A link so profound she was able to 'see' with her inner eye the images that fell upon his retina, hear the same sounds, smell the same odours, and share his feelings of intense joy or fear in moments of mortal danger. And also the pain, for when his flesh was pierced so was hers, the wounds – unlike his – miraculously healing within hours.

A new batch of wide-eyed travellers streamed out of the subway station under John Wayne Plaza as Roz and Annie walked down the ramp and made their way through the turn-stiles onto the outbound platform. The incoming shuttle had already gone down-line into the depot where it would switch tracks and pick up another crew before gliding back to pick up Annie and the other passengers, some of whom would be riding to the western terminal at Jackson/Phoenix in the newly-incorporated Outer State of Arizona.

Roz searched the platform but could see no sign of Uncle Bart.

'He won't arrive till we're due to leave,' said Annie. 'Bart don't wait for trains – they wait for him.' State Provost-Marshals, like other high-wires were allotted a special compartment which Annie had shared on the way in and she would be travelling back the same way. 'You don't have to wait if you've got better things to do.'

'I want to stay,' said Roz. 'We don't see each other all that often and . . .'

'I know,' Annie gave a sad smile. 'And now that Poppa Jack's gone . . .'

They gazed at each other silently for a while then Roz said: 'Things have been happening to me. I can't explain but . . . I may be going topside.'

Annie looked dismayed. 'But what about your studies? Does this mean you'll be quitting medical school?'

'I don't know. Maybe they'll let me re-enter the second year. You know how it is. I got word I'm needed elsewhere.'

Annie looked over her shoulder then dropped her voice to a whisper. 'Is this somethin' to do with Steve?'

Roz nodded.

Her guard-mother mulled the news over then appeared to come to a decision. She checked the nearest time display then led Roz by the arm into one of the passageways linking the two platforms. 'You were never meant to know this, but after what you said back at the shrine about Stevie bein' alive an' what you just told me, I've got to get somethin' off my chest. 'Specially as we might never get to see each other again.' Whatever she was about to say was obviously making great emotional demands on her.

Roz went to interrupt. Annie gripped her hands. 'No! Hear me out. I done my best to rear the both of you by the Book an' be everythin' a guard-mother should but with Poppa Jack away so much it wasn't easy. I can remember times when I could have been kinder and more carin', an' I knew you wanted me to be but . . . I held back.

'You know why? There was somethin' about the two of you. The way you seemed to talk to each other without sayin' anythin' that frightened me. Maybe I was just imaginin' things but it was like – when you were together – me an' Poppa Jack an' the rest of the world was shut out. Like you were different. Special. D'you know what I'm talkin' about?'

'Yes . . .'

'Well you *are* special. Don't ask me how and why. Nobody told me. There was a lot of things they didn't tell me, but I found out anyway,' Annie took a deep breath and laid her hands on Roz's shoulders. 'I didn't carry you inside me, honey. Not you *or* Steve.'

'Oh, Annie –'

'Hush now! You've done some of your doctor trainin' at the Life Institute . . .'

'Yes, but not in obstetrics. That's a Family matter.'

'But you know roughly what happens. I mean – how people get born . . .'

'Of course. We saw a whole series of video-graphics.'

'Well, when you go into the delivery room, they give you this gas. It's supposed to ease the birthin' process and usually knocks you out but it didn't work properly with me. It made me feel sick, but because I was frightened I might throw up over the doctors and add to the mess that was happenin' down below, I kept my eyes closed and pretended it was workin' so's they wouldn't pump more of it into me.

'Nobody guessed I was peekin' out on the sly. Both times were the same. I *saw* the babies they took outta my belly. They weren't the ones I was given a couple of days later in the nursin' ward.'

'Are you sure?' Roz felt confused, but in a curious way, not surprised.

'Just like you're sure about Stevie bein' alive. *How* I know's a different matter. You were both given to me to look after. But you came from somewhere else. That's maybe why I've always had this feelin' you were special – an' it looks as if I was right.'

'Does this mean that Stevie's not really my kin-brother?'

'I can't answer that. But there's no reason why he should be.' Annie smiled. ''Cept for the fact you two've always been closer than the top and bottom deck of a bean-burger.'

As they hugged each other, Roz kissed Annie on both cheeks. 'Thanks for telling me. But it doesn't change the way I feel about you. You *were* kind and you *were* caring and I won't allow you or anyone else to say that you weren't. It doesn't matter who carried me. *You* are the one who raised me.'

'Just doin' my job,' said Annie.

'You did more than that, and as far as I'm concerned we'll always be kin. And if Stevie was here he'd feel the same way.'

Annie stepped back and pulled out another tissue. She dabbed at both eyes then blew her nose. 'Where're you headed – State U?'

'Yes, but there's no hurry. I've been excused classes until to-morrow.'

'I'd rather you went now,' said Annie. Her voice was close to breaking. 'The shuttle'll be along soon and well – I don't want to upset your Uncle Bart. He hates to see people cryin'. So, go on – shoo!' She carefully folded the tissue and wiped her eyes again.

Roz shouldered her overnight bag then took hold of Annie's hand and backed away slowly until finally, she was forced to let go. 'G'bye, Annie . . .'

Her guard-mother lifted the hand that was still stretched out towards her in a last gesture of farewell.

Roz turned and walked down the passageway onto the in-bound platform. When she looked back, Annie was gone. Roz saw the white TransAm express with its sidebands of red and blue glide slowly past the opening and stop. She put her head down and strode towards the exit ramp.

Although the platform was crowded, there was no jostling for seats; everyone had reservations. Annie made her way down the length of the shuttle towards the VIP compartment and waited for Bart and his small entourage to appear.

She was glad she had shared her long-kept secret with someone. Poppa Jack had died without knowing but since he had only been the children's appointed guardian, it wouldn't have meant all that much. But having now told Roz, Annie wondered if she had done the right thing. She hoped she had. If, as Roz had hinted, the Family had different futures mapped out for them, it might help to know that they had been planted on her. It would be *their* task – if they were so minded – to find out why. And where they had come from.

As Annie caught sight of Bart being driven down the ramp in a wheelie, she realized that she had let Roz go without extracting a promise to never reveal what she knew to anyone other than Steve. But it was too late to do anything about that now. She would have to rely on Roz's good sense.

Having shared this knowledge, Annie might have been ex-pected to feel that a weight had been lifted from her shoulders but the burden remained. She had not told Roz the whole story. How she had known – beyond all doubt – that Steve and Roz were not the babies she had given birth to.

Feigning unconsciousness, she had watched through an imperceptible slit in her eyelids as the crinkle-faced tight-fisted infants had been eased out between her splayed thighs then held upside down and slapped into life. On both occasions, they had responded with the choking, squalling cries that all baby Trackers made in the first moments of their life. But instead of the usual greyish-mauve bodies that rapidly change to creamy pink as the lungs fill with air, the light skin of both her new-born children had been covered with irregular patches of black, brown and olive.

Only these children had been created, like all children now being born, by the seed of George Washington Jefferson the 31st, the current President-General . . .

There was only one explanation. Either she or the President-General was tainted by Mute blood. That was the shameful, bewildering secret she could share with no one. And would carry with her when the bag-men fed her body to the flames.

'Now tell me. Can you see Steve?'

'Yes . . .'

'Clearly?'

'I am there with him,' said Roz. 'He stands near the centre of the eight rings.'

'Eight rings?'

'Huts set in circles one inside the other. The hut he has been given is part of the inner ring. He stands outside it, watching the great fire . . .'

Karlstrom, seated on the corner of his desk saw her closed eyes shut tighter still. She seemed to be trying to blot out the received image. Her lips drew back, revealing clenched teeth.

'*She* is with him.'

'Clearwater? Good. How about Cadillac?'

'He too . . .'

'How do they feel about him?'

'There has been much anger but they still trust him.'

'Hmmm . . . this place where they're spending the winter. Can you tell me where it is?' Karlstrom eased Roz's chair towards the desk and placed her hands on the large map depicting the pre-Holocaust states to the west and south of the Great Lakes. 'I know all that snow is causing problems but try and describe the area.'

Karlstrom watched intently as Roz's forefingers inched slowly up and down the western shore of Lake Michigan as if reading a Braille manuscript. Her breathing abnormally slow and deep. The anger had been replaced by an expression of rapt concentration.

'There was a great city here once. Tall towers of shining metal and glass that shone with all the colours of the rainbow . . .'

'Navref Chicago,' said Karlstom, anxious to hurry things along. 'Is that where he is?'

'I am not sure if that picture comes from him or the map . . .' Her head drooped slowly until her chin touched her chest then, after a while, she lifted it again. 'Now I understand. The clanfolk of his Mute friends are linked to this place. The M'Calls are from the bloodline of the She-Kargo.'

'That's right,' said Karlstrom. 'But we already know that. Try again. He must have *some* idea where he is.'

Roz frowned. 'Trees, snow . . . high ground . . . to the west of the water.'

'That's better. Can he see the water from where he is?'

'No. Those who shelter him live in the middle of a great white forest.'

And there's plenty of them . . . Karlstrom controlled a sudden urge to slap the blank-faced girl across the face. He put the desk between them. 'But he *is* near Chicago . . .'

'Near, yes. Beyond that I cannot say. To his eyes, everywhere looks the same.'

'Yes, okay. Let's leave that for a minute. Does he know you're inside his head?'

'Yes . . .'

That's something at least . . . 'Is he trying to shut you out?'

'No, not this time . . .'

'What kind of shape is he in? Mentally. What's his state of mind?'

Roz breathed deeply and concentrated. 'He's worried. About a message. From a dead man. He had two names. The first begins like yours . . . Kar . . . Kall . . .'

'Kelso . . .?'

Roz nodded slowly. 'The second name is connected with a song.' She frowned, hesitating over the unfamiliar word. 'Mex . . . mexican . . . mexico?'

Karlstrom quickly changed the subject. 'What was the message?'

The President-General gazed thoughtfully out of the curved windows of the Oval Office at a screened image of his second favourite landscape then looked sideways at Karlstrom. 'Do you believe her?'

Karlstrom met the question with raised eyebrows. 'She's delivered the goods up to now.' His voice was tinged with doubt.

Jefferson the 31st, whose antennae were finely tuned to such nuances, eyed him shrewdly then resumed his seat at the big desk. 'It also fits in with your reading of Brickman's game-plan.' He gestured to Karlstrom to pull up a seat.

'Precisely. That's why I want your approval before acting on this information. There's a lot at stake here.' Karlstrom had not forgotten the steely pressure the P-G had applied to his shoulder earlier in the month.

Jefferson reacted with amusement. 'In other words, you want me to take the rap.'

'No. I want your advice. If it goes wrong, I'll be held responsible anyway. That's part of the job profile. I just want to make sure we've covered all the angles.'

'Okay, Let's go over it again . . .' The President-General turned his chair towards the VDU on the side table to his left and scanned the salient points of their conversation so far. In a simultaneous process, a voice-transducer had been converting the standard tape recording into binary code that came up as lines of text on the screen. The central processing unit, which was programmed to recognize their voice-prints, added their names to the alternate blocks of dialogue printing Jefferson's words in blue and Karlstrom's in red to facilitate read-out.

'So . . . according to her, the *real* reason why Brickman disabled the pick-up team at Long Point was because he was worried about the damage Clearwater might do once she got inside the Federation . . .'

Karlstom nodded. 'That's the underlying concern that caused the apparent change of heart. I take it you've read the edits of Jodi Kazan's debriefing sessions covering their escape from the Heron Pool?'

'Yes. Amazing stuff. But is she telling the truth?'

'She had every incentive.' Karlstrom could not resist a smile. 'I don't know quite how it happened but she seems to have gained the impression that – if she cooperates fully – she could be in line for a full acquittal and reinstatement as a Trail-Blazer.'

'And our contacts in Ne-Issan . . .?'

'The word is that the Heron Pool project was the first stage in an abortive coup by the Yama-Shita family against the Shogun. Our contacts are unable to corroborate Kazan's story in any precise detail. Most of those on the losing side who survived the actual event were executed or took their own lives soon after. And the Toh-Yota are keeping the whole affair under wraps.

'But by all accounts, some very strange things happened and, if our friends are to be believed, that Mute bitch is like a walking volcano. If you want my opinion, Brickman did us a favour. We sent him out to capture her but not enough consideration's been given to exactly how she was to be kept under control or –'

'– why we want to bring her back alive, along with her Mute boy friend, in the first place . . .'

'The question did cross my mind.' Karlstrom tried to keep a straight face. 'I imagine you'll give me the answer when it's time to let me in on the big secret.'

Jefferson's expression was that of a father forced to chide his favourite son. 'No one is closer to me than you are, Ben. But there are some things it's better for you not to know. It's not a question of trust – after all, you helped put me behind this desk. It's the Brickman girl. None of us really know what she's capable of. If she was able to get inside your head – and you knew everything that I know – we could lose the ball-game.'

'She says she can't but . . . I take your point.'

'From the conversations I've had with our shrinks over at The Farm, they seemed to think they could keep Clearwater damped down with drugs.'

'Assuming she's obliging enough to let someone stick a needle in her arm . . .'

'Yes, well, there are other ways. Isn't that why Brickman has gone to such lengths to worm his way into her confidence?'

'Above and beyond the call of duty,' laughed Karlstrom. 'Nevertheless, he's a worried man. And after what's alleged to have happened at the Heron Pool, he has every reason to be.'

The President-General scrolled quickly through several blocks of text on the VDU screen. 'Which brings us back to Roz . . .'

'Yes. She says she can neutralize Clearwater's powers. *If* she can get close enough.'

'Face to face . . . Is it possible?'

Karlstrom shrugged. 'Since we don't have a tame summoner for her to practise on, we won't know until she tries. But the motivation's there. Every time she picks up an image of Brickman with Clearwater she practically has a fit. The problem is we have to take her claim to be able to do this on trust. She can't explain the mechanics of how she's going to defuse this Mute bitch. She just has this gut feeling she can.'

'Not exactly an ideal basis on which to mount an operation of this importance . . .'

'I agree, but we don't have a lot of choice in the matter.'

'But you *are* sure she's totally committed to us . . .'

'Absolutely. She can't bear the idea of her kin-brother shacking up with a Mute. She's ready to draw blood'

'Hell hath no fury like a woman wronged', observed the P-G, paraphrasing an ancient saying. 'And that's as true now as it ever was.'

'You should know . . .'

The President-General let this allusion to his private life pass without comment. Few other people could have gotten away with such impertinence – or even dared contemplate making such a remark. 'So what's the plan?'

'Roz claims that she and Brickman are equally gifted. He's got the mental power to put the blocks on Clearwater – if only he would open up that side of his brain. The trouble is, the normality aspect of his conditioning is so deep-rooted, he's doing his utmost to keep it shut down.'

'Maybe that's because he's reverted and he doesn't want us to find out . . .'

Karlstrom shook his head. 'Roz says he's still with us. He's always known he had this gift but he's frightened of it. Being Brickman, he gets a high out of being different but he doesn't want anyone to know about it. In a society like ours, which is based on confirmity and has outlawed all talk of magic, there's absolutely no joy to be had by revealing you're a telepath. But Brickman's *real* problem is that he doesn't like the idea of anyone getting inside his head. Not even Roz. Our golden boy likes to be in total control.'

'I know the feeling,' said Jefferson.

Karlstrom didn't rise to the bait. That rejoinder was part of the P-G's 'I'm just one of the boys' routine'.

He picked up the thread of the conversation. 'We now have a clearer view of Brickman's intentions. I've touched upon his basic concern – the possible danger to the Federation. His thoughts are now focused on ways and means of getting Clearwater and Cadillac safely to Wyoming. And by doing so, in spite of our efforts to intercept him, he hopes to win their total trust – and prove to Mr Snow that he's a man of his word.'

'And then . . .?'

'He's going to lay a trap for all three. Which was his original assignment. He'll have crossed the continent to do it but . . . Mr Brickman is one of those young men who likes to follow through.'

'I knew we'd made the right choice. Didn't I tell you things would work out just fine?'

'You did,' admitted Karlstrom. 'You also told me to watch him "like a fucking hawk".'

'Ahh, no . . . they were *your* words, Ben, not mine. But to be fair, they did describe the kind of thing I had in mind.

Vigilance does not imply a lack of trust. In these troubled times it's merely a sensible precaution.'

'I agree. Anyway . . . here's how it plays. Roz is going to maintain contact with Brickman. He's planning to move west next spring. She'll track him when he does, and with the snow gone she should be able to get an accurate fix on his position. In Ne-Issan, it worked like a dream. We were able to alert Side-Winder to the possibility of a rendezvous and – hey, presto – in walks Brickman, dressed as a road-runner, just like she said!'

'Yes . . . it's frightening.'

Karlstrom threw up his hands. 'I'm as unhappy about it as you are. But whatever it says in the Book, we both know that Mute magic is for real. The only way we're going to get a handle on it is to fight fire with fire. I haven't been allowed access to their full bio-data – despite the fact I'm working with these two kids – but isn't this why they were raised? Why else would they be on the Special Treatment List?'

'Good question.' But it wasn't one the President-General was ready to answer. 'Okay . . . what happens in Wyoming?'

'Two things. Neither of them had been worked out in detail.' Karlstrom listed them on his fingertips. 'First, Brickman will renew his acquaintance with High-Sierra. And second, he'll discover that his kin-sister is on board a wagon-train. She'll be shipping out as part of the medical team aboard Big Red One.'

Jefferson's eyes narrowed. 'That's an intriguing idea. Did she suggest that?'

Karlstrom was tempted to take the credit but decided to play it straight instead. 'Yes. She explained it like this. Clearwater's able to get inside people's heads and make them do things –'

'Sort of like post-hypnotic suggestion . . .'

'Yes. That kind of thing. She's done a number on Brickman. Nothing drastic. Fortunately, from the mental point of view, he's a tough nut to crack. But she's been able to create a conflict of interests. Roz says she needs to get as close as possible in order to blast away the emotional garbage that's clogging his brain. Being aboard Red River puts her close to the action but at the same time she remains totally secure.'

'I hope so. I'd hate for us to end up losing both of them.'

'No chance.' said Karlstrom. 'If it goes according to plan and Brickman does his stuff, our boys will be rolling home with all three lumps in the bag.' He rose to his feet and gave Jefferson a brief outline of the projected operation, pacing up and down as he did so.

The President-General listened intently. He also watched Karlstrom's hands. The incisiveness of his gestures was a measure of the confidence he had in whatever plan he was proposing. When the presentation was concluded, Jefferson swivelled his chair gently to the right and gazed out of the windows at the snow-covered peaks of the Rockies set against a cloud-flecked sky of the purest, deepest blue. The definition and colour fidelity of the computer-generated image projected on the huge curved screen was amazing. The next best thing to being there.

Karlstrom waited expectantly.

After several minutes of silent contemplation, during which time the P-G gnawed at, and closely inspected his left thumb, he returned to face his cousin. 'Sounds good, Ben. Let's go for it.'

CHAPTER NINE

As spring approached, and the snow melt filled the high rock gullies with cold, sparkling water, Mr Snow's thoughts turned once again to the fate of Cadillac and Clearwater and the cloud-warrior who had promised to rescue them. Despite the fact that no Mute had ever escaped from the Fire Pits of Beth-Lem he had no doubt that, one day, they would return. But would he be there to greet them?

Some time before his journey to the Eastern Lands, Cadillac had drawn images of his teacher's death from a seeing-stone. The event, news of which Mr Snow had accepted with as much good humour as he could muster, was to have taken place during The Yellowing of the previous year. But the season had come and gone and his old bones had weathered yet another winter. The White Death had begun to relinquish its icy grip on the land and here he was, alive and well – and with no plans to return to the place by the two rivers where the stone had been found.

Had Cadillac misread the images in the stone, or had he quite simply fixed upon the wrong year? Prior to the battle with the iron snake he had given ample proof of his powers as a seer but he was, nevertheless, still a relative novice. Both past and future events were recorded in the stones and it was often hard to tell which was which. But even when the seer recognized the shape of things to come, it was extremely difficult to establish, with any degree of accuracy, *when* a future event would take place.

The white-haired wordsmith did not fear death. The Path was drawn. The Wheel turned. When it was time to go to the High Ground he would leave the world content in the knowledge that his two pupils would survive the perils ahead until they fulfilled their joint destinies. What irked him was the thought of being removed from the scene just when things were beginning to get interesting.

Cadillac and Clearwater were the Sword and Shield of Talisman. The Sky Voices had made this clear on a number of occasions, and they had also spoken of Brickman, the cloud-warrior whose presence had been detected in the stones lying beneath the path of the iron snake. Brickman had an equally important part to play, along with the young female he thought of as his kin-sister.

These four, who had yet to discover their true relationship with one another, were The Chosen. That much he knew. But the precious gift of this knowledge did not ease his growing frustration at the lack of precision concerning the time and place of his own demise. In Cadillac's reading it had been linked with scenes of unparalleled carnage. Scenes which seemed to presage the total destruction of the clan. Some days later, when he and his two young charges had watched the cloud-warrior rise into the sky on blue-mirrored wings that glinted like sharp iron in the dawn rays of the sun, Cadillac had spoken more directly: 'the cloud-warrior would return in the guise of a friend with Death hiding in his shadow' and carry Clearwater away 'on a river of blood'.

Well, the cloud-warrior *had* returned in the guise of a friend and had offered to rescue Clearwater and Cadillac from the clutches of the Iron Masters. Since they had been chosen to prepare the way for Talisman, Mr Snow was convinced that they would be returned unharmed to the Plainfolk. But if Cadillac had got the date of his own teacher's death wrong by at least a year, perhaps he had misread everything else. The Great Dying – the bitter conflict which presaged the birth of Talisman and would demand massive sacrifices by the Plainfolk might prove even more costly to their enemies: the sand-burrowers and the dead-faces. The 'river of blood', for example, instead of flowing from the bodies of M'Call warriors, might spring from the veins of the Iron Masters when Cadillac, Clearwater and the cloud-warrior made their escape.

And what if Cadillac's words had been tainted by jealousy and unwarranted feelings of inadequacy? Brickman's return 'in the guise of a friend with Death hiding in his shadow' suggested he harboured murderous thoughts against those who had saved his life and made him welcome. But would he remain an enemy when he learned his true identity? Mr Snow planned to tell him upon his return – but when would that be?

Drawing his fur cloak closely around his body, Mr Snow laid a talking mat on one of his favourite rocks high above the settlement. Squatting down cross-legged, he turned his closed eyes upwards and directed his mind towards the spirit world beyond the sky. An hour later, his sole reward was a frozen backside. The Sky Voices, like all cosmic intelligences which have guided the faltering steps of humankind since the dawn of Creation only communicated what they wished to make known; they were not running a citizen's advice bureau.

Eleven hundred miles to the east, Carnegie-Hall, the word-smith of the Clan Kojak, and his allies on the council of elders were considering seeking advice from the same source in the hope of resolving the dilemma that now faced them.

The story of the 'Chosen Ones' was something that Carnegie had concocted based on the background information provided by the Iron Master, Izo Wantanabe. The dead-face, who spoke from behind a fearsome mask, had crossed the Great River to seek the aid of the Clan Kojak just after the first onslaught of the White Death. The deal they had struck involved a massive search operation well beyond the southern edge of the Kojak's turf for five 'travellers'. If found, they were to be lured into 'protective custody' with a well-nigh irresistible offer of food and shelter for the winter. And without arousing their suspicions, their departure was to be progressively delayed until early spring when Izo's masters would send a strong force of warriors to seize them.

If all were captured alive, the Kojak would be richly rewarded with tools, cloth and other materials, and powerful sharp iron. And the dead-face had left caged birds that were to be released at specific moments. Izo had given the word-smith short lengths of various coloured ribbons that were to be tied around one of the bird's legs before release. The colours represented various simple messages and Carnegie-Hall had already released one bearing a white ribbon, knotted in five places to indicate the number of 'travellers' that had fallen into their hands. A drop of blood placed on both sides of the fifth knot indicated that one of the 'travellers' Izo sought was badly injured.

It was with this detail that Carnegie's problems had begun for in his eagerness to make trade with the Iron Masters, and thereby gain an advantage over his neighbours, he had launched the plump messenger bird soon after his warriors had returned with the first pair of travellers but *before* he learned that his guests were a wordsmith and a summoner, plus a third whose powers were, as yet, unknown. Singly or jointly, in a terrifying demonstration of power, they had succeeded in destroying four arrowheads, and their two companions had sacrificed their lives, shattering the body of one of the feared iron snakes with sky-fire and earth-thunder.

Its forced withdrawal had increased the standing of the Clan Kojak in the eyes of its neighbours but it had given Carnegie-Hall little cause for satisfaction. The wordsmith now realized that the story he thought he had plucked out of the air had been placed on his lips by Talisman. By their actions, the three smooth-boned Mutes had proved beyond doubt they really *were* The Chosen and he was now faced with having to choose between two, equally unpleasant courses of action.

What was he to do? Should he conceal his lies behind an increasingly nervous smile and risk the wrath of Talisman? If The Chosen discovered they had been betrayed, the terrible power that Clearwater was able to summon could destroy not only him but the whole clan! The alternative was to throw himself on their mercy, confess all, and expose the clan to the murderous wrath of the Iron Masters when they landed in the spring and found that two of the five were dead and the other three had been allowed to escape!

Steve, Clearwater and Cadillac had also been pondering the future. Only in their case, it was not the metaphysical connection with Talisman that concerned them, but the simple down-to-earth mechanics of getting from A to B. The distances involved were enormous but what worried them most was the realization that the journey from Lake Michigan to the high plains of Wyoming would take them across an unknown number of hostile turfs, jealously defended by clans from the bloodlines of the D'Troit and C'Natti – sworn enemies of the She-Kargo.

'I don't know why you can't bring yourself to admit that I've come up with the ideal solution,' said Cadillac, when they met for the umpteenth time to discuss their next move. 'Even Clearwater agrees that it makes sense. We stay here until it's time for the Plainfolk to walk on the water, then we go north with the Kojak delegation to the trading post, join up with our own people – who'll probably be led by Mr Snow – and when it's all over, go home with them to Wyoming. The truce will cover us all the way. What could be simpler?'

'Nothing,' replied Steve. 'It's a brilliant idea. In fact, I wish I'd thought of it myself.'

'I wish you had,' grumped Cadillac. 'Because I would've agreed and that would've put an end to all these pointless arguments!'

'There's just one thing wrong with it. If we do it your way, it means hanging around until the end of May. Towards the end of the period you call the New Earth.'

'So . . .?'

'A lot can happen in three months.'

'Brickman. How many times do I have to tell you this. *Nothing* is going to happen to us.'

'So why wait? Why don't we just head on out and take whatever comes our way?'

Cadillac answered with a tired sigh. 'Because there's no point in tempting fate.' He raised a hand to silence Steve. 'Yes, I know what you're going to say, but my view on the importance of our role in the overall scheme of things are not rendered invalid by a desire to take sensible precautions.'

Steve turned to Clearwater. 'And this is the guy who accused me of being sinuous . . .'

'I'm not *being* sinuous. I'm merely stating a fact.'

'Of course. Okay. If there's any room inside that fat head of yours for any original ideas, hang on to this. Maybe the three of us *were* born in the shadow of Talisman – although why he should pick on me is something of a mystery – and maybe that explains why we've gotten this far. Perhaps we *have* been put here to accomplish something, but as far as I know, nobody's explained what that something is.

'The point is this. Here you are, strutting around thinking you're fireproof but has it occurred to you that we might have *already done* what was required of us? If so, what happens then? Do we become surplus to requirements? Does your big friend in the sky withdraw his protection?' Steve was deadly serious but it was worth it just to see Cadillac's face. Denting the Mute's new-found authority gave him great satisfaction. 'Think about that . . .'

'I will. But you just shot yourself in the foot. What you've just said is the best argument I've yet heard for taking the safest road home. Via the trading post. In three months' time.'

'We can't afford to wait that long.'

'I see. Despite your suggestion that we might no longer enjoy the protection of Talisman, you'd rather we throw caution to the winds and just . . . ride off into the sunset.'

'I'm aware of the risks,' said Steve. 'But it's not just us. If we don't act fast, a lot of other people could get hurt.'

Cadillac rolled his eyes. 'Is this going to take long?'

'That depends on whether you can keep your mouth shut.'

The Mute invited him to proceed.

'I can't stop worrying about that Jap boat we flew over,' said Steve. 'If he saw us we could be in trouble.'

'I don't see how, but no doubt you're going to tell me.'

'The Yama-Shita have the exclusive license to trade on the Great Lakes. Which means that boat was one of theirs. The two buildings I glimpsed on shore suggests it's a permanent mooring. I have no idea what they're up to but the Japs aren't going to put a unit that far out without some means of communication. My guess is it's either a link-boat or –'

'Carrier-pigeons . . .' Cadillac eyed Clearwater. 'So if they *did* see us –'

'– you can bet your last meat-twist that the news has reached Sara-kusa.'

The palace at Sara-kusa was the headquarters of the Yama-Shita family.

'But,' began Clearwater. 'Lord Yama-Shita is . . .'

'Dead. I know.' Steve laid a reassuring hand on her arm.

'But his family aren't. So what does that mean, Caddy? You're the one who got into the heads of these people.'

The question fuelled Cadillac's annoyance at Steve's constant opposition to his plans. 'They will seek revenge. But how does that affect us? You are just building on this wild supposition to try and get your own way! We are no longer in Ne-Issan and even if the crew of this boat saw us fly overhead, which I doubt, I can't see what would lead them to connect those aircraft with our escape from the Heron Pool. And even if by some miracle of deduction they did, it will get them absolutely nowhere!'

'Unless, of course, they happened to come across the wreckage we left on Highway 30. And whatever we might have left inside . . .'

'Okay. Assuming they had connected us with the Heron Pool, I admit the remains of those two Skyriders would tell them we're now moving on foot but they still have no way of knowing we are *here*.'

'Let's hope so. That's one good reason for not hanging around. And we'd be in even bigger trouble if we went to the trading post.'

'Why?!' cried Cadillac.

'Because there's going to be three wheelboats packed with red-stripes and samurai belonging to the Yama-Shita family! All armed to the teeth and looking to get even!'

'So what? They're not going to recognize us. For most of the time Clearwater and I were in Ne-Issan, we were clear-skinned.'

'But I wasn't!' cried Steve, pounding his chest. 'How many Mutes are there with blond hair?!'

'Then dye it!'

Steve exploded. 'Jeez, what a nitwit! D'you think that's all I'm worried about? They *know* you two are from the Clan M'Call! If they don't nail us beforehand, d'you think those Japs are gonna let your people walk away without a mark on them?! Christo! I saw 'em shoot four of their own guys just to demonstrate how good their fucking rifles were! For all we know, they may be planning to chop the M'Call trade delegation into little pieces!'

Cadillac hid his concern behind a scornful smile. 'Be serious, Brickman. The Old One's not going to allow anything like that to happen.'

'Terrific. Supposing he has an off-day?'

'Then the other delegations will come to our aid.'

'The She-Kargo clans, maybe. But what about those belonging to the D'Troit and the C'Natti. They'd be glad of the chance to jump on your bones. I was at the trading post last year. The wordsmiths hit it off, I grant you that, but a lot of their warriors were just spoiling for a fight. If the M'Calls and the rest of the She-Kargo were no longer allowed to trade, it would be to their advantage.

'You know what it's like. On the surface it's all smiles, but underneath it's dog eat dog. You guys are so busy trying to do each other down, the Japs score every time they do a deal. I know 'cos when I wasn't looking for you two, I watched 'em do business. In fact, it wouldn't surprise me if they got some of the bad hats from the D'Troit to stick the knife in for them.'

'Then that's all the more reason for us to go there. If the Old One's strength fails him, Clearwater will take his place. You saw what happened at the Heron Pool. She will do the same and more!'

'And what if she finds she can't? You've lost the gift of reading the stones. Supposing she suddenly discovers she can no longer make rocks jump into the air? What do we do then?'

Cadillac shrugged. 'We must accept the will of Talisman.'

'Not good enough. I want to be in a position to be able to do something about it.' He indicated Clearwater. 'You can't proceed on the assumption that she is going to come to the rescue every time we get into a tight corner.'

'Oh? Why not?'

'Because I'm not going to allow it!' cried Steve. 'Each time a summoner cuts loose he dies a little. I know because Mr Snow told me. Those forces are like a lethal charge. The damage to the summoner's body is directly related to the power channelled through them. When I picked her up after she had done her bit at the Heron Pool, it was like lifting a dried corn husk.' He looked into her eyes. 'You were unrecognizable. I thought you were going to die on me.'

'Yet here I am . . .'

'I know.' He gripped her hand. 'And you took on a small army and won. But I don't want you to have to go through that again – which is what might happen if we go to the trading post. From here on in, any plan of action we come up with has got to work without relying on earth magic. That's a bonus. Our ace in the hole.'

Cadillac laughed dismissively.

Steve rounded on him angrily. 'I mean that, friend. I'm not going to let you put us into a situation where she has to let her body be ripped to pieces inside just to save your miserable ass!'

Cadillac accepted this with a mocking bow. 'So much for the blood pledge of loyalty and friendship! But then, such things are meaningless to one who is not of the Plainfolk!' He squared up to Steve. 'It is not for you to say what will, or will not be. The Path is drawn and we must follow.'

His eyes rested briefly on Clearwater. 'Ask her. You may have entered her heart and soul but she has not surrendered her being because it is not hers to give. The Great Sky-Mother has placed it alongside mine in the hands of Talisman. And if he asks her to lay down her life she will do so. Willingly.'

This was followed by a pitying smile. 'But that is something a sand-burrower, who believes in nothing he cannot see, will never comprehend.'

'You're wrong, blood-brother. I'm tuned into a lot more of this stuff than you think. I'm hearing a lot of talk about sacrifice but what's missing is any expression of willingness on your part to lay down *your* life to save hers.'

'If you had known me for as long as I have known her,' said Cadillac, 'you would realize there is no need to declare what has always been understood from the moment she and I met as children.'

Ouch! thought Steve. I really walked into that one. He appealed to Clearwater for moral support. She responded with an expression of gentle forbearance; like a mother watching two much-loved children engaged in a pointless squabble.

'Come on, say something! You're the reason why I'm arguing with this goon! What do *you* think we ought to do?'

She turned to Cadillac. 'The cloud-warrior is right. We should head westwards as soon as the grass has swallowed the snow. We must warn the clan what might happen at the trading post *before* the Old One and the others leave.'

'It will give them a chance to decide whether or not to go to the trading post,' explained Steve. 'If they *do* go, then at least they'll be forewarned. They can beef up the delegation with more warriors – and alert the other She-Kargo Mutes as to what might happen.' He paused expectantly. 'What d'you say?'

Cadillac eyed them both like a man betrayed. 'Before I answer, I'd like to hear just how you plan to get to Wyoming without being challenged. What have you got up your sleeve – some pills to make us invisible? Come on, Brickman. Amaze us with your brilliance!'

Steve mastered the constantly-recurring desire to sink a fist into Cadillac's face. 'Don't worry, I'll come up with something.'

For Steve, the winter months spent with the Clan Kojak were probably the happiest of his life but also the most frustrating. He was grateful of the opportunity to consolidate his relationship with Clearwater, especially as it was now legitimized by Cadillac's unspoken assent, but no matter how agreeable your partner, a young man, especially one like Steve, cannot remain endlessly locked in a loving embrace. He needed to be up, needed to be doing something, but the heavy layer of snow that blanketed the ground from mid-November to the beginning of April seemed to have brought the world almost to a standstill. Almost, but not quite. Two or three times a week, weather permitting, small groups of Kojak braves went out hunting and Steve went with them, as a keep fit exercise and to familiarize himself with the lie of the land.

One of the more interesting discoveries he made was that not all Mutes were frightened by large expanses of water. This appeared to be a characteristic of clans like the M'Call, who roamed the high plains. The Kojak, living alongside Lake Michigan – part of what the Mutes called 'the Great River' – fished the inshore waters using primitive catamarans, narrow-hulled craft made of oiled buffalo skin stretched over a wooden frame. Lashed across the hull amidships were two curving saplings with shaped log floats attached to the ends to provide extra stability.

The boats, which usually held a crew of four, were propelled and steered by paddle power. The fish were caught on hooked lines, or in hand-woven nets dragged between two boats. If a large shoal of fish were encountered, several pairs of boats would work in unison, first surrounding the shoal then corralling it into a smaller and smaller area by overlapping their nets, drawing the noose ever tighter until the fish surfaced in one great wriggling, slithering mass. Those not entangled in the nets were speared out of the water and it was only the fish with enough sense to dive under the nets that escaped.

During the winter months, the Kojak boats were hauled up the beach, turned upside down, and securely anchored against the howling winds by piles of rocks. Old nets were repaired and new ones woven during the long hours of darkness spent huddled round firestones in their triangular tents. In extremely cold weather, a thick layer of ice formed round the edges of Lake Michigan, but even when it was ice free, the bitterly chill winds that drew thin jagged lines of foam across the steel-grey water and the lowering cloud-filled sky that seemed as if it was about to fall upon the earth and crush all life upon it was sufficient to keep the Kojak fishermen onshore.

When the trees' central heating system finally managed to shift the snow from their leaves and branches and the falling droplets pitted the stubborn white carpet beneath, it was time for the fishermen and their families to move their tents down to the shore. Sweeping the snow off their boat hulls, they set to work, checking seams and joints, replacing split timbers and waterproofing the buffalo hide with animal fat.

The fishing season ran from early spring to late autumn and provided enough fish to satisfy daily needs plus a surplus that was dried like the M'Call's meat-twists and consumed during the winter. Quantities of dried fish were also the Kojak's principal item of trade with the Iron Masters.

In the Old Time, the lake had been slowly poisoned, but the nine centuries that had passed since the last gallon of chemical waste was pumped had allowed the healing hand of Time to give the dying waters the kiss of life and they now provided plentiful catches for anyone with a net and the necessary persistence.

This was the other interesting fact that emerged from Steve's conversations with the boat-men; 'the Great River' was regarded as no-man's land by the clans whose turf bordered Lake Michigan. In practical terms, it meant that boats from otherwise hostile clans often fished in sight of each other without the crews feeling the need to cut each other's throats.

At the time, Steve merely stored this along with everything else he had learnt about the Kojak. It was only later, after Cadillac made his own startling discovery, that this sidelight on the *mores* of Mute fisher-folk provided him with the germ of an idea.

The breakthrough quite unexpectedly came when Steve and Clearwater coaxed Cadillac to come down to the lakeshore to watch the activities of the boat-men. As a true high-plains Mute, Cadillac did not regard fishing as a fitting activity for a *real* warrior – although he was careful to conceal his feelings from his hosts – and he could not understand what there was to be gained by gazing out across dauntingly large expanses of cold water.

Clearwater was less worried with the matter of 'standing' than he was, but with her own journey across the Great River still fresh in her memory, she shared his antipathy towards the grey, fathomless deeps. She was there at Steve's request, and it was also to please him that she had persuaded Cadillac to cut short one of his interminable conversations with the Kojak wordsmith and join them. Like the mule he was, he evinced little interest in the activities of the fisherfolk, turned down the opportunity to go out and work with the nets, and only perked up interest when fires were lit on the beach at sunset and he was offered a warm seat and a piping hot portion from the day's catch – which Steve had helped bring in.

As they ate, the darkness gathered round them, and the leaping flames from the fire tinted the paler parts of their faces with an orange glow. Steve, sitting between two of the boat-men who had invited him to join their crew, looked across at Clearwater. She'd made sure Cadillac stayed onshore till he returned, and they were sitting together now. Her eyes were on Cadillac. But he had stopped eating, and was turned away from her, staring at something on the beach some yards beyond the chattering group of fisherfolk. Steve looked in the same direction but saw nothing of any interest in the flickering circle of light, or in the shadows beyond.

Cadillac rose and walked off into the darkness. Clearwater's eyes met Steve's, signalling him to follow. The boat-men and their women continued eating and jesting. There were several similar fire-circles and ever since cooking had begun, people had been wandering to and fro from one group to another.

Some fifteen yards beyond the light cast from the fire, Steve saw Cadillac kneel down and lay his hands reverently upon a large pebble. He squatted down beside him. After slowly caressing the stone for a while, Cadillac lifted it gently onto his knees.

'What is it?'

'A seeing-stone,' breathed Cadillac. 'Do you not see how it glows! The gift has been returned to me!'

All Steve could see was a smooth lump of rock the size of a baby's head. He looked up as Clearwater joined them. He could see from her face that she knew the whole story.

'Not here,' she said. She ushered Steve and Cadillac behind the upturned hull of a nearby boat where they were shielded from the Mutes sitting round the fire. 'For the moment it is better that this gift is known only to us.'

'What happens now?' whispered Steve as they sat down facing each other.

Clearwater motioned him to remain silent.

Cadillac closed his eyes and appeared to go into a trance. His head dropped forward then a short while later he raised it and, at the same time, lifted the seeing-stone in his cupped hands and placed it against his forehead.

'He draws out the images,' whispered Clearwater.

Steve held his breath.

Keeping his head erect, Cadillac brought the stone back to its starting point on his knees. His eyes were closed but his attention was focused on something that only he could see on the great expanse of water behind Steve and Clearwater.

'Red sky . . . blood and fire upon the water . . . horses rising from the waves . . . ridden by dead warriors . . . with banners of flame . . .'

Dead warriors . . . or dead-faces . . .?

Clearwater reached forward and touched the stone that lay in Cadillac's hands. 'Where do these warriors come from?'

'The Eastern Lands . . . Ne-Issan . . .'

It was just as Steve feared. He'd been right all along.

Clearwater posed the question on his lips. 'Do they seek us?'

'Yes . . .'

'When will they come?'

'Soon . . . they know we are here . . .'

'How?' asked Steve.

'Treachery . . . some who smile upon us are false friends . . .'

Steve looked at Clearwater and nodded. 'Snap.' He could tell, without asking, that they both knew who the culprit was.

Over the next five days they each kept a discreet watch on Carnegie-Hall, noting his movements, and timing his journeys with the aid of the digital watches taken from the two mexicans at Long Point. Whenever possible, they tailed him at a safe distance, often losing him in the process. Despite this, a pattern began to emerge. In general, Carnegie acted quite naturally and was apparently unaware he was under surveillance but there was one moment, early in the morning of every second day, when he appeared to exercise a degree of caution.

This was a thirty minute journey which took him into the woods surrounding the settlement. The route he took meandered aimlessly through the concentric rings of lodges. On each occasion he entered and exited from the trees at different points but always returned to his own lodge by a much more direct route, stopping now and then to exchange a word with various clanfolk as they emerged from their lodges to greet the rising sun and take in huge yawning mouthfuls of fresh air.

The next day, while Cadillac kept Carnegie-Hall occupied by a marathon 'down memory lane' session in which they took turns to relate great chunks of their respective clans' history, Steve and Clearwater moved stealthily into different segments of the woods, timing their journey to determine the limit of the wordsmith's outward journey. Once his 'combat radius' had been established they spread out in a line and slowly combed the perimeter until they found – or rather heard – what they were looking for.

Rising well before dawn on the seventh day, they tiptoed through the staggered pattern of lodges and entered the hide they had prepared. It had been agreed that Cadillac should stay behind to exchange his usual morning greetings with Carnegie-Hall so as not to arouse his suspicions, then join them after the trap had been sprung.

Sure enough, Carnegie-Hall appeared, moving silently along a cunningly disguised path through the tangled undergrowth. He stopped only yards away from where Steve and Clearwater lay hidden. They watched with bated breath as he parted the branches of a tall bush covered with forever leaves, revealing a portable woven bamboo and straw pigeon-basket – identical to the type Iron Masters used for carrying small numbers of birds to market.

Answering the soft cooing of the birds, Carnegie opened a feeding flap then fished a small sack of grain from the inside pocket of his fur cloak. The sack, like the basket, had been made in Ne-Issan.

Clearwater brought her palms together silently in front of her lips and uttered one of the trilling bird cries that the M'Call She-Wolves used to communicate with each other.

The cry evoked a similar response followed by the sound of someone crashing through the undergrowth. Carnegie-Hall whirled around. The initial surprise on his face turned to utter dismay as Steve and Clearwater revealed their presence. Cadillac arrived a few moments later.

The wordsmith wavered, as if about to run then froze as he saw the warning flare in her ice-blue eyes and the outflung arms whose linked fingers now pointed at his chest. Fingers that could unleash a force greater than the striking power of a thousand cross-bow bolts. The bag of grain dropped from his trembling fingers but he made to attempt to retrieve it. His treachery now exposed, Carnegie had no wish to test the forebearance of Talisman by making any move that could be misinterpreted as a foolhardy gesture of defiance or – more foolish still – the prelude to an assault on his accusers.

As Steve inspected the contents of the pigeon basket, Cadillac assumed his severest expression and gazed reproachfully at its keeper. The wordsmith, in return, attempted to look suitably contrite whilst retaining some vestige of his former dignity. It was a delicate situation. Carnegie-Hall was older – and therefore took precedence over younger colleagues, he also bulked much larger than Cadillac and despite everything, had been a genial host.

But, on the other hand, Carnegie had betrayed the trust of those to whom he had offered shelter. Such hospitality was not unknown but it was not often extended to members of another clan, and even more rarely to those from another bloodline. But the rigid code of the Plainfolk to which most clans subscribed did not permit treachery. If a clan harboured ill-intent against those seeking shelter then it drove them away or quite simply killed them. But if like the Kojak it received them into their fire-circle and lodges then custom required the host clan to treat them as soul-brothers and sisters.

To do otherwise would be to act without honour, causing the guilty parties to lose all standing. A fate worse than the death that would surely follow. It went without saying that the recipients of such hospitality were expected to observe the same strict rules of behaviour.

'How many?' asked Cadillac.

'Two . . .' Steve closed the feeding flap and prised the basket loose from its hiding place among the branches. He placed it at the wordsmith's feet.

Carnegie-Hall eyed Clearwater's outstretched forefingers. They were still pressed together and aimed at his chest like the barrels of the fearsome rifles he had seen demonstrated by the Iron Masters at the trading post. Yes . . . he should have known better than to mess with The Chosen Ones. So severe! So unsmiling! If this was a taste of what was to come, he was glad that Mo-Town, the Great Sky-Mother had not saddled him with some lofty destiny. Oh, well, you win some you lose some . . .

Ignoring the damning evidence at his feet, he spread his

hands philosophically and tried to disarm his principal accuser with a smile. 'What can I tell you . . .?'

Steve got there first. 'Everything.'

Back in the lodge he shared with Clearwater, Steve gazed at the pigeon-basket and mulled over Carnegie-Hall's disclosures. One of the birds, carrying a ribbon to indicate that the 'travellers' were still 'in custody', was due to be released when the snow melted; the second was to be held in reserve in case something unexpected happened.

The basket lay between him and Cadillac. Clearwater sat cross-legged in the open doorway with her back to them so she could see what was happening outside. Having freely confessed everything, Carnegie-Hall had begged for and received forgiveness but it was by no means certain that he, and the clan elders could be trusted. On the other hand, having listened to his side of the story, Cadillac and Steve could not bring themselves to condemn him out of hand. In the final analysis, they too had been guilty of a little mild deception.

'I think we should send the message the Japs are waiting for.'

'Why?' asked Cadillac.

'Because they're going to help us get to Wyoming.'

Cadillac looked puzzled. 'Wait a minute. I thought you wanted to avoid them. Wasn't that what all the fuss was about?'

'Yeah. But something you said when we were arguing has given me an idea. You talked about riding off into the sunset.'

'And . . .?'

'That's how we're going to get to Wyoming. On horseback.'

'On horseback . . .' Cadillac could hardly believe what he was hearing. 'You want us to stay here and take on a whole boatload of samurai *just* to get hold of three horses . . .'

'More than three. As many as we can get.'

Cadillac caught Clearwater's eye. 'You see what happens when people mess about with boats? Their brains become waterlogged!'

'Listen!' cried Steve. 'They already know we're here. They may even decide to pay us a visit even if the pigeon Carnegie-

Hall's supposed to send *doesn't* arrive. For all they know the birds could have died of cold or got eaten or something.'

'In that case, we should stick to your original plan and leave today!'

'We can't do that either.'

'Sweet Sky-Mother, why not?' cried Cadillac.

'Well, we just can't pull out and leave these guys to get it in the neck. If it hadn't been for them, we'd never have made it though the winter.'

'What are you talking about?! They were just fattening us up for the kill!'

'Oh, come on! Show a little gratitude. That may have been their original intention but that's not the way it worked out. Carnegie-Hall explained all that. If you're supposed to help unite the Plainfolk, shouldn't you start by displaying some solidarity yourself?'

'If you say so.' Cadillac eyed Steve warily. 'I didn't realize you had such a forgiving nature.'

'A tactical decision. With a boatload of Japs on their way, we don't need these guys on our backs. We want them fighting alongside us.'

'I agree, but can they be trusted?'

'Trust doesn't enter into it. You saw Carnegie's reaction to Clearwater. They're scared shitless at what might happen if she decides to cut loose. This clan hasn't raised a summoner in over two decades but they know one when they see one. Don't worry. All she has to do is flash those eyes of hers and they'll fall into line.'

'You're kidding yourself, Brickman. The only thing we can be sure of is they'll stand back then join the winning side. You heard what Carnegie said. He's willing to commit the clan to an attack on the Iron Masters *provided it doesn't fail.*'

'Yeah. There must be no survivors – because that could mean a second punitive expedition. That's not unreasonable. What I understood him to say was that the clan would offer us every assistance but we had to come up with a plan of attack which – if it *did* go wrong – would not implicate the Kojaks.'

'In other words, we have to do all the hard work.'

'Caddy, these guys are living on the front line. The nearest

Iron Masters are only eighty miles away. *We're* the reason why those Japs are coming.'

Cadillac banged his fists on his thighs. 'But they wouldn't be coming if the Kojak hadn't betrayed us!'

Steve motioned him to stay calm. 'Water under the bridge. If you're honest, you'll admit we're as much to blame as they are.'

'So what d'you suggest we do?'

'You've already supplied the answer.'

'What are you talking about?'

'Your reading of the stone. 'Blood and fire upon the sea . . .' We get on board the Jap wheelboat and set fire to it as it approaches the western shore.'

'Just like that . . .'

'Yeah,' said Steve, warming up. 'We blow a hole in the bottom. It starts to sink . . . the Japs abandon ship . . . men and horses swim for the shore and . . . the Kojak pick 'em off with crossbow bolts on the way in . . . or as they come out of the shallows and up onto the beach. What d'you think?'

Cadillac's face turned sour. 'Brilliant. But aren't you over-looking something? We don't know when the wheelboat is coming and even if we did, how do we get on board *before* they get here?'

'Don't worry, we'll figure something out. It's a pity you used up our last three wads of explosive. Never mind . . . we'll have to make do with whatever material we can find when we get on board.'

'You're crazy . . .'

'No – listen. If it's a big wheelboat it'll have cannon mounted in the side galleries. So they'll be carrying black powder. And they're bound to have some rockets –'

'You hope . . .'

Steve didn't react. He could see it all. 'We can arrange a firework display inside the ship to create a diversion, then we'll use the black powder to put the boiler through the roof and set fire to the log store –'

'And we finish her off by blowing a hole in the bottom of the hull . . .' The note of sarcasm failed to register.

'Yeah. When I came to get you, I stowed away in the

221

engine room so I know the general layout. With the boiler gone, she's a sitting duck, and even if they put the fire out –'

'She'll still sink . . . Yes. I must say you make it all sound very easy but somehow, I don't think it's going to be that simple.'

'Well – it's obviously going to take some time to set up.'

'Exactly. And time is what we haven't got. It's what – eighty miles from here to the mooring at Benton Harbour?'

'Could be a little bit more.'

'And what's the speed of the wheelboat? Ten miles an hour?'

'Depends on the weather. If there's a headwind –'

'Okay, let's say eight. That gives us ten hours. I assume that you and I will be working together on this . . .?'

'That was the general idea.'

'Good. We know from the stone that the boat will arrive under cover of darkness. The best time for a surprise attack which, I imagine, will probably be launched at dawn.'

'That's what I'm banking on. But we may have more than ten hours. Depends on how slow the boat is.'

'Doesn't make any difference. The days are getting longer. If the Japs don't come for several weeks, we may not have even *ten* hours of darkness! Or are you planning for us to wreck this boat in broad daylight!'

'No. But when you get right inside the ship it's much darker.'

'I'll have to take your word for that. But okay, let's assume we *do* have ten hours of darkness. Apart from the problem of getting on board, we have to find our way around the ship, locate the powder room and the rocket store, break in, steal what we want without the theft being detected, plant the charges and get the hell out without being caught. Tell me – what are the Japs doing all this time? Standing watching us, with their arms folded?!'

Steve exploded. 'For chrissakes, Caddy! I said it could work! I didn't say it was gonna be easy!'

Cadillac shook his head. 'We're going to have to think of something else, Brickman. It's a great idea, but it's just too difficult.'

'Difficult? It's fucking impossible! But we're going to do it anyway.'

'How?'

'Don't ask me how! I don't know yet! I just know *that's* the way it's going to happen! Maybe not quite the way I've explained it but we're gonna sink that boat! And you wanna know *how* I know? Because when you were drawing those images out of the stone, I started seeing pictures inside my head.' He paused. 'D'you know what I saw? You. On that boat. And I was right there with you, in this cabin – with water comin' up through the floor.'

Cadillac appeared to take this revelation seriously. 'Is this true?'

'I kid you not, blood-brother.'

'Did we escape?'

Steve shrugged. 'Can't tell you. We're gonna have to wait and see.'

After another day spent offshore, hauling in nets, Steve found the solution to the seemingly intractable problem of intercepting the Iron Masters' wheelboat. It was so obvious, he felt like kicking himself for not thinking of it before. He was so excited he leapt out of the boat as it ran ashore and didn't wait for the firelight fish supper he'd earned for himself and Clearwater.

Taking her aside, he quickly explained the plan he'd worked out. Still bubbling over with enthusiasm at his own cleverness, and without asking for her reaction, he ran off inland towards the main settlement, calling upon her to follow.

Clearwater caught up with him, matching him stride for stride as he settled down into the loping pace that Mutes were able to maintain, if need be, for twelve hours at a stretch. Steve had never had occasion to test his endurance for that length of time but he had been pleased to discover that, with training, he could keep up with the M'Call warriors who had allowed him the unprecedented honour of running with them on hunting trips.

Prizing Cadillac loose from the serpentine embrace of his three over-hospitable bed-mates, Steve silenced his protests and marched him over to where Clearwater sat waiting in front of the lodge they shared. She had already put wood on the firestone, and the flames were bright enough for them to read the plasfilm map she held out to Steve. He sat down on one of the spare talking mats.

Cadillac sat down on his left, opposite Clearwater, completing the triangle. He eyed them both with an aggrieved expression. 'This had better be good . . .'

'It's brilliant. Right?' Steve looked to Clearwater for confirmation as he refolded the map to expose the section he wanted.

'That depends on whether you like boats.'

Steve twisted the map round for Cadillac to read the right way up and pointed out navref Chicago. 'Okay . . . this is where *we* are and the Jap boat Clearwater and I saw . . .' His finger moved across to Benton Harbour. '. . . was somewhere around here.

'Carnegie got a good look at the boat when the man in the iron mask called here to set up the deal to capture us and from the description he gave me I reckon it's the same one. He reckons there were twenty, maybe twenty-five people on board, including some women and children – plus whoever they left behind to guard the mooring. Judging from the size of the boat, he doubts it could be more than fifty, all told. You mentioned seeing fire on the water. Did you get any clear images of the boat?'

'Only that it was huge – like those at the trading post.'

'That squares with the inside view I got. The cabin we were in was like the one Side-Winder had, forward of the engine room. Which makes sense. If these guys at Benton Harbour were going to try anything, they'd have been here long ago.

'No. After what happened at the Heron Pool, they'll be coming in strength. Not just for us, but to cover themselves in case the Kojak have a last-minute change of heart. The Japs'd be crazy to land a pint-sized force on the turf of a clan that can field close to a thousand warriors. But before they drop in on us, they'll call in here first.' Steve indicated navref Benton Harbour. ''Cos these guys are the only ones who know exactly where we are . . .'

'And *that's* when we climb aboard . . .'

'Yeah. What d'you think?'

'Well, so far, not a great deal. I'd already worked out that bit by myself. Apart from the problem of getting there, we still don't know *when* the wheelboat is going to arrive.'

'You're right. We're just gonna have to wait there until she shows up.'

'At Benton Harbour . . .'

'Or thereabouts. If we're going to do it, we ought to leave in the next couple of days.'

'I see . . .' Cadillac had good cause to be wary of Steve's steam-roller tactics. 'Suppose this wheelboat doesn't turn up for weeks. What do you propose to do – ask these Japs at Benton Harbour to give us board and lodging?'

'No. You and I are going fishing.'

'Fishing . . .' Cadillac exchanged glances with Clearwater then said: 'But neither of us know how.'

'We will by the time we get there. A couple of Kojak boatmen will be coming along to show us the ropes.'

'And Clearwater?'

'I'll be staying here,' she said.

'As a hostage?'

'No. As our last line of defence. If we don't manage to sink the wheelboat –' Steve left the rest unsaid.

'So you're not *totally* opposed to using earth magic,' said Cadillac mockingly.

'That's up to her. But if she chooses to do so, it will only be after you and I have tried everything else – and failed.'

Cadillac turned to Clearwater. 'And I suppose you agree . . .'

'I would prefer to come with you, but otherwise yes. Can you think of a better way?'

Cadillac met her challenging look then turned his attention back to the map. 'I have no qualms about embarking on a suicide mission – I just object to dying before we get a chance to engage the enemy. These ramshackle constructions the Kojaks use are not designed to cross an expanse of water like this.'

'We're not going across,' said Steve. 'We're gonna go round the edge.' With the aid of the map, he explained the plan to his unwilling shipmate. They would work their way around the curving southern shore of the lake, staying in deep water but keeping in sight of the shore.

As weather protection, skins and furs would be draped over a wooden frame to create a dry space in which they would take turns to sleep. Steve also proposed adding a mast and sail, like the small Iron Master boats they had seen on the Hudson River. The sail would be made by sewing several talking mats together. The rectangular mats, made of woven straw, were one of the items bartered by the Japs at the trading post.

For food, Steve proposed to take a supply of dried fish, to be supplemented with whatever they managed to catch on the way. This would have to be done by trailing lines over the side because his intention was to keep moving day and night. They would take the nets as proof they were simple fisherfolk but these would only be used if their passage round the shore aroused the suspicion of other lake-dwellers.

Once they were at Benton Harbour, they would station themselves off-shore then, having carefully spied out the land with the aid of their 'scopes, they would cast their nets then approach the mooring and try to sell the Japs some of their catch.

This, explained Steve, was where Cadillac's special gifts came into play. If this ruse could be repeated, Cadillac could use his command of the Japanese language to eavesdrop on the crew's conversation in the hope of picking up some indication of when the wheelboat carrying the punitive expedition was expected to arrive. By the time it appeared on the horizon, they would, with luck, have become a familiar sight and would be able to stay close by when it dropped anchor without arousing suspicion.

Once having inspected their prey, it would be a relatively easy matter to get on board – a feat Steve had already accomplished the previous year. Their first hiding place would be on top of the piles of logs stacked around the engine room. From there on in, they would have to play it by ear. 'Okay, that's the plan as far as it goes. Now pick holes in it.'

Cadillac stared into the fire and considered Steve's proposals. The idea of spending just one day rocking back and forth in one of the Kojak's frail fishing boats was awful enough; the prospect of being trapped on board for several weeks didn't bear thinking about. But he was obliged to put on a brave face in order not to lose the initiative. Although flawed, the plan had much to recommend it for once they got aboard, everything hinged on his linguistic skills – and that would put him back in the driving seat . . .

It was time to redress the balance. 'Has it occurred to you that there might already be a clan of boat-men living near Benton Harbour? If they're already trading with the Japs, they might get a little upset if we try to horn in.'

Steve shrugged off the objection. 'We'll tell 'em we lost our way. Winds blew us off course.'

'Okay, suppose they offer to show us the way back?'

'That's something we'll have to work out when we get there. Come on, Caddy. The Japs may have chosen that spot precisely because there *wasn't* anyone in the neighbourhood.'

'They might have. Suppose they aren't interested in trading with us. The Japs are pretty good fishermen themselves.'

'There's no harm in asking. Christo! We've got to take a *few* chances! When I said pick holes in the plan, I meant major flaws. The points you're raising are piddleshit!'

'I've only just started. But, okay, I'll give you one major flaw. Using a sail of straw matting. The Kojaks haven't developed sails which, if you think about it, means that none of their neighbours have either. The wheelboats that visit the trading post are propelled by steam-powered paddles. The only place a Mute could have seen boats with square-cut sails made of woven straw is Ne-Issan. If I was the captain of that Jap boat at Benton Harbour and I saw some Mutes come sailing in I'd be a bit suspicious, wouldn't you?'

Steve's eyes narrowed as he ran through the scenario. 'Good point . . . I'm glad you thought of that.'

'I've got another idea which might work better than trying to unload a pile of unwanted fish.'

'Okay, let's have it.'

'Instead of sending that pigeon the Japs are waiting for, why don't *we* carry the message instead?'

'You mean from Carnegie-Hall?'

'Yes. We take the two pigeons back alive and the remaining ribbons to establish our bonafides –'

'And confirm that the Kojak are still holding the five travellers . . .'

'And that the one who was wounded is making a recovery.'

'I like it,' said Steve, warming to the idea. 'And we can give 'em a crash helmet and a couple of the spare handguns as a little taster.'

'Good idea. But here's the best bit.' Cadillac paused, relishing the moment. 'We explain to the Japs that – for some reason we'll invent later – the clan has moved its settlement further inland and we've been sent as guides to lead the Iron Masters onto their quarry. Which means that our two crewmen can paddle off home and . . . we get a free ride on the wheelboat –'

'Until which time, we're guests of the Jappos – and have the free run of Benton Harbour . . .'

'And Clearwater will know in advance that we're in position and, maybe – if we get a lucky break – when the wheelboat is due.'

Steve saw it all in glorious videocolour. Even if they rode below decks, they would not be travelling as stowaways. They would be right at the heart of the action, with Cadillac able to eavesdrop on everyone within earshot. Steve hid his annoyance at being upstaged once again, 'Not bad,' he admitted.

'Not bad?' exclaimed Cadillac, mimicking his rival. 'It's absolutely fucking brilliant!'

Clearwater hugged them excitedly. They both slid an arm around her waist and closed the circle by gripping each others' wrists. Like true soul-brothers . . .

CHAPTER TEN

Despite some squalls en route which left the outrigger ankle deep in water, the trip from navref Chicago to Benton Harbour was accomplished without any major incidents. Boats from other clans had been sighted, but on each occasion, as Steve predicted, they were able to pass unchallenged.

The first half of the voyage had been made with the help of a mast and a sail hoisted on a primitive yard-arm; the remaining stretch was covered by paddle-power alone. It was a punishing exercise. For a while it felt as if their arms were being torn loose from their shoulders but their tough, young bodies were able to take the strain.

The hardest thing to cope with was the motion sickness. Steve felt queasy for the first couple of days but managed to arrive in reasonably good shape; Cadillac, on the other hand, spent most of the trip with his head hanging over the side. What little food he ate was regurgitated as soon as it reached his stomach, but even when his digestive tubes had been emptied, he continued to groan and heave in such an alarming fashion, his shipmates began to think he was trying to turn himself inside out.

Worried by the impression they might make if Cadillac – a supposed representative of a clan of hardy fisher-folk – staggered ashore pallid and weak-kneed, Steve persuaded the Kojak boatmen – Raging-Bull and Death-Wish – to beach their boat overnight south of navref Benton Harbour before presenting themselves to the Japs. The break allowed Cadillac to consume hot food and drink and gave his stomach time to digest it while he slept soundly for several hours on terra firma.

At dawn, they put to sea with the rising sun on their backs then circled round to approach the out-station from the south-west – a manoeuvre designed to give the Iron Masters the impression they had crossed Lake Mi-shiga without making landfall. The sea which had churned their stomachs during the previous four days was either mercifully calm or ominously flat depending on the degree of optimism with which each member of the intrepid quartet viewed the next crucial stage of the operation.

Raging-Bull and Death-Wish had been instructed to convey Steve and Cadillac to their chosen destination then return home, bearing news of their safe arrival and any additional message they were given. Neither of the boatmen knew of the plan to sink the wheelboat. This was not because of lack of trust – the two Kojaks had already taken a big risk delivering them to Benton Harbour. It was a simple safety precaution in case things went seriously wrong. The less they knew, the better it was for everybody concerned.

Izo Wantanabe, the pint-sized pipsqueak in charge of the 30-strong unit at Benton Harbour came ashore to meet them without his mask and after the usual bowing that characterized the face-to-face encounters between Mutes and Iron Masters at the trading posts, the Jap listened civilly while they relayed Carnegie-Hall's message then presented him with the remaining lengths of coloured ribbon and the two caged pigeons. Wantanabe appeared to accept their story at face value but his unchanging expression gave no clue to what he was thinking. It was only when they unwrapped the two Tracker hand-guns, and one of the crash-helmets taken from the AMEXICO pilots at Long Point that his interest quickened. One of the guns had an empty magazine, but when Wantanabe pressed the trigger, an explosive blast of air shot from the muzzle. *CHU-wii-CHU-wii-CHU-wii!!*

Hawwwwwww!

The Jap was taken by surprise, but fortunately he held onto the gun and covered his confusion by laughing loudly as Steve and Cadillac leapt into the air with expressions of mock terror. The watching soldiers men joined in the laughter at the exaggerated antics of the grass-monkeys, neatly avoiding a loss of face.

Taking care not to appear too knowledgeable, Cadillac explained that the second gun still contained 'long sharp iron' which was thrown through the air by a fierce wind demon imprisoned in a bottle concealed in the part Wantanabe held in his hand. After firing one triple volley into the water, the Jap watched his sergeant fire several more then pronounced himself satisfied. His approach to the the hi-tech crash helmet was more revealing and reminded Steve of the way Noburo Nakajima, the tough but amiable leader of the *ronin* had shied away from the inner workings of the radio-knife.

Wantanabe could see it was a warrior's helmet of some kind but he also knew – as he had known when he surveyed the interior of the winged chariot – that the polished, bone-hard blue plastic shell with its soft padded lining, silvered visor, earphones, filters, mike and jack plug sockets were unknown forms from an alien world where the Dark Light held sway. Guns were one thing, but this was bad news.

Steve watched with quiet amusement as Cadillac offered the helmet for examination, turning it this way and that as Wantanabe directed. But the guy wouldn't touch it. After he'd given it the once-over, he told Cadillac to wrap it up again then ordered his sergeant to take charge of it. The soldier produced his *kubibukoro* – the bag used for carrying the severed head of an enemy. Cadillac placed the wrapped helmet inside, leaving the sergeant looking as happy as someone holding a timebomb with ten seconds on the clock.

After thanking them in a rather stilted fashion, Wantanabe returned to the houseboat. Having listened in while Wantanabe gave orders concerning them, Cadillac already knew what was coming next but he nevertheless listened respectfully as the sergeant announced they would be provided with food and shelter.

The food turned out to be strips of raw fish and boiled rice; the shelter was a corner of the wooden hay-barn next door to where a small number of horses were stabled. A cluster of small shacks – accommodation units with raised floors – were under construction nearby. When Steve had passed overhead in November only the stable and the barn had been in place. This new onshore expansion was a clear sign that the Japs were settling in. Were they just building a bigger shop window – or staking a claim to the territory?

The plan had been for the Kojak boatmen to rest up for two or three days during which time Cadillac would eavesdrop on the Japs in the hope of picking up some indication of when the wheelboat was due. Rumours were plentiful but there was no hard intelligence. Cadillac did however glean a certain amount of anecdotal information. The sea-soldiers, he discovered, regarded Benton Harbour as the asshole of the world and were equally uncharitable about their boss. Despite his appearance, his faultless command of Japanese and upper-class diction Wantanabe was known as 'The Chink', and his Chinese wife had been dubbed 'The Yellow Peril'.

Yumiko, by all accounts, was a pushy hard-faced bitch who was even more ambitious than Izo Wantanabe. And that, apparently, was saying something. On the few occasions that Steve caught a glimpse of her bland oval face and submissive public stance in the presence of her husband, he found it hard to fit the image to the reputation but as he knew only too well, appearances could be deceptive.

Within an hour of their arrival, Steve caught sight of Wantanabe releasing a carrier-pigeon from the bridge of the wheelboat. The bird flew several wide circles around the out-station, rising higher and higher with each revolution then headed north-eastwards.

Steve was certain the message referred to the continued detention of five 'travellers' by Kojak but he wondered who it was addressed to. Despite the death of Lord Yama-Shita, his family were not only still in business, they were expanding their trading empire. The decision to establish out-stations had been taken long before his own arrival in Ne-Issan. Steve, of course, could not be expected to know that, or have any inkling of the whirlwind of retribution he and his four collegues had unleashed by destroying the Heron Pool.

But his gut feeling that the family would seek to get even had proved to be correct. The identity of the person who had taken over the reins of power was, in the present circumstances, of marginal importance. The real question was no longer 'Did they intend to get even?' but 'When?'

Five days later, the news he and Cadillac had been waiting for came home to roost. Through his sergeant, Wantanabe had given them permission to keep themselves occupied with some inshore fishing provided they did not stray too far from the houseboat. His master, explained the sergeant, did not want the waves to swallow the men on whom so much depended. Which was fine by Steve. Staying close at hand was the whole point of the exercise.

Cadillac was the first to spot the incoming bird. He and Steve rapidly hauled in the fishing lines then, assisted by powerful strokes of the Kojak boatmen, they paddled silently but swiftly towards the houseboat. Steve had already observed that Wantanabe and his family occupied the forward part of the deckhouse immediately below the bridge and that on warm days, the sliding wall panels on the southward-facing port side were left open to let in the spring sun.

As they approached, they caught sight of Wantanabe entering the pigeon coop atop of the rear deckhouse. Cadillac signalled the others to bring the outrigger to a halt. Moving their paddles in and out of the water to avoid attracting attention to themselves, they drifted to and fro until Wantanabe emerged from the coop and hurried back to his quarters.

Cadillac directed them to move forward again. Using his paddle as a rudder, the Kojak boatman in the stern eased the outrigger alongside the houseboat until the left-hand float was only inches away from the hull.

To anyone watching their movements onshore, the occupants of the Mute vessel appeared to be letting it drift up to the beach while two of them gazed up in wonderment at the houseboat. As well they might, for the superb fit of the timbers and the details of its design and construction underlined the unbridgeable gulf between its makers and the primitive society whose best efforts was this four-seat ramshackle tub which had all the grace of a floating pig-trough – and smelt like one too.

It was no easy task to block out all the background noise and chatter and listen at the same time to the conversation taking place immediately above them. Cadillac heard a strangled cry of excitement followed by a muttered exchange between Wantanabe and a second person with a higher-pitched voice – probably that of his wife, Yumiko. The thump of swaggering footsteps, then Wantanabe's voice again, this time loud and clear, summoning Kurabashi, the sergeant-at-arms.

Cadillac sat down and picked up his paddle as Kurabashi, a square-cut man with a face that looked as it had been hewn from weathered ship timber, came thudding along the deck and entered through the open screens without noticing the outrigger parked directly below. Cadillac stood up again. This time, as Wantanabe raised his voice and adopted a more official mode of address, he was able to hear everything. The wheel-boat captained by Ryuku Kawanishi would arrive at Bei-tanaba in ten days time, carrying a raiding party under the command of Samurai-Major Morita.

This second name sounded vaguely familiar but Cadillac was unable to place it. He carried on listening as Wantanabe told Kuribashi the numbers and types of soldiers involved. As he stood with one ear craned upwards, a small boy-child clad in a padded cotton jacket and trousers toddled to the rail and stared down at him.

The boy was quickly joined by a girl, about five or six years old. She put one hand on her brother's shoulder to prevent him falling through and spoke to him in Japanese. 'Look!' she cried, pointing at Cadillac. 'Monkey! Monkey! Poo! Smelly! Say "Go away, nasty monkey!"'

The boy-child imitated her aggressive clenched-fist gesture.

A second later, Wantanabe and the sergeant appeared at the rail behind the children. Neither had the slightest reason to suspect that anyone in the boat below understood a word of Japanese but both stared down accusingly.

Fortunately, Cadillac and Steve had already worked out their next move. Bowing from the waist, Cadillac offered up the two plump fish he was holding. Steve rose, bowed, and did the same.

The Plainfolk had learned to treat the Iron Masters with respect but they were not required to avoid eye-contact and prostrate themselves like the Mute slave-workers in Ne-Issan. 'Free-range' grass-monkeys might be regarded as inferior beings but they were also allies and trading partners. Strategic and commercial considerations made it necessary to adopt a more relaxed attitude towards them. It was only when the annual batch of new recruits – known as 'journey-men' – stepped aboard the wheelboats and the anchors were lifted, that the smiles vanished and the whipping-canes appeared.

'Fresh from the waters,' said Cadillac. 'A gift from the Kojak to grace the table of the great warriors from the east.' He bowed again then looked up expectantly.

Wantanabe treated them both to another impassive stare then told his sergeant to summon the cook from the galley. The cook – a fat Chinese dumpling – appeared with two assistants and lowered a basket over the side on the end of a rope.

'How-ah many you ah-give?' asked Sergeant Kurabashi.

'As many as you want,' replied Steve.

'Good,' said Wantanabe. 'We take all.' He lifted his son Tomo away from the rail, snarled briefly at the female servant who was supposed to be looking after him then handed him over. 'But from ah-now after you keep away from ah-this boat. If you ah-wish speak or make trade, ah-do so on shore. Unnah-stan'?'

Steve and Cadillac bowed again. *Yeah, we unnah-stan', you ah-firat-faced ah-rittar creep . . .*

As darkness fell, Cadillac, Steve and the Kojak boatmen shared a stew made from their reserve of dried fish and some rice provided by Wantanabe's cook. It wasn't exactly a generous helping considering the number of fish they'd handed over but this was not the time to get pushy. Especially after the beady looks they'd drawn.

They bulked up the meal by tossing stale pieces of flatbread into the stewpot – acquired, like so many domestic items, from the trading post at an exorbitant exchange rate. There was no doubt about it; the Iron Masters really knew how to gouge the natives.

When the two boatmen hit the hay, Cadillac and Steve stayed by the fire until the glowing embers collapsed and began to turn grey.

'What d'you think?' asked Steve.

'About Wantanabe? He certainly didn't give much away.'

'No. But I'm willing to bet my last meal credit he wasn't thinking about fish. That guy's brain was in overdrive.'

'He's certainly no dum-dum,' admitted Cadillac. 'But even

if he didn't like us sneaking up on his boat, there's no way he could figure out we were listening in.'

'Let's hope not.' Steve stared into the fire and weighed up the situation. In the light of what Cadillac had overheard, their chances of sinking the wheelboat appeared to have diminished considerably. With so many troops and horses on board, it sounded as if it was going to be standing room only. How, in sweet Christopher's name, were they going to be able to move around?

'I've got a feeling we're in big trouble, good buddy.'

'Wrong. *They're* the ones who are in trouble,' said Cadillac confidently. 'We'll manage it somehow. But first, we've got to send 'Bull and Death-Wish back to warn the others.'

'Better wait a couple of days. It's running things a little tight, but providing they make the same time on the return trip Carnegie and Clearwater should have enough time to get the reception committee organized. If they take off straight away it might look suspicious. We don't want Flat-Face connecting their departure with us hanging around underneath his window –'

Cadillac nodded. 'Good thinking . . .'

As a wordsmith, Cadillac was endowed with a phenomenal memory but he appeared to have forgotten that ordinary Mutes were not the ideal carriers of verbal messages – especially ones containing precise numerical information. Since Mutes had no written language they were unable to read; with two exceptions – Cadillac and Clearwater.

Cadillac had gained the ability to read when he had used his extraordinary mental gifts to tap into Steve's fund of acquired knowledge, and during the last three months as guests of the Kojak, Steve had taught Clearwater what Mr Snow called 'silent speech'. At the time, it had been nothing more than an agreeable exercise; a way of being together without necessarily having to be in bed. Looking back, it had been a smart move for besides helping to deepen their relationship, her new skill was now going to help save lives.

Despite her eagerness to learn, Clearwater's written vocabulary was still limited. But it was not her fault. Steve, like all Trackers, had learned to read at a very early age but he had never learned to write. There had been no need. The focal point of his education had been video-screen with its host of interactive teaching programmes and to make use of them, Trackers acquired keyboard skills.

The verb 'write' was only used in the context of writing computer programmes – a task rarely performed by anyone outside the First Family. Trackers used the verb 'key' instead. Paper, pens and pencils as used in the pre-Holocaust era were unavailable. The only thing to write with was a light-pen, the only surface, a computer screen. Any drawing was done the same way, coloured by selecting shades from a palette offered by COLUMBUS. There were no books, paintings, prints, no photographs except those stored in the video archives. The only 'hard copy' available were the plasfilm navref maps issued to overground units. From Day One, everything a Tracker knew about the world and the meaning of existence came through the screens of the video-network controlled by the First Family.

Apart from word of mouth, there was only one subversive medium – 'blackjack' – unofficial, and therefore illegal, music secretly recorded onto tapes and discs. Sometimes it was accompanied by bizarre images but usually there was just a sound-track recorded onto blank videotapes. Copies of copies of copies of countless copies of thousand-year-old masters.

Not everyone had access to the necessary equipment but those that did heard a mix of husky, snarling, raucous, plaintive vocals about seeking, finding, losing, yearning, backed by wild, soaring urgent harmonies and underscored with a spine-tingling rhythmic beat. The words mirrored the dreams, some bright, but more often broken, of an imperfect world where the freedom to love, to be and do anything, was both a boon and a curse. A world full of hope yet beyond salvation; lost forever in the fires of the Holocaust.

No one knew who had started the trafficking or who was behind it now. And Steve, who had always steered clear of the stuff had not inquired further. Handling blackjack was a Code One offence: a one-way ticket to the wall.

So ... although Steve knew the shape of each letter, its sound value and was able to spell, until he began to teach

Clearwater, he had never actually *formed* words using anything other than a typewriter keyboard. So he had traced the outlines of letters in the snow and when darkness fell, he drew them on smooth pale-coloured stones using a charred stick from the fire.

To provide a more permanent record of the alphabet, Clearwater had sewn the letters onto the sleeves of her cotton tunic using an Iron Master needle and thread; thirteen letters running in two rows down the left hand sleeve, the remainder running up the right hand sleeve. She began by identifying each one as Steve called them out in random order and then progressed to spelling out the names of objects around her.

The first words she wanted to write were 'cloud-warrior' and her own name. He tried to explain that his given name was Steven Roosevelt Brickman but she was not interested. Cloud-Warrior was his name of power and that was how she, like all Mute women, wished to address her chosen soul-mate.

The first tentative sentence produced entirely unaided read: 'Clearwater gives to Cloud-Warrior her long life heart loving.' Using the inside of a piece of tree bark, Steve scratched a reply with the point of his knife. 'It is a gift I will always strive to be worthy of.' Not exactly a vibrant piece of prose but Steve had never written a love-letter before.

Inside the haybarn, out of sight of the Iron Masters, Steve got to work on another small piece of bark. Congratulating himself on having had the foresight to teach Clearwater basic arithmetic as well as reading and writing, he scratched out a cryptic message using symbols she would be able to decipher.

This was the first time he'd ever drawn anything without the aid of a computer and he enjoyed doing it. And apart from the mathematical signs, the symbols were not borrowed from COLUMBUS's vast store of graphic elements: they were entirely his own creation.

It was a strange feeling and it reminded him of the artisans he'd seen at work during his time as a road-runner in Ne-Issan. Men who drew pictures on paper-covered screens with brushes and pots of coloured water.

Not pictures composed by soulless circuit boards, but created *out of their own imagination* – of forests, snow-capped mountains and mist-shrouded valleys. Horsemen hunting wild

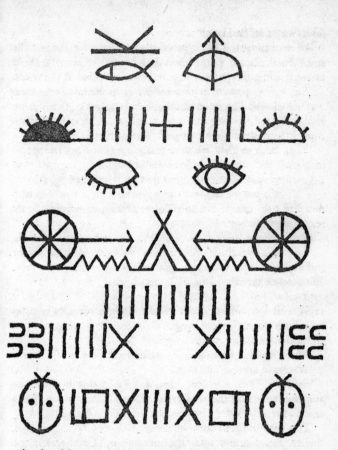

animals with spear and bow, birds perched on branches heavy with pink blossom, or wading on long slender legs through reedy marshes. Courtesans in richly patterned *kimonos*, some with their chalk-white faces half-hidden by parasols, poised daintily on the edge of lily ponds where plump red and white fish rippled the surface with their noses.

Compared to the marvels they produced his efforts were pitiful but now, at least, he knew that some human beings had the potential to produce such things – no matter how brutal their society might be. And if the Iron Masters could do it, why not Trackers?

After cutting the last line of the message, he opened the small earthenware pot of powdered dark brown dye he'd brought along to keep his hair from going blond at the roots. Mixing a little powder with some water in the lid, Steve used a sliver of wood to stain the knife cuts to make them more legible. Satisfied with the effect he had achieved, he then copied the original onto a second piece of tree bark.

When both medallions were ready, he gave Cadillac one to look at. 'Think she'll be able to understand that?'

Cadillac studied the engraved message then read it back: 'Is this . . .? Oh, yes, a K on its side, making an arrow pointing down to fish. Got it . . . the Kojak. Drawn crossbow . . . Be ready? On your guard?'

'Keep going . . .'

'Five plus five. Suns . . . one dark one light. Must be sunset and sunrise . . . ten days . . . you will wake to see – mmmm, quite clever. Are those meant to be wheels?'

'Yes.'

'Wheelboats coming over water to lodges. Arrows coming from both sides. Surrounding . . .'

'Settlement.'

'Five times ten times five . . . what are these – hoofprints?'

'Who ride horses?'

'Samurai. Yes . . . neat idea. I take it this next set of numbers refers to the red-stripes. Doesn't look much like a mask.'

'You got it didn't you?'

'Yes, but I know what the message is.' Cadillac handed back the medallion. 'Wouldn't it have been simpler to write it in Basic?'

'Of course it would! D'you think I did this for fun?!'

Cadillac made a soothing gesture. 'Don't get irritated. It's very ingenious. The thing is – with something this crucial – we don't want any misunderstandings.'

'There isn't gonna *be* any misunderstandings,' said Steve heatedly. 'Has it occurred to you that Wantanabe might be able to read Basic? Better than he can speak it? Obviously not. Suppose he takes it into his head to search the boat and our two friends before they leave? Unlikely to happen, I grant you, but having gotten this far why take chances?'

'You're right. But in that case, won't he be suspicious of anything that looks like a hidden message?'

'It's not going to *be* hidden. I'm planning to hang these round their necks. They're good luck charms. That's why I've only used ones, plus signs, X's and square noughts. Any other numerals would give the game away.'

Steve's worries were not entirely groundless. Wantanabe's suspicions *had* been aroused upon finding them lurking directly below his quarters on the houseboat while he was discussing information that would be of use to an enemy. But the more he thought about it the more he realized there were no grounds for believing the Mutes were up to some mischief. Even so, he felt a certain unease. There was something about the two guides the Kojak wordsmith had sent him. Something about their eyes, their demeanour. They looked ... What was it? Too ... astute? On the other hand, that might be the reason why they had been selected.

In Ne-Issan, slaves were forbidden to make eye-contact with persons from the upper classes. They were dealt with by persons of inferior rank. Perhaps it was his *own* attitude that was incorrect. Perhaps they weren't *all* as dumb-looking as the two that were leaving, and the majority of Mutes he'd met since arriving in the outlands. Yes ... Clearly, there was still a lot to learn.

Two days later, the two Kojak boatmen sought permission from Sergeant Kurabashi to return to their settlement in order to confirm the safe arrival of the guides. Kurabashi told them their request would receive due consideration and strode off to check up on the new building work. The japs had negotiated a deal with their nearest Mute neighbours to supply timber and were employing a sixty-strong gang working under close supervision to saw the logs up into planks and do other labouring jobs using Iron Master tools. The Mutes had brought along their women and children and they were now camped in a mini-settlement about half a mile inland. It was a neat arrangement. The Japs didn't have to feed or house their work force, and they didn't have them under their feet after the whistle blew.

Steve and Cadillac helped 'Bull and Death-Wish prepare the out-rigger for the voyage home then sat down on the beach near the gangway to the houseboat. When Kurabashi returned, they looked up at him expectantly but he walked on board without giving them a second glance.

Cadillac watched the sergeant enter Wantanabe's quarters then eyed Steve. 'What's going on?'

'You tell me, you're the expert. You know what these guys are like. They like to make a big production out of everything. He's probably trying to make us sweat a little.'

If that was Kurabashi's intention, he succeeded. Half an hour later he reappeared with Wantanabe, and followed him down the gangway. Steve, Cadillac and the two boatmen scrambled to their feet and bowed but the Japs walked right past them and on up the beach. And so it went on all through the morning. It was as if they had suddenly become invisible and although they joked about throwing themselves across the foot of the gangway there seemed no way of attracting the Jap's attention without giving offence – and that would have been counterproductive.

The midday meal-break came and went and it was not until the late afternoon, when Steve was becoming increasingly anxious at the thought of losing a day off an already tight schedule, that Wantanabe and his hatchet-faced sergeant condescended to address them.

Kurabashi was carrying the pigeon-basket they'd brought back. The two birds were inside and the remaining ribbons were looped through the woven cane. The two Kojak boatmen bowed as he placed the basket in front of Raging-Bull. Death-Wish was on his left then Steve and Cadillac, forming two sides of a square.

Wantanabe drew himself up to his full height and adopted his severest expression. It was difficult to impress your authority on loutish savages when you were obliged to look up their nostrils. It was also extremely annoying. In Ne-Issan, these monkeys would have been grovelling at his feet with their noses in the dirt.

'Tell your ah-wordsmith we ah-will soon thank him in-ah person for his ah-sistance. Tell him also he mus' ah-send back bird with message as we ah-range.' He glanced sideways at Steve and Cadillac but they were careful not to react.

'Bull and Death-Wish bowed. As they straightened up, 'Bull's bark medallion swung out of the v-neck of his leather overshirt. Steve's earlier assurance vanished as he saw Wantanabe's eyes light up. Pointing to the medallion, the Jap snapped his fingers then opened his palm. 'Bull took it off his neck and handed it over.

Wantanabe scanned the symbols scratched in the bark, checked the other side, took another closer look at Steve's handiwork then passed it over to Kurabashi. There was a muttered exchange that Cadillac failed to get the gist of.

The head Jap turned back to Raging-Bull. 'What is ah-meaning of this?'

'It's a good luck charm,' replied 'Bull. 'It contains magic to ward off evil spirits.'

'Ah-so . . . we no see before. Who ah-give this thing?'

'Our clan elders. To guard us on this dangerous voyage. No one from our clan has ever crossed the Great River before.'

Well done, 'Bull. Keep going . . .

Wantanabe grunted. 'These ah-marks which bring good fortune. These suns, these eyes. What is it they ah-say?'

The boatman bowed and spread his hands apologetically. 'I cannot tell you, master. They are sky-signs. Only our wordsmith knows the language of Mo-Town, the Great Sky-Mother.'

Wantanabe accepted this with a nod but the set of his mouth showed he was far from happy. He turned to Death-Wish. 'You also carry necklace to bring you good fortune?'

The second boatman produced his bark medallion but didn't remove it from his neck. Wantanabe compared it to the one he held in his hand then beckoned Steve and Cadillac to step forward. Steve tried to think of a convincing answer to the question he knew was coming as Wantanabe planted himself in front of them and held out his hand. How stupid not to have made two more copies!

Cadillac came to the rescue while Steve was still struggling to put words together. 'It is only our clan-brothers who carry the magic amulets charged with the power of Mo-Town for it is they who must cross the Great River. We do not need the sky-signs to protect us. The Great Sky-Mother has placed our lives in your hands.'

Wantanabe inclined his head graciously. 'You speak well. The Kojak have ah-tongues as slippery as eels.' Turning on his heel, he issued a rapid stream of orders to Kurabashi.

The sergeant relayed them to an underling on the deck of the houseboat and within seconds, Steve and the three Mutes were surrounded by eight armed soliers.

'What in hell –'

'Don't say or do *anything*!' hissed Cadillac.

Two soldiers grabbed Death-Wish by the arms and forced him to kneel. Two more grabbed Raging-Bull. A fifth handed Sergeant Kurabashi a short wooden stick then joined the three who stood poised ready to cut down Steve and Cadillac should they be rash enough to interfere. Kurabashi stepped behind Death-Wish, slid the stick through the knotted leather thong onto which the bark medallion had been threaded and twisted it round to take up the slack.

Death-Wish began to choke as the necklace became a garrotte.

'Tighter!' cried Wantanabe, in Japanese.

The crewmen who were not working on shore appeared at the rail of the houseboat and watched impassively as Death-Wish started to turn purple. His eyes bulged and his tongue was forced out of his mouth as Kurabashi applied another turn, forcing the leather noose to bite into the Mute's neck. The carved bark medallion was now stuck hard against the underside of his chin.

Wantanabe turned to Steve and Cadillac and affected an air of puzzlement. 'Your frien' seem to have ah-problem. Good luck charm does not appear to be ah-working.' He returned to his victim and watched calmly as Kurabashi applied more pressure then, when death was only seconds away, he called it off with a dismissive wave of his hand.

The sergeant rapidly unwound the garrotte, revealing an ugly purple weal, scored through a bright red line where the sharp edge of the leather had cut through the skin. The two soldiers dragged the semi-conscious Mute face-downwards to the outrigger, his toes trailing in the sand and dumped him unceremoniously into the forward part of the hull.

When they had returned to stand on either side of Wantanabe he waved the medallion he had taken from Raging-Bull under the noses of his captive audience. 'Let that be ah-lesson to all of you! The sky-signs of your gods ah-worthless against pow-ah of Iron Masters! Mo-Town and ah-this Talisman of who ah-you speak cannot save you. Future of Plainfolk in ow-ah han's!'

His Basic pronounciation got worse the more angry and excited he became. 'Only we have pow-ah to defeat san'-burrow-ah! We give help to those who obey – kirr aw who defy or seek-ah to betray us! Resistance totaree useless! Thousan' grass-monkey die for each one Iron Master who fall!' He threw the medallion towards Raging-Bull. 'Terrah-this to yoh peepaw!'

'Bull caught the medallion and bowed. Steve and Cadillac helped him haul the outrigger into the water under the gaze of the Japs. Death-Wish was still flat on his back but he was still alive and his lips were no longer blue. Steve moistened them with some water. 'You gonna be all right?'

Death-Wish massaged his throat and nodded weakly. He tried to pull himself upright.

Steve restrained him. 'Lay there a while. 'Bull's taking you home. I'm sorry about what happened but you'll have a chance to get even with these guys. That's a promise.' He waded back to where Raging-Bull sat in the stern. The bark medallion hung around his neck. Steve kissed two fingers and laid them on the carved message. 'Make sure Clearwater sees this.'

'Bull nodded and lifted his paddle over the side. Steve and Cadillac got behind the outrigger, gave it a last push then walked up onto the beach and watched as it headed towards the sun – a pale golden orange disc growing bigger by the minute as it curved down to meet the watery horizon.

'Think they'll make it?'

'I don't see why not,' said Cadillac. 'In fact, now they're out of the hands of that lunatic I'd say their chances of getting back in one piece have improved considerably.' He glanced over his shoulder and saw Wantanabe strutting up the gangway followed by Kurabashi and the soldiers. 'Wish I could say the same about ours. We must have been mad to think we could pull this off.'

Steve answered with a dry laugh. 'A while back, *you* were the one who was reassuring *me*. We'll make it. Wantanabe was just trying to show us who's the boss. He may come on a little heavy but he's not going to do anything drastic. He's got too much riding on this. As far as he knows we could be a key part to this operation. But he isn't sure. That's why he's on edge. All we have to do is avoid rubbing him up the wrong way.'

'And how do we manage that?'

'By not saying or doing anything that could give him the impression we think he's a complete and utter shithead.'

Cadillac bristled. 'Is this your way of suggesting that Death-Wish was almost killed because of something *I* said?'

'Listen, I'm glad one of us said something. My brain just locked solid.'

'Exactly. Considering it was completely off-the-cuff I thought it was a rather clever reply.'

'Too clever by half. But it wasn't so much what you said as the way you said it. C'mon, Caddy. You and I have both been there. You know how the Japs feel about uppity Mutes. From now on, we act smart and play dumb. Okay?'

Cadillac sighed wearily. 'If you say so, Brickman. The last thing I want is another argument. You lead, I'll follow . . .'

Hugging the eastern shore of Lake Mi-shiga, the giant wheel-boat commanded by Ryuku Kawanishi headed south towards Bei-tanaba, the last of the five out-stations established during the previous year. The glancing rays of the rising sun turned the calm waters on the port side into a sheet of hammered gold, while to starboard, the dark shadow cast by the multi-storeyed superstructure stretched away towards the heartland of the Plainfolk – their ultimate destination.

The head of station at Bei-tanaba was a certain Izo Wan-tanabe, and it was the report of this sharp-eyed functionary which had led to the operation now in progress, a punitive expedition designed to capture, alive, the five assassins who had murdered Domain Lord Yama-Shita and engineered a hideous conflagration which had killed and maimed hundreds of others.

On the bridge, alongside Captain Kawanishi, stood Samurai-Major 'Tenzan'. Morita *Tenzan*, the Japanese word for lightning was a nickname derived from his skill as a swordsman and the speed with which he reacted to tactical situations. Morita was, in other words, an experienced field commander, and this was the reason why he had been chosen to lead the two hundred and fifty samurai now quartered in the cabins running off the galleried upper decks.

Their horses were stabled in specially-constructed stalls on the cavernous through-deck together with their grooms and three hundred red-stripes – foot-soldiers of inferior rank and birth whose martial skills had earned them the right to carry a mass-produced version of the *tachi*, the curving long-sword. In Ne-Issan, where only samurai were permitted to carry both the *tachi*, and its shorter companion the *wakisashi*, this was regarded as a great honour.

The five assassins had spent the winter with Mute fisherfolk and, according to the last report from Wantanabe, were now trapped like flies in a honeyed web of deceit and flattery. The plan was to seize them as they slept or were still in the grip of the yawning stupor that precedes the state of wakefulness. Their Mute hosts had pledged to cooperate fully with the invading force and, most important of all, they had promised to remove any poisons, weapons and other potentially dangerous implements possessed by the assassins on receipt of the signal that a landing was only hours away. This was not because Morita and his men feared for their lives; it was to ensure that the assassins were deprived of the means to kill themslevves in the crucial moments between realization that they were about to be captured and the act itself.

During his visit to the clan, Izo Wantanabe had furnished the Kojak's headman with a simple notched wooden calendar to mark the passage of the days. From the end of the first week in April, the clan was to maintain a nightly watch of the eastern sky. If they saw three red stars shoot heavenwards in quick succession it would be a sign that the raiding force was in position and intended to land at sunrise. In return, the Kojak would ignite a green rocket provided by Wantanabe to signal that all was well.

These arrangements were further proof of the commendable foresight and ingenuity which Wantanabe had displayed from the moment he had sighted the flying-horses passing over his out-station.

Aishi Sakimoto, the chief surviving member of the Yama-Shita family's Inner Council and uncle of the murdered domain-lord had emphasized that the assassins were to be brought back yoked and chained but otherwise unharmed. Once they were incarcerated in the Yama-Shita's palace-fortress at Sara-kusa they would be subjected singly and collectively to the most exquisitely painful tortures that could be devised.

Past experience showed that this process, patiently applied, could loosen the stubbornest of tongues. And prior to the removal of that particular organ – but only after it had been pierced by red-hot needles – Sakimoto hoped to discover the full story behind the destruction of the Heron Pool. The role of the sand-burrowers and their Mute lackeys, the clan M'Call had already been clearly established; what was of crucial importance was the degree of involvement – active or passive – of the Shogun, Yoritomo Toh-Yota and Ieyasu, his wily Court Chamberlain who, despite his advanced age, was still the power behind the throne.

The death of Lord Hiro Yama-Shita and the subsequent redistribution of the family's trading licenses had been a severe blow to their long-term plans to displace the Toh-Yota and assume the leadership of Ne-Issan. The exclusive right to westward trade with the grass-monkeys had given the Yama–Shita virtual command of the slave trade and only their boats had the right to use the canal which divided their domain and formed the link between the Great River and the Eastern Sea.

This trading monopoly had been the source of the family's power and influence, but with the posthumous charge of high treason levelled against Lord Yama-Shita by the Shogun things had changed dramatically. Their neighbours, the Ko-Nikka and the Se-Iko, erstwhile-friends and secret allies had joined with other powerful domain-lords in supporting the charges against them and had eagerly seized upon the Shogun's offer to grant them equal trading rights and, as a result of their cowardly defection, the family now faced the prospect of losing at least half its revenues.

The death by execution and suicide of Lord Yama-Shita's immediate family, his principal retainers and some two dozen relatives judged to be implicated in the conspiracy had been a bitter blow. In time, the house of Yama-Shita would recover and exact a terrible revenge but for the moment, patience and stealth were required.

Morita's expedition had been assembled and despatched in great secrecy for two reasons: to prevent the Shogun from learning what was afoot, and because the intended action was illegal. If it came to light, it could lead to another round of punitive sanctions being imposed upon the family. An edict laid down by the Toh-Yota shogunate expressly forbade 'foreign adventures'. The seventeen domain-lords of Ne-Issan owed – in theory – total allegiance to the Shogun. Their private armies were – again in theory – his, and movements of all units were supposed to be reported to the resident Consul-General, the principal representative of central government stationed in each of the domains.

Prior notification of all troop movements was one of the many mechanisms employed by the Toh-Yota to maintain the status quo and it had helped keep the peace for over eighty years. Yoritomo, the present ruler of Ne-Issan, would have taken a dim view of the unreported despatch of five hundred fully armed men into the outlands – especially when the aim of the operation was to bring back evidence that would help nail him and his family to the wall.

Passing through the straits of Hui-niso, Kawanishi's massive three-storeyed vessel had made overnight calls at the four out-stations dotted round the broad peninsular separating Lake U-ron from Mi-shiga. Supplies and mail had been unloaded, written reports on the progress made in establishing permanent links with the grass-monkeys inhabiting the hinterland were collected together with the latest airborne message from Wantanabe, and the future toasted with copious drafts of *sake*.

And now, at last, they were on their way to Bei-tanaba — the anchorage from which the attack would be launched.

Steve and Cadillac were filled with a mixture of excitement and trepidation as they saw the wheelboat appear on the horizon. Up to this moment, everything had gone far better than they dared hope. But what they had accomplished with the help of the Kojak boatmen was nothing compared to what lay ahead. Success or failure, life or death — all now depended on what happened within the next forty-eight hours.

In a short while, they would become accredited members of the military expedition now steaming towards them. Both were aware that one wrong move could spell disaster but their thoughts were focussed on the difficulties they would encounter once they'd managed to get on board. Neither had any inkling that their plan to sink the glittering vessel was about to lurch sickeningly off course before they had even set foot on deck.

CHAPTER ELEVEN

After checking with the aid of a spyglass that the wheelboat was flying the insignia of the house of Yama-Shita, Izo Wantanabe clambered down the ladder from the roof of the bridge and told his sergeant to organize a hot bath and a change of clothes for the two Mute guides. If the commander of the military expedition, or one of his subordinate officers, wished to question the grass-monkeys it was necessary to make them presentable. That meant changing their stained, greasy 'walking-skins' for clean trousers and tunics, and making sure they smelt of nothing stronger than soap.

Kurabashi summoned Steve and Cadillac onto the deck of the houseboat and gave them the good news. The bad news was that they were not permitted to use the facilities on board. They had to remove one of the big wooden tubs from the bath-house and carry it down onto the beach, using the stout pole provided.

The tubs were normally shifted by four men with two poles but by threading it through on the diagonal they achieved the right balance – then almost ruptured themselves lugging it off the boat.

'Sheehh! Jack me!' gasped Steve, after they'd staggered up the beach and shed their burden on the spot indicated by Kurabashi.

'Could've been . . . worse,' panted Cadillac, hanging limply over his end of the pole.

'Yeah?' Steve straightened up and probed his right collar-bone to make sure it was still intact.

'Yeah, it could've been full of water.' Cadillac recovered his breath and withdrew the carrying pole. 'Still – at least it's down-hill on the way back.'

'Save the jokes. Kurabashi's getting impatient.'

They ran back to the houseboat and collected twenty

buckets of boiling hot water, two at a time, at the double. Kurabashi dogged their footsteps, screaming angrily each time they spilt some on the deck. He was swearing at them in Japanese but military-style abuse has a familiar ring that transcends the barrier of language.

The last trip was to collect a bar of soap, scrubbing gloves and two towels. 'Wash body from-ah head to toe!' barked Kurabashi. 'Hair, face, everything tip-top! Smell mus' go! Quick, quick! No time! No time!'

Steve and Cadillac bowed then raced down the gangway. Pausing only to add several cooling buckets of water from the lake, they stripped off their walking-skins, grabbed the soap and a scrubbing-glove and side-vaulted into the steaming tub.

Steve sank down up to his chin, savouring the all-embracing warmth. 'Hope he's not going to scrub our backs . . .'

Cadillac laughed as he joined him. 'You worried he might laugh when he sees your –'

'Idiot! It's not down there I'm thinking about, it's up here.' Steve tapped the dirty strip of rag tied around his forehead.

Cadillac was also wearing one. Stitched into the first few inches of the strip – the layer lying nearest the skin – were some flat-bottomed pebbles which, when concealed by the other layers of rag, created the characteristic bulges that had prompted Trackers to refer to Mutes as 'lump-heads'.

Their body-markings, which were authentic reproductions of the variegated skins the vast majority of Mutes were born with, would not come off no matter how hard they scrubbed with soap and water; only the chemical action of the oily sap from crushed pink finger-leaves could alter the permanence of the specially-formulated vegetable dyes. But because their skins were free of the usual rough patches of vein-like ribbing and gathering – the third deformation that set Mutes apart from their fellow-humans – they had adopted the 'lump-head' look to hide the fact that they were also straight-boned.

It was this need to blend in with their Kojak hosts which had led them to choose Raging-Bull and Death-Wish from amongst a host of volunteers. Apart from having 'tree-bark' veining on their forearms, the two boatmen were virtually smooth-skinned. The lumps on their foreheads – bone-tumours arising from a hereditary defect in the Mutes' genetic code – had also been covered by ragged strips of cloth to give all four a similar appearance.

As a child of the Federation, Steve had been showering daily ever since he'd been able to stand on his own feet but Cadillac had never experienced the luxury of washing in hot water until landing in Ne-Issan. The communal tub favoured by Iron Masters provided imaginative bathers with a range of delicious opportunities and the twice-daily encounters with his 'scrubbers' had been one of the most pleasurable aspects of his stay. The other great discovery had been the libido-loosening effects of *sake* – the pale yellow liquor made from fermented rice. The warm embrace of the water brought back memories of both, and with it, the sharp realization that his body still craved for a bracing shot of alcohol. Cadillac fought down the sudden thirst that gripped his throat and as he tried to banish all thought of *sake* from his mind, Steve's voice cut across his reverie.

'Caddy! Take off your headband and wash it now while nobody's around!' Turning his back to the house-boat, Steve dunked his head repeatedly while he scrubbed the dirt out of his own strip of rag.

Cadillac did the same then wound it back over his wet hair. Steve was just knotting his into place when they saw Kurabashi heading towards them followed by two of the female domestics. The first was carrying a neat pile of clothes, the second some rolled straw mats. Kurabashi had his whipping cane under his arm. He usually carried it around as a symbol of his authority when dealing with the Mute construction workers. So far they hadn't seen him use it but the threat of a beating was always there.

Having received a sound thrashing during his time as a road-runner, Steve was in no hurry to earn himself another. He rubbed soap in his hair and quickly worked up a lather.

When the straw mats had been laid down a couple of yards from the tub, the first Thai woman placed a pair of rope-soled sandals and a neatly-folded white cotton tunic and trousers on each one. Both women then bowed to Kurabashi and scuttled back to the boat. The clothes – a wide-sleeved V-neck wrapover tunic fastened with a sash, and boxy, calf-length trousers were almost identical to those Cadillac had been given to wear at the Heron Pool.

Kurabashi took the whipping-cane from under his arm and placed it behind his back. Holding it in his clasped hands, he paced slowly around the tub. In Iron Master bath-houses, the tubs were set into holes in the planked floor to permit easy access and to allow the bather's back to be scrubbed by somebody kneeling outside: here on the beach, the rim of the tub was level with Kurabashi's armpits.

'You ah-wash feet – backsides, grass-monkey?'

'Yes, Iron Master!' they chorused.

Kurabashi jerked his head. 'Outside! Do again for-ah me to see!'

Steve and Cadillac leapt out and scrubbed themselves from toe to waist under the sergeant's beady gaze. Fortunately, Steve had taken the precaution of dying his pubic hair dark brown as well. He had very little chest hair whereas Cadillac's formed a dark shadow that ran down through his navel from breastbone to groin. His lower legs were well-covered too.

Kurabashi, like all Iron Masters, had no body hair, and apart from a meagre scattering of short pale eye-lashes had no hair on his skull either. He surveyed them with a mixture of curiosity and distaste then brandished his whipping-cane. 'Hoh-kay! Back in-ah water! Wash rest of-ah body!'

They went over their chests, arms and faces, scrubbed each other's backs then started to rinse the suds out of their hair.

Kurabashi rapped his cane sharply on the rim of the tub. 'No! No! No good!' He prodded Cadillac's head-band. 'Remove ah-this before wash hair!'

Cadillac and Steve exchanged a loaded glance.

'Looks like we've got some explaining to do . . .'

'Then you'd better come up with something good.' Steve slipped off his headband and sank beneath the water. Cadillac did likewise then emerged and started to wash his hair.

As Steve surfaced he heard Kurabashi say: 'Grass-monkey . . . why you no more have lumps on-ah your face?'

With their skins still tingling from a brisk towelling, Steve and Cadillac were marched up the gangway in their clean dry clothes and halted on the fore-deck of the houseboat. After telling them to lay down their straw mats, Sergeant Kurabashi left them under the watchful gaze of four armed sea-soldiers and strode off towards Wantanabe's quarters. When the head Jap emerged some ten minutes later he did not look too pleased.

Following Cadillac's lead, Steve fell to his knees on the mat beside him and bowed his head as Wantanabe confronted them, thrusting one of the ragged headbands under their noses. It had been folded to expose the section into which the pebbles had been stitched. 'So, grass-monkeys . . . you ah-wish to explain this-ah deception?'

Now that he had the advantage in height, he had ditched the aggressive bullfrog act: now it was the velvety-steel inquisitor. The old cat-and-mouse routine . . .

Cadillac clasped his hands together in supplication and threw a sideways glance at Steve. The message spelled out by the eyes read: 'Okay, smart-ass, you want to show me how it's done? Start talking.'

Sonofabitch . . .

'No deception intended, Iron Master!' began Steve. 'Stones were only to, uh . . . to, uh –'

Cadillac bailed him out. '– to cover our shame! We were given the skin of the Plainfolk, but to punish us for wrongdoing in former life, the Great Sky-Mother did not give us the same bodies as our clan-brothers. Ever since we were born, our mothers kept our heads wrapped with stones – for our shame was also theirs. And so what they began, we have continued to this day.'

Not bad, Caddy . . . not bad . . .

Wantanabe stepped back and conferred with his trusty sergeant. Cadillac managed to catch most of the exchange. The head Jap had swallowed his story but it was a reluctant decision, influenced by the fact that the wheelboat was drawing closer by the minute.

Wantanabe gave the headband back to Kurabashi. Steve and Cadillac held their breath and kept their eyes averted as he paced slowly up and down in front of them. 'Good story. But is it ah-true?'

Cadillac bowed lower still. 'Plainfolk speak only truth to Iron Masters. A Kojak warrior who lies to save his life is without honour. This is the law of my people.'

Ethical codes of conduct were something an Iron Master could understand. 'The Kojak *are* great warriors,' admitted Wantanabe. 'I also know of-ah shame that can come from unfortunate-ah circumstance of birth. This can explain many things.'

Cadillac sat back on his heels and bent his head to touch the clasped hands resting on his chest. 'Iron Master possess great wisdom and forgiving heart.'

Easy, Caddy. No need to overdo it . . .

'But present difficulty-ah remains. Truth of matter can only be verified by-ah Kojak wordsmith. Until then must find way to prevent further monkey-business!' Wantanabe laughed loudly at this witticism and everyone else joined in. In Ne-Issan, when the boss-man laughed, you laughed even louder and you kept on going until the smile left his face.

On Wantanabe's signal, Kurabashi moved to the foredeck hatchway and yelled to someone below. Three soldiers appeared. One was carrying chains, the other two lugged heavy square wooden boards. They were made of jointed timber about three inches thick and had a hole in the middle, lined with a strip of iron. Steve and Cadillac were handed the chains and told to shackle each other's ankles and wrists. When they'd handed over the keys and were back kneeling on their mats, it became clear why the boards were made in two halves with a simple hinge on one side and a closing bolt on the other. They were neck restraints.

The boards, some four inches wider than their shoulders, were locked around their necks. The chain connecting their wrists was pulled through a slot at the front of the board and fastened to it by means of another small bolt. It was brutally simple and fiendishly clever. To balance when standing upright, you had to adopt a stooping posture and in order to ease the pressure of the iron collar on the base of the neck, the wearer was forced to support the weight of the board with both hands.

Wantanabe stood in front of them for a few moments to

savour their predicament then, satisfied that they were unlikely to cause him any further upset, he returned to his quarters. Kurabashi told Steve and Cadillac they could, if they wished, sit cross-legged on their mats.

After the sea-soldiers had gone off to prepare for the arrival of the wheelboat, Steve tried to find the best position for the neckboard. There wasn't one. 'This is killing me . . .'

'Me too,' whispered Cadillac. 'What in Mo-Town's name are we going to do if they put us on board the wheelboat trussed up like this?'

'Let's just get on it first. 'We'll figure out the rest later.'

'But –'

Steve cut him off. 'Listen to me. Did they kill Death-Wish?'

'They came pretty close.'

'Yeah, but the point is they *didn't*. This is all part of their campaign to keep us guessing. It's a tried and tested technique. If you're in charge of an operation and you haven't a clue what to do next, then the best way to maintain control – and conceal your own uncertainty – is to throw everybody else off balance. Never fails.'

'I hope you're right. Sounds to me as if you're pissing in the wind . . .'

'Caddy! For crissakes, snap out of it! Every time we run into a sticky patch, you throw a downer! Just hang in there. Things always go from bad to worse before they get better. I can read this guy like a vid-screen. Hell! You're the one whose supposed to be the expert. Can't you see the state he's in?'

'He's worried, yes –'

'Worried?! The guy's crapping himself! He's set up this whole raid, he's told whoever's out there that he's got two guides ready to lead the way and now he finds we're not quite what we appeared to be. Nothing he can really put his finger on but enough to set the alarm bells ringing. And you know what? I bet my last meal-credit he's beginning to wonder about those medallions 'Bull and Death-Wish sailed off with. Were they just good luck charms or were they a secret message tipping off the bad guys? Whose side are the Kojak on now? And I bet you something else. He's not going to say a word about this to the guys on that wheelboat.'

'If I were in his position, I don't think I would either.'

'Because he's not a samurai. Which means no quick way out. If this raid goes down the tube and he has the bad luck to survive . . .'

Cadillac nodded. 'And something equally nasty could happen to his family. Yes, I take the point. Just one thing – you say "If this raid goes down the tube". Don't you mean "When"?'

'Of course!' snapped Steve. He let the board rest on his neck in order to stretch his aching arms. '*You* know what's gonna happen, and *I* know what's gonna happen –'

'But *he* doesn't . . .'

'Exactly. Satisfied?'

'Never felt better.'

They sat there in silence, bearing the irksome weight of the neckboards without further complaint, and watched the wheelboat draw closer. To the east, the yellow dawn sky had been bleached silvery-white and was now turning eggshell-blue. The flecks of gold scattered across the water by the rising sun had sunk without trace in the endless rippling expanse of grey. Some time later, when the surface of the lake changed, chameleon-like to match the deepening blue of the sky, they heard the hushed, rhythmic beat of the wheelboat's engine; the faint opening bars of a slow, stately crescendo whose hypnotic four-note cycle gradually became more distinct as the square menacing bulk of the wheelboat bore down on them.

'I've suddenly thought of something,' said Cadillac.

'If it's not good news I don't think I want to hear it. But tell me anyway.'

'Supposing there's somebody on that boat who was part of the Yama-Shita delegation that came to see our first test flights at the Heron Pool?'

'You mean . . . somebody who . . . might recognize us?'

'Yes. Look at me. I'm wearing almost exactly the same outfit.'

'But your hair was shorter and you were clear-skinned.'

'You weren't.'

'No, but my hair was –'

'Blond. That's right, but only at the roots. The rest of it was dark brown – as it is now.'

Steve mulled over the implications. It was unbelievable. How could he have overlooked the possibility of something like this happening? 'We could have a problem . . .'

The pounding of the engines was enveloped by the plunging thundering sound of water being churned to foam beneath the massive blades of the rear-mounted paddle wheel, then cascading off them as they rose high into the air.

Now they could see, in ever-increasing detail, its gilded, blood-red superstructure and as it drew closer still, the figures crowding the rails of the forward galleries. As yet, the faces were pale, featureless blobs but soon they would acquire noses, mouths and eyes. And one of those pairs of eyes could soon prove to be their undoing.

In the middle of the afternoon, when the wheelboat captained by Ryuku Kawanishi had anchored close inshore, Izo Wantanabe and his wife stepped into a dory and were rowed across by two sea-soldiers wearing newly-washed uniforms. Both Izo and Yumiko had taken great pains to dress up for the occasion and so had Sergeant Kurabashi who stood in the bow holding a bamboo pole bearing the house flag of the Yama-Shita.

The wheelboat was anchored with its port side parallel with the shore, a standard manoeuvre which brought half its battery of cannon to bear on the land surrounding the out-station. No attack was expected but Iron Masters always remained alert to potential sources of danger. In a country where suspicion and intrigue was rife no one who sought to challenge the authority of the Shogun could afford to relax their guard – especially in view of the betrayals that had followed the debacle at the Heron Pool.

The same rules applied here in the outlands. The primitive weapons of the grass-monkeys – most of which the Iron Masters had supplied – were no match for samurai steel but there were other dangers; dark forces that could not be quantified but which were, nevertheless, very real.

Disembarking from the dory, Izo and Yumiko made their way up the wide port bow gangway which had been lowered into the water for that purpose. A samurai from Morita's personal staff and a junior ship's officer greeted them as they reached the deck. Sergeant Kurabashi and the dory were already on their way back to the house-boat to pick up the two troublesome Kojak guides.

After the usual long-winded ritual of polite, self-effacing exchanges and a series of bows that brought the Wantanabes' noses closer and closer to the spotless *tatami*, they finally found themselves facing Captain Ryuku Kawanishi and Samurai-Major 'Tenzan' Morita. Izo's wife, who had been invited to be present as a mark of the esteem in which the couple were now held by the family, paid her respects to the high-ranking figures on the dais then shuffled backwards in her snow-white cotton socks to a kneeling position at the rear of the room and took no further part in the proceedings.

Wantanabe answered Morita's questions promptly and, in the opinion of Captain Kawanishi, with admirable economy. When Morita had been brought fully up to date on the situation and the personalities involved, Wantanabe told him about the guides Carnegie-Hall had sent to lead the attacking force to their target.

'I wish to question them,' said Morita.

Uncrossing his legs, Wantanabe acknowledged the oblique order with a bow. 'Your wish to do so was anticipated by my humble self. I ordered them to be brought to the wheelboat. In chains and neckboards.'

Morita exchanged looks with the wheelboat captain then said: 'I assume there is a good reason for this?'

Wantanabe bowed again. 'A precaution, sire, but they have not been harmed I assure you. They were impudent and their conduct made me feel uneasy. I came to the conclusion that a certain amount of restraint was necessary to make them more, ahh . . . responsive.'

Morita nodded. 'The wrist chains will suffice . . .'

'What did I tell you?' said Steve, as the neckboards and leg shackles were removed.

Cadillac raised his chained wrists in reply.

'Some people are never satisfied,' said Steve, trying to lighten the mood.

'Silence!' barked Kurabashi. 'No more speak until ah-spoken to! You go meet commander of-ah expedition. Big Iron Master! Much powah! Show respect otherwise ah-bad things happen!'

Steve didn't need to be reminded – not since Cadillac's thunderbolt had dropped out of the blue. Wantanabe and a samurai were waiting for them at the top of the gangway with six red-stripes who positioned themselves in front, behind and alongside the manacled pair. The samurai led the party up to the second floor of the three side galleries and down a wide companion way with guards stationed at each end and halted outside a large stateroom located amidships. The samurai entered first, the double doors sliding open and shut behind him as if operated by a magic eye. Wantanabe, Steve, Cadillac and their escort waited in silence outside. The dink's face gave nothing away but he was several shades paler than usual and the veins on either side of his forehead stood out: dark mauve squiggly lines that throbbed in unison with his beating heart.

It wasn't the only one that was pounding.

The two square box-panelled doors slid apart to reveal the samurai. As they opened wider still, Steve caught sight of the mechanism – two guards positioned just inside. Yumiko knelt on a mat over to the right. Two more samurai sat cross-legged on either side of the room. Straight ahead, blocking off the rear half of the room was a folding screen with a red-stripe poised on one knee at either end. Two brown mats lay side by side in front of the screen flanked by two plain ones edged with white.

The samurai had already taken off his sandals. Wantanabe signalled Steve and Cadillac to do likewise. 'You ah-follow me,' he whispered. 'When I bow, put head to mat. When you ah-sit up, keep eyes down. Stay on knees whole time. Do not answer questions directly. Give answers only to this samurai. Unnah-stan'?'

'Yes, Iron Master . . .'

They followed Wantanabe into the room and took their places on the brown mats. It was a rather appropriate colour, thought Steve, considering the shit they were in. Wantanabe positioned himself to Steve's left, the samurai to Cadillac's right. The six-man escort stayed outside.

As the doors swished shut behind them, the two red-stripes folded up the screen and carried it to the left side of the room revealing the top brass, in full armour and the usual paraphernalia seated imposingly on the dais flanked by eight richly-dressed aides. They made an impressive sight and to intimidate their two primitive guests even further, they now wore the snarling, bulging-eyed masks that had caused the Plainfolk to refer to the Iron Masters as 'dead-faces'.

Steve and Cadillac put their noses to the floor and kept them there until they saw the people around them straighten up.

Even if they had been allowed to look directly at the people on the dais the masks made it impossible to recognize any of them. The two men seated in front of the others were obviously giving the orders. One of them was Samurai-Major Morita but Steve and Cadillac had no way of knowing they'd already met him. The thought that all eyes in the room were upon them while they could look at no one plus the fact that, at any time, someone might recognize them made the pressure almost unbearable. Once again, Steve's brash confidence had led them to overlook dangers which, on mature reflection, should have been blindingly obvious.

Speaking in Japanese, Morita began his questioning of the two guides using the samurai as an interpreter. The samurai, who spoke faultless Basic, then gave running translations of their replies. Cadillac's knowledge of the language gave him a head start since he knew what was coming as soon as the interpreter did. It was this unexpected advantage – and not a desire to pass the buck – which had prompted Steve to suggest that Cadillac should provide as many of the answers as possible.

Morita asked for an explanation of how the five 'travellers' had fallen into the hands of the Kojak. This was no problem. Claiming to have been one of the search party, Cadillac gave him an edited version of the real events, omitting the 'Skyhawk incident', the blasting of the wagon-train, and the fact they had been collected in two instalments.

He went on to recount how one of the five – a man – had been badly injured. Unwilling to abandon their colleague, the group had opted to stay together and take advantage of the hospitality offered by the clan. It had taken all winter for the injured man's bones to join together. Thanks to the skill of the healing-women he was now on his feet but not yet able to undertake a long, arduous trek.

Did they, inquired Morita, know the place to which the 'travellers' planned to return? Cadillac replied they did not. He and his companion were just simple fishermen. Perhaps Carnegie-Hall knew of these things. The wordsmith had spent many days and nights talking to their guests about strange matters and devices using words which he, Cadillac and his companion 'Motor-Head', did not understand.

Morita then enquired when they had last seen the 'travellers'. Cadillac told him, via the samurai, that it had been on the day before they had set sail.

Steve cursed silently and Morita, who could obviously speak Basic, was equally quick to spot the blunder. Set sail? What did the Kojak know about 'sailing' and who had taught them this word?

Cadillac hurriedly extricated himself by explaining that the term 'to set sail' meant to begin a journey across the water. The word, like everything else they knew, had come from the mouth of Carnegie-Hall. Steve, who'd been registering every word sensed they were heading into trouble. It was like being trapped on a raft drifting downstream and knowing that round the next bend there was a stretch of killer rapids.

'So,' said the samurai, translating for Morita, 'the Kojak hold three males and two females.'

Cadillac, who'd imparted this information earlier, confirmed this was so.

'Describe them,' said Morita. 'In detail.'

This was the moment Steve had been dreading. He glanced sideways at Cadillac. He must have known this question was coming but from the expression on his face it was clear he'd been hoping it wouldn't be asked. How much did the Iron Masters really know? Who, exactly, were they looking for? Four long-dogs and one Mute – as they had appeared to be at the Heron Pool? Four Mute slaves and one courtesan – their owner – who had travelled from Ari-bani on one of the

Yama-Shita wheelboats? Or the five 'Mutes' who had disappeared from the slave-merchant's compound at Bu-faro?

Cadillac realized that they had played it wrong from the first moment they had landed. What had been required was low, animal cunning, not an articulate intelligence. His gifts as a wordsmith and his overweening conceit had led him to believe he could out-think his adversaries when he should have been acting dumb. Had they done so from the beginning, they could have avoided answering potentially dangerous questions by claiming they – like their fellow Mutes – were unable to remember. How ironic that he, of all people, should have forgotten that! And now it was too late . . .

As it happened, Morita was now aware of all three combinations. The full story had not been available when the first messages had been exchanged by Wantanabe and the palace at Sara-kusa but during the winter, further inquiries had established that the assassins had been given an 'assisted passage' out of the country.

Their journey from the Uda-sona river port of Ari-bani through the canal to the slave-merchant's compound at Bu-faro had now been reconstructed. Their subsequent 'escape' from the compound – duly reported to the authorities – had coincided with the disappearance of the Mute overseer from the wheelboat which had carried them to Bu-faro. The two events were clearly linked, and the overseer's disappearance was proof that the Yama-Shita's enemies had managed to plant their agents amongst the crews of vessels which, up to now, the family had believed to be totally secure.

The slave-merchant's activities had come under scrutiny from time to time but the investigations had been concerned with the possible non-payment of taxes. In all other respects his conduct had been unremarkable. None of the informers employed by the Yama-Shita had ever filed a report that gave the family cause to suspect he might be a secret agent of the Toh-Yota. All the information gathered in Bu-faro after the event, had come from two of his shipping clerks who had been pressured with the help of bribes into revealing the circumstances surrounding the arrival and departure of the assassins. It was only then that the family had discovered one of the outlanders spoke fluent, upper-class Japanese and had had the effrontery to impersonate a courtesan!

Prior to the death of Lord Yama-Shita, the merchant would have been arrested and forced, under torture, to reveal the extent of his complicity, but in the present hostile political climate with the family no longer the unchallenged master of its own house this would have been counter-productive. It was far better to leave him in place and hope to turn him into a double-agent . . .

Cadillac's fear that they might be recognized was not without foundation. Samurai-Major 'Tenzan' Morita *had* watched the ground trials and the proving flights of the rocket-powered glider conducted by its long-dog designer and builder and his Mute protégé. And the more he looked at the two grass-monkeys kneeling in front of him, the more he was convinced he'd seen them somewhere before. But where? At the Heron Pool? The attack upon the assembled dignitaries and the installations had been conducted with breathtaking audacity but even so . . . Would anyone be so bold as to . . .?

Morita dismissed the idea. It was inconceivable. Yet there was something about the voice of the one answering his questions . . .

'We are waiting,' said the samurai.

Cadillac moistened his dry lips. Reasoning it out, as Steve had done, he had come to the conclusion that it was safer to stick to the last known permutation of five 'Mutes' since such a group was more likely to be offered – and accept – hospitality from another clan.

The Japs appeared to know exactly who they were looking for and he knew from Carnegie-Hall that they'd found the two Skyriders. Should he throw them off the scent by describing five Kojaks picked at random? Would that stop them sailing to She-Kargo or would they press on regardless? On the other hand, if the Japs called the raid off because his descriptions didn't match the people on their hit list, what would happen to him and Steve? If they were released – and it was a big IF – how were *they* going to get back? They would have to walk, unarmed, the long way round and that could prove as dangerous as sailing across on the wheelboat.

His dilemma seemed to have resolved itself. They needed to hitch a ride back across the lake and they needed the Iron Masters' horses when they got to the other side. That meant telling the man on the dais who'd been asking the questions what he was waiting to hear. It was an interesting problem because sooner or later, he was going to have to supply descriptions of Steve and himself!

He began by detailing Kelso and Jodi, then moved on to Clearwater. None of the Japs who'd gotten close to her at the Heron Pool had survived but his interrogator might have obtained a more-detailed description from Lord Min-Orota. Cadillac, of course, did not know he and the Yama-Shita were no longer on speaking terms. In the wake of the Heron Pool disaster and the ensuing revelations about their joint plans to conjure up the Dark Light, Min-Orota had promptly switched sides, leaving his former allies to take the full heat.

As Cadillac began to describe Clearwater's face, and its most noteworthy feature, her blue eyes, he came up with a genial solution to his remaining problem – how to describe himself and Steve without being recognized. He would mix up their physical characteristics and make two new composites which would match *parts* of the 'wanted' portrait the Iron Masters had composed but would *not* – and this was the risky bit – describe the two people kneeling in front of them. The chances of pulling it off were slim but there was no time to come up with a better idea. Cadillac took a deep breath and went for it.

When Steve understood what Cadillac was trying to do, he mentally took his hat off. It was a wild gamble, but what the hell? They'd already stretched their luck to breaking point. Even if, by some miracle, they emerged from this session with their heads on their shoulders, they still had to find a way to blow up the boat!

Morita listened intently as the samurai relayed Cadillac's descriptions of the last two travellers, and after a whispered exchange with his armoured colleage, pronounced himself satisfied. He gave orders for Steve and Cadillac to be taken out of the room.

'Congratulations,' muttered Steve, as they took their place

between the red-stripes standing in the corridor outside. 'You did a terrific job.'

'Noh-spikk!' snapped the nearest red-stripe.

The doors slid shut with Wantanabe and his wife still inside. As they stood in their stockinged feet, Cadillac tried to hear what was being said inside the room but the voices remained tantalizingly indistinct. Fifteen, twenty, twenty-five minutes later – it was hard to tell, the doors slid open. The folding screen was back across the centre of the room and the people on the near side of it were still in place.

Steve and Cadillac returned to their mats and endeavoured to look suitably humble. They heard people moving around on the other side; the clack of armour plates and the swishing sound of heavy silk cloth. Probably the top brass returning after their tea-break.

The screen was taken away, revealing the masked figures of Morita and Kawanishi seated on the dais, as before, with their aides. What, in Mo-Town's name are they going to ask us now? wondered Cadillac. He and Steve put their noses to the floor as everybody bowed in greeting.

Morita's samurai-interpreter stood up and summoned two of his lower ranking colleagues from the back of the room. They came up behind Cadillac and before he knew what was happening, they seized him by the arms and swiftly looped a stick through the chain attached to the iron cuffs round his wrists. The stick was passed behind his neck and in front of both wrists to form a yoke to which his hands were pinned at shoulder height. This brought the middle portion of the chain tight across his throat.

A second later, Cadillac saw the tips of the samurai's razor-sharp short swords poised on either side of his head. The blades were just a hair's breadth away from his skin. His stomach froze as his mind pictured the hideous wounds the swords could inflict on his face.

'We think you have not been telling us the truth,' said the interpreter. 'You must therefore be punished.' The blades were withdrawn as the two samurai behind Cadillac each took hold of an ear.

Keeping his eyes on the helpless Mute, Samurai-Major

Morita leaned towards Captain Kawanishi and asked in Japanese. 'Which one shall we cut off first?'

'The right one.'

Morita signalled for it to be done and as he did so, Cadillac flinched in anticipation of the blow, drawing his head to the left.

But there was no cut. No searing pain. It was a trick. And his lack of nerve at the crucial moment had given him away.

Morita slapped his thighs and laughed heartily as he nudged Kawanishi. 'What did I tell you? He understands every word! Isn't that incredible? I *knew* I'd seen this dog before.' He pointed to Steve. 'And I wager that one with the blue eyes was at the Heron Pool too!' He called out to the interpreter. 'Look closely at his hair and tell me what you see!'

Steve couldn't understand what Morita was saying but when the samurai walked over and made a close study of his head he didn't need a translation. They'd blown it . . .

Given the maelstrom of death and destruction they had unleashed at the Heron Pool Steve expected, at the very least, to be savagely beaten as a prelude to something infinitely nastier, but to his surprise they were conducted from the room with their skins intact. They were not even roughed up by their escort – something that defaulters in the Federation could look forward to from the moment they fell into the hands of the Provos.

On reaching the foredeck, where Sergeant Kurabashi had been catching up on the latest happenings back home, the ankle chains and neckboards were replaced. One of the red-stripes congratulated the sergeant for his part in spotting that the two Mutes might be 'wrong-un's'.

Steve found it hard to read Jap faces but Kurabashi gazed at them with what appeared to be a mixture of grudging admiration and regret. 'Ah-rong-dogs brave but ah-so very-ah foo-rish.' He smiled and drew a finger quickly across his throat.

The red-stripes took them below, down two sets of step-ladders and locked them in a small, darkened cabin whose door opened onto the forward passage to the engine room. The only light came through a latticed hatch in the main deck above the ladder-way at the end of the passage to their right. Very little of it reached their temporary cell but Steve didn't need bright lights to examine their surroundings. The wheel-boat was built to the same pattern as the vessel he'd stowed away on, and the cabin matched the one on the other side of the narrow corridor where he'd lain hidden in the long-box under Side-Winder's bunk for the greater part of the voyage.

He was also familiar with the layout of the engine-room at the far end of the passageway; the logs stacked eight feet high against the forward bulkhead and both sides of the hull. The huge boiler in the middle with its ever-hungry furnace, framed by iron platforms and catwalks, its gleaming brass valves, pumps, the maze of copper pipes, and the huge steel pistons whose driving force, transmitted along two massive wooden, iron-strapped beams turned the stern-mounted paddle-wheel – twenty feet in diameter and over thirty feet across.

Steve knew it was possible to get out through the engine room by crawling up one of the shafts housing the drive beams onto the rear deck. But when he'd made the journey in the reverse direction the beam hadn't been moving. They could go up the ladder-way onto the through-deck above them where the samurai's horses were stabled and get out through one of the square ports. But they weren't going anywhere so long as they were weighed down with chains and neckboards.

The ring holding the keys to their chains, boards and cell had been hung on the wall outside but it was only possible to push a finger through the stout lattice in the padlocked door. To reach the keys they would first have to smash the lattice, and even if they found some way of doing that, it could not be attempted while there was a guard stationed at each end of the passageway. By putting his face as close as he could to the lattice Steve could just see bits of the right arm and leg of the guard standing by the forward ladder. The Jap by the engine room was beyond his angle of sight but Cadillac had heard him being ordered to his post. Since when, like all soldiers on guard duty, he'd been exchanging the occasional word with his companion to relieve the boredom.

Steve turned his back on the problem. 'Not good, still . . . could be worse.'

Cadillac sat dejectedly on the large, wooden bunk in the semi-darkness. 'What's that gloo–gloo–slop–slop noise?'

'Oh, you'll get used to that. This cabin's below the water-line.'

'Wish I hadn't asked.' Cadillac tried to stretch out on the bunk but the board round his neck made it impossible. He found the only comfortable position was to sit against a wall with the front of the board resting on top of his knees.

'I'm sorry. It was stupid to get caught out like that.'

'Could have happened to anyone,' said Steve. 'If *I'd* been answering those questions I couldn't have kept the ball in the air for as long as you did.'

'Yeah. But you wouldn't have flinched when the Jap told them to cut off your right ear.'

'I would if I'd known what was coming,' laughed Steve. 'What d'you want me to say? "You blew it"?' He dismissed the question with a shrug. 'We gambled on being able to outsmart these guys and we lost. That's all there is to it.'

Cadillac nodded gloomily. 'I'm surprised they . . .' He left the sentence unfinished. 'Better not to talk about it. Might bring bad luck.'

'Yeah, well, if it's any comfort I think we're all right for a while. The way I see it, the number one task for these guys is to collar the rest of us. The pain comes later . . .'

'What's going to happen now there's no chance of sinking the wheelboat?'

'You tell me . . .'

'Do you think Clearwater will . . .?'

'. . . be able to get us out of this jam? She might,' said Steve. 'It depends.'

'On what?'

'On quite a lot of things. Such as whether 'Bull and Death-Wish got back safely with the message and whether she under-stood it. And then there's Carnegie-Hall. Is he still backing her up like he promised or is he just making the right noises while getting ready to dump us if things go the wrong way?'

Cadillac's spirits rallied. 'No. That won't happen. He's too scared of what she might do.' He adjusted the neckboard and stood up. 'She'll get us out of this, I know she will.'

'I wish it were that simple,' said Steve. 'I've as much faith in her as you have but –'

'But what?'

'It's not going to work!' cried Steve. He grabbed Cadillac's arm. 'Hear me out – and for crissakes keep your voice down!' He forced the Mute to sit on the bunk beside him. 'To begin with, she doesn't know we're in this mess. Let's assume she's waiting where Wantanabe landed at the end of November and that the guys above us on the bridge have managed to aim for exactly the same stretch of beach –'

'Okay –'

'So it's dark. As arranged. They stop the engines. Fine. But suppose they don't *drop* anchor and wait till dawn like everyone's expecting? Suppose they let the forward momentum of the boat carry her forward? Before Clearwater and the others realise that it's not gonna explode, they could have the bow of this boat halfway up the beach!'

'But that wasn't the plan!' hissed Cadillac. 'You heard what Carnegie said. 'They were going to arrive under cover of darkness, heave to offshore and exchange signals! Red and green rockets!'

'There aren't going to *be* any signals! Do you think the Japs are going to trust the Kojak after sending *us* two over as guides?! C'mon!'

'Yes . . . I suppose you're right.'

'Of course I'm right! They're going to steam in hard and come charging off this boat like buffaloes with rockets up their ass! In a situation like that, anything could happen. She might get hit by an arrow or go down under a horse before she has time to react.'

'That's stupid. You saw what happened at the Heron Pool.'

'You mean when she had all those samurai coming for her.'

'Yes! When the power is upon her she cannot be harmed by man-made weapons! Talisman is both sword and shield!'

'I'm not arguing about that. I'm talking about before she warms up. But okay, let's say she gets her act together and succeeds in doing what we've failed to do. She blows this wheelboat apart, far enough out so that the Japs wearing armour are in deep shit but close enough in so that any horses who survive can swim ashore –'

271

'I know what you're going to say. This cabin's below the water-line.'

'*Exactamente*. When it starts to pour in, we'll be the first to start treading water. But with all this junk on us, that won't be for very long.' Steve stood up. 'From the weight of this board I'd say it floats like a slab of concrete.'

Cadillac's new-found confidence began to ooze away. He fell back against the plank wall behind the bunk. 'This was what you foresaw when I read the stone – us drowning.'

'Wrong. Not drowning – *about* to drown. There's a big difference. All this talk has brought us right back to where we started. We can't expect Clearwater to do everything. Her job is to help the Kojak deal with any Iron Masters who get ashore. The rest is down to us. We've gotta wreck this boat and then we've gotta get out of here.'

'Shouldn't that be the other way round? How can we –?'

Steve cut him off. 'Look – I'll fix the boat, okay?'

'But how?!'

'Never mind how! If what I have in mind works, this thing is gonna go sky-high. But with luck, she won't sink until everything above the main deck is ablaze. *That's* when we leave – at the moment of maximum panic. So you've got from now till then to figure out how to get us out of this box – given that situation.'

'Brickman, the sun was setting when they brought us down here. If they keep to their original schedule and sail this evening we have –'

'Less than ten hours. I know.' The cards were stacked against them but there was one person who might be able to help.

Roz.

It was time to try a little magic of his own . . .

CHAPTER TWELVE

After taking leave of his wife and children, Izo Wantanabe was escorted back to the wheelboat by Kurabashi. A female domestic and a sea-soldier selected to accompany him as attendants sat with the baggage in front of the rowers.

The unmasking of two assassins – a direct result of his initial suspicions – had served to raise him further in the eyes of Samurai-Major Morita and Captain Kawanishi. The three other assassins would soon be brought to book and the treacherous Kojak would be taught a bloody and dreadful lesson that would serve to remind their Plainfolk neighbours of what awaited those who betrayed their benefactors.

All in all, the future could not have looked rosier. But Wantanabe was assailed by a nagging doubt that pricked his conscience like a sharp thorn. The discovery that one of the assassins understood the language of the Iron Masters had raised the possibility that the strength and timing of the raid might now be known to the enemy. Wantanabe knew that, besides being unable to read or write, Mutes were afflicted with unreliable memories and he now realized with the benefit of hindsight that the bark medallions carried by the returning boatmen could have contained a coded message for the other 'travellers'. How stupid not to have confiscated them!

But how could he have known one of these fake grass-monkeys was able to speak Japanese? It was absolutely forbidden, under pain of death, for slaves to utter a word of the sacred language of the Sons of Ne-Issan. Where had the outlander gained such knowledge? The answer to this and other questions would, without doubt, be elicited in the torture chambers that rumour placed beneath the palace of the Yama-Shita family at Sara-kusa.

Wantanabe would have liked to inflict a memorable measure of pain on the two assassins himself for having created the gnawing anxiety which had ruined his sleep since he'd found them lurking below his quarters on the houseboat. Their unmasking had relieved him of most of that anxiety but he now faced a difficult choice. Should he confess that he might – albeit unwittingly – have allowed vital information to be taken back to the enemy or should he say nothing? The truth might bring in its wake a charge of negligence and seriously damage his future prospects, whereas if he remained silent, as his wife Yumiko suggested . . .

Why risk everything? Even if the Kojak Mutes *were* alerted to the impending arrival of the wheelboat, how could they, a bunch of savages, and the three remaining assassins – two females and a semi-invalid male – resist the overwhelming might of the Iron Masters?

When lines from the dory had been secured to the gangway of the wheelboat, Sergeant Kurabashi bade a respectful farewell to his master, wishing him fair wind and good fortune. Wantanabe, who had formally passed over command of the out-station before the assembled crew of the houseboat, thanked him in a haughty tone that hinted of the preferment to come and urged him to take the utmost care of Yumiko and her two children. Not that there was any likelihood of them being neglected in his absence; Kurabashi knew that despite being named as the officer in charge, he'd be kept on the hop like everyone else.

Wantanabe supervised the unloading of the baggage by his two attendants to make sure that nothing had been forgotten then strode imperiously up the ramp with his left hand resting on the hilt of the single sword thrust through the dark sash around his waist. A sword which, as far as Kurabashi knew, had never drawn blood.

The sergeant, whose fighting experience ranged from drunken back-street brawls to murderous clashes with river-pirates, watched him mount the deck with mild amusement. These half-castes were all the same; always trying to prove something. He nevertheless wished him a safe and speedy return; the prospect of being saddled for more than three or four days with a sharp-tongued shrew like Yumiko was distinctly unappealing.

*

Throughout the same day, the Kojak had been preparing their defences along the stretch of beach on which the Iron Master landing was expected to take place. Having never seen horses, they had never fought against mounted warriors and it was here that Clearwater's experience was invaluable. She described the appearance of the two-headed, six-legged beast and assured the Kojak warriors that although a line of charging horsemen was a fearsome sight they could be defeated if the warriors held their ground. Those who stood firm were in less danger than those who turned and fled like startled fast-foot. They could not outrun their pursuers and with their backs to the horsemen's swords they could not defend themselves. To help meet the coming threat she showed them how to make halberds using the blades of their machetes and long staves then taught them how to counter and deliver blows using the knowledge she had gained from watching Steve practise with his quarterstaff.

The actual landing was due to take place just before dawn – a propitious moment for the Iron Masters because of their mythical links with the rising sun – but the Chosen Ones had promised that the wheelboat would be consumed with fire while it was still dark. With their great vessel ablaze and sinking, the dead-faces would be at a disadvantage as they struggled out of the shallows. Better still, they would be silhouetted against the flames whilst their attackers would be cloaked in darkness.

Given this situation, the beach formed the ideal first line of defence and it was here that the Kojak warriors hoped to inflict the maximum damage. Being hunters as well as fishermen they were already well versed in the art of digging pits to trap game and in a short while, the beach was dotted with a mixture of potholes and trenches designed to bring down rider and horse. The holes were overlaid with a light framework of branches strong enough to support criss-crossed layers of leaves and a thin topcoat of sand and shingle. When each one was completed its position was marked by thin twigs stuck upright in the sand but in the grey pre-dawn twilight the pitfalls they enclosed would be invisible.

A second line of defence was erected using the clan's fishing nets mounted on poles that leaned towards the water. Stretched out along the beach, with the bottom edge raised high enough to enable a warrior to duck underneath it, they too would be invisible until horse and rider found themselves entangled in the coarse mesh.

Close to the water's edge, a small fire would be built. Around it, a group of Kojak fisherfolk would lie asleep alongside their up-turned boats while two of their number kept watch in the normal manner. It was known that the dead-faces had hollow brass sticks containing magic eyes through which they could see distant objects as if they were only an arm's length away. The fire, built close to where Wantanabe had landed, would — it was hoped — draw the wheelboat towards the same spot; the centre of the beach defences.

The peaceful scene — with two sentinels watching for the red fire that was to appear in the night sky — was designed to lull the Iron Masters into thinking that the clan were adhering to the original plan. But underneath the hulls of the upturned boats, Kojak warriors with crossbows would be lying in wait, ready for any false move.

The return of Raging-Bull and Death-Wish with details of the coming attack gave a physical and temporal dimension to the danger but did little to reduce Clearwater's anxiety. For Cadillac and the cloud-warrior, reaching the out-station was only half the battle. The livid scar round Death-Wish's neck from his near-strangulation underlined the unpredictable nature of the enemy. The Iron Masters' thinly-disguised contempt for 'inferior persons' placed Mute slaves under constant threat of death. Cadillac and the cloud-warrior were not officially in that category but as long as they remained in the clutches of the Iron Masters they were in mortal peril — especially in view of what they had set out to do.

She offered prayers to Mo-Town for their deliverance but she knew that they first had to sink the wheelboat. She was tempted to use her powers to help them but because they were on board and she was on shore, only they could choose the moment. Did they realize, she wondered, how much depended on them?

Clearwater had penetrated Carnegie's mind and strengthened his will to resist. The wordsmith, in turn, had passed that resolve on to those around him but she could not control the whole clan. Even though they were in awe of her powers she could not *force* them to fight – and that was another source of anxiety.

Their reluctance had its roots in the past. Apart from a few initial skirmishes, the Plainfolk clans had avoided armed conflict with the Iron Masters. The decision had caused individual clans a great deal of heart-searching as it gradually became clear that the little yellow men from the eastern lands had no territorial ambitions. Their landings on Plainfolk turf had only one purpose: trade – an exchange of goods and bodies beneficial to both parties, but which gradually became weighted in the Iron Masters' favour.

The early confrontations had demonstrated that the deadfaces were highly-disciplined, well-armed warriors with no qualms about taking on a force several times their number. Plainfolk Mutes were justly proud of their courage and prowess as warriors but they quickly realized that, in attacking the Iron Masters, they had – to use a Mute phrase – bitten off more bone than they could chew.

Conflicts over disputed turf were usually small-scale affairs involving bands of warriors numbering no more than two or three hands. Ambushes and 'zaps' – hit-and-run attacks – favoured by some of the D'Troit clans, were frowned on by the She-Kargo who adopted a more flamboyant style. Combat was preceded by a lengthy verbal confrontation in which each side exchanged taunts, mocking each other's manhood, and this was accompanied by a great deal of aggressive posturing; a process known as 'strutting the stuff'.

The ensuing battle usually consisted of individual conflicts and where one side outnumbered the other those without an opponent did not enter the fray unless one of his clan-brothers fell. This ritualized style of combat was not always adhered to in clashes between warriors of different blood-lines and when fifty or more were involved on either side the battle that ensued often became a sprawling, messy affair.

Unless they were led by a gifted wordsmith – and not always even then – Mute clans did not fight in disciplined formations and never evolved a tactical battle-plan. This lack of a coherent military command structure was probably the reason why large-scale conflicts rarely developed between rival clans. The last one involving the M'Calls had been fifteen years ago when Clearwater's father, Thunder-Bird, had kissed the sharp iron of the D'Vine during the battle of the Black Hills.

With room enough for everyone in a world where the resourceful and energetic need never go hungry, Plainfolk clans had no desire to annihilate each other. The important thing was to maintain their 'standing' – the recognition, by his peers, of a warrior's courage. But a warrior with a knife, however brave, was no match for a sword-wielding samurai and once this had been established, along with the benefits to be derived from regular trading contacts, a cautious partnership had developed. A partnership on which the Mutes had come to rely, for besides a range of useful domestic items, the Iron Masters supplied better knives with sharper cutting edges to replace the precious relics handed down through countless generations, cross-bows for hunting and, last year, rifles – to be used against the Mutes' *real* enemy, the sand-burrowers.

Clearwater was acutely aware that this deferential relationship and material dependence, built up over several decades, was at the back of the clan's collective mind along with the realization that they were about to ruin it. It was not courage they lacked but conviction.

Having seen proof of their power, the clan had welcomed them as The Chosen. The initial deceit, concocted by Carnegie-Hall, had become a reality. The thought that they, the Kojak, had been plucked from obscurity to play a key role in the events that heralded the birth of Talisman had been thrilling. But now the euphoria had worn off. Cadillac's promise that their name would be linked forever with the advent of the Thrice-Gifted One had gradually lost its appeal as the fatal day approached. The clan had worked hard to construct the defences that Cadillac and the cloud-warrior had planned before leaving, but as the day drew to a close, she sensed they were becoming increasingly concerned about the long-term consequences of defying the Iron Masters.

Moving from group to group she had made their eyes glow

by telling them of the weapons they could seize and the treasures to be recovered from the wreck of the sunken vessel. This, she knew, would persuade them to take up their positions on the shore but it would not keep them there. Only a brilliant coup by Cadillac and the cloud-warrior could put the iron back into their souls.

On board the wheelboat, Captain Kawanishi and Samurai-Major Morita stood on a portable dais in the centre of the through-deck and watched as four pairs of *Shinto* priests and their acolytes worked their way around the stalls where the two hundred and fifty samurai stood by their saddled mounts.

The ceremony was designed to render Morita's troops invulnerable to the evil *kami* called into being by the 'white witch' at the Heron Pool. Morita was the only man there who had witnessed the terrifying effect of her power upon the troops assembled there. No sword, arrow or spear could harm her. Seeing this, many turned tail and fled; those samurai who held their ground perished. Had he not been trapped in the shattered grandstand, he would have perished with them. But not this time. After delving into ancient documents, the priests had prepared a number of powerful incantations guaranteed to turn the witch's magic back upon herself.

Morita and his officers had already been blessed in a private session and soon it would be the turn of the three-hundred red-stripe infantry. Being of lower rank, they would receive a simultaneous blessing from all eight priests at group rates.

Izo Wantanabe, who had been in the back row when Morita had received his spiritual armour plate, watched from the sidelines. Despite his grand title of Emissary to the Outlands, he was only an administrator and a relatively junior one at that. Unless they were involved in a last-ditch stand during a civil insurrection, administrators did not usually wage war with anything sharper than a writing brush. Their swords were badges of rank but their function was not purely ceremonial. At a certain awkward moment, when your career as a functionary took a sudden downturn, they provided a quick and efficient way of saving yourself and everyone else from further embarrassment.

As a special honour, Captain Kawanishi had given Wantanabe permission to watch the coming landing from the bridge. Once the three remaining assassins had been safely locked away below, he would go ashore to witness the execution by beheading of all captured Mutes and the impaling of their treacherous wordsmith. Only one man, woman and child would be spared to relate what lay in store for those who dared to challenge the Sons of Ne-Issan.

When all the troops had been blessed, Morita drew a cheer from their throats with a short, upbeat address then returned to the bridge with his aides and personal guard. After being assured that they were still on course for a dawn landing, Morita called for a celebratory cup of *sake* for everyone on the bridge then retired to his second floor headquarters in the centre of the galleried superstructure.

Passing his helmet and swords to a retainer, Morita lowered his armoured-plated body into a reclining chair which he always took with him on military expeditions, closed his eyes and fell asleep. It was a knack he had acquired many years ago. In two hours it would be time for the troops to assemble for the landing. The same knack would wake him, without prompting, in an hour and a half and he would spring from his chair ready for action.

His staff tip-toed away and made themselves as comfortable as they could around the walls of the room. Up here, on the second floor, they were partially insulated from the constant rumbling beat of the engine that filled the lower levels and made the hull timbers quiver. With all external lights now extinguished, and only a masked lantern illuminating the compass on the bridge, the wheelboat ploughed on, its churning wake blue-white under a fitful moon. A stiff headwind furrowed the water across its path, lifting spray from the crests onto the foredeck as they collided with the under-slope of the square-nosed bow.

Wantanabe, who occupied a small cabin on the floor below, also tried to catch some sleep. The wind, gusting around the posts of the gallery outside kept him hovering on the edge of consciousness. He consoled himself with the thought that it would carry the sound of the boat's engine away from the approaching shore.

*

Guided onto their target by a Skyrider mother-ship, four Skyhawk Mark Two's fitted with long-range fuel tanks caught sight of the wheelboat when it was some two miles west of navref Chicago. The Skyrider, loaded with an imposing array of pin-point navigation devices and image intensifiers passed low over the boat, skimming dangerously close to the tall funnels before releasing two parachute flares to starboard. The blinding white light threw the boat into silhouette; a huge dark rectangle like a pre-Holocaust apartment block perched on a broad flat hull. Impossible for the quartet of Skyhawks to miss. Sweeping in from the south-west, they lobbed their first string of explosive napalm canisters into the portside galleries and flitted overhead like giant grey bats vanishing into the darkness beyond before the exploding fireballs could illuminate their passage.

The Skyrider mother-ship climbed to eight hundred feet and began to circle the wheelboat. The pilot and master-navigator saw the diamond formation of nav-lights turn left onto a northerly heading then continue round back towards the ship. The navigator spoke to the planes below. 'Fire-Chief to Fire-Crew. Strike Two.'

The gyro-compass on the instrument panel of the lead aircraft turned and steadied on a heading of 225 degrees. And now, as the parachute flares lay guttering in the water, it was the starboard side of the wheelboat that was thrown into sharp silhouette by the mushrooming flame-cloud beyond. A second low pass, which forced the tight formation to jink right and left of the twin funnels as the napalm canisters were released, created a second wall of fire.

The attack-coordinator came on the air again as the formation reformed. 'Fire-Chief to Fire-Crew. You're doing a great job down there. That turkey must be really feeling the heat. Let's go roast his big fat ass. Strike Three! Strike Three! All planes break sharp right after release. Reform and circle line-astern at five hundred, on the rank. Watch those funnels and flagpoles on the run-out. Don' wanna lose you after coming this far. Over.'

Fire-Crew Leader acknowledged the order. A few moments later, the stern deck and rear galleries erupted into flame.

The bow-section and forward galleries were now the only parts of the boat where fires were not raging. There were two very good reasons for this: first, the pilots from Karlstrom's private air force knew that one of their number was imprisoned below decks in the forward part of the vessel and second, the initial attack had been designed to force the crew and their military passengers to abandon ship.

The two wide bow gangways were now the only exit down which an orderly evacuation could be made. At that moment, the giant paddle wheel was still turning, driving the stricken vessel towards the shore. When the time came to sink it, the circling Skyhawks would deliver the *coup de grace* using the eight 50-lb bombs which made up the other half of the surprise package they'd brought, with the compliments of Karlstrom, all the way from Texas.

On the wheelboat, the initial moment of paralysis was rapidly replaced by growing pandemonium as would-be fire-fighters discovered the grisly adhesive qualities of the napalm gel. Fanned by the stiff breeze, the individual fires quickly became one huge conflagration and within minutes three fifty-foot high walls of fire were spreading inwards towards each other, consuming everything above the main deck.

The explosive nature of the fire that had suddenly engulfed the crowded boat, its scale, intensity and the probable cause was beyond comprehension. No one had ever experienced a napalm strike and apart from Morita and Izo Wantanabe, none of the soldiers or sailors on board had ever seen an aeroplane before; the only man-made flying object they were familiar with were kites.

The strike force, painted in the dark grey used by AMEXI-CO for covert operations was swallowed up in the surrounding darkness. The speed and unexpected nature of attack had given the Iron Masters no opportunity to realize what had hit them. Only the wing-tip and tail navigation lamps, and the red wink-lights above and below the fuselage sliding through the darkness like slow-motion meteors identified the source of the trouble. But if you didn't know what they were, you were none the wiser, and the sound of their motors, only briefly heard before the first string of napalm canisters exploded, was now blanked out by the roaring rush of flame, the screams and shouts, the crash and thud of timbers.

Samurai-Major Morita, wakened by his aides a few seconds after they themselves had been shaken by the first muffled blasts, rushed out into the passageway to be greeted by a searing wave of heat. Flames now engulfed the exit to the portside gallery. The four red-stripes guarding the entrance to the stateroom – unable to leave their post without orders to do so – were milling around indecisively. Their nervousness was aggravated by the burning body of one of their colleagues who had been caught by the sudden eruption of flame whilst guarding the port entrance to the passageway. The head and shoulders burned in places down to the bone were charred beyond recognition but from mid-spine to thigh he was still alight and the flames had spread to his surroundings.

And yet, incredibly, despite his horrific injuries, he was still alive – or, at least, part of him was. All four limbs jerked spasmodically and he seemed to be trying to crawl blindly towards his terrified companions. But they had turned away to greet Morita with a low bow.

The samurai-major ordered one of them to put the poor wretch out of his misery. As he did so, the red-stripe guarding the starboard exit came running towards them screaming something about giant green-eyed night-birds. Something dark hit the floor behind him and the rest of his warning was drowned out by a sudden thunder clap of sound. The entrance to the passageway was filled with an exploding wall of flame that rolled forward engulfing the guard.

As Morita recoiled, he saw the red-stripe's body flare briefly like a moth caught in a candle and an instant later, as his aides hustled him towards the other end of the stateroom, the fiery tidal wave swirled around the other red-stripes. With their screams ringing in his ears, Morita hurried towards the second, forward exit to the stateroom.

Reaching the stairs beyond, he ordered his personal guard to proceed forward and aft, and to the floors above and below to check the extent of the fires. He himself was going up to the bridge and they were to report to him there. Just as they were about to disperse, two officers dispatched by Captain Kawanishi to fetch him came hurrying down the stairway. At this point only the side galleries were ablaze but as Morita listened to their report he realized that, barring divine intervention, there was little hope of saving the vessel. Seamen using hoses spraying water pumped from the steam engines below were being deployed but the scale of the fires and the speed with which they had spread had already outstripped their resources.

With both sides of the superstructure alight the blaze could only be fought from the foredeck and the stern and from below using the internal companionways. The side decks were now impassable; the only access between the front and rear of the boat was via the cargo deck where the horses were stabled and the bilge deck below where the engine room was situated.

As they gave a breathless account of the devilish nature of the fire – how it stuck to flesh, or any other surface, and could not be extinguished with water, the boat shook under the impact of the third strike on the stern. The two officers excused themselves hurriedly and ran down a passage alongside the stateroom only to find that the far end was in flames. Shouting to his personal guard to assess the situation as ordered, Morita dispatched his second-in-command to take whatever action he judged necessary to save the cavalry and horses then clattered up the stairs to the bridge with his remaining aides.

He was met by Kawanishi, his face ashen-grey. Not with fear but the grim realization he was about to lose both his vessel and his command. That in itself was bad enough, but his shame was compounded by the realization that the entire expedition could go to the bottom without striking a single blow at the enemy.

Morita shared his concern. Their only chance of salvaging some shred of honour was to press on at full speed in the hope of beaching the stricken vessel before it sank.

Kawanishi agreed and told him he had already sent a trusted officer and a squad of sea-soldiers to the engine room to make sure the stokers and engineers stayed at their posts.

But what, demanded Morita, was the cause of it all? Were the explosions accidental – the result of gunpowder stored on board being accidentally ignited – or had the vessel been sabotaged? Or – something even more difficult to accept – had it come under attack? Morita recounted what the red-stripe had shouted about giant night-birds in the brief instant before his obliteration by fire.

Kawanishi pointed to a cluster of twinkling lights moving backwards and forwards in the darkness to starboard. 'There are your night-birds! Fire-breathing sky-demons spawned by the white witch you seek! Accursed priests! How foolish we were to imagine that their empty gestures and worthless vapourings could protect us!'

One of the bridge officers reported that the system of signalling wires to the engine room had ceased to function.

'How far are we from shore?' demanded Morita.

Another bridge officer, who had a powerful spyglass trained on a group of Mute fishermen standing round a fire, told him they were now less than three-quarters of a mile from the beach. Morita doubted whether horses wearing battle harness and carrying fully-armed warriors could swim that far.

A smoke-blackened runner sent from the through-deck reported that flames were beginning to curl round the ceilings beams in the aft portion of the deck space. The horses were becoming more difficult to restrain. Any further delay might cause the panic-stricken beasts to run amok. Parts of the galleried superstructure had already started to collapse and there was a growing danger that burning debris might start crashing through the ceiling. The deputy task-force commander, continued the runner, acting upon the powers given to him, had ordered the evacuation of the through-deck before the worsening situation made it impossible.

Morita gave the decision his approval and sent the runner back with a new order. The infantry were to strip themselves of all inessentials but were to keep as many weapons as they thought they could swim with. The rafts and dories – which, in any event, would have only provided berths in an emergency for the wheelboat's crew – were all blazing fiercely in the side galleries. Morita also gave instructions for the senior officers leading the mounted samurai to wait until last.

This was not out of a deep concern for those they led, it was a purely pragmatic decision. The first waves to ride into the water would probably founder with their exhausted horses before they reached the shore whereas the last to leave would be closer to the beach and in better shape to organize the survivors into a coherent force which he would then lead into battle.

Kawanishi, he imagined, would go down with his ship. As to his own fate, Morita viewed it with indifference. Samurai rose each day ready to embrace death. Their only concern was to die with honour. Perhaps the ruling deity, Amaterasu-Omikami, who watched over the world ruled by the Sons of Ne-Issan, had frowned upon this enterprise because it ran counter – for some reason that he, Morita, could not as an ordinary mortal comprehend – to the greater good of the nation. So be it. He would kill as many grass-monkeys as he could then take his own life rather than suffer the indignity of dying at the hands of an inferior being.

Speaking of which, there were two inferior beings below who richly merited death. A sword thrust was too good for them. Before leaving the boat he would have them brought up from their cell and cast into the inferno that raged behind him . . .

A cry from one of his aides standing on the gallery outside the bridge cut across his thoughts. Morita moved quickly through the open doorway and sighted along the aide's out-flung arm. A dark stiff-winged shape with a glowing red eye embedded in its belly was moving across a moonlit patch of sky almost directly overhead. It vanished against the dark underside of the cloud base but the baleful red eye continued to wax and wane as the 'night-bird' circled above the wheel-boat.

Except it was not from the natural world, or a creature summoned by sorcery from The Pit. It was twin-brother to the flying-horse Izo Wantanabe had sketched in his first message to Sara-kusa. The wheelboat had been attacked by long-dogs from the south. But how could they have known where it was going and, more importantly, when? There was only one explanation. The long-dogs and the grass-monkeys were working hand-in-glove. Somehow the assassins had gained access to the contents of his last dispatch to Bei-tanaba and, despite his suspicions, Wantanabe had allowed them to depart. It was an act of incredible folly, of criminal negligence, for which, if he was still alive, he must pay. Now. Instantly.

Morita summoned his three aides and began to give the fatal orders. Two were to fetch the chained assassins with the help of the soldiers guarding their cell, the third was to seek out Izo Wantanabe and behead him.

The door to Izo Wantanabe's cabin on the port side was the impact point of one of the canisters dropped in the first strike but he had escaped death by seconds. Unable to sleep, he left his cabin and walked onto the foredeck as the four aircraft suddenly appeared off the port bow and flashed overhead. A second later, all three galleries erupted into flame.

As he stood there, in a state of shock, staring at the inferno that only a moment before had been the cabin in which *he* had been lying, cursing his inability to sleep, the starboard side exploded. He caught a brief glimpse of four dark shapes with red eyes, illuminated by the flames as they passed overhead but by the time he had recovered from his surprise and turned around, all he could see were points of light moving against the blackness of the sky.

Unable to decide whether to advance in the hope of being of some assistance, or retreat further from the searing heat, Izo Wantanabe watched in horror as screaming crewmen stumbled out onto the blazing galleries and leapt overboard, their bodies totally enveloped in flames. Human torches.

It was a dreadful sight, but what chilled him was the sickening realization that the boat was being attacked by what Morita had described as 'flying-horses' – ridden by long-dogs from the south. Allies of the assassins imprisoned below . . .

As he watched the flames spread he remembered the words used by Aishi Sakimoto when warning him not to act until reinforcements arrived. His message had contained the chilling phrase: 'The riders have powerful friends and secret means to summon them in the twinkling of an eye'. So be it. Death would overtake them just as quickly. If he and his comrades were destined to perish in these god-forsaken outlands then he would personally make sure they were not spared.

Grasping the hilt of his sword, he ran towards the forward companionway and promptly collided with the first of several dozen soldiers who came swarming up the steps and onto the deck. A hand grasped his arm. Turning, Wantanabe found himself face-to-face with a samurai-officer, his face blackened and blistered, his clothes burned in several places and still smouldering.

'Quickly! Help these men lower the bow ramps!'

'Are we abandoning ship?' cried Wantanabe.

'Not yet! We have to get the horses ashore first! We're not going down without a fight!'

Sammy-Jo Mackinnon, the attack-coordinator and master-navigator who had shepherded the four Skyhawks from the AMEXICO air-base outside Houston-GC decided it was time to stop the Japs dead in the water. For several minutes, men and horses had been streaming out of the through-deck and down the bow-ramps lowered close to, but not quite touching the water. The wheelboat, now less than half a mile from the shore, had not reduced speed despite the massive fire-damage it had sustained.

What she and the other pilots didn't know, along with Morita, was that the engine room of the boat was itself a raging inferno. The crew, ordered to stay at their posts, and the soldiers sent to make sure they did just that, were now unrecognizable lumps of bubbling fat and over-roasted flesh, buried amidst the glowing embers at the heart of a growing pile of collapsed timbers which had come crashing down into the rapidly-emptying through-deck like a cloud-burst of celestial fire. A few minutes later, the flaming mass cascaded into the engine room swamping everyone and everything below.

Yet, miraculously, despite the searing heat which had caused spontaneous combustion of the fuel logs and the falling pressures as fractured pipes and burst joints hissed steam, the pistons shunted doggedly back and forth, and the iron-strapped beams — themselves now ablaze — had shouldered the debris aside and were continuing to power the paddle-wheel. More slowly, and with increasing difficulty, but on they went, up and down, like the failing muscles lifting the thighs of an exhausted marathon runner, driving him on when the whole point of the race, of existence, has been lost in the all-consuming fog of pain and only one thought remains. *To keep going forward, forward, forward ...*

In the belly of the boat, Steve and Cadillac had also heard the detonations despite the drumming background roar from the engine room at the end of the passageway. They had also heard the shouts of alarm and glimpsed the growing confusion as the squad of sea-soldiers rushed past on what was to prove a suicide mission. And they heard the thunder of hooves as the horses on the through deck above became increasingly restive and then, as more explosions sent shockwaves through the ship's timbers, were ridden up and out across the bow deck into the relative safety of the sea.

Steve had known what was going to happen for several hours but the promise of help was not the same thing as help actually arriving, on time and in a form that would ensure their deliverance. So far, Roz had performed brilliantly. It was like being on a two-way radio circuit. From the moment of making contact, she had delivered regular, reassuring progress reports and then, as the four Skyhawks lined up on their target, she came through to warn him what was about to happen. He was to keep calm and stay tuned. A few seconds later, a series of muffled detonations had shaken the boat from bridge to keel.

Steve had already decided not to tell Cadillac what was going to happen. If he wanted to, he could work it out for himself. Not that it mattered greatly. Knowing *why* the boat was on fire and sinking would not aid their escape, and by the time they managed to get out, the Skyhawks would — Steve hoped — have disappeared. In which case Cadillac would credit Mo-Town or Talisman with their deliverance. Steve was happy to leave it that way. To reveal that he had set up the attack with the aid of Roz would only have led Cadillac to ask the kind of questions he was not ready to answer.

The two guards stationed in the passageway were still on duty but the one stationed near the engine room had moved towards his companion and the ladder which was now the only escape route. And although the cause remained a mystery, Cadillac was now aware from the questions and answers put by the guards to anyone who passed overhead that the fire raging above was now totally out of control and the order to abandon ship would come at any moment.

As far as the guards were concerned the order could not come a moment too soon; a feeling that Steve and Cadillac shared. A chorus of hoarse screams cut across the sonorous drum-beat of the engine. There was a brief, chilling groan and crack of timbers then both sounds were eclipsed by a sudden thunderous roar as the central section of the blazing superstructure crashed down into the engine room burying everyone beneath. Only two sea-soldiers and a stoker, naked to the waist, who had been within reach of the forward door managed to stumble to safety pursued by a shower of red-hot embers and a brief orange tongue of flame.

Smoke seeped through the lattice of the door. 'We've gotta get out of here,' said Steve, as the survivors staggered past. 'C'mon. Do your stuff!'

Peeking though the lattice, Cadillac glimpsed the two guards and the sea-soldiers clustered around the foot of the step-ladder. Screams of agony came from the inferno at the other end of the passageway. Someone, a colleague of the stoker, trapped near the doorway, was calling out to him, begging to be pulled clear of the flames. The stoker hesitated, then went back to rescue him. The braver of the two guards followed. The others shouted at them to come back.

The confusion of sound and voices gave Cadillac the opportunity he'd been looking for. Standing back from the door, he adopted the commanding tone of Samurai-Major Morita and shouted: 'Release the prisoners! Release the prisoners! Bring them on deck!'

The two sea-soldiers and the guard at the foot were not sure where the order had come from but they recognized an officer's voice when they heard one. The guard grabbed the key ring off the hook on the wall and started to unlock the door.

Steve grabbed Cadillac by both arms. 'You're a genius! Y'know that?' He pulled him down onto the bunk bench. It was better not to crowd these guys by the door. They might get the wrong idea.

C'mon, c'mon, c'mon! Oh, what an idiot! The dink had inserted the wrong key!

There was another thunderous crash of timbers as more of the superstructure collapsed into the engine room sending a gust of smoke-laden red-hot air rolling up the passageway. The guard and the engineer, their faces raw and blistered, reappeared dragging a blackened, smoking body.

'This is hopeless,' croaked the guard. 'He's finished!'

'You're right . . .' The engineer laid his colleague to rest with his hands placed neatly across his body. 'Come on. Let's get out of here before she breaks in two!'

The two sea-soldiers started up the step-ladder.

'Wait a minute,' cried the second guard. 'We've got to get these two monkeys out of here.' Having dropped and retrieved the key ring with trembling fingers he was trying, yet again, to open the lock with the wrong key.

'Sod them!' shouted his companion. 'Let the bastards drown!' The sea-soldiers led the scramble up the step-ladder onto the through-deck.

Cadillac heard a voice shout. 'Moto! Quick! This whole deck is on fire!'

So far, Steve and Cadillac had been incredibly lucky not to have been burnt to a crisp or asphyxiated by smoke. Two things were working in their favour. The ten-foot high piles of tightly-packed timber, stacked several rows thick against the forward bulkhead was acting as a kind of fire-wall. The outer stacks were blazing fiercely and the rest were close to flash-point but they had not yet caught fire. The flames generated by the collapsed superstructure were being funnelled upwards out of the gaping hole above and were being fuelled by air sucked down the hatches and along the passageway past the room in which Steve and Cadillac were held. Any smoke was thus being drawn away from them but they could still feel the heat and knew that, at any minute, the fire could spread suddenly and dramatically to engulf them and the fumbling idiot outside the door on whom their lives now depended.

'What are you doing?' demanded Izo Wantanabe.

The guard jumped nervously to attention. 'Evacuating the two prisoners, sir! As ordered!'

'Who by?'

'Can't say exactly, sir.' The guard gestured towards the hatchway. 'I think it was an officer up there!'

Wantanabe nodded. 'Good. Off you go. Hurry! Get out while you can.'

'But, uh – what about the prisoners, sir?'

Wantanabe took charge of the key ring. 'Leave them to me . . .'

The three aides detailed to execute Izo Wantanabe and drag Steve and Cadillac from their cell to be cast into the flames saluted Morita and turned to leave. As they did so, the first 100 pound bomb struck the forward gallery directly underneath the bridge. The second crashed through the gallery below, several feet further to the right. The next four fell into the yawning furnace that had once been the midships section, and the last two struck the stern, blasting the paddle-wheel apart.

Morita, his aides, Captain Kawanishi and the remaining bridge officers heard a deafening roar and felt the floor lift beneath them as the top half of the unburnt forward galleries blew apart then collapsed inwards and backwards. Morita experienced one last brief moment of lucidity in which he realized his body was one of several tumbling head over heels towards the blazing heart of the funeral pyre he had chosen for the assassins then his brain froze in horror as the glowing mass exploded like the sacred Mount Fuji, tearing him apart with tentacles of fire.

It was this explosion – the almost simultaneous detonation of the four 100 pound bombs planted amidships – that finally ripped the guts out of the boat and stopped her dead in the water. For Steve and Cadillac, this final convulsion brought them deliverance but came close to killing them in the process.

As the bombs were falling towards their target, Izo Wantanabe flung the door open and stood there, sword grasped firmly in both hands, silhouetted against the wandering pool of light cast by the lantern near the steps.

Steve eyed the quivering point of the sword as he and Cadillac rose to their feet. The dink was as frightened as they were. All the more reason to hang loose. In this confined space he'd have to thrust, not swing. Even so, this didn't look good. Steve grasped the sides of his neck-board. Properly angled, he might just be able to parry a cutting blow, creating an opportunity for Cadillac to move in . . .

Wantanabe hesitated, trying to decide which of his victims was the most dangerous. The one who spoke Japanese or his more strongly-built companion? He jabbed the blade at Cadillac, savouring his moment of power over the two treacherous dogs who had ruined him then pulled back to make the killing stroke.

Using the powers of mimicry he had first displayed whilst impersonating the courtesan Yoko Mishima, Cadillac stepped towards the blade and screamed: 'Husband! I beg you! Don't! These are the Shogun's men! Think of me, your wife, and the little ones!'

Momentarily stunned at hearing Yumiko's voice issue from the mouth of the assassin, Wantanabe faltered and lowered his sword.

And it was in that same instant, as Steve and Cadillac hurled themselves towards him, that the four bombs exploded amidships and broke the wheelboat in two. Wantanabe staggered and fell against the back wall as the bow lifted under the weight of water flooding into the gaping hole where the engine room had been. Steve and Cadillac fell on top of him. Steve, who'd moved in first, got the top half, pinning Wantanabe's throat against the boards with the right side of his neck-board while he tried to hammer the sword loose from the Jap's hand. Cadillac fell across Wantanabe's legs, grabbed his other arm and held it at full stretch while pressing one corner of his own neck-board into the Jap's groin.

A torrent of water was now rushing up the passageway and flooding into the room.

Steve used his shoulder to ram his neckboard up hard under Wantanabe's chin. 'Right – I've got it.' he grunted. 'Let me at the fucker!'

Cadillac rolled aside as Steve staggered to his feet. The Jap realized he was done for, but he wasn't taking it lying down. Leaning against the wall, he hauled his soaking wet body clear of the water – now calf deep. Steve hefted the sword.

'Watch him!' cried Cadillac.

'It's okay! If he wants it standing up, that's the way he's going to get it!'

But Wantanabe wasn't quite finished. Before either Steve or Cadillac had time to react, the Jap threw himself towards the open door, seized hold of the precious keys that still hung in the lock jerked the door clear of Cadillac's outstretched fingers and pulled it shut behind him.

'Steve!' screamed Cadillac. 'For chrissakes! Stop him!'

Reversing the blade to put the curved cutting edge on top, Steve raised the blade level with the ceiling then plunged it downwards with all the force he could muster. The blade sliced through the lattice and sank deep into Wantanabe's chest before he could turn the key but as Steve withdrew it and his body slid into the rising water, his dead hand pulled the keys from the lock.

'Shit!' cried Steve. The water was now up to the level of the lattice and with the steepening downward tilt of the floor most of the back wall was under water. Passing the sword to Cadillac, he forced the door open and went in nose first to hunt for the key ring.

Cadillac, who had found the reckless courage to face the fearsome Shakatak D'Vine, tried to master the wave of panic that was rising as fast as the water he was floundering in. This was the moment Steve had foreseen. The moment he had been dreading. The gut-ripping pain of cold steel was infinitely preferable to the nameless horrors that awaited the souls of those who drowned.

Mutes from the high plains were always very cautious about getting out of their depth. If you were unlucky enough to die in the water, your spirit was dragged down into a black whirlpool at the centre of the earth instead of rising into the arms of the Great Sky-Mother. A whirlpool full of poisonous scorpions from which you never escaped . . .

Steve's hand rose out of the water, clutching the key ring. His head followed, gasping for air. 'Do my hands first!'

Cadillac took the keys and freed Steve's wrists.

'Okay. Let me do yours . . . and now the neckboard . . .' The water was now up to their chests. 'Terrific. Now mine. Can you reach?'

'Yeah, but what about –'

'I'll do the feet. Don't worry!' Steve threw off his neck-board, grabbed the keys and sank out of sight.

Cadillac waited but nothing happened. Why was Steve taking his own leg shackles off first when it was he, Cadillac, who couldn't swim? There was only a thin wedge of air space left in the room. The panic returned as he started to tread water. Hands grasped at his thrashing feet, pulling him under. The shackles' chains dropped away from his ankles then he felt Steve's arm curl round his neck from behind pulling him deeper still. Into the blackness. He kicked wildly, trying to break Steve's hold but all he managed to do was crack his own shins on the top of the door frame as he was dragged through. Water filled his mouth and nostrils –

Oh, Sweet Mother! They were going to drown!

On shore, Clearwater and the Kojak Mutes who lined the beach defences heard or saw nothing of the wheelboat until it burst into flames, lighting the surrounding waters with an orange glow. The clan-folk roared with delight.

Heyyy-yaaaAAHH!! This was proof, yet again, of the power that Talisman had placed in the hands of The Chosen! And the Kojak would show themselves to be worthy and courageous hosts!

Since the first three rapid strikes against the boat had been made in almost total darkness when it was just under two miles from the shore, Clearwater had no inkling that the havoc had been created by an outside agency. And even when the boat drew closer, and the presence of the drifting red star-fires were registered by the sharp-eyed Mutes the Kojak were none the wiser.

It was only when the boat was struck by the final salvo of bombs and Clearwater glimpsed grey bird-like shapes flitting in and out of the furnace glow that her excitement became edged with fear. And she began to wonder if the moving points of light in the sky signalled the presence of a darker power – the sand-burrowers. Had the cloud-warrior summoned them to his aid? She decided it did not matter whether the agency was human or divine as long as the wished-for result was achieved. Talisman had power over all things and exerted his will in mysterious ways.

Shouts from further down the beach turned her thoughts back to the matter in hand. The fishermen standing by the decoy fire at the water's edge had seen the first dark shapes of men and horses swimming towards the shore. The warriors, who had come out of their hiding places beneath the upturned boats when the Iron Master's vessel had gone up in flames to cheer and strut exultantly back and forth along the beach, fell on one knee and took careful aim with their crossbows.

Zzhhh ... zzhhh ... zzhh-zzhonk! Zzhhon-zzhhon-zzhhonk! Six samurai in the first wave were blown out of their saddles into the water. But although the Kojak had the advantage of firing from the cover of darkness, the traffic was not all one way. Many of the advancing samurai had drawn their bows, and long feather-flighted arrows were finding targets illuminated by the decoy bonfire on the beach. As soon as they realized the source of the danger, the nearest Mutes picked up two of the fishing boats, turned them on their side and held them one on top of the other in front of the fire while it was quickly smothered with sand. Then, having discovered the boats could be used to hide behind as well as under, they laid them down several yards further back and started firing again, ducking out of sight to reload.

The protection afforded by the skin-covered boats was more imaginary than real as several Mutes were to discover. The spear-pointed samurai arrows punched straight through the slatted roundwood floors and between their ribs before stopping but the notion they were safely hidden from view kept their colleagues in the firing-line.

Seizing the halberd she had fashioned from a machete and a

strong sapling, Clearwater led a group of similarly-armed warriors down from the dunes and onto the beach. The clan's morale had been boosted by the wheelboat's fiery demise and by placing herself in the forefront of the battle she hoped to inspire them even further by demonstrating that the much-feared Iron Masters bled and died just like ordinary motals.

Karlstrom watched with mounting concern as Roz arched her back over the chair and began to choke. Her chest heaved convulsively. Her left arm was raised and bent at the elbow back towards her body, with the knuckles jammed against the base of her neck; the clawed fingers of her right hand were raised in the air as if she was trying to grab something hanging from the ceiling. Her eyes, as always, were tightly shut.

He moved closer, ready to catch her if she fell off the chair. Now her left arm unfolded. She seemed to by trying to lift or push something heavy away from her, then she collapsed forwards across the top of the desk coughing and spluttering as she gasped down lungfuls of air.

Karlstrom saw her eyes flutter open as part of her mind returned to her present location. 'Are you okay?' He prided himself on being a pretty cold fish but no matter how many times he watched Roz do her stuff it disturbed and impressed him. He came away from these sessions filled with a sense of wonder: a feeling that he was a privileged observer of a process which – to use a word that had never crossed his lips – was little short of, well . . . miraculous.

'Yes . . .' Her voice was a hoarse whisper, her face drained of all colour. She used her hands to push herself away from the desk. 'He's out . . . they're both out. They're safe . . .' She slumped back in the chair and let her head fall forward, hunching her shoulders as her exhausted body was wracked by another bout of coughing.

'Would you like me to call a medic?'

Roz raised her eyes to his and greeted the question with a rueful smile. 'I *am* a doctor – or, at least, I was.' She took several deep, calming breaths and, as the colour returned to her cheeks, her exhausted body was rapidly transformed into its normal healthy self.

It was, reflected Karlstrom, really quite remarkable. Once again, Roz had demonstrated her ability to not only be aware of, but to mirror – with her own body – Brickman's current physical or mental state. Their minds had to be linked at deep trance level but in moments of intense stress, such as when his body suffered traumatic wounding, that telepathic connection was made instantly and without warning.

What stunned and mystified the First Family surgeons who had observed the psychosomatic woundings that Roz had endured was the incredible speed with which they healed, the absence of any scars or need for convalescence and the level of pain that would normally accompany such injuries.

When Brickman had made his escape from the Heron Pool, Roz had been walking along a corridor in her medical school with a group of student colleagues. They had noticed she was tense but with vital exams coming up, who wasn't? Without warning, her right leg suddenly buckled, throwing her to the ground, where she lay, clutching her thigh.

As friends helped her up they noticed blood seeping through her fingers. She shrugged off the incident but was carried protesting into the first aid room where Family medics investigators assigned to her case found a three-inch deep wound caused by a bladed metal projectile which had sliced through the muscle with considerable force. Roz, who had been sharing Steve's gut-wrenching anxiety during the destruction of the Heron Pool, had also been wounded by an invisible replica of the arrow that had split a wooden strut before burying itself in Steve's thigh. An invisible arrow brought into being and delivered with the same force and in the same moment of time through the power of their linked minds.

It was not surprising that Karlstrom felt uneasy. He had no cause to doubt Roz's loyalty and dedication, but like all members of the First Family, he didn't like depending on people or things over which he did not have total control.

But it had to be admitted that in this latest affair, Roz had performed brilliantly. Within seconds of Steve making contact, she had carded herself into a closed video-booth and placed a call to Karlstrom using the special high-priority number he'd given her to memorize. And within an instant of keying in the last digit, COLUMBUS had activated the bleeper in his Karlstrom's pocket and put a flash notification of her call on the nearest screen.

From their brief on-screen conversation Karlstrom had gotten enough information to order the commander of AME-XICO's airforce to make immediate preparations to despatch five of his aircraft – four Skyhawks and a Skyrider mothership – on a long-range mission. The pilots were to go on red alert; course and target details would follow later.

By the time Roz arrived by shuttle at AMEXICO's headquarters with fuller details of Steve's predicament, the aircraft on the overground base near Houston-GC was being armed and refuelled, the pilots were kitted up and gathered in the briefing room, and Karlstrom had a map of the lower half of Lake Michigan spread out on his desk.

From there on in it had all gone like clockwork. If Karlstrom had harboured any doubts about putting Roz on the Red-River wagon-train to help her kin-brother bring in Clearwater and the other two targets they vanished on receipt of 'Fire-Chief' Mackinnon's radio message that the wheelboat had been deep-fried and was now settling into the water some four hundred yards from the shore. Properly handled, this girl and her brother were dynamite. And it was beginning to look as if he had taken too jaundiced a view of Brickman's reliability. He was a devious sonofabitch, but then so was every successful agent. His intelligence was unquestioned and his performance in the field had proved he was tough, resourceful and courageous. He was also very lucky. In fact, considering the jams Brickman had been in and the one he'd just gotten himself out of, one could almost say – if you believed in magic – that he led a 'charmed life' . . .

This was not quite how Steve saw it but he was, nevertheless, glad to be alive. The bomb blast had ripped the lantern from its hook on the ceiling of the passageway outside their cell, but the glare from the blazing roof timbers ahead of the shattered engine room had provided enough light to unlock the neckboards and wrist shackles.

After that, darkness had descended and he'd had to feel

his way out of the sinking boat whilst fighting to keep hold of Cadillac at the same time. The rush of water rising up the passageway from behind had carried them through the hatchway onto the deck above where they both had a chance to gulp down some more air before being pushed back under by an avalanche of assorted debris that came sliding towards them as the front section of the boat tipped backwards at a steeper and steeper angle.

There was a timeless moment when Steve had no recollection of anything except a strong impression that he was going to die then to his utter surprise, his head bobbed out of the water and he realized that (a) he was still alive, (b) he still had his left arm round Cadillac's neck, and (c) a fire-blackened upturned dory and an oar were both floating within reach.

Righting the dory with the aid of the oar whilst trying to keep the unconscious Mute's head above water was no easy task but Steve finally managed it. Getting Cadillac aboard was even harder but, having taken the precaution of throwing the oar in first, he succeeded in doing that too. When the Mute was balanced on his navel over the back-board, Steve clambered in over the bow, hauled the rest of his colleague out of the water and laid him in the bottom of the boat.

A few minutes hard pumping got his eyes open and most of the water out of his lungs. Cadillac rolled onto one side and vomited weakly. 'I think I'm going to die . . .'

'I doubt it.' Steve rose, inserted the oar in the stern rowlock and fishtailed the boat southwards, parallel with the shore. It was time to steer clear of any further trouble.

From the shrieks and cries and the unmistakable ringing clash of steel carried by the wind across the water, it was clear that the Iron Masters who'd made it to shore weren't going down without a fight. Steve felt a twinge of guilt but Cadillac, for one, was in no shape to start trading sharp iron. It was time for the Kojak to show what they were made of. If things got sticky, there was always Clearwater. She would pull some magic out of the air and blow the Japs back into the water. Or whatever.

Nyehhh . . . to hell with it. They'd done enough for one night . . .

CHAPTER THIRTEEN

Stu Gordon, a Tracker renegade guarding the eastern approaches to his group's temporary campsite, set the 'scope on distant focus and began another slow, patient sweep of the seemingly limitless landscape. Another breaker, Nick Walsh, lay on his back beside him, his eyes trained on the sky while he waited for his turn at the 'scope. Stu was on the look-out for any roving bands of Mutes, Nick was searching for what the Mutes called 'arrowheads' – Skyhawks sent up as forward scouts by the wagon-trains.

The name, which had been derived from the standard tailless, delta-winged configuration, was no longer strictly accurate. This year, a new, more powerful aircraft had appeared in the skies, one with straight, constant-chord wings and trim tails perched on the end of narrow booms sprouting from the trailing edge of the wing on either side of the rear-mounted engine. An aircraft that also packed a more powerful punch: a fixed forward-firing six-barrelled gun.

It was a quantum leap from the lone rifleman in the sky and their appearance was a sign that the Federation meant business. In the spring of the previous year, the wagon-trains had made their first penetration of Plainfolk territory, a vast area which, up to then, had provided uneasy sanctuary for groups of breakers like the one Nick and Stu ran with.

The constant fire-sweeps launched from the wagon-trains and way-stations in the New Territories of Colorado and Kansas had driven most of the groups northwards. Some breakers had decided to try and find one of the westward trails that were said to lead over the Rockies but their group had voted to try and continue their nomadic existence on the high plains of Nebraska and Wyoming. To go west would be to enter uncharted territory. There would no longer be any threat from the Federation but there would be no pick-ups either.

Renegades were scavengers who lived off what the wagon-trains left behind. They were like seagulls who hovered constantly above the sterns of ocean-going liners. Except they weren't looking for food. What they needed were compressed air bottles to power their rifles and hand-guns, clips of needle-point rounds, torch batteries, first aid kits, knives, tools, uniforms, boots – any useful item of equipment that would add a few creature comforts to their rough and ready existence.

But of course this kind of stuff didn't just *fall* off wagon-trains. Good sense suggested you should get the hell out of any area where a fire-sweep was in progress but that was exactly where you stood the best chance of picking up some goodies. When wagon-trains were stalled by the terrain, they sent out combat squads in pursuit of the lump-heads with Skyhawks riding point. But the Mutes had a habit of hitting back with crossbows and they rarely missed.

Luckily, each bowman only had a few bolts and he relied on getting them back. That's when renegades got lucky. Provided you were able to move in quick enough, and the lump-heads were driven off or killed, you could strip the kit off the corpses and cut out the crossbow bolts to trade with the Mutes who were also in the business of pillaging corpses. Despite this there was no serious conflict of interest. The Mutes were trophy hunters. It was the severed heads of Trail-Blazers and their combat knives that were the real collectors' items. The lumps had no use for rifles or handguns. Like breakers, they took everything they could lay hands on but provided they had a few bits and pieces to hang round their necks or sew onto their leather body armour they could be persuaded to part with precious air bottles and spare magazines.

It was a dangerous game because you could get your own ass blown off while you were waiting to pounce. And there was an even greater risk of that happening if you decided to ambush linemen on their way to the wagon-train when they were most likely to have used up most of their ammo – or thrown it away to cut down on the weight they had to carry.

Breakers like Stu and Nick had no qualms about attacking Trail-Blazers. Renegade Trackers and lump-heads were bracketed together as vermin: to be exterminated – which was probably why the Mutes allowed the 'redskins', as they called them, a certain amount of elbow room. Provided you didn't set up a permanent camp on a clan's turf, and hunted game in an economical fashion, the lumps left you pretty much alone for most of the year. There was only one danger period – the last three weeks in April and the first week of May – when the Mutes made their annual cull of renegades. That was when breakers went to ground. If you didn't lie low, you risked being captured, or killed if you used force against your pursuers. Those that fell into the net were traded at the Mutes' annual jamboree on Lake Superior and shipped to an unknown destination in the east.

The lumps looked on the annual round-up as a game which, even if those being chased didn't think it funny, was conducted in a free and easy fashion and with evident goodwill. If you gave 'em a good run before being captured they sometimes let you go. But for many breakers, who had risked everything to break free of the Federation's claustrophobic regime, death was preferable to a life of slavery.

That was why Stu Gordon and Nick Walsh were on lookout duty along with six other guys covering the north, south and western approaches to their camp overlooking the North Platte River in Nebraska.

But there were additional dangers breakers faced which were harder to identify. Besides the general hazards of surviving on the overground, avoiding wagon-trains and the annual Mute round-up, there was the threat posed by the roving presence of FINTEL squads – Trackers whose job it was to gather field intelligence to help the planning of wagon-train operations and, worst of all, undercover Feds, disguised as breakers, and working singly or in small groups.

These slimy bastards were the *real* ememy. Their job was to shaft breakers whenever the opportunity occurred and their preferred method was to boobytrap dead bodies with small-anti-personnel mines. They also left ration packs laced with cyanide, poisoned water filtration kits and first aid bags containing hypodermics filled with junk designed to kill, not cure.

All in all, a nice bunch. But while the threat they posed was strictly bad news, their presence on the overground did bring one positive benefit. They were maintained in the field by air-dropped supplies which were fed into a network of small underground dumps. These were always extremely well-concealed but they could be found if you knew where to look and what to look for. It needed a lot of experience but the leader of their group – a guy called Malone – had a real nose for it. But even his years of experience did not mean the group was totally fireproof. Last year over thirty guys had been lifted by the M'Call, a big Mute clan whose beat – depending on the time of year – ran from navref Caspar in Wyoming down the line of the North Platte to navref Kearney.

Stu Gordon grunted as he picked up something in the 'scope. 'What the eff-eff we got here . . .? Hey, Nick! Take a look.'

Walsh took the 'scope and aimed it in the direction indicated. 'What am I lookin' for?'

'Three guys and a bunch of animals. Follow the line of the river beyond that second bend there, see? You'll come to a clump of trees on the bank to your left –'

'Got it . . .'

'Now pan left – easy now. There's a faint trail. If you're lookin' at more trees you've gone too far.'

'I have. Wait a minute . . . Yeah, okay, I'm on it.'

'Good. Now follow that line up towards the horizon.'

Walsh found the target. A group of strange four-legged animals. The first three had men astride their backs. The head of one of them was covered by a helmet with a wide sweeping brim. He and another guy were carrying what looked like green flags on the end of poles but at this stage, they were still too far away to make out any details.

During their time before going over the side – the breaker term for what the Federation called desertion – neither Gordon nor Walsh had spent a lot of time tuned into the Archive channel or hung around with anybody who had. As far as they were concerned it was 'now' that counted, the only history they were obliged to be familiar with was that of the Federation, beginning in 2051 AD. Any reference the obligatory lessons made to the pre-Holocaust period concentrated on its negative aspects – all of which had been eliminated by the Federation, a point which their teachers and the supporting video-programs were at pains to stress. *Ad nauseam* . . .

This meant that neither renegade realized they were looking at a herd of some eighty horses – part of the spoils of the Kojak's great victory over the Iron Masters – led by three riders sitting proud in the saddle. As they had every right to be.

Walsh lowered the 'scope. 'D'ja ever see anythin' like that before?'

'Never.' Stu Gordon slithered down the sloping rock face to take himself off the skyline then sat up and waved to attract Malone's attention. 'Hey, Chief! Somethin' here you might wanna see!'

Malone handed the map he'd been examining back to one of his four lieutenants and clambered up towards Gordon and Walsh. Walsh handed him the 'scope and went back to his skywatch. Guys on guard duty who failed to remain alert soon found out why Malone had remained the *honcho* of one of the largest and best-equipped bands of renegades for so long. The hard way.

Malone focused up on the advancing herd. Some of the riderless horses had saddles with raised pommels and seat backs. They were grouped in a loose V-shape behind the lead animals with a few strays running wide on each side and to the rear.

From his almost head-on view of the herd it was difficult to judge their speed but from what he'd seen of buffalo on the move they appeared to be covering the ground at a fast clip. The horses were, in fact, moving at the canter but Malone's knowledge did not embrace the technical terms used to describe their gait. He lowered the 'scope. 'Hmmmm . . . interesting.'

'D'you know what they are, chief?'

'Yeah. They're horses.'

'Horses? Ahh, I know the *word*,' said Gordon. 'I didn't know it was the name of an animal. I thought it was –'

Malone interrupted with a knowing smile. '– just another name for your prick.'

A word which, in its turn, was yet another drawn from the vast lexicon of slang for the male and female sex organs and the adjacent orifice which, in the pre-Holocaust era, a significant and tenacious minority had elevated from its humble function as a drainpipe through which fecal matter was pumped from the bowels into an object of veneration. 'Putting the horse between the shafts' – a phrase mainly employed by Young Pioneers – was one of a host of euphemisms spawned over the centuries by man's compulsive need to simultaneously embroider and deride the coital act.

'If you'd spent more time checking the picture archives 'stead of playin' arcade games you wouldn't need to ask,' continued Malone. 'Even so it's a surprise. According to the stuff I scanned, horses were one of several kinds of domestic animals that were wiped out during the Holocaust.'

Gordon frowned. 'What does "domestic" mean?'

'Tame. People used to raise 'em and feed 'em. Some of them they used to eat, others – dogs for instance, that was kind of like a wolf – were trained to hunt game and guard the homesteads. Sounds hard to believe but people used to live with 'em in the *same* room.'

The two breakers laughed disbelievingly.

'Sounds crazy, I know. But that's the way it was. And before we invented trains, planes and wheelies – when there weren't any engines to move things – folks used horses for transportation. For thousands of years there were big herds of wild horses roamin' the plains. The way the buffalo do now – only horses are a lot brighter. Guys would round 'em up and break 'em, knock 'em into shape, so they know who's boss. When you've got animals haulin' a load they gotta stop when you want and move when you say "Move" – right?'

'You mean like the D.I.'s at boot camp.'

Malone smiled. 'Exactly. Break 'em then remake 'em. It's the only way to deal with animals like you. That's how the First Family keep us tied to their wagon. Horses were used to haul carts – cargo wheelies. Only they were the traction unit. That's how we got the term "horse-power" for measuring an engine's output.'

'Really? I didn't know that,' said Gordon.

'Well, stick with me. You'll learn somethin' every day. But as well as hitching 'em to carts and ploughs, people also used to ride on their backs – like those three guys are doing now. Question is – where the hell did they come from?'

Malone rolled over onto his belly and raised the 'scope to his eye. The riders were continuing to advance towards the hidden campsite and now, he could see that one of the riders was female. She was carrying a ragged green and yellow flag with the bottom end of the pole resting in her left stirrup. And the guy at the head of the pack had a strip of the same green material wrapped around his forehead..

Behind him, to the left of the picture frame, was the third rider who was also carrying a green and yellow flag. His face was shadowed by the wide-brimmed helmet. All three were dressed in a curious assortment of clothes and bits of body-armour of a type that Malone had never come across before. But it was also their skin colour which aroused his curiosity.

'Jack me . . . they're lump-heads!'

Gordon reached for his carbine. 'What are we gonna do, chief – take 'em out?'

'No, invite 'em up for a little chat. I want to find out just what the hell's goin' on.' Malone handed the 'scope back to Gordon. 'Well done, Stu. If they stay on their present heading, there's a good chance they'll come through that defile below us. Keep your eyes peeled but stay well under cover. If they suddenly change course, send Nick down. Okay?' Malone scrambled to his feet. 'I'll go and organize a reception committee . . .'

Malone was not the only one to have been intrigued and impressed by the cavalcade. Since leaving the Kojak to celebrate their hard-won victory over the Iron Masters, Steve, Cadillac and Clearwater had crossed the turf of seventeen other clans. All of them, after listening to their story, had given them a heroes' welcome and after an exchange of tokens they had been escorted in triumph to the boundary of the no-man's land that, by tradition, lay between the turf claimed by neighbouring clans.

Mounted on strange beasts, with tasselled harnesses and

decorated saddles, dressed in a mixture of soft Mute leathers and Iron Master armour, and with their green and gold silk banners fluttering proudly from the top of the long thin poles, they were an imposing sight. And the same melodramatic mix of words and magic that brought the Kojak off the fence and into the fray had worked on every clan they had encountered, including those from the bloodline of the D'Troit, mortal enemies of the She-Kargo.

Even Steve, who was struggling to maintain a healthy disbelief in pre-destination and the all-embracing power of Talisman was increasingly tempted by the idea that perhaps it *was* true. He had always nourished the idea that he was a cut above the average and destined for great things. And the 'otherness' he shared with Roz marked them out as something special. There could be no denying that the mind-bridge that joined them had allowed him and Cadillac to escape from the wheelboat and he had seen with his own eyes the power of Clearwater's magic. Scientific explanations might help you sleep more soundly but they weren't necessary. It *worked*. End of story.

Except of course it wasn't. Deep down, Steve wasn't ready to hand over control of his life to anyone. But if Cadillac's act was going to get them to Wyoming, then that was a good enough reason to conceal any reservations he might have and play his part with total and utter sincerity.

Cadillac, who had assumed the role of spokesman, was now in his element. The embarrassing moment of panic during the escape from the sinking wheelboat had been totally forgotten. He was back on top and, what was more, he actually believed what he was saying. This wasn't just a story; this was a divine revelation. The light of Talisman, the radiance of his power, as bright as the noonday sun, had entered the world. He, Cadillac Deville, was the torch-bearer and his allotted task was to kindle the flame of collective resistance. Stirring stuff.

This message, delivered with messianic fervour, plus their unusual appearance, led the normally-hostile scouting parties who barred their path to extend a cautious invitation to address the clan's circle of elders. After repeating this impressive preamble, Cadillac would raise their silvered eyebrows even further by revealing that before them stood The Chosen; the first of the Lost Ones to return *as prophesied* from the Eastern Lands and the dread Fire-Pits of Beth-Lem.

How had this been achieved? How had *they* managed to escape from the world of the dead-faces beyond the Great River – something that no one had ever succeeded in doing before? By the power given to them by Talisman! And here, on Cadillac's signal, Clearwater and Steve would display some of the Iron Master swords, bows and armour they had brought with them. Was this not proof, demanded Cadillac, of a stirring victory?

It was indeed. *Heyy-yaaahhhh . . .*

The first of many, declared Cadillac. The Plainfolk need never walk in fear of the dead-faces again! And here he would launch into an edited but highly graphic account of how they, The Chosen, had destroyed the assembled might of the Iron Masters at the Heron Pool and then, with the help of the clan Kojak, had sunk and killed an entire boatload of samurai. With a sweeping gesture Cadillac then drew the attention of the elders – as spellbound as the clan seated behind them – to the patient group of horses. These magnificent animals were just a few of those who had been ridden into battle by the yellow war-lords whose heads now adorned the poles outside the lodges of the Kojak!

Heyyy-YAHHHH!

And now it was Clearwater's turn to demonstrate a skill that Steve had not known about before the sinking of the wheel-boat.

In the harsh light of dawn, Steve and Cadillac had made their way northwards along the shore to the battleground. The hairless corpses of Iron Masters lay everywhere. In the shallows where the water lapped the pebbled shore, half-buried in the pit-falls, strewn along the beach, and hanging from the fish-nets – the last line of defence before the dunes. A number of horses had also fallen victim to the clan's spirited defence of the beach. Most were dead, but some lay mortally wounded, their life-blood draining from their heaving flanks, while others, with limbs broken by stumbling into the pitfalls, thrashed about in wild-eyed panic. Moved by the piteous sound they were making, Steve persuaded Cadillac to help him put an end to their misery.

The Kojak had lost a hundred and eighteen warriors and scores had been wounded. Some of these might yet ask to kiss sharp iron but it was still held to be a famous victory. *Mo-Town thirsts, Mo-Town drinks.* The Iron Masters had lost three times that number. Many of the samurai and red-stripe infantry who succeeded in reaching the shore were on the point of exhaustion but all had fought with a reckless fury until they were cut down. Others, finding themselves surrounded like wild animals at bay had chosen to fall on their own sword before being hacked to pieces. The rest, including the crew of the wheelboat, had perished in the water.

The work of stripping and beheading the corpses had already begun, and out on the lake, the crews of a score of outriggers were busily salvaging anything and everything that was floating on the water. The two halves of the burning vessel had sunk without trace but a storm or two would complete its destruction and bring another rich harvest ashore.

But where was Clearwater? If she had survived unharmed, should she not have been there, on the beach – showing some concern for their fate? Gripped by a sudden anxiety, Steve and Cadillac hurried inland, through the dunes in the direction of the settlement. It was then that they saw the horses – clustered round Clearwater like bees around a bee-hive.

Steve called out to her but she did not respond and when they reached the circle of horses and tried to catch her eye she looked right through them. As they watched her move amongst the animals, touching their heads and speaking softly to them, it quickly became apparent they were witnessing an extraordinary act of communion. Clearwater was oblivious to everything beyond her group of four-legged admirers, who patiently waited their turn to make contact.

Cadillac had known for some considerable time that Clearwater was able to exert a certain mastery over animals but he had never suspected she could control so many. Steve, to whom all this came as a great surprise, could only marvel at the range and depth of her powers. What other surprises did she have up her sleeve?

Ever since he had proposed the idea of capturing a number of Iron Masters' horses he'd been grappling with the problem of how the three of them could keep control of the riderless mounts during the journey west. He and Cadillac had already agreed that if a sufficiently large number of horses were captured, they would give two – one male, one female – to every clan they encountered on the way home. Always provided, of course, there were enough of each to go round. Clearwater had provided the solution. The horses were ready to follow her anywhere and proceeded to do so, instantly obeying her spoken and unspoken commands.

It was this skill which Clearwater would then proceed to demonstrate to the delight and consternation of her Mute audience. By pointing and snapping her fingers and with sweeping movements of her arms she could make individual horses, or groups of any number she chose, trot round the assembled clan in either direction following the leader nose to tail, then call them to halt and turn inwards. A further command would cause them to bow their heads to the circle of elders and paw the ground in salute. It was masterly display and always drew roars of approval from the delighted audience.

And then it was Steve's turn. The only card up his sleeve was the one he wasn't yet ready to play. Besides which, a telepathic connection with an absent party was hardly likely to win him a sustained round of applause. The horses were a hard act to follow, but Clearwater had lent his number her magic touch and, apart from Cadillac's final rousing address, he now topped the bill with a death-defying feat that tested his own credulity and courage to the limit.

While three woven straw mats were being rolled into tubes by a trio of elders and secured by knotted twine, Cadillac and Clearwater planted two six-foot long poles in the ground just in front of Steve but about eight feet apart. Two of the rolled mats were then slid onto the top of the poles. Spreading his legs in a fighting stance, Steve would draw the samurai sword he now carried and, with a sudden yell, shorten the tightly-rolled straw mats with four lightning-fast strokes. It was easy for his audience to imagine the sword slicing through someone's neck with the same chilling ease.

Cadillac would then call upon the clan's paramount warrior to enter the circle whereupon Steve would present him with the sword and invite him to do the same. Despite their unfamiliarity with the weapon, the chief head-collectors rarely failed to duplicate the power and speed of Steve's killing strokes; all they needed were a few trial swings.

When the top gun had lopped a few more inches off both rolls and satisfied himself that he was holding a lethal weapon, Steve took a deep breath and proceeded to the show-stopper. When he had taken up a firm stance with his feet spread apart, Clearwater offered him the third rolled mat. Grasping it firmly at both ends, Steve raised it above his head and told the paramount warrior to cut it in two with one blow.

This always brought a murmur of alarm from the crowd. They had already seen how the superbly forged weapon sliced through the rolled mats without encountering any perceptible resistance. If the warrior accepted the invitation to strike the mat, the sword would cleave open the head of the Chosen One!

The same thought had passed through Steve's mind when Cadillac had dreamed up the idea. Clearwater assured him he would be under her protection and safe from harm but Steve, somewhat understandably, had taken some convincing. Sure, he believed in magic. He had total confidence in her abilities. But supposing Talisman had an off day? With the kind of stunt they were suggesting, if the magic didn't happen, you could die at the first rehearsal. If Cadillac was so sure it would work, he argued, let *him* do it.

To his great surprise and subsequent embarrassment, Cadillac had volunteered to hold the rolled mat while he, Steve, gave it his best shot. It worked. That was the good news: the bad news was that Steve was then obliged to swap places. All he had to do was believe in Clearwater but it was no easy thing to stand there while Cadillac got ready to cleave him in two. Things might be all right between them on the surface but underneath there was a festering layer of jealousy and resentment that could burst through at the slightest provocation. If Cadillac was looking for a chance to put an end to their rivalry, this was it. The fragile oath they'd sworn to be blood-brothers wasn't worth a pigeon's fart; only Clearwater could stop that sword . . .

And she had. And the power given to her by Talisman had kept him from harm again and again as they progressed westwards. When the paramount warrior of each clan steeled himself to make the killing stroke, some invisible force brought the blade to a shuddering halt just before it touched the rolled mat Steve held above his bare head. Then it vibrated wildly, tore itself loose from the stunned warrior's grasp and flew back over his head, burying its point in the ground.

It was time for Cadillac to move centre stage. Behold! Now you see with your own eyes the power of Talisman! Even the weapons of the Iron Masters dare not harm The Chosen! The Lost Ones are on the homeward march, brothers! Nothing can stop the rise of the Thrice-Gifted One!

So far this had never failed to bring the clans to their feet. *Heyyy-yaaahhh! HEYYY-yaaahhh! HEYYY-Y AAAAHHH!!*

The buffalo trail they'd been following curved away from the river and rose towards a narrow pass. Bringing their horses to a halt, they scanned the high ground on either side of the defile then walked the herd up the slope.

Steve's mind was still on the events of the last few days. Yes . . . there had been sweet moments. It didn't really matter whether it was true or not. If it was what the Plainfolk wanted to hear, if it helped get them through the day – what the hell? It was better to believe in something than in nothing. It was the dream of a return to a cleansed Blue-Sky World that had sustained Trackers down the centuries. And maybe the First Family too.

Everyone needed something to hang onto. His dream was that somehow he'd find a way to reconcile his own mixed-up hopes and desires with the conflicting demands that other people kept making. He wanted to be with Clearwater – but what kind of a life could they make together out here? And there was Roz. With her life now in jeopardy because of his involvement with Karlstrom's ultra-secret operation she needed him too. If he hadn't gone back in she wouldn't have gotten involved in this mess. But he had, and she was.

The only way he could secure her chosen future was to bring in Clearwater and Cadillac. Or their heads on a plate. That was the least Karlstrom would settle for. But despite the constant desire to throttle Cadillac, Steve could not break his promise to return them unharmed to Mr Snow. He could envisage only one solution: by some means or other, Roz had to be brought out of the Federation. But if by some miracle he *was* able to free her, she and *Clearwater* would be at each other's throats!

It was an impossible situation, and on top of all that, Steve had another cause for concern. Throughout the journey Cadillac had been delivering spell-binding performances but he was back on the *sake*. When the wheelboat had broken up, several dozen small casks of the potent brew had floated up from the hold. Cadillac who, by Sod's Law, just happened to be there with Steve when the first cask was brought ashore, tore it from the hands of the unsuspecting fisherman, sniffed the bung then clasped it to his bosom.

Were there more? Indeed there were. Steve's heart sank. The sunken vessel had released a veritable bonanza of booze and the pressing need to recover every last drop instantly transformed the inveterate landlubber into a bright-eyed, bushy-tailed sea-dog who proceeded to trawl the waters for the next seven hours without once feeling sick.

Watching with growing dismay as the casks continued to pile up on the shore, Steve realized the truth of what he'd been told while training to be a mexican at Rio Lobo. If you had the right mental attitude, the right motivation, you could endure anything.

Several casks had been opened to help give an extra swing to the Kojak victory celebrations – with predictable results. Those who overdosed ended up completely legless. And while it loosened a few libidos, it also unleashed a certain amount of aggression; something which never happened when Mutes opened their heads to the sky with the help of a pipeful of rainbow grass. The combination of top grade *sake* and grass left everyone who'd been hitting heavily on both lying flat on their backs nursing blinding hangovers. Those who manged to haul themselves upright found that their eyes were being stabbed cruelly by sharp daggers of daylight, and that any jarring movement produced the painful sensation of being kicked in the head by a buffalo.

Practice, as the saying goes, makes perfect, but as a result of this salutary experience, most of the clanfolk were unwilling to try again. The general consensus was 'Thanks, but no thanks', which left them with a small mountain of unwanted booze. Faced with the possibility that Cadillac might insist on staying put until he'd drunk it all, Steve had helped him load up several pack-horses with an absurdly generous supply of the yellow fire-water.

The prospect of Cadillac once again drinking himself nightly into insensibility went against the grain, but Steve had no desire to stir up any more arguments. They'd already had enough run-ins. Cadillac seemed to sense Steve's concern and promised to restrict himself to a modest nightcap and remain reasonably sober until they got to Wyoming. And, in all honesty, Cadillac had done his best. He hadn't lost his place in the script, or fallen nose first into his pot of stew but Steve – who'd watched him put it away before – knew the alcohol was back in his blood. Sooner or later that could only mean trouble . . .

But right now, they were facing trouble of a different sort. Entering the defile at the top of the rise, they suddenly found the trail barred by a line of ten armed renegades. There was another twenty or so standing further back. A quick backward glance confirmed they were surrounded. Those at the rear were still moving down the side slopes but a hasty retreat was out of the question. Only Clearwater's magic could level the odds against so many rifles. But even if, by some miracle, they broke free without getting hit, many of the horses ran the risk of being killed or wounded, and that was not the object of the exercise.

'Leave this one to me,' muttered Steve as he dismounted. He handed the reins of his horse to Cadillac then walked forward, unslinging his halberd. Fitted with an Iron Master blade, it was a later model of the turbo-charged piece of lightning she'd bequeathed to him before flying to Ne-Issan. And she had poured the same electrifying power into the one he now held.

A blunt-featured man, in the centre of the group of riflemen ranged across the trail, stepped forward ready to fire from the hip and called out: 'Hang up the sharp iron, friend.'

Steve halted about ten yards away from the line and did as he was told.

'Okay.' The speaker put up his rifle. 'This aint gonna hurt. Just step forward, nice and slow.'

The men on either side reacted as they got a closer look at what Steve was wearing: the travel-stained white, wide-sleeved cotton jacket, walking skins – the Mute name for their soft leather trousers – and on his feet, the boots worn by mounted samurai. Protecting his chest, back, shoulders and forearms, various pieces of samurai armour. Like the renegades who faced him, Steve's hair was now long and unkempt and he'd stopped dyeing the blond roots. Holding it back from his face was the green and gold silken headband. Every inch of exposed skin – like the bits they couldn't see – was covered with the irregular blotches and swirls of light olive-brown, dark brown and black. Lightened here and there by steaks of pinkish ochre. The legacy of the Holocaust that separated the Mute from the rest of humankind.

Steve had been wearing these colours for almost a year. They had become like a second skin. There was nothing to distinguish him from Cadillac and Clearwater and, in fact, he looked even more genuine than they did because his face bore the scars of a warrior who had 'bitten the arrow'. The Mute badge of courage. The Kojak had accepted him without question and so had the clanfolk they'd encountered on their journey westwards. With pools of water and polished knife blades providing the only reflections of himself he had few opportunities to study his appearance and had not paused to consider the possible reaction of other Trackers.

As the renegades gave him the once-over, Steve studied the man who'd called him forward and was stunned when he realized they'd already met. The square, deeply-lined face with the pale piercing eyes, and the blunt squashed nose: the camouflaged headband, and the long brown hair tied on the nape of his neck with a torn strip of the same material belonged to Malone, leader of the renegade band that Jodi, Kelso,

Medicine Hat and Jinx had run with before being captured and sold down the river. Malone, the hard-faced sonofabitch who had punched the shit out of him before ordering him to be posted – tied kneeling upright to a stake, face-to-face with a week-old corpse. Fresh from a shallow grave Steve had dug himself. Despite his own protestations of innocence and Jodi's appeals for clemency, Malone and the rest of his gang had just walked away and left him to die.

But things had worked out very differently. And now Malone was on the hit list. Not now. But one day, yes . . . his turn would come.

Steve forced a smile onto his lips. 'Small world . . .' He extended his hand. 'We had a little misunderstanding last year.'

Malone eyed him suspiciously. 'Yeah?'

'Yeah.' Steve left his hand on offer. 'But afterwards you changed your mind and sent Kelso and Jodi to let me off the hook.' He paused then added. 'Brickman. You posted me last April – up by Medicine Creek.'

Malone frowned in surprise, walked slowly round Steve then stood in front of him again and thrust his face closer. 'Well, jack me! So it is. What the hell you doin' dressed up like a piece of lumpshit?'

Steve swallowed the reply on the tip of his tongue and said: 'It's a long story.'

Malone jerked his head towards Cadillac and Clearwater. 'And those two?'

'They're part of it.'

Malone pointed to the hilt of the samurai sword thrust through the sash around Steve's waist then flicked the front edge of the small square shield attached to Steve's right shoulder. 'Where did all this junk come from?'

'We collected it on our way out.'

'Out of where?'

'Ne-Issan. Where the Iron Masters live. They're the guys who trade with the Mutes – and ship any breakers they've captured back east.'

'Christo,' breathed Malone. 'Is that where you've been?'

'Yeah. With Kelso and Jodi. They and I were collared

at the same time. And a couple of other guys. Medicine Hat and Jinx. You lost about thirty guys – remember?'

'I'm not likely to forget. What happened to 'em?'

'Can't say. After they landed Kelso and Jodi were in the same yard as Medicine Hat and Jinx for an hour or two then they were pulled out and bunched with us.' Steve shrugged. 'Never saw any of the others again – and my guess is you won't see 'em either.'

'Sounds like bad news . . .'

'Ne-Issan? Yeah, it is. Once you're there, it's almost impossible to get out. But it can be done. We're proof of that.'

'So what happened to Kelso and Jodi?'

'They got away with us but, uh – we got hit by some 'hawks from a wagon train and . . .'

Malone got the message. 'When was this?'

'Last year. Sometime around the end of November.'

Malone registered the news with evident disbelief. He eyed his henchmen then said: 'Are you telling me those suckers are sending out wagon-trains when there's *snow* on the ground?!'

'You'd better believe it.'

Malone chewed this over then reached out and curled a set of steel fingers round Steve's right arm, just above the elbow. It was meant to be a friendly gesture, but it didn't feel like one. 'Go tell your fancy-looking friends to join us, cuz. You and me have got some serious talking to do.'

Dressed in camouflaged Trail-Blazer fatigues and a wingman's crash helmet, Roz climbed nervously into the passenger seat of a dark grey Sky-Rider. The plane, its engine running, stood facing the closed hangar doors. The AMEXICO pilot sat waiting with his hands on the controls, the dark mirrored visor of his helmet closed to preserve his anonymity.

As Roz fastened her safety harness with the help of one of the ground crew, Commander-General Ben Karlstrom stepped through a side door and approached the cockpit.

'How do you feel?'

'Excited, sir. But a little nervous too.'

'That's understandable. But Steve adjusted very quickly. I'm sure you will too. Your performance so far has been absolutely magnificent, Roz. We're very proud of you. And now we're counting on you even more to help Steve complete his assignment. Do you think you're going to be able to do it?'

'Yes sir. There's never been any question about that. It's just . . .'

Karlstrom smiled. 'I know. The overground. No matter how many video pictures you see, they can never do justice to what's waiting for you out there. For the first few minutes you'll be overwhelmed by the sheer scale of everything. You may experience a degree of disorientation, of panic even. There are people who can't take it. They suffer from space-sickness no matter how much exposure they get. But you'll be okay. You're special, Roz. If you weren't I wouldn't be here to see you off.' Karlstrom gripped her gloved hand briefly then stepped back and saluted. 'Have a safe trip – and good hunting!'

Roz returned the salute. 'Thank you, sir. Can't wait!'

As the motors controlling the hangar doors whined into action, Karlstrom strode back to the side entrance. One of the hanger staff closed the door behind him and spun the wheel to activate the air-tight seal. The Skyrider pilot lowered the bubble canopy and locked it into place, then checked that Roz was correctly plugged in to the intercomm.

'You receiving me?'

Roz held up both thumbs. 'Loud and clear.'

'Good. There's nothing to be frightened of. Just sit back and relax. If you start feeling queasy or anxious, close your eyes and breathe deeply. We're gonna be airborne for several hours so you've got plenty of time to get adjusted. Just take it a step at a time. Okay?'

'Yep . . .'

'Right, let's go.' The pilot signalled the ground crew to remove the chocks from under the main wheels, opened the throttle and released the parking break.

In front of them, the doors were sliding back to reveal a huge sloping slab of concrete topped by a narrow rectangle of brilliant blue. The sky above the overground . . .

Although she had never been higher than Level Four-4, Roz had already been there. Her mind had merged with Steve's on his first solo flight over the dazzling white sands of New

Mexico. She had seen what he had seen, experienced the same dizzying emotions, the confusion, the sense of liberation, the awareness of 'coming home'.

But even the intensity of that experience could not compare with actually *being* there herself. As the Skyrider taxied out the hanger and up the sloping ramp the full majesty of the overground engulfed her senses. Raising her visor, she gazed in awe through the tinted canopy at the dazzling radiance of the sun as it lifted over the eastern horizon into a cloudless sky.

The pilot turned the plane onto a concrete runway and put the nose wheel on the dashed white centre line as he exchanged clipped signals with the tower.

'How're you doing?' he inquired.

'Fine,' murmured Roz. The plane surged forward. Roz felt her stomach drop a little as it lifted into the air then climbed steadily, its engine working hard to lift the added burden of the external long-range tanks fitted under each wing. And now as the ground dropped away, the vast, seemingly limitless expanse of the surrounding landscape was revealed. Pink, red and orange, mingling with the brown of the earth, colours that were the violent legacy of the Holocaust.

There was a song from the Old Time which spoke of 'the green, green hills of home'. One day, perhaps, things would return to the way they were but to Roz, who had never known anything else, the overground was stunningly beautiful. She felt it embrace her, like a mother gathering a long-lost child to her bosom. Her heart and mind seemed to blossom, bursting painlessly from the confines of her physical body to unite with the One-ness of all creation.

And like Steve, she heard voices. But Roz did not try to shut them out. She listened, and she understood many things . . .

CHAPTER FOURTEEN

Malone and his four closest henchmen seemed reasonably satisfied with Steve's account of the escape from Ne-Issan. He dropped all mention of the ill-fated Heron Pool project, the intervention of Skull-Face's agents and the incident at Long Point from his narrative and substituted a perilous voyage as stowaways on a wheelboat which had taken them to the new outstations the Iron Masters were establishing on the eastern shore of Lake Michigan. It was, he claimed, during the crossing to establish a new trading base at navref Chicago, that he and his friends had managed to blow up and sink the wheelboat and a Mute clan had completed the job by killing every Jap who managed to reach the shore.

The horses, weapons and other booty explained Steve, was their share of the loot and to blunt any piercing questions from Malone or his sidekicks, Steve swiftly offered them a celebratory taste of *sake*. It had the desired effect but Malone was quick to spot the dangers of operating in a hostile environment with a group who were permanently smashed out of their skulls. The next morning, when Cadillac awoke with one arm draped fondly over a half-empty cask, he discovered to his horror that the rest of the stock had been systematically destroyed.

Malone's unilateral action left Steve outwardly sympathetic but secretly relieved. Clearwater felt the same way. The casks of *sake* they'd been lugging around had, in their own way, the same kind of destructive potential as four dozen kegs of dynamite. Steve watched him wander disbelievingly among the smashed casks littering the banks of a nearby stream, fiercely clutching the sole survivor of the massacre to his breast. When he returned he was still speechless. A broken man, silently nursing broken dreams.

If he felt any anger, he did not show it. Or perhaps did not dare. Faced with a sullen undercurrent of protest, Malone promptly challenged anyone who was not happy with his decision to step forward and say their piece. Two breakers who had unwisely appointed themselves as spokesmen for the parched-throat majority had accepted his invitation and Malone shot both of them before they could open their mouths.

Apart from the Iron Masters swords and bows Steve's party had brought with them, the sole remaining item of interest was the herd of horses. There were no animals of any kind in the Federation and this had bred an antipathy towards them. Which wasn't a problem for renegades since the idea of making friends with one rarely entered their heads. Animals were there to be killed and, as a last resort, eaten.

Loyal Trackers, living inside the Federation, did not eat animal flesh. That was one of the disgusting things Mutes did and, in any case, overground animals were contaminated with radiation. The 'beef' burgers served in divisional mess-halls were soya-bean derivatives. Their diet included rice, various kinds of beans and root vegetables but basically it was a hi-tech laboratory product – bland-tasting, highly nutritious junk-food. Renegade Trackers had to adapt quickly or starve but it was not easy and not everybody was able to do so. Old habits died hard, and despite the risks, abandoned ration packs were still preferable to anything the overground had to offer.

All of which meant that the renegades were curious about the rapport Steve, Cadillac and Clearwater had developed with the herd of horses, the way they used them as a means of transportation, and the uncanny way Clearwater could make them obey her. For Steve, her skills provided a useful focus of attention, drawing the interest of Malone and his men away from his own adventures, his present appearance and the true nature of his involvement with his travelling companions.

Working with the horses also helped draw the renegades' minds away from the fact that, despite being marked like a Mute, Clearwater was a strong, beautiful woman with a great body. The only female among seventy-odd hairy-assed renegades and probably the last they'd gotten a sniff of since Jodi was captured. Not every guy was ready to bounce beaver but Steve was willing to bet that, given the right opportunity or sufficient provocation, a good half of them would be ready to try.

If they did, he and Cadillac wouldn't be able to stop them. Clearwater would have to call on outside help. But Talisman had done nothing to protect her from the attentions of Nakane Toh-Shiba, and he might not help her now. After falling from a height of two thousand feet, the fat Consul-General had dug a satisfyingly deep hole in the ground but the sweet vengeance did not prevent Steve being wracked by jealousy at the thought of Clearwater in his sweaty embrace. It was all very curious. She was supposed to be under the protection of Talisman but he had done absolutely nothing to prevent her being jacked up and generally abused by anyone who took a fancy to her. It was one more reason for approving Malone's decision to liquidate Cadillac's private stockpile of joy-juice.

Since there were more than enough horses to go round, Steve suggested to Malone that it might be a good idea if Clearwater gave him and his men a few riding lessons. Malone, who could see that it was a skill that might have useful applications, agreed to give it a whirl. When outlining the possible benefits, Steve omitted to say that besides occupying their minds they would discover that several hours of bouncing up and down in a saddle was guaranteed to leave them hobbling about bandy-legged with their thighs and butts on fire. And it would also banish any thoughts of a quick bunk-up.

Cadillac, of course, was no longer a happy man. The stories which had held Mute clans spellbound were of absolutely no interest to Malone's renegades. And had he spoken of these things they would have undermined Steve's account of their escape. After having been the life and soul of the party for a few glorious weeks, it was extremely annoying to be suddenly relegated to the sidelines. It was now Clearwater and her stupid horses who were the centre of attention and he found that irritating too. Gritting his teeth, Cadillac had acquitted himself manfully mile after painful mile but the bad sailor had revealed himself to be an even worse rider and as a consequence horses had now superseded boats at the top of his list of Least Favourite Things. It peeved him that Clearwater not

323

only had this magical affinity with these stupid beasts but that she was also a far better rider than he was. On top of which, to add insult to injury, Brickman was once again dominating the action – well, temporarily anyway.

The bunch of cut-throats he was trying to cosy up to had made no attempt to hide their distrust of Mutes. In itself, that was understandable, but it quickly dawned on Cadillac that *he* was the only one who was being cold-shouldered! Clearwater was besieged by her pupils and Brickman – despite being dressed like a Mute from head to foot – was constantly being invited to confer with the renegades' leader!

And – worst of all – the one thing that might have helped him bear these insults to his person and his position as leader of The Chosen had been taken from him. These vandals had smashed every single cask of *sake* bar one! And that was half empty. He now faced the agonizing choice of seeking solace a few drops at a time and remaining depressingly sober, or splurging the lot on one glorious burst of oblivion. His inability to decide, plus the knowledge that he had allowed his need for alcohol to gain a new foothold, plunged him into a black, vengeful mood.

Yes . . . It was time for someone else to suffer . . .

To avoid any trouble, Steve, Cadillac and Clearwater had laid their sleeping furs around a small fire in a shallow cave beneath the brow of the hill. Their nearest neighbours were the sentinels who had taken over the post previously manned by Gordon and Walsh. The main body of renegades were camped some eighty yards to the west of them, among the trees at the bottom of the slope. Steve and Clearwater had unsaddled the horses and let them roam free to graze at will. Now firmly attached to their new mistress, they would not roam far. When the time came, all she had to do was throw back her head and call to them using a warbling cry which caused them to neigh with delight and brought them galloping towards her.

It was a strange evocative sound. The first time she had summoned them, the cry had sprung fully formed from her lips. Steve concluded that it must have lain dormant in her memory since birth but who had put it there? And why did fleeting visions of another world, another existence, pass through his mind each time he heard it. Yet another mystery . . .

Late in the afternoon of the third day Steve returned to the cave to find Cadillac sitting with his knees drawn up to his chin and staring morosely into the flames. The small cask of *sake* stood close by. Steve decided it was better not to enquire whether it was now empty.

'Nice of you to drop in . . .'

Steve added more kindling to the fire and settled down facing him. 'You don't have to sit here by yourself.'

Cadillac responded with a sneering laugh. 'No . . ? Well, never mind, we won't go into that. Perhaps you can tell me when we'll be moving on. Or have you and Clearwater been too busy to think about that.'

'On the contrary. I've given it a great deal of thought.'

'So when do we leave?'

Steve grimaced. 'As soon as we can.'

'And how soon is that?'

'Dunno. Another two or three days.'

'Why not tomorrow? Or tonight?'

'It's not that simple.'

'It never is.'

'Listen! Don't start, okay?' Steve pointed to the camp at the bottom of the slope. 'There are upwards of seventy breakers down there and Malone's got guards posted all round. So far we've kept things nice and friendly but we're not out of the woods yet.' He shook his head in puzzlement. 'Something's going down. Don't ask me what, I can't put my finger on it. But we've got to tread lightly.'

'It's Malone who needs to tread lightly.' replied Cadillac. 'I'd kill him if I got the chance, and I'm sure you would too.'

'Maybe. But now's not the time to get even. It's Malone who's holding this bunch of misfits together. He and his four side-kicks are the only ones with enough brains to figure that by helping us on our way, they may be able to cut a deal with the M'Calls at the next annual round-up.'

'Is that what you told him?'

Steve shrugged. 'I didn't promise anything. But if they

decide to earn themselves a few brownie points by escorting us the rest of the way . . .'

'But we don't need them. Everything's gone according to plan up to now. How will we explain their presence? All it does is add an extra complication!'

'Listen! Things *haven't* gone according to plan – not unless you'd already decided to run into these guys –'

'Oh, come on. Don't be stupid!'

'Precisely. *They're* the ones who've complicated everything, not me. I'm just trying to find a neat way out.'

'Brickman. It's very simple. We just leave!'

'Yeah, but, uh . . . they're beginning to think it might be a good idea to keep the horses.' Steve paused to let the news sink home then added: 'All of them.'

'I see . . .'

'That's why I need a few more days to find out what their intentions are. If we can't part on good terms, the next best thing is to take them with us. Think about it. If the worst comes to the worst, the M'Calls can always sell them down the river.'

Cadillac eyed him, hardly able to credit what he was hearing. 'You'd do that to your own kind?'

'Don't you?'

Cadillac hid his annoyance at being outwitted. 'Yes, I suppose we do . . .'

'Look,' said Steve. 'I know you've been getting the treatment from these guys but you're not the only one. They rate lump-suckers even lower than Mutes. It's not only *your* ass I've been protecting. I've been having to do some fancy footwork myself.'

It was the opening Cadillac had been looking for. 'Yes, well, when it comes to fancy footwork, you're in a class of your own.'

The heavy sarcasm was not lost on Steve. 'What's that supposed to mean?'

'It means that despite saving my life, and swearing on oath to be my blood brother, you are still playing a double game!'

Steve met this accusation with a dry laugh. 'What the hell are you talking about!?'

'The wheelboat! When it caught fire and blew up so fortu-
itously, I assumed – since you said nothing to the contrary –
that it was the work of the Talisman! You can imagine my
surprise when I eventually got Clearwater to talk about it –
and it wasn't easy, I can tell you – to discover that she believed
the boat was attacked by arrowheads. Aircraft from the
Federation!'

Steve, wrong-footed by the sudden jump in the conversation, instinctively gave an evasive answer. 'Where'd she get
that idea?'

'Are you saying she's wrong?'

'Not exactly.'

'Okay, Brickman, just what, precisely, *are* you saying?'

'That you're drawing the wrong conclusion.'

'So, in other words, Clearwater was right. The wheelboat
was attacked by aircraft!'

'Look, uhh – I'm not sure what your problem is. We got
out, didn't we? And you've been in the spotlight ever since.'

'So . . .?'

As he posed the question, Clearwater returned. Sensing the
atmosphere, she sat down between them without saying anything and warmed her hands over the fire.

Steve threw her a loaded glance then said: 'So why should
it matter *how* the wheelboat sank? It did. And that's all there
is to it.'

Cadillac smiled pityingly. *At last . . . A chance to get his own
back.* 'How typical! You're so riddled with lies and deceptions,
you are incapable of admitting the truth. I'll ignore that sneering remark about me being in the spotlight, except to say I've
not forgotten the fact that if you hadn't saved my life, I
wouldn't be here. But that's not the issue. What we need to
establish before we go a step further is which side you're on.'

'Isn't that obvious?'

Cadillac threw up his hands and appealed to Clearwater.
'You see what I mean?'

Clearwater's eyes locked onto Steve's. 'Tell me, Cloud-
Warrior – the burning of the wheelboat – was this the work of
your friends in the Federation?'

'Yes . . .'

'And did you summon them?'

Steve hated having to lie to Clearwater. Unless he could quickly find a way to sidetrack this line of questioning he was going to be forced to come clean. He nodded. 'In a manner of speaking.' He saw her expression. 'Yes, okay, I did! But I'm not working with them. I *used* them. It was the only way we could escape from the wheelboat – and we only just managed that!'

'I agree,' said Cadillac. 'It was a master-stroke.'

'Good.' Steve slapped his outspread knees. 'Let's leave it there. The Kojak are happy, you guys are on your way home, and Talisman got all the credit.' He eyed them both. 'What more do you want?'

'I want to know *why* they did, Brickman. We blew several holes in one of their wagon-trains, remember? For which you were supposed to get the blame. It's obvious that someone – and it might even turn out to be you – has put the record straight.'

Steve frowned at his tormentor. 'What makes you say that?'

'Oh, come on! I'm not that naive! If your masters were prepared to send –' He sought Clearwater's help, 'What was it – four?'

'Five . . .'

'Five aircraft over nine hundred and fifty miles to burn that boat, they must think you're still working for them. I can't think of any other reason, can you?'

Steve shrugged off the veiled accusation of treachery. 'You tell me. You're the one with all the answers.'

Cadillac's patience began to wear thin. 'That's 'cause you're not coming up with any!' He upended the cask of *sake* and took a quick swig.

Steve gazed at Clearwater for a moment then said: 'Ask her. She knows where I stand.'

Cadillac's voice soured. 'Does she? I wonder.'

'Listen, I really don't need this – okay?' Steve got to his feet and made a strenuous attempt to keep calm but some of the bottled up anger found its way into his voice. 'We're even. I owe you nothing. And that includes an explanation! I've done my bit to help us get this far. If that's not good enough, then tough shit! I'm getting sick of pulling your nuts out of the fire.' He pointed to the western hills. 'Wyoming's thataway! Go ahead! Ride off into the sunset! I'm bailing out!'

Clearwater seized his arm as he turned away. 'Cloud-Warrior!'

'Forget it. I've had it with this guy! He's been on a tightrope to disaster ever since he got his nose back in that stuff!' He looked over her shoulder at Cadillac. 'Keep taking the medicine, pal! You're doing just fine!'

Cadillac scrambled to his feet and started to gather his belongings together. 'Come on, let's go! We're safer without him!'

Clearwater grasped Steve's hands before he could make fists out of them to smash into Cadillac's face. 'This is madness! What will you do?'

'I'll stay with these guys. What the hell? At least they're my own kind!'

'But they are not your kind any longer. Look at your hands! Do you think they will let you live amongst them marked like this?'

'Aww, c'mon, honey! It's just *paint*! I'll find some pink finger leaves and scrub it off. Christo! It's not going to be *that* difficult!'

Clearwater greeted this with a sad smile. 'Do you think their minds will change as swiftly as the colour of your skin? I have seen the way they look at us. They call you "lump-sucker" –'

'Yeah, I know –'

She tightened her grip on his hands. 'In their eyes you are unclean – as we are. You will not be safe with them. These men may have fled from the dark cities, they may parley and barter with the Plainfolk, but in their hearts they hate and fear us.'

'Then maybe I'll be able to teach them a thing or two – show them it's possible for your kind and mine to live together. It's not quite what I had in mind but it's better than having to listen to *that* asshole sounding off!'

Cadillac's temper flared. 'I couldn't have put it better myself!' He beckoned to Clearwater. 'Come on. Let's pack up and get out of here before I do something we may both regret!'

Clearwater drew back. 'No! I shall not leave unless the three of us are together!' She stamped her foot angrily. 'Make peace with your blood-brother! Now!'

Cadillac raised his clenched fists and turned his eyes to the sky. 'Sweet Sky-Mother! What a bitter cup you have poured me!' He flung an accusing finger at Steve. 'I shall not ride with this lying toad until he swears on *your* head to tell us the truth!'

Clearwater's blue eyes fastened on Steve. It was amazing how they changed hue depending on her mood. This time, they were a deep azure, liquid pools that invited his soul to plunge towards the very centre of her being. 'Do this for me . . .'

'Okay,' said Steve lightly. 'Cross my heart and hope to die.'

She took his hand as he made the sign of the cross and laid it on her breast. 'It is *my* heart that will be pierced, Cloud-Warrior. If your words are untrue they will kill me, not you.'

Steve had an uncomfortable feeling she meant it. They all sat down again. Clearwater picked up the small cask of *sake* and passed it to Steve. Amazingly, Cadillac did not object. Or did not dare to. Steve would have liked to pay him off by swallowing the lot but he contented himself with a couple of sips to lubricate his tongue then handed it back and used the Japanese word for 'Cheers!' he'd picked up from the leader of the *ronin* Noburo Naka-Jima. '*Kanpai!*'

With great reluctance, which sprang from his ingrained habit of keeping his true thoughts and feelings to himself – plus any information which, if kept secret, might confer a tactical advantage, he told them about the telepathic gift that he and Roz had been born with. A gift that was, as far as he knew, theirs alone.

And he described how, when he crash-landed after his arm had been pinned to his helmet by Cadillac's cross-bow bolt, the same wounds had appeared in Roz's right arm and scalp: only to disappear without trace some hours later. This led, inevitably, to explaining how this deep rapport which they had kept to themselves since early childhood had forged an unbreakable bond; 'one-ness' that went far beyond the most

330

intimate bonds of friendship and which he could not adequately describe.

His deep secret now revealed, Steve lapsed into embarrassed silence, hoping that Clearwater might understand what he was talking about. And praying that she might also understand the message he sought to convey with his eyes: his equally profound feelings for her. Clearwater had opened up a totally different side to his nature, had aroused emotions that, at first, he had been unable to describe. She had taught him both the meaning and the language of love. He had told her this many times. And he wanted to tell her again but was unable to do so in Cadillac's brooding presence.

'Do you love her?' asked Clearwater.

'Not the way you mean.'

'And what way is that?'

They both ignored Cadillac's question.

'And Roz. Does she love you?'

Steve paused, thinking of Santanna Deep. 'Do I have to answer that?'

'You already have. How does she feel about me?'

'She doesn't understand.'

'In other words she regards me as a threat.'

'It's my fault for not explaining things properly,' said Steve 'You know what I mean – the difference between *our* relationship and the way I feel about her.'

'Is there a difference?'

'Hey, c'mon!' laughed Steve. 'You're already skinning me alive. What d'you want?'

Cadillac lowered the cask from his lips. 'The truth!' He wiped the back of his hand across his mouth. 'So . . . your masters *know* of this bond between you.'

'Yes. Ever since you put that arrow through me. But at the beginning, they didn't know we were able to send thought-messages to each other. It was just this shared stress phenomenon – what the medics called "psychosomatic trauma".'

'But they know you can talk to each other now,' insisted Cadillac.

'Of course! Roz *had* to tell them! It was the only way she could help us.'

331

'Obviously. What also strikes me is the extraordinary faith they appear to have in your kin-sister's abilities, and the speed with which they reacted. And the organization and effort required to send those five planes over that distance, to make a pin-point attack in the dark! Just to save your life. Amazing . . .'

'Of course, they don't know you're no longer a loyal subject of the Federation. But they must think Roz is reliable. Why else would they go to so much trouble? I can only think of one explanation. She must have proved her worth before this. You say they are holding her hostage to ensure your obedience but it's clear they must know it was not you who blew up the wagon-train. Otherwise they'd have killed her to get back at you. What other messages have you been sending, I wonder?'

'None! The only time we had the same depth of contact as on the wheelboat was when the five of us and Side-Winder were heading towards Long Point in those powered inflatables. The words, or the thoughts –' Steve searched for an apt description, '– the totality of the experience which comes through all of a piece and tells you everything you want to know, only comes through – according to her – when *I* open up. In moments of high stress the contact occurs on an involuntary basis, otherwise it's down to me. Unless I switch on, she can't reach me.'

This was not strictly true but Steve was not aware of the progress Roz had made in the period since their ill-fated rendezvous – arranged with the connivance of certain members of the First Family – at Santanna Deep.

'And what did she tell you on the way to Long Point?' asked Clearwater.

'That what I'd decided to do was the right thing.'

'And what was that?'

Steve turned to Cadillac. 'Stay with you, steal the planes and head west.'

'Why?'

'Because that was the way things had been planned.'

'Who by?'

'She didn't say.'

It was Clearwater's turn again. 'Have you talked to each other since we left the Kojak?'

'No.' Steve hesitated then said: 'I've tried to keep that side of my mind shut down. Unless we got into another impossible jam I was going to stay off the air until you were safely back home. I, uhh – well, to be honest, I didn't want to risk giving our position away. Roz wouldn't betray me but, uhh – the thing is, I just don't know what kind of pressure she's under.'

Clearwater nodded but it was impossible to tell whether she believed him or was merely acknowledging receipt of the information. Steve stared defiantly across the fire at Cadillac. 'Satisfied?'

'Yes. For the moment.'

And fuck you too . . .

When night fell, they curled up around the fire in their individual sleep furs. Clearwater lay within arm's reach of Steve but by tacit agreement they'd stayed out of each other's beds so as not to cause further hurt to Cadillac's wounded ego. At the Kojak settlement it hadn't been a problem: Cadillac had been provided with his own lodge and an ample supply of what the fishermen called 'night bait' to dress his hook. But the situation became more delicate when the guy whose girl you'd taken over was lying on his jack less than three yards away – and might not even be asleep.

Tonight was different. Steve woke to find Clearwater easing her body beneath his furs. 'Whaa –?'

Her fingers sealed his lips. 'Sshhh . . .' She caressed his face then kissed him hungrily. She was naked except for the threadbare cotton undervest she'd brought out of Ne-Issan. Her hand slid down his chest and found the knotted drawstring of his walking skins. Steve got the message and started to wriggle out of his trousers while she ran the flat of her hand over his stomach.

A swift pull on the side ties of his triangular loincloth cleared the decks for action. Clearwater slithered on top of him and sat crouched forward, astride his belly while she lifted her vest over her head. Steve lying beneath her managed to lift his as far as his armpits.

Drawing the top fur blanket over her shoulders, she brought her breasts to within reach of his eager mouth then, hooking

333

her feet inside his calves to force his legs apart, she slid her body downwards until the moist lips of her vagina came to rest against his stiffening penis. Steve felt her firm thighs close round him.

Hhooo-hhoooo-hhooo! Ohh, Sweet Sky-Mother . . !

Clearwater silenced him with another devouring kiss that left his mouth and roamed over his face and neck. It was as if she was trying to eat him alive.

Steve responded in kind, his hands roving up and down her spine, into the cleft between her buttocks then back up over her hips and slim waist to touch the sweetly curving sides of her breasts.

'Hold me!' she whispered fiercely.

He locked his arms against her spine, and held her tightly.

'Harder!' she begged. 'Tighter!'

They lay cheek to cheek, locked together from head to toe. Her thighs continued their gentle massage, squeezing rhythmically against the pulsing beat of the blood surging through his body. Steve could feel her sex quivering as it sought to embrace him. Burning. Melting. Dissolving into one. Delicious. Unbearable.

She put her lips to his ear. 'Now, Cloud-Warrior! Now! Oh, oh, ohhh! My love! My Golden One! Quickly! We have so little time!'

In that brief glorious moment when his brain exploded like a supernova, Steve also had a blinding revelation. He had coupled with two women, not one. Roz had been inside his head from the moment of penetration and she had played a dual role – merging with Steve's psyche to become the male partner in the sexual act and, at the same time, the mental projection of her own female psyche had superimposed itself on Clearwater's half of the action.

Put into blunt Trail-Blazer language, she had screwed both of them simultaneously. Not just in her mind, but *with* her mind

Steve knew he wasn't imagining things. This wasn't inspired by any feelings of guilt or betrayal. Roz had *been* there. But not as a jealous rival. There had been no anger. Desire, yes. A burning physical need to be held in a warm embrace, to merge

334

ogether as one, but above all, transforming and elevating the whole experience, was an overwhelming feeling of love. Of sharing. Of understanding.

And in that same lightning-strike of illumination Steve also realized Roz was physically within reach. She was here. On the overground. Aboard an approaching wagon-train. Red River . . .

Steve and Clearwater lay in each other's arms, their legs entwined, their loins still inflamed with the sweet fever. Clearwater's head nestled in his shoulder. She brushed her lips against his neck then whispered: 'She was here, wasn't she?'

'Yes . . . But –'

She sealed his lips. 'You don't need to explain. I wanted her to be with us. I called her into my mind and into my body. There is no more hatred. While she was imprisoned beneath the earth her mind was darkened by a cloud of unknowing. But now that has lifted. She knows we are not rivals but soul-sisters. The power that binds you and her binds all of us.'

'But how could –'

'Sshhh! When you are ready, these things will be made known to you.'

'Okay. But what did you mean – "We have so little time"?'

Clearwater stroked his face then hugged him tightly. 'Before the dawn, Cloud-Warrior. Before the dawn . . .'

As he lay silently watching the cloaked movement of their bodies, Cadillac found himself unable to adopt the objective detachment that was the mark of a true warrior. As the Leader of The Chosen his mind should have been grappling with more lofty concerns; matters of great moment, not the doubtful pleasures of the flesh. But it was precisely the bitter-sweet memory of *those* pleasures which had been resurrected by his reintroduction to *sake*. He had been happy in Ne-Issan – until Brickman had come along to spoil everything. Yet again.

In his present sour mood, Cadillac's new role, however important that might eventually become, did not compensate being totally deprived of sex and, barring a few last precious mouthfuls, *sake*. It was the latter which had removed his inhibitions with regard to the former, transforming him from a tenative lover – burdened with secret lusts but tongue-tied by fear of rejection and thus doomed to fail – into a liberated, super-confident cocksman.

It was ironic that his first love and chosen mate, the child-woman he had grown up with, had been drawn by Fate – and perhaps by an unrequited hunger – into a relationship with a duplicitous slick-tongued adventurer when he, Cadillac Deville, had finally acquired *real* standing, had been given a leading role befitting his talents, and was also capable of satisfying her as a man. In triplicate.

Yes . . . As Mr Snow had often reminded him, being born in the shadow of Talisman was a great honour bestowed on a few rare individuals. An honour he must constantly strive to be worthy of. Cadillac was doing his best, but Mr Snow had omitted to mention that, at times, being a Child of Destiny could be a real pig . . .

When Steve and Clearwater woke next morning, Cadillac was still asleep. To avoid waking him, they took their breakfast down to the renegades' main camp and ate with Malone. Afterwards Clearwater resumed her riding lessons. Steve stayed with Malone and his lieutenants and tried to glean some information about their next move. Malone's side didn't give much away. They were more interested in questioning Steve about the Iron Masters.

It was around mid-day when Steve walked back up the slope to find Clearwater kneeling by the fire, cooking a meal for Cadillac. The Great Helmsman was perched on a nearby rock, staring moodily out into space. He didn't even acknowledge Steve's arrival.

Steve and Clearwater exchanged silent greetings. The small cask of *sake* lay on its side. Empty. Steve glanced down at it then aimed a questioning glance across the fire. Her eyes begged him to tread carefully.

Steve went over and broke the news about Roz. He had no idea how Cadillac would react but he had expected some sign of interest. What he got by way of response was a mocking, belligerent laugh. Steve let it ride and tried to get a fix on

336

what was going on behind the eyes. The Mute wasn't drunk but he had been drinking.

Steve tried again. 'I don't think you quite realize what this means. She's out! Up here in the real world!'

'So . . .?'

'It's the break I've been looking for! If we could find some way to spring her from the wagon-train –'

Cadillac slid off the rock and started down the slope. 'And just how do you propose to do that?'

'I haven't worked that out yet. But there must be a way. If Malone and his breakers got together with the M'Calls –' Steve was interrupted by a call from Clearwater.

'Caddy! Your meal's ready!'

'Later! I'm going down to the stream for a wash. Okay?'

Steve seized Cadillac's arm as he went to move off. 'Forget the wash. This is important!'

'To you maybe. But not to me. This bunch of no-hopers are *your* friends, Brickman. You want to work with 'em? Fine! Just leave my people out of this. There will be no deal.'

Clearwater, sensing an argument was brewing, came down to join them.

'Wait a minute. Just listen, will you? I know it seems a far-fetched idea but –' Steve held up his hand to prevent Cadillac interrupting '– suppose, if a way could be found, we *did* manage to capture a wagon-train. To the M'Calls it would be nothing more than a large heap of junk. All they'd do is tear pieces off it. But with the help of these guys, you and I could actually *use* it! Can you imagine the edge it would give us?'

Cadillac snorted derisively. 'A pipe-dream! Grow up, Brickman! You've involved us in enough of your lunatic schemes!'

'Yeah, sure,' snapped Steve. 'They were lunatic. But *your* ass is still in one piece – in spite of the fact you did your best to fuck things up!'

Cadillac started to turn away. Steve pulled him back. 'What's the matter? Having trouble facing facts? Has your courage run out with the joy-juice?'

'You don't need to lecture *me* about courage! Cloud-Warrior . . . Hahh! You are not worthy of the name!' jeered Cadillac.

He turned to Clearwater. 'You should have heard your Golden One when he felt the flames licking round the wings of his Skyhawk.' He mimicked a weak version of Steve's voice: '"Help me . . . please!!" No sign of the all-conquering hero then! Just a pitiful whining wretch! No Mute, worthy of the name would have ever begged for mercy from an enemy! He would have died – proudly!'

'Like you on the wheelboat . . .'

Cadillac's lips trembled. 'That was different! I wasn't trying to save my life. I was trying to save my soul!'

'That's a good one. I must remember that line.' Steve turned to Clearwater. 'And he calls *me* a devious sonofabitch!'

'How can you, a sand-burrower, who believes in nothing, possibly understand what the Plainfolk mean by honour and courage?'

'I'm trying the best I can. Which is more than can be said for you.' This was almost followed by 'You drunken bum', but Steve just managed to stop his tongue in time.

'Then understand this! The M'Calls have *attacked* one of the great "iron snakes"! The one you rode into battle. More than three hundred clan-brothers and sisters kissed sharp iron that day. Men women and children. Shot and burned and torn to pieces by its angry white breath!'

'Yeah, I know. That super-heated steam is a real killer. But you know about all that now. And you've got a hundred guns! No one – not even the M'Calls, who are renowned for their bravery – can succeed by attacking *en masse* in broad daylight! We've got to use our brains! Figure out some way to get aboard. I don't know . . . maybe in disguise. Think positive! There's got to be a way!'

Cadillac remained unmoved. His voice suddenly cold. 'There's no way, Brickman. No way that you are going to drag me, or Clearwater, or any of my people into attacking Red River just to free your kin-sister!'

Steve clawed air. 'Christopher Columbus! She's not the *only* reason!'

'But she's the main one . . .'

Steve appealed to Clearwater. 'Talk to him, will you? Make him understand.' She didn't respond. He turned back to Cadil-

338

lac. 'We've got to go for it, Caddy. We may never get another opportunity like this again!'

'And neither will your masters . . .'

Steve frowned. 'What d'you mean?'

Cadillac laughed bitterly. 'Don't play games, Brickman. Why d'you think your kin-sister is on that train?'

'You're the smart-ass – why don't you tell me?'

'She's the bait on the hook! They figure you'll either make an attempt to free her, or –' Cadillac caught Clearwater's warning glance.

'Or what? Come on, let's have it.'

'You'll sell us down the river.' Cadillac's voice was muted but his eyes didn't budge from Steve's.

'I see. You think they brought her out here to bring pressure on me.'

'Can you think of a better reason?' The defiant tone matched the look. 'Isn't that why you came back out? You agreed to try and capture us because they were going to kill her if you refused!'

'In other words, in spite of everything we've been through so far, you *still* don't trust me.'

Cadillac weighed up his reply. 'Let me give you the bottom line, Brickman. I don't think you trust yourself.'

'What kind of an answer is that?'

'The only one you're going to get. You fed me the same kind of line often enough. All right if I take a wash now?'

'Yes, I think you should,' said Clearwater. 'It's time you both cooled down. This isn't getting us anywhere.'

'On the contrary,' snapped Steve. 'It's about time we cleared the air.' He jerked a thumb towards Cadillac. 'Wanna know what is *really* pissing this guy off? He can't bear competition. He'd like us all to step back and let him run the show. Well it ain't gonna happen.' He squared up to Cadillac. 'The Number One spot has to be earned, *amigo*. You get to be king of the hill by being better than everybody else. Tougher, meaner, smarter –'

Cadillac waved Steve's words away and went to step past him.

'Stay!' commanded Clearwater.

'Maybe you're right about me not trusting myself,' Steve continued. 'I certainly don't where you're concerned. For a long time I felt I owed you one for saving my life – since when I've pulled your ass out of the fire *twice!* Not because I wanted to but because I had to. If it wasn't for Clearwater and Mr Snow, I'd have left you behind long ago.'

'Really? You'd have left *me* behind? If it wasn't for the deal I did with the Kojaks, you'd be hanging in strips from their lodge-poles! Who was it who saw that wheelboat coming? Who was it who came up with the best idea of getting on board?'

'Yeah. And once we did, who fucked it all up by losing his nerve?! Falling for the simplest trick in the book! Who'd be out there now with the fishes feedin' off his face if I hadn't got him ashore?'

Cadillac's mouth trembled as he tried to control his anger. 'I don't owe you anything, Brickman! My people have repaid that debt ten times over, and what they didn't give you've taken. Saving your lying snake-hide was the worst thing I ever did.'

'Yeah. And you know why? Because you finally found yourself up against some *real* competition – instead of those dumb, slack-jawed pieces of lump-shit who've been listening to you all these years!'

Clearwater seized Cadillac's knife arm and held on as he tried to wrestle free.

Steve continued to taunt him. 'You know what your problem is? You've never forgiven me for dragging you out of your cosy little corner at the Heron Pool. Upending bottle after bottle of *sake* and sticking it to those slant-eyed body slaves. What a sweet little number! You were so busy enjoying yourself you couldn't see it was only a matter of time before they pulled the rug out from under you. No. You were the big man on the campus.

'But who got you the job?! *I* did! You've never had an original idea in your whole fucking life! Everything inside your head that's worth knowing was stolen from me! Everything you knew before that was given to you by Mr Snow, and all that Japanese junk you've got tucked away was another reel-to-reel job!' He laughed derisively before delivering the *coup-de-grace*. 'You want the truth? Well here it is, friend. You've got a second-rate brain full of second-hand ideas. You think you're born to lead The Chosen? I wouldn't put you in charge of a pile of buffalo-shit!'

Clearwater saw Malone striding up the slope towards them. A handful of renegades followed, several yards behind. Clearwater stepped in front of Cadillac and tried to stop the fight before Malone arrived. 'Listen to me! Let the wind carry away these hot words. Do not answer them with sharp iron!'

Her appeal went unheeded. Blood-brothers they might have sworn to be, but these insults were too much to bear. They must be avenged! Cadillac broke loose with an angry roar, his blade a sliver of white fire as it caught the afternoon sun.

Steve drew his combat knife and got ready to parry his opponent's first lunge.

Clearwater turned as Malone reached them. 'Please –!'

The breaker backed off with raised hands. 'To hell with it. I don't know what this argument's about but if they want to work it out the hard way, let 'em.'

Clearwater attempted to intervene. 'Have you both gone mad? Stop this! Now!' Once again her appeal fell on deaf ears. Both men thrust her aside and continued to circle one another, jabbing and feinting to test each other's reactions. Clearwater realized she had to do something – but what?

The answer came from within. A surge of power that rode on the back of her anger, fuelling a blood bloodcurdling scream.

Malone saw her eyes gleam with blue fire. Her two arms flashed forward and outwards, the raised palms of each hand aimed towards the heads of the duellists. He prided himself on being a hard man but the sound that issued from her lips was so terrifying, he came as close as he'd ever been to crapping himself.

The effect on Brickman and the Mute was even more startling. For a split second, they seemed to be transfixed, open-mouthed, the knives dropping from their splayed fingers then in the next instant they were lifted bodily off the ground and hurled several yards through the air in different directions. Both landed heavily and lay sprawled on the ground, winded by the fall and the invisible hammer-blow Clearwater had delivered.

Malone had never seen anything like it. How on earth could she have . . .? He never found out. As he turned back to her, his amazement turned rapidly to wide-eyed dismay. Above and behind Clearwater a low-flying Federation Skyhawk soared up over the ridge like a wide-winged death bird and dived straight towards them.

Malone pitched himself sideways into the cover of a nearby rock as several other breakers whose attention had been drawn to the knife-fight raised a ragged chorus of alarm. But it was too late. The stream of needlepoint rounds being pumped out by the six-barrelled gun under the nose of the Skyhawk was already ploughing a deadly furrow through the grass and dirt towards Clearwater, chipping flakes off the rocks and pebbles and sending whining ricochets in all directions.

Instead of throwing herself down, Clearwater turned as if to challenge their attacker and was caught on the turn. A cloud of rock powder and earth erupted around her –

Chu-wii-chu-wii-chu-wii-chu-wii-chu-wii-chu-wii-chu-wii!

Even if they had been on their feet, Steve and Cadillac were too far away to pull her out of the line of fire. Clearwater's arms and head jerked wildly as she was struck by several rounds in quick succession then she too was hurled to the ground as the hail of bullets swept down the slope.

NO-oh-oh-OH! With not an ounce of breath left in his body, the scream of anguish remained sealed inside Steve's brain. But it was sufficient to trip the circuits that opened the channel to Roz.

Oh, Bless you, Sweet Sky-Mother! Roz! If ever we meant anything to each other, help me now!

Clearwater rolled slowly onto her back and tried to raise her left arm towards the Skyhawk as it skimmed over their heads. But the only thing that issued from her lips was blood. Her arm fell sideways, the fingers stretched out towards Steve.

Steve dragged himself upright with the aid of a nearby rock and staggered over to where she lay with her feet pointing up the gentle slope. Malone joined him. Blood was seeping through the tunic and trousers of her faded blue cotton slave outfit. The undyed sections of her skin had turned greyish-white. She wasn't dead but she soon would be, unless . . .

Yes, little sister, I hear you. I understand . . .

CHAPTER FIFTEEN

Malone concluded a preliminary survey of Clearwater's wounds with a pessimistic grunt. 'Pity Medicine-Hat isn't still with us. Difficult to know where to start.'

'Yeah ...' Steve choked back the tears. He stroked Clearwater's face and tried to connect with her half-open eyes but there was no reaction. She was unconscious. Probably in deep shock. He grasped her hand and squeezed hard, trying to will his life into her body. His mind pleaded with her to live. Begged her to forgive him. If he and Cadillac had not become involved in that senseless argument which had been triggered by the Mute's refusal to even think about freeing Roz from that wagon-train, they might have seen the Skyhawk earlier. Then none of this would have happened.

But all was not lost. Not now that Roz was here ...

Steve gripped Malone's arm. 'This is out of my league. Can you do anything? Can you stop the bleeding?'

'I can try. We still have a few odds and ends. But it'll only be a delaying action. If you've gotten hooked on beaver I advise you to start looking for another piece.'

Steve didn't rise to the jibe. Falling out with Cadillac was enough for one day. 'We've got to try and keep her alive.'

'On account of that amazing stunt she pulled on you two?'

'For all kinds of reasons. Do what you can ...'

'Okay. But I've also got another little piece of business to take care of.' Malone turned and bellowed at two of his side-kicks. 'Andy! Jake! Take some of the guys and bring those two fuckers Gordon and Walsh down off that point!'

It didn't sound as if Malone was planning to hand out medals.

As Andy and Jake led a handful of armed men toward the lookout post, Steve hobbled over to where Cadillac still lay sprawled on the ground. He was out cold too. Griff, one of

Malone's breakers knelt over him. He had pulled open Cadillac's tunic and was looking for the source of the blood.

Steve hunkered down beside him. 'Bad?'

'Nahhh, just flesh wounds. He'll live.' Griff pointed to where single needlepoint rounds had sliced across the outside curve of Cadillac's left thigh and the left-hand side of his belly, then closed his tunic and rolled him over to show Steve where two more rounds had torn jagged furrows in the right-hand side of his ribcage before burying themselves in the ground beneath.

A lump raised on the back of Cadillac's head by a nearby rock explained why he was out cold, and Steve discovered a fifth grazing wound in the back of Cadillac's right calf. The Mute had been incredibly lucky to have been struck glancing blows from the finned rounds. The .125 copper-jacketed steel-tipped darts were designed to keyhole on impact, causing explosive wounding. The damage sustained by Clearwater's body didn't bear thinking about.

'Got any sulfanilamide?' It was an antiseptic powder used for preventing the infection of open wounds.

'Yeah. But I ain't wasting it on any friggin' lump-heads.'

Steve seized Griff by the front of his tunic. 'Do it, friend. We need this guy in good shape. He's our ticket to a trouble-free future.'

'Yeah?' Griff didn't look impressed.

Steve relaxed his grip. 'You want the Mutes off your back, don't you?'

'It'd make life a lot simpler.'

'This is the guy who can fix it. Look after him.' Steve patted Griff's soldier and stood up. The party dispatched by Malone was on its way back, pushing Gordon and Walsh ahead of them. Both men had given up trying to protect themselves from the rifle butts that were being jabbed into them from all sides. They obviously knew what was in store for them and it wasn't long in coming.

The party halted in front of Malone. Walsh's face was scuffed and bruised, one eye was rapidly closing. Gordon's right trouser leg was soaked in blood from a wound in his thigh.

'He tried to make a run for it,' explained Jake.

Malone pulled the three-barrelled air-pistol from his shoulder holster and moved closer to the luckless breakers. 'Know what this is about?'

No reply.

'Two dead and three wounded on account of you not seein' that Skyhawk!' He gestured towards Cadillac. 'Not these lump-heads. Your buddies – that you scumbags were supposed to be lookin' out for!' He tapped his chest. 'And I was only a whisker away from gettin' my own ass blown off! What the fuckin' hell were you doin' – watchin' the fight?'

Stu Walsh straightened up defiantly and croaked. 'Wasn't everybody?'

Malone placed his pistol against Walsh's throat and blew a hole right through his neck. He moved on to Gordon. 'Got somethin' you wanna get off your chest?'

'Yeah. I'm sorry I ain't gonna be around when you get yours.' The breaker spat a gobbet of blood and spittle in Malone's face.

Malone wiped it off with the back of his hand then holstered his pistol and drew his combat knife.

Everybody held their breath.

'So,' he said quietly. 'You wanna try and take me?' He grabbed Gordon's right hand and placed the butt of the knife in his palm. 'Here's your big chance.' Malone took a couple of paces backwards. 'Okay! Let him go!' He beckoned the breaker with both hands. 'Come on, Gordy. You got the edge, let's see you use it!'

Gritting his teeth against the pain in his wounded thigh, Gordon tightened his grip on the knife and made a desperate lunge towards his tormentor. Malone was solidly-built but he was fast. Throwing his weight onto his left heel he made a half-turn, leant away from Gordon and delivered a high pile-driving kick.

KUH-CHERAKK! Steve, no stranger to violence, winced as the heel of Malone's right boot struck Gordon under the jaw, snapping his head back and breaking his neck at the same time.

'Strip off their gear and clothes and dump 'em . . .' Malone retrieved his combat knife without bothering to check if Gordon was dead then turned to Steve. 'This way, friend . . .'

The renegade had enlisted the help of two other breakers to help staunch Clearwater's wounds. Being old hands, they hadn't stopped to watch Walsh and Gordon have their cards cancelled. Still unconscious, Clearwater lay on a folded straw poncho. The blood-stained tunic, loose trousers and v-shaped cotton loincloth had been removed but she was not naked; close to half of her blood-smeared body was covered with field dressings.

'How're we doing?'

One of them – a guy called O'Keefe – wiped his hands on her torn tunic. 'We've blocked the holes but she's still bleeding internally. Only one thing can save this beaver – major surgery.'

'Yeah . . .' Steve rolled up her clothes to pillow her head and covered her from chin to toe with his sleeping furs. Gazing for a moment into her unseeing eyes, he brushed a hand across her forehead then rose and took Malone aside. 'I need to talk.'

'What's the problem?'

Steve hesitated. After what he had just seen he had to choose his words carefully. If he didn't get it right first time, he could end up dead before he'd had time to explain. 'That was a Mark Two Skyhawk. See the red wingtips? Means it came from Red River.'

Malone eyed him suspiciously. 'How come you know so much about Skyhawks?'

'I used to be a wingman – remember? Class-mate of mine let me look over one at the Pueblo way-station. Before I got into trouble. We were lucky. That guy must have been on the end of his drum. But he'll be back – and so will his friends.'

'In that case we'd better get going.'

'Not me. I'm staying.'

'With that beaver? What'n the hell for? She's finished, *amigo. Terminada.*

'You're wrong. She's going to live.' Steve led Malone out of earshot. 'I'm gonna get her on board that wagon-train.'

Malone did a double-take. 'Come again?'

The guy was good, there was no doubt about that. But then he'd had years of practice ...

'It's her only chance,' said Steve. 'She's less than fifty miles from where we're standing, and she's carrying a combat surgical team and a fully-equipped operating theatre.'

Malone greeted this with a dry laugh. 'What good's that gonna do her? Do you seriously think those guys are gonna waste their time trying to save a lump-head — even one built the way she is?'

'They'll save this one. She's special.'

'I'll buy that. But how're you —?'

Steve lowered his voice. 'They're already on their way.'

Malone's face hardened as he studied Steve through half-closed eyes. 'Jack me ... I had you figured right the first time. You *are* a fuggin' Fed!'

Steve caught Malone's hand as it went across his chest towards his pistol. 'That makes two of us, *compadre*. But being a wet-back, it took me a lot longer to get your number.'

'Yeah ...' Malone dropped his gun arm.

Steve slid his forefinger behind his left ear and pressed the tiny transceiver hidden under the skin at the edge of his skull. A gentle on–off pressure was enough to transmit HG–FR in Morse code.

Malone scratched his neck and sent back his own four-letter call-sign: HH–SA. Steve's unit — the size of a quartz watch battery — translated the series of dots and dashes into a high-pitched humming noise and fed it directly to his inner ear.

The renegade then introduced himself by disclosing his full code-name. 'High Sierra.'

'Hang-Fire ...'

'Mother said you might be in touch.'

'How much do you know?'

'As much as you wanna tell me.'

Watch yourself, Stevie. This is one cagey sonofabitch you got here ...

Malone jerked a thumb towards Cadillac. The Mute was just starting to come round. 'Is he on your shopping list too?'

'Yeah. But I need to keep him back to help me collect the rest of the consignment. *Etiende?*'

348

'*Perfectamente*. Anything I can do to help?'

'Yeah, there is. Got any morphine?'

'I already gave her a jab.'

'I meant for him.'

Malone looked surprised. 'But they're just scratches! You've got to take an arm and a leg off before a Mute starts hollerin' and most of them don't utter so much as a squeak even then. Way you're cosied up with these two I'd've thought you'd know that.'

'That's not why I asked. It'll make things easier all round if he's damped down for a few hours while you ship him out of here.'

'In that case, since he can swallow, we'll slip him some Cloud Nines.' Summoning Griff, Malone fished out a bubble-card of pills from the first aid bag and told him to give Cadillac a double dose.

Cloud Nine, the standard pain-killing sedative dispensed in pill form by the Federation had helped to make Poppa Jack's last years of life easier to bear.

Steve gazed across at Clearwater's inert body. Had she known what was going to happen? Was this what she meant when she had whispered 'We have so little time' . . .?

'You were saying . . .'

Steve snapped out of his reverie. 'Huhh?'

'The lump. Ship him out – to where?'

'Ohh, yehh, I, uhh – want you to run him home for me. His clan hangs out up around navref Caspar, Wyoming. If you follow the North Platte river –'

'I know the way. How do we find 'em when we get there?'

'Don't worry. They'll find *you*. The M'Calls control that area. It was their warriors that lifted Kelso, Jodi, and the other guys who went missing during last year's round-up.'

Malone nodded. 'I'm beginning to get the picture . . .'

'Cadillac's a wordsmith.'

'No kidding?' Malone looked genuinely interested. 'I thought they were all old guys.'

'Not when they're born,' laughed Steve. 'He's next in line for the job. That makes him important. So important you'll be able to cut your own deal. All you've got to do is deliver our friend in good condition and you could earn yourself a stack of credits. Go in under the white smoke and talk to Mr Snow. He's the main man – and this guy's teacher. If you tell him I sent you, I guarantee he'll do business. Handle it right and you need never play hunt the redskin again.'

'Would certainly make life a lot easier . . .'

'Then go for it.'

'Okay.' Malone grimaced thoughtfully. 'This Mr Snow. Is he "the rest of the consignment"?'

'This is my operation, *amigo*. When you need to know more, I'll tell you.'

'Just asking . . .'

'The first priority is to deliver Cadillac to the M'Calls. If you can then use that contact to get cosy with 'em, that'll be even better. That way they won't suspect anything when I call you in to help make the hit.'

The prospect of a well-engineered betrayal twisted Malone's mouth into a thin smile. 'Sounds good. What about the horses?'

'If your boys are game, take 'em. All I need is mine and a couple of spares.' It was Steve's turn to smile. 'If you find you can't ride 'em, you can always try eatin' 'em. And I suggest you tie Big-Mouth to the saddle and rope his feet together under the horse's belly.'

'Does that mean he's gonna give us trouble?'

'Not once you've got him away from here.'

'What do we tell him when he wakes up?'

'Good question.' Steve thought it over. 'Tell him that, thanks to his desire to kill me, we were jumped by a Skyhawk and the last time you saw me, Clearwater was dying in my arms. That'll give him something to think about. Might even shut his mouth too. You can also say I'm aiming to catch up with you as soon as possible.'

'But you don't want me to tell him you're puttin' the beaver on the wagon-train.'

Steve concealed his growing irritation at Malone's repeated use of this pejorative word to describe Clearwater. 'Not yet. If she doesn't survive . . .'

'Yeah, I see what you mean.'

'I'll break the news to him as and when. And listen, bear with him, huh? I know from experience how you feel about people giving you lip but, uhh – don't damage the merchandise. You may need his help to talk your way across the turf of any Mute clans between here and navref Caspar.'

Malone nodded. 'I'll bear that in mind.' He broke away to confer with his two chief lieutenants. While they went off with the other breakers to round up the horses, Steve and Malone made a rough stretcher and carried the unconscious Clearwater back to the shallow cave under the rock ledge where, less than eighteen hours before, she had been in his arms, gloriously and vibrantly alive . . .

Steve tried to hide his feelings as they stepped outside.

'So –' Malone fisted his left palm, '– you gonna wait here until . . .?'

'Yeah. I've been to the end of the world and back for this one. I wanna stay and see it through.'

'Sounds reasonable . . .'

'You got a radio?' asked Steve.

'Why?'

'Don't you think you ought to get Mother to call the 'hawks off? That guy who hit us today obviously didn't know who he was aiming at.'

Malone shrugged. 'We have to take our chances like everybody else. AMEXICO keeps us supplied by stashing small packs of goodies around the landscape but some of us also come close to getting our asses blown off. If we didn't, some of the *real* breakers who are running with us might get suspicious.'

'And when they do?'

'That's my problem. How'd you get onto me?'

'Process of deduction,' said Steve. 'When I ran into you guys last year you came down on me pretty fast. For a breaker you seemed to know a great deal about undercover Feds. Too much, in fact.'

'Yeah. I'll have to watch that.'

'But it wasn't until Kelso came out of the woodwork that I finally put it together. He and Jodi wouldn't have dared come back to rescue me if *you* hadn't decided it was time to cut me loose. Once I knew he was Rat-Catcher, I started to back-track over what had happened and ended up more or less convinced that you must be working for Mother too.

'Watching you and O'Keefe and that other guy at work on Clearwater clinched it for me. The rest of the boys had made it pretty clear how they felt about Mutes. If they found one dying of thirst they wouldn't even piss on him! I had to twist Griff's arm to get a wound dressing for Cadillac. You wouldn't have spent time on her unless she was important. And you knew she was.'

Malone wasn't someone who smiled a lot but he managed a steely grin. 'Just for the record, it wasn't my idea to post you. We all get taken right to the edge – either that way, or some-thing just as unpleasant. It's part of the graduation ceremony. Nothing personal – you understand?'

'Sure. Was it you who arranged for Jodi to leave me the knife?'

'Not directly. Through Kelso. But getting themselves cap-tured by the Mutes wasn't part of the plan. Real shame about Kelso. Dave could be a real pain in the ass but –'

'You're telling me.'

'But he could be good company too. Medicine Hat . . . Jodi. Not much to look at but –'

'She was one tough lady.'

'More'n that, sonny.' Malone's eyes glinted knowingly. 'When she got that sweet little jolly-box of hers fired up she could put a real shine on your pin. Know what I mean?'

Steve hid his surprise. 'Yeah,' he said, thinking how strange it was that in all the time they'd been together he had never given a moment's consideration to that side of Jodi's nature. And he wondered why disclosure of it made him feel un-comfortable.

'Yep . . .' Malone grinned reflectively. 'There were some good men among that bunch but – that's the way it goes.' He rummaged in the first aid bag and produced two pre-packed syringes of morphine. 'I don't think she's gonna wake up again but then this is not your average run-of-the-mill beaver. So keep those handy in case the medics don't get here. She may need 'em when the shock starts to wear off.'

'Thanks.'

'That's okay. We're not all as bad as we're painted.' Malone grinned at the unintentional joke then slapped Steve's shoulder. 'Take care, *amigo*.'

Steve watched Malone walk down the slope to where his band of breakers now waited with the remaining horses. Some had decided to ride in the saddle, others had elected to lead a string of roped horses. Cadillac sat slumped on the back of his mount with his wrists and feet secured as Steve had suggested. The ragged column set off westwards without a backward glance and was soon lost from sight among the trees.

He wondered how many of them, besides Malone, were working for AMEXICO. Jodi was right. You couldn't trust anybody. Nothing was what it seemed. He himself was a prime example: a Tracker who was not only decked out like a Mute but had actually taken one for a bunkmate. A trusted envoy of the President-General who felt more at home with his enemies. He had already mentally deserted the Amtrak Federation and if a way could be found to spring Clearwater from Red River – and Roz too – he was now ready to spend the rest of his life in the Blue-Sky World.

But freedom had its downside. Once you started to challenge the accepted order of things, you could no longer be certain of anything. If there *was* such a thing as truth, you couldn't be sure what the word meant or whether the truth about anything – final, absolute and indisputable – could ever be established.

Most Trackers went through life without ever considering there might be an alternative mode of existence. They knew about Mutes, of course, but Mutes were sub-human. If you were a Tracker, you obeyed orders, believed what you were told, and never questioned the wisdom of the First Family. That was the way you survived.

The trouble started when you deviated from the norm. Once you strayed from the path laid down by The Manual, you found yourself sinking into a morass of fear, uncertainty and doubt. To avoid going crazy, a person needed something to believe in, an objective to aim for, a dream to cherish. The Family had one, but Steve no longer shared their vision of a purified Blue-Sky World purged of all those who did not conform to the chosen image.

Trackers were fired with an unshakeable belief in the rightness of their cause but it was a certainty based on blind ignorance. The Mutes were equally convinced they were destined to triumph over their oppressors, but they were merely defending their right to exist; the conflict had been started by the Federation.

In material terms, the Plainfolk Mutes led an impoverished existence, but in other intangible ways their life-style was more rewarding and less restrictive. Warriors of rival clans subscribed to a common code of honour and there was a generally accepted set of rules governing social interaction which each clan adopted to suit its particular circumstances. The punishment for transgressing these rules could be as harsh as that meted out by the Federation but the rules themselves were not oppressive and – as Steve knew from experience – and they were not always strictly applied.

Compared to their underground counterparts, Mutes possessed an enviable degree of freedom and they also enjoyed an instinctive, harmonious relationship with everything that made up the fabric of the Blue-Sky World and the invisible beings who – they believed – watched over it and them from a spirit-realm beyond the clouds.

The Federation did not deal with such intangibles. The notion of individual liberty, the idea that the human body might carry within it a spiritual element – a kind of guidance mechanism that could not be dissected, analysed or weighed simply did not arise. The word-concept 'soul', along with 'freedom' and 'love' did not form part of the Tracker vocabulary.

Love . . .

Kneeling down, Steve laid a hand on Clearwater's forehead. It was cold. Her eyes were now closed. After making sure she was well covered, he set about gathering some wood to make a fire. When darkness fell, it would serve to guide the medics and the soldiers who would come with the wagon-train.

With Roz . . .

Adopting the cross-legged style favoured by Mutes, Steve sat down by Clearwater's shoulder and watched the flames spread through the layers of chopped branches. The wood popped and crackled and hissed as the sap boiled, the tiny jets of steam mixing with the drifting plume of white smoke. A fire like this on a late afternoon under a cloud-filled sky was something the majority of Trackers now alive had never seen and would probably never experience.

Until a short while ago, his kin-sister had had to content herself with a filtered version of his own vivid experiences. Not any more. She had gazed upon the *real* world with her own eyes, and from the enhanced 'colour' and depth of the word-images now reaching over the mind-bridge Steve knew that she too had felt as if she was coming home.

Would she be afflicted by the same uncertainties? Would she be able to reject everything she had been taught to believe in and accept without question the secret knowledge now flooding into her heart and soul? How would she cope with the process of unlearning – of deciding where the *real* truth lay?

Despite everything Steve had gone through he was no closer to resolving the problem. He *still* felt torn between the two cultures. The attitudes inculcated over seventeen years of in-doctrination could not be eradicated overnight. He no longer regarded the Mutes as either sub-human or the enemy but deep down he still believed himself to be – in some undefined way – superior. But there had been *some* improvement. Only two short years ago he had berated Roz for daring to suggest that the Mutes had a right to exist!

From the moment Steve had emerged onto the overground for his first flight over the white sands of New Mexico, his perceived view of the world had begun to change; a process which had accelerated following his capture by the clan M'Call. Cadillac and Mr Snow and, above all, Clearwater had helped him discover unsuspected depths of feeling, a sense of wonderment and an affinity with the Blue-Sky World.

At first, the inner conflict between these new emotions and what he, as a Tracker, knew to be right had crippled him with guilt. This was followed by a growing realization that he had been reared on a steady diet of lies and that what he was now discovering was the *true* state of things and a new self. He felt drawn to the Plainfolk. Emerging onto the overground had been like 'coming home'; a phrase he had used many times since. He knew, deep down, precisely what it meant, but in terms of his Trackerhood it made no sense at all. Home had been Roosevelt/Santa Fe, but he no longer belonged there.

The trouble was, despite his warm attachment to Mr Snow and his continuing desire to be with Clearwater he was no longer sure *where* he belonged. The last two years had provided ample proof that his life was being shaped by forces he did not understand. He had seen with his own eyes the power of earth magic flow through Clearwater and had watched Cadillac read the future in the stones – had even caught a glimpse of it himself. Yet he still could not accept unreservedly, as the Mutes did, that every action was predestined, that past and future events were shaped by a collection of invisible beings.

Despite everything that had happened, despite the fact that he had invoked the name of the Great Sky-Mother on more than one occasion, he retained a healthy scepticism. Talisman, Mo-Town, the Sky Voices, the lesser spirits who rode the wind, dwelt in the forests, the rocky crags, the rivers, lakes and streams were agreeable fantasies dreamed up by past generations of Mutes over pipefuls of rainbow grass to explain known geophysical phenomena.

The Eastern and Western Door in the sky through which the sun entered and left the world each day was a classic example. Mutes had attached a mystical significance to events for which there was a straightforward, rational, scientific explanation. Admittedly, there was, as yet – as far as he knew – no basis in science for the special gift he shared with Roz, or the powers possessed by Clearwater, Cadillac and Mr Snow, but one day there would be.

In a sense, they were both right. If you believed, like Trackers, that everything could be explained or, like the Mutes, that nothing happened by chance, then life – the totality of existence – had to have meaning. And if it had meaning, then it had a logical structure which, in turn, meant that one day everything, including Mute magic, would be understood. All would be known.

Yes . . . the intervention of Talisman in moments of danger was what Trackers called 'good luck'. Nothing more than a fortuitous conjunction of events which conspired to put the right person in the right place at the right time. Or vice versa. Cadillac could claim The Path was drawn, but it was equally true that if you had a clear objective, if you analysed all the elements of a situation and their impact, in various permutations, on a chosen course of action then – nine times out of ten – you ended up knowing what to do. Assuming, of course, you had enough brains to reason things out in the first place.

Steve knew the Blue-Sky World was where he wanted to be, but despite the occasional urge – usually in moments of utter desperation – to let whoever was upstairs run things, he believed that the future was shaped down here on earth. By people like himself. The feeling that he was destined to accomplish great things might, as Cadillac claimed, have been put there by Talisman, but it could have also been there all the time, a product of his own genetic make-up, slowly maturing as his physical and intellectual abilities were honed by endless hours of training exercises and study.

The tests of courage and endurance he had undergone in the past two years had strengthened his resolve but he did not imagine he was invincible; what had just happened to Clearwater was a timely reminder that a well-aimed bullet or crossbow bolt could stop him dead in his tracks. But deep down he was convinced that nothing would.

He piled some more branches on the fire and took another look at Clearwater. No change. He wanted to cradle her in his arms – kiss her, breathe life into her, soothe the pain away, but he knew that in her present condition she should only be moved by skilled medics.

Oh, Mo-Town! Sweet Mother! If you or Talisman are REALLY up there why don't you DO something?! Are you just going to sit there on some stupid fucking cloud and watch her die when you could reach out a hand and wipe the hurt away?!

George Washington Jefferson the 31st, President-General of the Federation, closed the book he was reading and used the handset to cancel the soft but insistent bleep-bleep and bring up the incoming call on the nearby video-screen. Karlstrom's personal call-sign was replaced by a close-up of the man himself – beaming exultantly.

'Evening, Ben. It's a long time since I've seen your face crack open like that. You must have some good news for me.'

'Not exactly good news. Let's just say promising.'

'Spit it out, Ben. Even I like to have a little time off now and again.'

'I'm calling with an update on OPERATION SQUARE-DANCE. Steve Brickman. D'you want to pull the file?'

'No. As the saying goes, "I remember him well". Didn't you put his kin-sister, uhh – whatshername ... Roz – on board Red River?'

'That's her, yes. Amazing. What with everything that's going on topside ...' Karlstrom shook his head. 'How do you do it?'

'I don't keep tabs on them all, Ben. Just the ones where our collective asses are on the line.'

'Yes, well – we just heard from High Sierra – one of my top men. We used Roz to track Brickman from navref Chicago. Once she'd established they were moving along the North Platte, we moved High Sierra's group in ahead of them.'

'And?'

'My hunch paid off. Brickman came clean. He's back on track. In fact, he was never off it. Roz has been picking up positive signals for some time and High Sierra has just confirmed it. He's enlisted Sierra's group to help complete his original assignment.'

'So when can we can expect to hang out the flags, Ben?'

'Not for a while yet, but it's looking good.'

'Now give me the bad news.'

Karlstrom's ebullient smile faded. 'What makes you think there is any?'

'There always is, Ben. There always is. You've laid these upbeat openings on me before. So let's have it.'

Karlstrom assumed his normal poker-face then said: 'In an hour or two from now, Clearwater –'

'Jefferson's interest quickened. 'The summoner that our young hero has been, uhh –?'

'Stiffing? Yes, the very same. He's arranged for her to be collected by Red River. Roz is making the pick-up.'

'Are they going to be able to . . .? I'd hate to think that train might be at risk.'

'That's not going to be a problem. One of Red River's 'hawks on forward air patrol spotted a bunch of hostiles and used up his last rounds on a strafing before turning for home. He reported seeing several targets go down. I guess he didn't realize who he was shooting at. Fortunately, Roz got the message within seconds of it happening.'

'How badly is she hurt, Ben?'

Karlstrom grimaced. 'Well, it's critical but High Sierra says it's not fatal – providing the medics get there in time. Two of the surgical team are going out to handle the transfer. She'll be flown in on a buddy frame.'

'And Roz?'

'She's going out too.'

'Have someone keep an eye on her, Ben.'

'Don't worry, she'll be well covered.'

'And Brickman?'

'Well, according to Roz, he wants to come aboard to coordinate the final stage of the operation. He's with Clearwater now. Everything's been prepared for her to undergo immediate surgery on board Red River. She's in no condition to travel any further. On the plus side, of course, she's in no position to do us any harm.'

Jefferson met this news with a satisfied nod. 'Okay, Ben, well done. Keep me posted N and D on this until she's off the danger list.'

'Will do. Goodnight, Mr President-General.'

'G'night, Ben.' Jefferson cleared the screen with his handset then picked up his book and gently fondled it's leather binding for a moment before turning to the page where he left the marker ribbon.

The book he held in his hands – about steam locomotives that once ran through Texas on the Southern Pacific and the Atchison, Topeka and Santa Fe railroads – was over a thousand years old. The history of the American steam locomotive was one of Jefferson's two private passions; the other was the cultivation of antique roses.

The First Family possessed a magnificent library of real

books covering both of these and many other subjects, and COLUMBUS, the guiding intelligence of the Federation, held the texts of virtually all the books ever written. But the time when their contents would be made known to a wider audience was still a long way off. The material they contained was not even available to all members of the First Family. The work Jefferson was reading was harmless enough but even the fact of knowing that such things as books existed could have an unsettling effect on those who served the Federation.

Books were beautiful things, but they were also dangerous.

Steve gently removed the bundle of clothes he made into a pillow and rested Clearwater's head on his thigh. The move enabled him to hold her right hand in his, while caressing her head. He was as close to her as he could get. Her forehead was still cold, her hair damp, her eyes were shut.

Seized with a feeling of hopelessness, he decided to direct his attention somewhere else. If he did that for a while then perhaps when he looked down at her again, their eyes would meet. It didn't matter how briefly. If she could just see that he was *there* — if he could just connect and somehow beam in the message that she was in safe hands — that she had to LIVE..!

He dragged his eyes away from her face and stared into the glowing embers. The next few weeks were not going to be easy. When Cadillac found out that Clearwater had been put aboard Red River he would go apeshit. But it had to be done. It was the only way to save her life. That was all Steve was concerned about. Only highly-skilled Federation surgeons using the advanced techniques developed by the First Family could rejoin ruptured flesh and rebuild shattered bone. Mr Snow would understand. Steve was counting on his wise, calm counsel to stop Cadillac bouncing off the walls. For his part, Steve was prepared to call a truce — was ready, in fact, to end all hostilities. Permanently. In the present situation, the one thing neither of them could afford was the luxury of another argument.

As part of the medical team aboard the wagon-train and

through her connection with Karlstrom, Roz would ensure that Clearwater got the best possible treatment. And at the very first opportunity, Roz would tell her that she had not been abandoned. Roz would also convince Karlstrom that Clearwater had to be kept on the wagon-train as bait to catch the others.

Karlstrom had to believe that Steve was utterly loyal to the Federation – as Roz had claimed. But it was not so. Federation medical skills would mend Clearwater's body but she would convalesce among the Plainfolk.

Somehow or other – and at the moment he hadn't the faintest idea how it could be accomplished – Steve intended to rescue Clearwater from Red River: the wagon-train with the best operational record and the highest kill-rate in the Federation. The task he had given himself was like trying to storm the Shogun's palace-fortress at Yedo single-handed. Ordinarily, he would have dismissed the idea as impossible, but with Roz on the inside, it was suddenly a whole different ball-game . . .

Steve reached out absent-mindedly for a rounded stone and held it in his palm, turning it this way and that, and wishing he had Cadillac's ability to read the future in the stones. Nothing happened. The stone did not come alive. But as he held it tightly in his fingers, he reflected on what Clearwater had told him about the prediction Cadillac had made as they stood on the bluff with Mr Snow watching him rise into the dawn sky –

'Will he come back?' Clearwater had asked as Blue-Bird turned towards the Dry Lands of the South.

'Yes, in the time of the New Earth,' Cadillac had replied. 'He will come in the guise of a friend with Death hiding in his shadow and he will carry you away on a river of blood.'

Whenever Steve had mulled over these words, he had always taken the phrase 'a river of blood' to signify a terrible battle – for which he would somehow be responsible – in which hundreds would die. Partly because that he would come 'with Death hiding in his shadow' and because before Cadillac had made the prediction, Motor-Head called him the 'Death-Bringer'.

But Steve now realized the lines could be interpreted in a completely different way. The 'river of blood' that Clearwater was going to be carried away on could be Red River! The wagon-train they were both about to board!

'Am I to die?' she had asked, '– in the darkness of their world? His world . . .'

'No,' Mr Snow had replied. 'You will live.'

Oh, Sweet Mother! Steve's heart almost burst as he realized that the answer had been there all the time! In the shock of the moment and the mental confusion that followed, the desperate need to deceive their enemies had pushed all other thoughts aside. He tossed the stone away, and put his arms around Clearwater's head and drew her as close as he dared. 'You will live!' he whispered fiercely. 'You will live!'

High above him, in the darkness, a ragged cluster of winking red lights slid across the sky.

Clearwater's closed eyelids quivered as Roz's inner voice cut through the pain and confusion that gripped her mind to reach the core of her being.

Greetings, soul-sister. We meet at last, under the stars that are our home. I bring you love and life. Be well. Be strong. The time draws near. Our work begins . . .